PROLOGUE

DANIEL Talbot wished he had his sunglasses. Squinting and blocking the sun with his hands, he could barely make out the two figures that were fast approaching across the desert from the east. They were men, Daniel was sure of that, for they weren't wearing the traditional flowing dresses and veils that women in that region of Iraq typically wore. And from their quick gait, Daniel could tell they were young and fit. These were not the decrepit beggars who sometimes wandered through the excavation site looking for handouts. These were young, strong men, approaching fast and with a purpose.

Are they carrying shovels? Daniel strained to make out the long object each man carried on his shoulder. A few weeks ago, a group of teenagers from a local village had shown up at the site with crude shovels and improvised picks, ostensibly looking for work. After a terse negotiation, Daniel had paid them each five dinars to go away. The last thing he needed was a group of kids hacking up his archeological site.

Perhaps word had gotten out that *the American* was paying people to stay away from the site. Daniel grimaced at that thought and wondered how many more villagers he would have to pay off to keep his site unmolested.

The *shamal*—a steady wind from the southwest—buffeted Daniel's back, whipping his loose khaki shirt and pants back and forth with a soft snapping sound. Swirls of sand rose off the desert floor in front of him and floated away quickly on the warm, dry wind. For a moment, the two men disappeared entirely behind an opaque cloud of orange dust. When they reemerged, they were about one hundred yards away and approaching quickly. Daniel could now make out more details. Both men wore pants, not robes. One wore a headscarf. And . . .

"Oh shit," he muttered. He could now see the men were dressed in desert camouflage fatigues and that each had a rifle slung over his shoulder. *Not good*, he thought. Instinctively, he turned toward his vehicle, parked just over the hill a few hundred yards away.

"*Erfaa yadaik!*" one of the men shouted, now about fifty yards from Daniel and jogging toward him.

Daniel froze, put his hands in the air, and turned around slowly. He stared in disbelief as the two men approached, each aiming a Kalashnikov AK–47 assault rifle at Daniel's chest. They stopped a few feet away.

Both men were taller than Daniel, who was just shy of six feet. And, unlike most Iraqis he'd encountered in this region, these men were thick and muscular. One wore a black ski mask over his face, the other a black-and-white Pakastani-style scarf that covered his mouth and head.

Daniel decided to speak first. "I have permission to be here," he said in broken Arabic. "*Government* permission." He slowly lowered his right hand to retrieve the official paperwork from his shirt pocket.

"*Erfaa yadaik!*" the man in ski mask shrieked, thrusting his gun forward menacingly.

Daniel put his hands back in the air, higher this time.

The two gunmen conversed in low, muffled voices. Daniel hoped they were discussing how to verify his paperwork. If they would just take the bundle of documents from his shirt pocket, they would see he had permission from President Al-Bakr himself, and from the Director-General of Antiquities in Baghdad. He was sure the situation would be quickly resolved.

The gunmen were not interested in checking Daniel Talbot's paperwork, however. The man in the scarf pointed to a rocky path a few yards away, which sloped uphill and disappeared into a thicket of date palms. Nodding to his subordinate, he ordered in Arabic, loud enough for Daniel to hear: "Check the vehicle."

Daniel lurched forward but was immediately halted by the muzzle of the lead gunman's rifle, now just an inch from his forehead. He fought the primal urge to tackle the man and pound his face with his fists. At forty-two years old, Daniel was in excellent physical condition and could hold his own in a street fight. But, as he stared down the barrel of the AK–47, he knew any such attempt would be suicidal. He stepped back, checked his rage, and slowly put his hands behind his head.

After a confirmatory nod from the lead gunman, the man in the ski mask trotted off toward the rocky path, which led over a small berm to a dirt road about two hundred yards away.

Daniel's heart sank as he listened to the man's shuffling feet disappearing down the rocky path.

On the other side of the hill, Daniel's Toyota Land Cruiser sat idling. Inside the vehicle, his wife, Becky, was studying archeological maps and preparing her equipment for the day.

It was 7:45 A.M.

Daniel shook his head in disbelief. Today was supposed to be *the day*. The day he and Becky had been looking forward to for nearly five years. The day they'd both quit their jobs for two years ago and dragged their young daughter halfway around the world for.

Now, something had gone horribly wrong.

He kept his eyes fixed on the AK–47, now held loosely against the lead gunman's hip. Out of the corner of his eye, he could see the ski-masked man disappearing into the date palms on his way toward the Land Cruiser . . . toward Becky. For a moment, he considered yelling for Becky to drive away, but he dismissed the idea quickly. The vehicle was too far away, and Becky almost certainly had the A/C on full blast. Besides, even if she did hear him, she would never just drive away without debate. She never did anything without debate. It was one of the reasons he loved her.

He opted for a different approach. Making eye contact with his captor, he asked in the most polite Arabic he could muster, "My friend, what is the problem?" If he could just find out what the problem was, he was sure he could work things out with these men, *whoever they were*.

The gunman said nothing. His eyes flitted back and forth between Daniel and the rocky path.

"Is there a fine to pay?" Daniel asked politely. "I have American dollars."

No response.

Then Daniel heard the sounds he'd been dreading. Becky's voice in the distance, a man's voice, then Becky's again. A car door slammed loudly, and Daniel's heart nearly stopped. Moments later, he heard his wife screaming in a bewildered, terrified tone, "Daniel! *Daniel!*" It grew louder as she made her way, at gunpoint, up the rocky path.

Daniel yelled to her. "It's okay Becky, I'm up here! Just do what he says!"

But things were definitely *not* okay.

Desperately, Daniel tried again to engage the lead gunman in conversation. "We have friends," he sputtered in Arabic, "very important friends in the government."

The gunman stared impassively.

"Do you know Mohamad al-Bitar, Chief Cultural Minister? He is a very good friend of ours."

No response.

"Also Hakeem Abdul Sargon. He is the Director-General of Antiquities. We had dinner with him last week. He will explain everything, if you will please let me call him."

"No, he cannot help you," the gunman replied in Arabic. His voice was calm and oddly polite given the situation. He seemed educated.

Daniel was relieved to finally have a dialogue with the gunman, but he didn't understand his reply. "Yes . . . Director Sargon knows us. Whatever the problem is here, I'm sure he can fix it. Please, just let me contact him. We can drive my truck to al Hilla and use a pay phone—"

"No," the gunman said abruptly, "Sargon is dead."

Daniel had little time to digest that shocking news, for, at that very moment, Becky emerged from the rocky path, the ski-masked gunman trailing directly behind her. She ran to Daniel and hugged him tightly, shaking uncontrollably.

"*Karay hona-alag!*" the junior gunman barked, poking his weapon into Daniel's ribs. Daniel obeyed the command and gently pushed Becky away.

"What do they want?" Becky whispered in a quivering voice.

"*I don't know . . .*"

The Talbots stood at gunpoint against the north wall of the Tell-Fara temple, the ancient and enigmatic structure that had consumed their lives for nearly five years. The temple was situated nine miles north of Babylon and eighteen miles southeast of Karbala, in an uninhabited area that had been known as Shuruppak in ancient Sumer. Twenty feet to their right was "the pit," a large opening in the ground, which had started two years earlier as a modest ten-by-ten-foot test square. It now measured twenty by sixty feet at the surface and descended seventy feet into the earth along the north wall of the temple. The pit was reinforced with steel scaffolding, and the three exposed earth walls were covered with gunite (sprayed-on concrete) to prevent them from collapsing. The fourth wall was formed by the glazed bricks of the exterior north face of the temple, which extended downward at a slight angle, such that the pit became progressively narrower as one descended into it. At the bottom, near the base of the temple, it was just six feet wide.

The gunmen conferred with each other in low voices, keeping their eyes and guns aimed at their hostages at all times.

Finally, the lead gunman pulled a piece of paper from his pocket and began reading aloud, holding his rifle upward with one hand. "All perfect praise be to Allah," he announced bombastically, "the lord of the worlds. I testify that there is none worthy of worship except Allah, and that Muhammad is his slave and messenger."

"Oh shit," Daniel muttered.

"This is the ruling of Ayatullah Ahangari, long may he live, concerning the desecration of holy Muslim sites by infidels."

"It's a *fatwa*," Daniel whispered to Becky.

"In the name of Allah the compassionate, the merciful, the prophet of mercy, Mohammad, son of Abdullah, may God bless him and his family, who was sent with a divine message that toppled the symbols of infidelity and polytheisms in order to elevate man's status in line with angels and virtuous people. Whereas infidels desire to put out the light of Allah with their ignorance and their impure acts . . ."

"Becky, listen to me," Daniel whispered. "At the count of three, run toward the pit."

"What?"

"Becky, they're going to kill us! Run toward the pit, and don't stop no matter what."

Becky nodded.

"Whereas the infidels have joined forces with the corrupt and despicable government and its corrupt and disgraced leaders . . ." continued the gunman in an absurdly official tone.

"One."

"Whereas the infidels have broken the sacred earth at Tell-Fara and defiled the sacred and holy monuments there . . ."

"Two."

" . . . it is *God's will* that those who have perpetrated such crimes be punished by death and . . ."

"Three!"

Everything happened at once. In unison, Daniel and Becky darted toward the pit, Daniel grabbing her hand as they ran.

The gunman in the ski mask screamed, *"Therna!"* and fired his weapon.

The lead gunman dropped the *fatwa*, shouldered his weapon, and fired at the Talbots just as they leapt, feetfirst, into the pit.

Two seconds later, Daniel hit the first wooden platform—ten feet below the top of the pit—landing awkwardly on his side. His left elbow shattered, sending a jolt of excruciating pain down the left side of his body. Everything was dark and spinning. But he could feel the weight of Becky's body next to his, and she was . . . sliding. *She was falling off the platform*, he realized. He reached out with his right hand and caught her arm just as she slid off.

Becky was now dangling from the uppermost platform, sixty feet above the bottom of the pit. Daniel had her arm, but he was losing his grip. And his other arm was numb with pain and totally useless. He looked down at his wife, who appeared unconscious.

"Becky!" he screamed. But she neither moved nor responded. With every measure of strength remaining in his body, Daniel attempted to hoist her up with his right arm. He rolled over onto his left side as he did, causing his elbow to explode anew with pain. He had almost succeeded in pulling Becky's limp torso across his chest when he heard a loud crack.

In an instant, the wooden scaffolding gave way, sending Daniel and Becky falling another ten feet to the next wooden platform. Daniel hit the platform hard with his back and felt Becky's arm slip out of his hand.

He knew, instantly, that she was gone. He tried to scream, but nothing came out. His diaphragm had been paralyzed by the force of the fall. For a few seconds, he wasn't sure if he could move at all. His body seemed to have shut down.

Then came the gunshots. The first bullet ricocheted off the brick wall above him. The second splintered the edge of the platform he was lying on. Instinctively, he rolled away from the shot, toward the gunite wall. Another bullet whizzed past the platform and ricocheted somewhere below him. *The gunmen couldn't see him in the shadows*, he realized. They didn't know where to shoot.

Thinking only of Becky, Daniel rolled over and forced himself, with incredible pain, into a crouching position. In agony, he lowered himself over the edge of the platform and onto the rickety steel-pipe ladder that led to the third platform. He nearly fell as he negotiated the first rung, for there was very little strength remaining in his right arm, and his left arm dangled uselessly at his side. Through sheer willpower, he held onto the ladder and descended, rung by rung, into the pit.

The gunmen continued firing sporadic shots into the pit. Then Daniel heard their muffled voices above him. *Were they coming down after him?* Terrified and desperate to reach Becky, he quickened his pace.

At the bottom of the pit, he found Becky's lifeless body on the ground. He knelt beside her and began to sob. For a moment, he forgot about the gunmen, the temple, the searing pain in his arm—everything around him except how beautiful she was and how much he loved her. *And now she was gone.*

As he wept, the shamal whipped across the opening of the excavation pit, creating a low, ethereal moan. He heard a soft thud on the ground next to him.

In the darkness, he could just barely make out the shape of the Iranian F–1 Fugasnaya hand grenade that had landed just inches from his leg. Frantically, he scampered backward toward the temple wall, though he knew the effort was futile. Seconds later, the grenade exploded.

When Daniel Talbot regained consciousness, his first realization was that he had no sensation below his waist. Badly burned and suffering from grave internal injuries, he lay pinned beneath a pile of rubble. He was confused and in total darkness. *Am I dead?* he wondered.

Then he saw a light. A single beam coming from somewhere behind him. It dimly illuminated his surroundings so that, for the first time, he could see where he was. And, for a fleeting moment—despite his grievous condition and the incredible pain he was in, despite the bastards with guns up above, and despite Becky's death—Daniel Talbot smiled.

He was *inside* the Tell-Fara temple.

Daniel had theorized for over a decade that there were chambers inside the Tell-Fara temple. His academic colleagues, however, had harshly criticized that theory as absurd. It was widely known, they pointed out, that ziggurats are solid;

they have no internal chambers. Ziggurats were not erected as tombs to house the mortal remains of beloved leaders. Instead, they were built as artificial mountains, erected of solid earth to bring an ancient people closer to their gods.

Daniel knew all of that. But his theory was that Tell-Fara was not a ziggurat at all. And the presence of an internal chamber—which he now saw for the first time *with his own eyes*—proved that beyond a doubt. Moreover, he and Becky knew what the Tell-Fara temple really was.

Daniel's smile quickly faded as he realized that no one would ever know of his discovery. No one would ever know the truth about Tell-Fara.

The beam of light drew nearer and became brighter until, finally, it shone directly in his face, blinding him.

"Daniel?" said a man's voice.

Daniel recognized that voice. Bewildered, he struggled to speak. At first, only labored gasps came from his throat. But, eventually, with great effort, he managed a weak whisper. "How . . . did . . . *you* . . . get . . . in here?"

PART I

And it came to pass, when men began to multiply on the face of the earth and daughters were born unto them, that the sons of God saw the daughters of men that they were fair; and they took them wives of all which they chose. And the Lord said, My spirit shall not always strive with man, for that he also is flesh: yet his days shall be an hundred and twenty years. There were giants in the earth in those days; and also after that, when the sons of God came in unto the daughters of men, and they bare children to them, the same became mighty men which were of old, men of renown.

—Genesis 6:1–4

CHAPTER ONE

Present Day. Rockville, Maryland.

DR. Kathleen Sainsbury peered into a twenty-four-ounce clear plastic container and frowned. She held it up to the light for a better view but still did not like what she saw. Inside, three black fruit flies were crawling over a brown, mushy slice of banana. It wasn't the crawling fruit flies that bothered her, however. It was the two flies that *weren't* crawling—the ones that appeared dead at the bottom of the container—that caused her great concern.

She tapped the bottom with her pen, and the two listless flies suddenly took flight, buzzing in tight, frantic circles. At that, Dr. Sainsbury smiled and made a quick notation on her clipboard. Then, as she did every morning, she moved on to the next container, and the next, and the next . . .

"Dr. Sainsbury?"

Kathleen turned to see Carlos Guiterez, the office manager at Quantum Life Sciences, entering the laboratory. "Oh, good morning Carlos. How are you?"

"I'm fine, Doctor. I just wanted to remind you about your interview at nine thirty."

"Got it, thanks." But Kathleen hardly needed a reminder about the interview. She'd arrived at work a full hour early just to prepare.

Tall and attractive, although in a bookish way, Kathleen looked much younger than her thirty-eight years. Her auburn hair was pulled back tightly in a no-nonsense ponytail. Her slender, athletic physique was more suggestive of a soccer player (which she'd been in high school and college) than a world-class biologist. Indeed, if not for the square half-rimmed glasses and lab coat that she habitually wore at work over her jeans and blouse, it would be easy to mistake Kathleen Sainsbury for anything but a serious scientist. And, for that reason, she'd become increasingly self-conscious over the years about her appearance. *An interview is fine*, she thought, *but why do they have to take pictures?*

Checking her watch, she was surprised to find it was already 9:15. She quickly finished collecting data and hung her clipboard on the wall beside the door. Before exiting, she turned and surveyed the laboratory with a weary but satisfied look. She was proud of what she'd built at Quantum Life Sciences. In addition to various computers and peripheral equipment, her state-of-the-art lab boasted a mass spectroscopy machine, two centrifuges, a DNA synthesizer and sequencer, a digital osmometer, a thermocycler, and a sophisticated microinjection microscope that allowed biological material to be injected directly into individual cells through an ultra-thin needle. She'd purchased most of this equipment secondhand from contacts she had at the National Institutes of Health, or from one of several "scavenger" companies that specialized in buying used laboratory equipment from failed biomedical startups and reselling it to new startups. *The ultimate recycling program,* she often mused.

Kathleen drew a deep breath and savored the faint smell of phenol that permeated the lab. It had a sweet aroma, which, at least to her, was oddly pleasant. She closed her eyes, exhaled, then turned and left the lab.

At 9:30, Kathleen was pacing nervously outside the front entrance of Quantum Life Sciences, Inc., one of forty-eight business suites in the Gateway Office Park on the outskirts of Rockville. It was a cold, damp morning in late March, with a dark gray sky portending rain.

As promised, a reporter and photographer from the *Washington Post* arrived exactly on time. Kathleen escorted them inside and led them to a small conference room, which doubled as QLS's supply room.

"Sorry about the mess," she said as she busily cleared stacks of paper from the chipped IKEA table that had once graced the dining room of her Bethesda apartment. "So how does this work?"

The reporter—tall and handsome, in his early forties—introduced himself as Bryce Whittaker, a business and financial reporter for the *Post*. He explained that he was working on a story about biotech startup companies in the Washington area and that he wanted to include Quantum Life Sciences in the story. After confirming that Kathleen was, in fact, the president and CEO, he launched into a series of questions.

"What's the business of Quantum Life Sciences?"

Kathleen responded quickly. "Our goal at QLS is to develop therapeutic products to fight Alzheimer's, dementia, and other age-related diseases." She'd given the same, well-rehearsed elevator pitch to hundreds of potential investors in the past two years. She could recite it in her sleep.

"And how did you get involved in that field?"

"I received a Ph.D. in microbiology from Johns Hopkins. Then, after my post-graduate work, I took a position as a research fellow at the National Institutes of Health, studying the biological processes of aging. When that fellowship was, uh . . . *finished*, I formed QLS, with the goal of continuing my research in that area." Kathleen was relieved that she'd remembered to say "finished" instead of "terminated."

"When was that?"

"About two years ago."

"And how many employees does QLS have now?"

"Well, at this point, just four. There's me and Carlos, whom you met, and two other biologists, Jeremy Fisher and Julie Haas."

"Does the company have any revenue?"

Kathleen smiled at that. Everyone in the business world seemed intensely interested in revenue, whereas science often seemed to be just an afterthought. "Not yet," she replied flatly. "We're engaged solely in early-stage R&D at this point, so we're not focused on generating revenue at this time. That'll be several years off, I would guess."

"So how's the company financed?"

"Private equity. Some friends and family, a few angel investors, but mainly venture capital."

This line of questioning went on for some time, which made Kathleen uncomfortable. She disliked the business side of QLS, preferring instead to submerge herself in her research. She was happy to let Carlos run the books day to day, and she dreaded her "business" responsibilities as CEO, such as preparing quarterly progress reports for the investors. Truthfully, the only financial number she cared about was the company's burn rate, the rate at which it was spending the 2.5 million dollars it had raised in its first round of financing. As far as Kathleen was concerned, her goal as CEO was to get as much research done as she could within that budget, so she could postpone the detestable process of begging for more money. To date, QLS had burned through more than three quarters of its first-round financing, and Kathleen was determined to make the remainder last as long as possible. For her, that meant long hours and weekends in the lab at little more than a subsistence salary.

So much for the glamorous life of a CEO.

"How close are you to developing a commercial product?" Whittaker asked.

Kathleen hesitated. She'd heard that same question from investors since Day One of QLS's founding. "I'm glad you asked," she said, seizing the opportunity to change the subject. "Why don't we go to the lab so I can explain what we're working on."

At that, the photographer piped up. He was a thin, pale slacker in his mid-twenties. "Great, I can get some pictures of you in front of your lab equipment. "

Yeah, great.

In the anteroom outside her lab, Kathleen pointed to a glossy poster titled "*D. melanogaster* Genetics." It included a large illustration of a fruit fly, with various body parts and characteristics linked and color coded to hundreds of genes. "Curly wings," for instance, was connected by a thin magenta line to "Cy0" on chromosome two. In the bottom left corner of the poster, a small circle of photographs was labeled "Life Cycle of *D. melanogaster*," depicting the seven stages of fruit-fly development, from embryo to larva to pupa to the fully developed fruit fly.

"Gross," the photographer muttered, eyeing the poster.

"Not at all," Kathleen countered. "It's actually quite beautiful. The genetic design of the fruit fly is both amazingly complex and beautifully simple."

Whittaker interrupted. "I thought you were

trying to cure Alzheimer's. What do fruit flies have to do with Alzheimer's?"

"Ah . . ." Kathleen smiled and arched her eyebrows. "First of all, I said we're looking for a potential cure for a number of age-related diseases, including Alzheimer's. We believe many of these diseases are manifestations of the same genetic defect. And fruit flies have *everything* to do with our research." She paused to allow Whittaker to finish scribbling in his notepad.

"Biologists have been studying the genetics of *Drosophila melanogaster* for almost a century. Like a lot of things in science, this field actually started by accident. About a hundred years ago, researchers at the Carnegie Institution began noticing that some of the fruit flies they were studying had offspring with strange vein patterns on their wings and other mutations such as dwarfism or white eyes. They quickly realized that they could control these mutations through selective breeding. Since then, generations of biologists have studied *D. melanogaster* and have identified thousands of repeatable mutations. There are mutants with every conceivable eye color— white, pink, purple, maroon, bright red. There are mutants with truncated wings, extra wings, missing wings, and miniature wings. Some mutants are extra hairy; some are nearly bald. More recently, biologists have bred mutant flies with legs growing where their mouths should be, or fully functional eyes on their wings, legs, or antennae."

"Whoa, awesome!" exclaimed the photographer, suddenly interested in their conversation. "Can we see some of those?"

"Sorry, we don't have any of those."

"Aw, man."

Kathleen continued. "Some mutants are uncoordinated and can't fly straight. Other mutants lack memory. Still others have no tolerance for alcohol. The list goes on and on. You get the picture."

Whittaker nodded.

"The important thing is that each mutation has been carefully traced to the specific location in *D. melanogaster's* DNA where the corresponding gene occurs. So, for instance," she pointed to the poster behind her, "we know that TM3 on the right branch of chromosome three controls whether a fruit fly will have long or short bristles.

"And Cy0 on chromosome two controls curly wings, right?" said Whittaker, pointing to the magenta line on the poster.

"Exactly." Kathleen was impressed and gave Whittaker a quick smile that said so. "So we now have a nearly complete, functional map of the fruit-fly genome."

"Wait a second," said Whittaker, holding up his pen. "Hasn't the entire *human* genome already been mapped? I remember covering that story several years ago. So what's the big deal about mapping the fruit-fly genome?"

"There's a *big* difference." Kathleen checked her voice, which had betrayed just a hint of defensiveness. She'd taken her fair share of ribbing from other biologists over the years for being a drosophilist—a "fly person"—which many biologists considered an antiquated field of study. "Although most of the human genome has been sequenced," she explained, "that only tells us what the human genome *is*, not what it *does*. It's like having billions of lines of computer code without knowing what any of it does. For instance, if you ask a human-genome researcher to locate the specific gene that, say, controls whether you will have long or short eyelashes, they can't tell you. Because the only way to figure that out is by doing what biologists have painstakingly done for the past hundred years with *D. melanogaster*."

"You mean creating mutants?"

Kathleen nodded, once again impressed with Whittaker's intuition. "The only way to figure out what a particular gene does in an organism is to switch it on or off—mutate it—and see what the consequences are. Easy to do with fruit flies. Not so easy with humans."

"Okay, I get that," said Whittaker. "But I still don't understand what the fruit-fly genome has to do with human diseases like Alzheimer's."

"One thing biologists have discovered over the years is that genetic mechanisms are surprisingly consistent from one living organism to another. Once evolution stumbles upon a genetic mechanism that works, it tends to use that same genetic code over and over again in many different organisms. These pieces of code are called 'conserved regions.' As a result, humans and fruit flies share much of the same genetic code."

The photographer's eyes widened. "So we're, like . . . related to *flies*?"

"Well, in a way, yes. That is to say, we're related to all living organisms through various portions of DNA that have weaved their way into virtually every living creature through the process of evolution."

Whittaker rubbed his chin thoughtfully. "So you're hoping to find a gene that cures Alzheimer's in fruit flies?"

"Well, not quite. Here, follow me." She unlatched the airtight door to her lab and led the newspapermen in, closing it behind them. "Temperature control is very important when you're working with fruit flies," she explained. "Their breeding cycle and life span are heavily influenced by temperature, so we keep this room at a constant temperature of twenty-five degrees Celsius, which is about seventy-seven Fahrenheit." She pointed to the digital temperature readout above the door. "In fact, we can refrigerate the eggs almost indefinitely until we're ready for them to hatch." She gestured toward a refrigerator in the far corner of the lab.

"The average life span of *D. melanogaster* at twenty-five degrees Celsius is forty-seven days. At sixty days, ninety-nine percent of a typical generation of *D. melanogaster* will be dead. At seventy days, the mortality rate is essentially one hundred percent."

Whittaker and the photographer glanced at each other and shrugged.

"Gentlemen, the fruit flies in this container are *one hundred and forty-four* days old."

Whittaker scrunched his eyebrows together, doing a quick mental calculation. "So that's . . . three times their normal life span?"

"Correct," said Kathleen, nodding.

"And how'd you do that?"

"These fruit flies have a genetic mutation. A dormant gene on one of their chromosomes has been turned on."

"What do you mean, 'turned on'?"

"Activated. Made functional. It's basically like turning on a light switch. You inject a vector into the fruit-fly embryo with a snippet of DNA that is designed to activate the gene. When it finds its target, it effectively turns that gene on."

"And by turning this gene on, you're able to make the flies live longer?"

"Exactly. The life span of these mutated flies is up to four times that of normal flies."

Whittaker was now scribbling furiously in his notebook. "So which gene did you turn on?"

Kathleen suppressed a smile. "It's called the *INDY* gene."

"Indy? Like Indianapolis?"

"No. I–N–D–Y. It stands for 'I'm Not Dead Yet.'"

Suddenly, the photographer's eyes lit up. "Like in Monty Python?"

Kathleen nodded.

"Oh man, that's classic! Bring out your dead!" he cried in a mock cockney accent. "Bring out your dead!"

Whittaker interrupted. "So are you saying you can also do this for humans?"

"Not exactly," said Kathleen hesitantly. "At least not *yet*. The INDY gene was discovered in fruit flies several years ago by a group at the University of Connecticut. Since then, researchers have been poring over the human genome looking for an INDY-like gene in humans. Unfortunately, no one's been able to find one. Which, frankly, doesn't surprise me given that the mechanisms of aging in humans are much more complex than in fruit flies. It may well be that the INDY mechanism doesn't exist in humans. Or, if it does, it may be spread over multiple locations in the genome, rather than conveniently packaged in a single gene, as it is in *D. melanogaster*. That would make it exceedingly difficult to find . . . at least without some sort of a road map."

Whittaker scratched his head. "Okay, now I'm confused again. What's the point of studying the INDY gene in fruit flies when you don't even know if it exists in humans?"

Kathleen nodded, acknowledging what she knew to be a very reasonable question. "One of the amazing things about these INDY flies is that their quality of life seems better than that of other flies. Not only do they live longer, but they're more energetic throughout their entire lives. The female flies can reproduce well into old age, and the males are, how should I say . . . *friskier*. They mate more often than their non-INDY counterparts, and well into old age."

"Way to go, little dudes!" whispered the photographer, giving a goofy thumbs-up to the plastic container.

"Anyway," Kathleen continued, "we're trying to understand—on a cellular and biochemical level—exactly what gives these INDY flies such vigor and longevity. Our goal is to eventually create a drug therapy that can stimulate those same biological processes in humans. If we can do that, then maybe we can give people a better quality of life as they grow old."

"How close are you to developing such a treatment?"

And there it was. *The Question*. The same question Kathleen had heard at every quarterly shareholder meeting for the past two years. She gave Whittaker the same response she gave the investors each time. "It'll be at least another three to five years."

"That long?"

Kathleen shrugged. "Science takes time," she said matter-of-factly. "Three to five years is our conservative estimate."

With that, the interview concluded. The photographer snapped some additional shots of Kathleen in the lab, in the anteroom in front of the *D. melanogaster* poster, and, finally, in the conference room where they'd begun an hour earlier. He then went to load his camera equipment into the news van, leaving Kathleen and Whittaker standing alone in the lobby.

Outside, a chilly rain had begun to fall.

"I have one last question for you," said Whittaker, inching closer to Kathleen. "Strictly off the record."

"Okay . . ."

"Is there a, uh . . . *Mister* Dr. Sainsbury?" He cocked an eyebrow impishly and smiled.

Kathleen was stunned by the question, which seemed to have come from nowhere. She shook her head no.

"Any chance you'd consider having dinner with a lowly newspaper reporter? Full disclosure: I got a C in high-school biology."

Kathleen laughed. "Well, I don't know . . . *maybe*." She immediately regretted that response. *She didn't even know this guy.*

"I'll take that as a yes."

"You did what?" asked Julie Haas in mock disbelief.

Kathleen, Carlos, Julie Haas, and Jeremy Fisher—the four employees of QLS—were seated at a booth at Azteca, a Mexican bar and grill a few blocks from QLS.

"I said I'd go out with him," Kathleen repeated, shaking her head remorsefully. "I honestly don't know what I was thinking."

"Hey, I think it's great," Carlos reassured her. "You said yourself you need to get out more."

The foursome never needed an excuse to come to Azteca after work for margaritas and chips and salsa. Today, however, they had a bona fide reason to celebrate, namely the upcoming story in the *Washington Post*. Like Dr. Sainsbury, the other three members of QLS each owned stock options in the privately held company, and they knew their big payday would come when QLS went public or, more likely, was acquired by a large pharmaceutical firm. Either way, some positive press in the *Washington Post* couldn't hurt.

And it couldn't have come at a better time. QLS was low on cash and fast approaching the end of its first-round funds. The investors were growing increasingly vocal about the company's lack of progress, and, unfortunately, Kathleen's constant refrain of "science takes time" was wearing thin.

QLS needed a breakthrough . . . and *fast.*

"What does he look like?" Julie asked.

"Like this." Kathleen pulled Bryce Whittaker's business card from her purse and handed it to Julie. In bold, gothic print, it read: BRYCE A. WHITTAKER, REPORTER, THE WASHINGTON POST. In the upper left corner was a professional black-and-white photograph of Whittaker in a dark suit with a serious, hard-hitting expression.

"Oh my God," Jeremy crowed, snatching the card from Julie's fingers. "Who puts a picture like *that* on their business card? This guy's totally full of himself."

"Hey, I think he's cute!" Julie retorted.

"He looks like an ass," Jeremy said.

Just then, a pitcher of Margaritas arrived, and Carlos filled everyone's glass. "Here's to QLS," he proposed, raising his glass.

"Here's to some good press," Kathleen added.

An hour later, the foursome exited Azteca and headed for their respective cars in the parking lot. Carlos walked Kathleen to her car. "Dr. Sainsbury?" he said as they reached her car. He never called her "Kathleen"—a sign of respect and a carryover from his twenty years in the Marines.

"Hmmm?"

"I meant to ask you earlier, but do you have plans for Easter Sunday? Ana and I would love to have you join us for dinner."

"Oh, thank you, Carlos, that's very kind." Kathleen genuinely appreciated the offer, though it made her feel vaguely sad. Carlos knew she had no family except for her elderly grandfather, so he always made a point of inviting her to spend holidays with his family. *A sweet gesture but totally unnecessary.* "I've already made plans," she lied. "Thank you, though."

"Well, if you change your mind, just let me know."

"I will."

"Good night, Dr. Sainsbury."

Across the street from Azteca, a black Lincoln Navigator was parked lengthwise across three parking spaces in a Burger King parking lot. Its sole occupant—Semion Zafer—sat motionless in the driver's seat, staring out the side window at Azteca's front door. The Navigator's dark tinted windows made him practically invisible from the street.

Zafer was tall and gaunt, with oily black hair and a pale, unshaven face. His dark eyes were deeply recessed above protruding cheekbones, giving his face an angular, skeletal appearance. His lips were thin and tight, expressionless.

Through the telephoto lens of his Hasselblad H2D–39 camera, he spotted Dr. Kathleen Sainsbury—his target—exiting Azteca with three other people. "Well hello," he croaked in a heavy Israeli accent, "aren't *you* a pretty one?" The corners of his mouth curled up slowly as he increased the zoom and surveyed Kathleen's slender body from head to toe. She wore tight jeans and a fashionable silk blouse that accented her figure tastefully.

Zafer quickly zoomed in on each member of the QLS foursome, snapping several face shots of Kathleen, Julie, Jeremy, and Carlos in a matter of seconds. He then followed Kathleen and Carlos with his lens as they walked to Kathleen's car, snapping several shots along the way.

Three minutes later, as Kathleen pulled out of the parking lot and turned right onto Route 355, Zafer snapped one last shot of her silver Subaru Outback, being sure to capture the license-plate number.

His work today was done.

CHAPTER TWO

LUCE VENFELD LEANED BACK in his plush leather chair and flipped open the business section of the *Washington Post*. He was a lean, serious man in his early fifties, with salt-and-pepper hair and a square, clean-shaven face. His appearance was refined in every respect, save for an ugly, purplish scar that ran diagonally across his left cheek, betraying a life that had once been far less luxurious.

Venfeld's K-Street office was spacious and beautifully appointed with expensive leather and mahogany furniture, an intricate Turkish rug, and several tasteful oil paintings on the wood-paneled walls. In a corner by the door, partially obscured by a Kentia palm, a half dozen framed photographs showed Venfeld posing with some of the most notorious characters of the past three decades. In one, he stood next to Manuel Noriega. The Panamanian dictator was smiling broadly, his arm draped casually over Venfeld's shoulder. In another, Venfeld was shaking hands with a handsome man with deeply tanned skin and white hair, dressed entirely in white. They stood before a palatial hacienda somewhere on the Mexican coast. The photograph was inscribed in blue ink: "Many thanks. —Guillermo."

Venfeld was a lawyer by education but had never actually practiced law. Instead, upon graduating from Georgetown Law School some twenty-five years earlier, he'd gone straight into the CIA, where he worked his way up from analyst to field agent. During his last ten years at the agency, he'd successfully infiltrated the business hierarchy of some of the most sophisticated drug cartels in Venezuela, Panama, and Mexico, posing as Joseph Browning, an international tax attorney with Langston and Darby of New York, London, Hong Kong, and Buenos Aires. His polished appearance and world-class education allowed him to mix easily into Latin-American society, where he casually collected information at cocktail parties and befriended key individuals, gaining their trust over a period of years.

The large window behind Venfeld's desk framed the Washington Monument and the federal buildings at Madison Place like a postcard. At this early hour, the morning sun was just breaking the horizon, backlighting Washington's famous limestone obelisk with a soft peach glow.

Venfeld read with mild interest the story that began on page one of the business section, titled AREA BIOTECH STARTUPS REACH FOR THE STARS.

The byline attributed the story to "Bryce Whittaker, Staff Reporter."

"In the past decade," the story began, "the Washington area has become a major biotech hub, with dozens of biotech and life-sciences companies establishing headquarters in Maryland, Virginia, and even the District."

The article went on to recount the numerous reasons for this rapid growth of the biotech sector around the capital beltway. For one thing, the Washington area offered easy access to important government resources such as the National Institutes of Health (NIH), the National Cancer Institute (NCI), the National Institute of Standards and Technology (NIST), and the Food and Drug Administration (FDA). The area boasted several universities with renowned health and life-sciences programs, including Johns Hopkins University and the University of Maryland. The Washington area was also incredibly wealthy, claiming four of the five richest counties in the United States: Loudoun and Fairfax counties in Virginia, and Howard and Montgomery counties in Maryland. Those affluent counties had each created tax-funded "incubators" to help small startup companies get off the ground, including many biotech, bioinformatics, and nanotech companies.

"Here," the article continued, "we will take a look at eight biotech startups in the Washington area, each hoping to ride the area's biotech boom to new heights."

Venfeld casually sipped coffee as he skimmed

the remainder of the article, which included a short synopsis of each of the eight spotlighted companies. He read with waning interest until he reached Quantum Life Sciences on page three, at which point he suddenly sat straight up in his chair, nearly spilling his coffee.

QUANTUM LIFE SCIENCES SEEKS TO EXTEND, IMPROVE HUMAN LIFE

Imagine living an active life for two hundred, three hundred, even four hundred years or more! It may be possible, according to the scientists at Quantum Life Sciences, Inc., a two-year-old biotech startup in Rockville. QLS has already isolated a gene in fruit flies that triples their life expectancy, while also making them more active and productive. Though it is unclear whether this gene—called "INDY" for "I'm Not Dead Yet" (a Monty Python reference)—occurs in humans, QLS is studying how the gene operates in fruit flies and hopes to replicate the same biochemical processes in humans to achieve a better quality of life in old age.

"Clinical tests are several years away," said Dr. Kathleen Sainsbury, QLS's founder and CEO, "but we feel we are moving steadily toward a meaningful treatment for Alzheimer's, dementia, and other age-related diseases."

QLS raised approximately $2.5 million in its first round of financing. The company had no comment on whether it plans to seek further private equity or make an initial public offering to finance its continuing research operations.

Venfeld studied the picture of Dr. Kathleen Sainsbury that accompanied the article. She stood, arms folded and smiling broadly, before an impressive array of laboratory equipment. The square half-rimmed glasses and lab coat did nothing to detract from her natural beauty.

He refolded the paper and tossed it onto his desk. "Maria!" he bellowed through the open door to his secretary.

"Yes?" she answered.

"Bring me the file on Dr. Sainsbury."

CHAPTER THREE

D**R.** William McCreary pressed his security badge against the infrared scanner that controlled access to a door marked OSNS at the Defense Advanced Research Projects Agency (DARPA). He was a youthful fifty-one years old, medium height, athletic build, but a bit pudgy around the middle. The infrared scanner beeped and, simultaneously, the heavy steel door magnetically unlocked with a loud *ka-chunk*. McCreary entered the restricted area belonging to the Office of Science and National Security and headed straight to his office. In an agency notorious for top-secret, black, and off-budget programs, McCreary managed one of the most secretive of them all.

He reached the door to his office and unlocked it with a key—there was no security scanner for this door. The sign on the door read simply LOGISTICS ANALYSIS. He smiled every time he read that sign, having purposely chosen the most mundane project name imaginable. For the past two years, "Logistics Analysis" had worked like a charm. No one at DARPA seemed to care very much about the boring activities that presumably went on behind this door.

And that was just the way he preferred it.

DARPA was established in 1958 in response to the Soviet's launching of Sputnik. DARPA's mission then—as it was today—was to ensure that the United States always maintained the upper hand in state-of-the-art military technology and was never again surprised by an enemy's technological advances. DARPA was specifically designed *not* to be a bureaucracy. Instead, its goal was to give brilliant (and often zealous) program managers nearly complete autonomy—and considerable financial resources—to pursue cutting-edge ideas that were often viewed as impracticable or downright crazy by the mainstream scientific community. Although many such projects failed, others succeeded beyond all possible expectations. The Internet (formerly DARPANET) was just one example of such successes.

McCreary entered the Logistics Analysis office and closed and locked the door behind him. The reception area was small and windowless. A plain, wooden desk dominated the center of the space, upon which sat the typical paraphernalia of a workaday government analyst—a computer and printer, graphs, charts, reams of data, and various binders and books. Seated at the desk was a large, muscular man of about thirty with bulging biceps and a protruding, square chin. He wore the uniform of a federal bureaucrat: khaki slacks, white, short-sleeve shirt, cheap necktie, and a security badge clipped to his shirt pocket.

"Good morning, Dr. McCreary," said the bureaucrat.

"Morning, Steve. I've got a secure video conference at nine fifteen."

"Right." Steve stood up, walked to the back of the office and typed in a nine-digit code on a small keypad beside a large, white panel in the wall. Suddenly, the panel shuddered and popped open about twenty inches, creating a narrow entryway into another chamber.

"Thanks," said McCreary stepping through the opening. "This shouldn't take long."

McCreary was now standing inside a stark, white room, eight feet long by five feet wide, with a seven-foot ceiling. He pressed a button on the wall and the steel door slid shut with a soft thud.

There were no paintings, drapes, or other objects hanging on the walls—nothing that could potentially conceal an eavesdropping device. The floor and ceiling were likewise clean and bare.

McCreary pushed another button on the wall, and the room suddenly filled with the whooshing sound of white noise. The walls were now being permeated with random frequencies so that nothing that was said in the room could ever be detected from the outside, even with the most sensitive eavesdropping equipment.

A Criticom secure video teleconferencing console sat atop the only piece of furniture in the room, a combination desk and chair constructed of high-strength plastic. At precisely

9:15, McCreary sat down at the console and pressed the ENCRYPT/TRANSMIT button. The equipment emitted a random series of beeps and blips as it worked through the process of synchronizing the outgoing signal with the recipient's console and authenticating the daily key code. Finally, the image of a man appeared on the screen.

"Good morning, Mr. Secretary," said McCreary deferentially.

"Morning," grunted Peter Stonewell, Assistant Secretary of Health and Human Services. He was sitting in an identical room twelve miles away at HHS headquarters on Independence Avenue in Washington, D.C. "Have you seen this story about the young lady with the mutant fruit flies?" he asked, holding up a folded copy of the *Washington Post*.

"Yes, sir."

"Is that the same Dr. Sainsbury who used to be at NIH?"

"That's her."

"So I gather she now has her own company?"

"Yes, sir."

"How long have you known about it?"

"About a year and a half, sir."

"Then how come I'm just hearing about it now!" Stonewell boomed, "and from the goddamn *Washington Post* of all places?"

McCreary swallowed hard. He'd worked for Stonewell long enough to know it would do no good to point out that Stonewell had, in fact, been briefed on Quantum Life Sciences eighteen months ago. Very little in this program was ever put in writing, so there was nothing McCreary could produce to verify that fact. Besides, trying to suggest to Stonewell that he was wrong about *anything* was, quite simply, out of the question.

"We're on top of it," McCreary said stoically, "and if I failed to mention it to you before, I apologize."

"All right," Stonewell said, apparently satisfied with McCreary's mea culpa. "What do you think about her research?"

"We've been tracking her closely, and it doesn't look like she's close to anything right now."

"How does she compare to the others?"

"Of the eight groups we're still watching, I'd say she ranks third or fourth in terms of likelihood of success. The University of Connecticut group is still the closest, but, as I've explained before, they're still several years away, in our opinion."

"Well, just last week, your friends at DeCode linked a form of glaucoma to a particular gene in the human genome, and it took them less than twelve months to do it. How do you explain that?"

"That's different, Mr. Secretary. DeCode is working with a small, heterogeneous population in Iceland, which shares much of the same DNA. When they set out to target a disease like glaucoma, they begin with a DNA sample from a person in the population who actually *has* that disease—in other words, someone who has a mutated gene in their DNA that causes the disease. By sequencing that person's DNA and then comparing it to members of the Icelandic population who don't have the disease, they can quickly pinpoint the genetic source of the disease."

Stonewell grumbled an acknowledgment.

"The INDY researchers don't have that luxury, Mr. Secretary. Because, as far as we know, there's no one walking around today with an intact INDY gene in their DNA. *That's* why there's no easy way for them to find it in the human genome. They have no road map."

Stonewell sighed. "All right. Well, I'm sure you'll keep me posted if anything develops."

"Of course, Mr. Secretary."

Across town, Peter Stonewell turned off his secure videophone and returned to his office through a narrow metal door. His secretary— a petite, mousy woman in her sixties—quickly drew a set of dark blue drapes over the metal door after it shut.

Peter Stonewell was a dinosaur in Washington—big, old, and powerful. He'd weathered five administrations as Assistant Secretary of Health and Human Services for Strategic Research and Planning, serving under both Republican and Democratic presidents. Other administrators at HHS had come and gone like the seasons, but Stonewell—shrewd, powerful, and at times ruthless—had always managed to stay put. His twenty-six-year tenure at HHS was an unprecedented feat in Washington, and one that had allowed him to amass considerable power.

The Department of Health and Human Services was a massive organization with vast governmental resources. Officially, it was the agency charged with protecting the health of all Americans and providing essential human services. The department administered more than three hundred government-funded programs, covering a wide spectrum of activities, including basic scientific research, immunization and disease prevention, food and drug safety, and medical preparedness for bioterrorism and other emergencies. HHS also controlled the National Institutes of Health, the world's premier medical research organization.

In Washington, power stems from money. And, by that measure, HHS had grown to be a very powerful agency indeed. It now consumed fully a quarter of all federal outlays, administering more grant dollars than all other federal agencies combined. Its Medicare/Medicaid program was the nation's largest health insurer, handling more than a billion claims per year and providing health-care insurance for one in four Americans. HHS employed more than sixty thousand people and controlled an annual budget of more than 700 billion dollars.

To say that HHS cut a wide swath through the U.S. economy was no understatement.

"What else is on my calendar today, Judy?"

"You have a nine forty-five with Michael Tate of the American Millennium Foundation, an eleven o'clock with Max Schneider and Roger Glick of Westpharma Corporation, and lunch with Senator Morris at the Army-Navy Club at one thirty."

"Christ, barely time to take a crap," Stonewell muttered under his breath.

CHAPTER FOUR

"**I MUST** say I've never eaten dinner in a chimney stack before," Kathleen said, gazing up from her grilled scallops.

Bryce Whittaker smiled and nodded knowingly. "Amazing, isn't it?"

They were seated in the Chimney Stack Room of Fahrenheit, one of Washington's most fashionable restaurants, near the Georgetown waterfront. The small, circular room circumscribed the base of a 130-foot brick chimney, built in 1932 as an incinerator. A skylight at the top admitted a small circle of moonlight, which mixed with the candlelight at their table to create a flickering, otherworldly glow.

"I'm impressed," Kathleen said.

"So am I. *With you.*"

"Aw, c'mon." Kathleen looked bashfully at her plate.

"No, really. You're smart, you're beautiful, you

run your own company. How could I not be impressed?"

Whittaker was tastefully dressed in a black suit with no tie. He was clearly at ease in the rarified atmosphere of Fahrenheit's exclusive, private dining room. After telling Kathleen to trust him, he'd confidently ordered lime-cured salmon and quail en croûte for appetizers and a 160-dollar bottle of wine, a 2000 Château Clinét.

"So tell me about yourself," he said, refilling her wineglass. "Where'd you grow up?"

"Great Falls, mostly," said Kathleen, referring to Great Falls, Virginia, a semirural suburb of Washington.

"Mostly?"

"Well, I moved there when I was seven."

"And before that?"

Kathleen poked nervously at her food with her fork.

"Sorry, I didn't mean to pry—"

"No, it's okay."

"I'm a reporter, you know. I never know when to stop asking questions."

"It's okay, really." Kathleen took a deep breath and launched into the same explanation she'd given so many times in her life that it now seemed rehearsed. "I was born in Boston. My parents were archeologists, so I moved around a lot when I was a kid. We lived in Egypt for a while. And when I was six and seven, we lived in Iraq."

"Iraq? Wow."

"Yeah, it was pretty wild. Anyway, my parents

died when I was seven, and after that, I lived with my grandparents in Great Falls. They adopted me, and I lived there until I graduated from college."

Whittaker's relaxed smile had turned to an expression of concern. "I'm sorry to hear that."

"It's okay. No big deal."

By age ten, Kathleen had adopted "no big deal" as her official motto whenever someone expressed sympathy about the death of her parents. "No big deal" always came in handy to save her the embarrassment and awkwardness of others' pity. In fact, she'd said it so many times in her life that she almost believed it herself. *Almost.*

"Well, anyway," Whittaker said, "I shouldn't have pried. Both of my parents died in a car accident while I was in college. I know how hard that is."

"Gosh, I'm sorry," said Kathleen.

Just then, a waiter entered the dining room, and Whittaker raised his hand to call him over. "The crème brulée here is amazing," he whispered across the table, "but we have to order it now because it takes forever to prepare. You want one?"

Kathleen declined, so Whittaker ordered one just for himself. "Last chance," he warned.

Kathleen shook her head.

When the waiter left, Kathleen seized the opportunity to change the subject. "So, where are you from?"

"Originally, Upstate New York. I went to college at SUNY Buffalo, and journalism school at NYU. I interned for the *Wall Street Journal* while I was at NYU then landed a job there when I graduated."

"Impressive," said Kathleen. She was happy to have turned the conversation away from herself.

"Thanks." Whittaker smiled humbly. "Anyway, I spent eight years at the *Journal*. It was a great job, but eventually I felt . . . you know, like I needed a change. So I sent out some feelers and, boom, I ended up at the *Post*. That was, let's see . . . about two years ago. I'm hoping to move from business to the national desk soon."

"Do you like it here?"

"Sure. There's a lot of opportunity at the *Post*. It's not like the *Journal*, where you have to wait until someone dies before you can move up—"

Kathleen interrupted, "I *meant* do you like living in Washington?" She smiled as she recalled Jeremy's comment a few nights ago about Whittaker's business card.

"Washington? Absolutely, it's a great city. It's not New York, mind you, but I really like it."

Thirty minutes later, as predicted, the crème brulée arrived, and the waiter blowtorched it beside their table with great fanfare. He also set two glasses of twenty-year-old Graham's Tawny Port on the table, which Whittaker insisted Kathleen try.

"I've been thinking about what you said the other day," Whittaker said, cracking the caramelized top of his dessert with a spoon.

"What's that?"

"You said when evolution finds something that works, it tends to stick with it, right?"

"In general, yeah."

"Okay, then why would a fruit fly have a suppressed gene that essentially cuts its life expectancy to a third? I mean, what possible advantage could that be for the fruit-fly race?"

Good question. Kathleen mulled it over awhile before answering. "Well, evolution theory would suggest there's some advantage to having the INDY gene suppressed."

"Right, but what could that possibly be? I mean, how could dying *younger* be an advantage?"

"Hey, I didn't say I knew the answer." Kathleen took another sip of her port wine, which was surprisingly tasty—and potent. "Maybe," she continued half jokingly, "the short-lived flies work harder because they know they have less time to live."

"Or maybe," Whittaker suggested, "it was just a mistake in the genetic code. You know, a mutation that got passed down through the generations."

Kathleen shook her head no.

"Why not?"

"According to evolution theory, there would still have to be some natural advantage to the short-lived mutation in order for it to completely replace the long-lived class over the course of millions of years. Otherwise, the short-lived mutation would eventually die out, or, at the very least, the population would become a mixture of long-lived and short-lived flies, with the ratio reflecting their relative ability to survive and procreate."

Whittaker smiled coyly. "You biologists and your *theory* of evolution." He formed air quotation marks as he said "theory."

Kathleen took the bait. "What, you don't believe in evolution?"

"Hey, *you're* the one who said evolution can't entirely explain the suppressed INDY gene in fruit flies."

"No. What I said was, I don't know the answer right now. That doesn't mean the theory's flawed. It just needs further study."

"Fair enough." Whittaker held up his hands up in faux surrender. "But I do have another theory about those fruit flies."

"Yeah? What's that?"

Whittaker savored the last bite of his dessert. Then he spoke in an absurdly dramatic tone, separating each word for emphasis. "God . . . hates . . . fruit flies."

Kathleen laughed. "What?"

"You heard me. God hates fruit flies. Admit it, they're annoying. They buzz around, eat people's fruit. They're a menace. So, my theory is, God *hates* them. And he punished them by shortening their life span."

Kathleen smiled and shook her head. "Interesting theory, but . . . I don't think so."

"Why not? It's just as viable as your *theory* of evolution." Whittaker once again formed air quotation marks around the word "theory."

Kathleen shook her head resolutely.

"What, you don't believe God would do that to the poor little fruit flies?"

"No," said Kathleen without missing a beat, "I don't believe in God."

CHAPTER FIVE

KATHLEEN unlocked the door to her apartment, stepped inside, and locked it behind her. She kicked off her high heels and hung up her cashmere overcoat, all while replaying the night's events in her head.

Dinner had ended just after at ten o'clock. Afterward, Whittaker had waited outside the restaurant with her while the valet retrieved her car. She'd insisted on meeting him at the restaurant instead of having him pick her up at her apartment. *Just in case the date goes badly*, she'd reasoned.

When it came to relationships, Kathleen had long accepted one unchangeable fact in her life. Namely, despite her numerous accolades, including being a brilliant scientist and founder of a high-tech company, she had a terrible track record with men. "Book smart, man dumb," one of her girlfriends had teased her in college. It was still true.

Kathleen recalled the precise moment at the end of the date, just as they were about to say good night, when Whittaker leaned into her car and surprised her with a quick peck on the lips. "Good night," he said softly. Predictably, Kathleen froze and said nothing. She drove away without another word, leaving Whittaker standing befuddled in the street.

Like everything else in Kathleen's life, Bryce Whittaker had proven to be a mixture of good and bad. A bit *too* smooth for her taste, she decided. But, then again, he was handsome, smart, sophisticated, and funny—*not bad qualities in a man*, she reasoned.

These thoughts were all swirling in her head as she walked into her small galley kitchen for a bottle of water. The message light on her answering machine was blinking. She pushed "play" on her way to the refrigerator. The machine beeped loudly, then a man's voice began speaking in an odd accent—part British, part Middle Eastern. It was one of those vague, "international" accents that typically identified a person as highly educated and well traveled.

"This message is for Kathleen Sainsbury," said the voice in a slow, deliberate meter. There was a long pause, as if the man were struggling for words. Meanwhile, Kathleen opened the refrigerator and searched for a bottle of water. "My name is Tariq Al-Fulani," the voice continued. "I was a friend of . . . your parents."

Kathleen stood upright and spun around, leaving the refrigerator door wide open.

"You may remember my daughter . . . Farhana."
Another pause. "You used to play with her at our
house . . . on Rashid Street . . . in Baghdad."

Kathleen raised a hand to her mouth. A vague
memory flashed of her and an Iraqi girl playing
with dolls in a large townhouse in Baghdad. She
was six or seven years old then. Her parents were
downstairs at a dinner party. She remembered
the reassuring hum of adult conversation wafting
upstairs, punctuated by laughter, as she and the
little Iraqi girl enjoyed a game of make-believe
house in two different languages.

"I have something . . ." The voice trailed off, followed by another long pause. It was clear the man
was having difficulty choosing his words. "I have
something for you," he said finally. "It is very important. My address is . . . 1810 U Street . . . in
northwest Washington. Please come tonight if
you can." There was another long pause. "It is *very
urgent*. Thank you. Good-bye."

Kathleen stood motionless as the answering
machine beeped three times and turned off with
a click. More than thirty seconds passed before
she realized the refrigerator door was still open.
When she finally regained her senses, she re-
played the message and jotted down the address.
Then she checked her caller ID to see if there was
a phone number she could call back. But the incoming number was identified only as UNLISTED,
WASH DC.

The digital clock above her oven read 10:33
P.M. A dozen thoughts ran through her head at
once. *Who is he? Why did he call me? What did he*

mean it was "urgent"? She sat down on the sofa and tried to clear her head, which was now churning with thoughts of her childhood, her parents, and the mysterious voice on the answering machine. After several minutes of sitting and standing, she finally made a decision—at least a partial decision.

She would drive to U Street and decide what to do when she got there.

She stepped back into her high heels, put her overcoat on again, and left the apartment.

Five minutes later, Kathleen turned right out of her parking garage onto Sandalwood Street, paying no attention to the black Lincoln Navigator pulling away from the curb a block behind her at precisely the same moment.

CHAPTER SIX

KATHLEEN parked in front of 1810 U Street just after 11:00 P.M. It was a three-story brick row house in a once rundown neighborhood that was now gentrified, though still not free of the bums and loiterers who had populated its street corners and parks for decades. The street was relatively quiet at this hour, save for an occasional passing car and the faint shouts of revelers several blocks away.

In its heyday, U Street had been known as Black Broadway and was home to some of the most important jazz venues in the country, including Club Bali, the Crystal Caverns, and the Howard Theatre. All the greats—from Billie Holiday to Louis Armstrong—had played on U Street at one time or another. The legendary Duke Ellington had grown up just a block away on T Street. In the 1960s, however, the D.C. race riots and widespread economic depression drove the U-Street corridor into shambles. It was not until the mid–1990s that it finally began to reemerge as the premier artistic, musical, and cultural center of the city. Today, U-Street was home to an eclectic mixture of residential row houses, avant-garde galleries, jazz clubs, and numerous funky bistros.

Kathleen sat behind the wheel of her car, debating in silent anguish for nearly five minutes. Twice, she put the car in gear to drive away but changed her mind each time. Eventually, she turned the ignition off and got out of the car. Her pulse was racing, her palms damp despite the chilly air. She looked both ways and saw no one on the sidewalk. Then she cautiously climbed the brick steps leading to the front porch of the house, ascending slowly until she stood in the yellow glow of the house's solitary porch light. It was a clear, breezeless night. The faint aroma of burning firewood from a nearby tandoori restaurant hung in the air.

The front door to the house was shiny and black. A polished-brass plaque beside it read:

DR. TARIQ KHALID AL-FULANI
TURKISH AND MIDDLE EASTERN ANTIQUES
BY APPOINTMENT ONLY

There were no lights on inside the house, and no sound. Kathleen took a deep breath, held it tightly in her lungs, and rang the doorbell.

A half-minute passed without any sign of life inside the house. With every passing second, Kathleen's anxiety grew more intense until it was nearly unbearable. She glanced repeatedly at her car on the street, reassuring herself that it was still there. Then, just as she was about to leave, the foyer light flicked on. Seconds later, the doorknob rattled, and she watched with breathless anticipation as the shiny black door swung slowly open.

The elderly man behind the door was thin and frail. He wore a crisp white Oxford shirt and dark blue slacks with black socks and no shoes. He was a short man of about eighty, his head nearly entirely bald except for a crescent of thin, silver hair around the back. His face was deeply wrinkled and covered with silver whiskers—too thick to be called stubble but not quite a beard. His shoulders drooped forward slightly, giving him a disarming and somewhat servile demeanor.

"Good evening," said the man in the same vague accent Kathleen had heard on her answering machine. His breathing was heavy and labored, as if the simple act of greeting her had taken great physical exertion. "I am . . . Tariq Al-Fulani." He bowed his head as he said his name.

Kathleen nodded slightly. "Kathleen Sainsbury."

"Yes, of course." Still breathing heavily, the elderly man made a sweeping gesture with his hand, as if to usher her into his home. "Please, come in."

Kathleen did not move.

"Ahhh . . . I'm sure you don't remember me. You were much too young." He flashed a toothy smile. "But I remember *you* . . . when you were just a little girl." He paused to catch his breath. "And now I see you have grown to be such a beautiful woman."

None of this made Kathleen feel any more comfortable. She stood motionless on the front porch, studying the man's sad eyes and odd expression.

"Please, come in," said the man insistently, motioning again with his hand. "I have something very important to give you."

With trepidation, Kathleen entered the house, glancing back at her car one last time as she entered the foyer. The car disappeared from view when the old man closed the door softly behind them. He offered to take Kathleen's coat, but she declined, stating that she preferred to wear it. Then he motioned for her to follow him to a large, rectangular room just off the foyer. She followed cautiously.

Stepping into the room, Kathleen felt as if she had been instantly transported to a different place and time. The room smelled of dust and old wool. Its walls were covered from floor to ceiling with antique Persian rugs, their stunning colors—deep crimson, cobalt blue, and dark gold—evoking the atmosphere of a Moroccan bazaar. The rugs obscured the only windows in the room and one of the two doorways, giving the room an enclosed, intimate feeling. It reminded Kathleen of a *suradeq*, the beautiful, embroidered traveling tents of Arabia, which she vaguely remembered from her childhood travels.

A large oval table dominated the center of the

room, draped with a lavish "tree of life" medallion tablecloth in rust red and black velvet. A pair of Moorish table lamps—dancing metal figurines topped with fringed silk shades—bathed the room in soft yellow light. Surrounding the lamps was an array of rare and unusual objects, which Kathleen surmised were Middle Eastern antiques. A white alabaster head immediately caught her eye. It was a life-sized depiction of a stern, bearded man with small holes carved into its eyes and long, curly beard.

"That is from the fourth century BC," the elderly man explained, noticing Kathleen's interest. He stood a few feet away, near the corner of the room. "Found in southern Iraq. Most likely part of a funerary niche. The holes would have contained precious stones, or perhaps glass or shell inlays."

Kathleen nodded in appreciation and continued surveying the astounding collection of artifacts. There was a pair of ancient Syrian mosaics, a second-century bust from Palmyra wearing a Romanesque tunic, Egyptian Pharaonic funerary pots, several gleaming pottery pieces from Persia—their blue, red, and gold patterns as brilliant today as they were in the twelfth century—and dozens of mosque lamps and other intricate glasswork from twelfth- and thirteenth-century Syria. Kathleen also noticed six or seven ornately sculpted silver boxes, some decorated with small stones and beads. She ran her fingertips across one of them.

"Quran boxes," the man explained from the corner of the room. "From eastern Turkey."

Kathleen nodded politely.

On the far side of the room was a low, wide sofa, upholstered in bright red velvet with gold fringed trim. A collection of embroidered pillows was scattered across the sofa. Behind the sofa, next to the wall, was a massive, hand-carved Turkish screen, its gleaming gold-leaf floral design reflecting the soft light of the table lamps. Mounted on the screen were two sixteenth-century Persian sabers, their crescent blades crossed. It reminded Kathleen of the Saudi royal seal.

"Please, sit down," the man urged, gesturing to a spot on the sofa directly below the swords.

Kathleen did not move. Something about the old man's voice and mannerisms seemed overly anxious, almost . . . *desperate*. She didn't like it.

"May I offer you some tea?"

Kathleen grew more uncomfortable by the second until, finally, she could no longer ignore the alarm bells in her head. "I should go," she announced, turning quickly toward the foyer.

"No!" the old man exclaimed. "Please don't go."

Kathleen ignored him and walked briskly toward the front door.

The man followed her into the foyer. "Please, this is very important!"

Kathleen turned suddenly to face him. "*What* is very important? Who *are* you, and what is so damned important?"

A tense moment passed as the old man obviously struggled to find the appropriate words. When none came, Kathleen turned once more to leave.

"Wait," said the man softly. He released a heavy sigh. "My *real* name is . . . Hakeem Abdul Sargon."

Kathleen stood motionless, facing the door.

"I was the Director of Antiquities in Iraq under Ahmed Hassan Al-Bakr until 1979, when he was ousted by Saddam Hussein. I knew your parents well. They were . . . great scholars. *And friends.*"

Kathleen turned slowly to face him.

"I remember you, too," Dr. Sargon continued. "You sometimes played with my daughter, Farhana." At the mention of his daughter's name, he looked down, evidently disturbed by some distant, haunting memory. "Please, stay and allow me to explain." He once again motioned with a sweep of his hand toward the living room.

Kathleen stood with her back to the door, her coat still on, car keys gripped tightly in her hand. If she wanted to go, she had only to turn around and walk out the door. She stared into Dr. Sargon's eyes for several seconds, uncertain of what to do.

Suddenly, her cell phone rang, piercing the uneasy silence. She fished it out of her purse and answered on the second ring. "Hello?" she whispered.

"Are you okay?" Carlos Guiterez asked in a concerned voice. Kathleen had called him earlier, while she was sitting in the car in front of the house, and had asked him to call her back in ten minutes. She hadn't explained why.

With the phone still pressed to her ear, Kathleen studied Sargon's face carefully. He seemed frail and sincere. *Or was it desperation and fear she sensed?* Either way, she decided she could trust him. *For now.* She whispered into the phone, "I'm fine, Carlos, thanks. See you on Monday." Then she tucked the phone back into her purse and gave Sargon a thin, nervous smile. "I *will* have some tea," she said finally, removing her coat.

Dr. Hakeem Abdul Sargon smiled eagerly and took her coat. Then he hurried off to the kitchen to fix some tea.

"I'm fine, Carlos, thanks. See you on Monday."

Semion Zafer closed his eyes and listened intently to Kathleen Sainsbury's voice emanating from a pair of noise-cancelling headphones secured tightly over his ears. The headphones had the effect of putting her feminine voice directly in his head, a sensation he found very pleasant. He turned up the volume on the specialized scanner/receiver to which the headphones were connected.

From Zafer's location at 16th and U, the modified Watkins-Johnson HF1000A scanner/receiver had no problem picking up Kathleen's cell-phone signal as she conversed briefly with her office manager, Carlos Guiterez.

Zafer jotted down some quick notes about the call and then settled back into the plush leather seat of his Lincoln Navigator.

He needed a drink. *Badly.* But then he thought about his boss, the man he knew only as "Joe," and recalled what Joe had told him nine months ago when he'd first entered his employ. "You're a drunk," Joe had said. "I've known plenty of men like you, and they usually end up dead. If I catch you drinking on the job, I'll cut your throat myself and dump your body in the Anacostia River. *Understand?*"

Zafer understood. And believed him. After nine months of working for "Joe"—the perquisites of which included a rent-free apartment, unlimited use of the Lincoln Navigator, and bimonthly envelopes of cash delivered to a Mail Boxes Etc. mailbox—all he knew of his mysterious boss was a single prepaid cell-phone number and an anonymous e-mail address.

And that's all he *wanted* to know.

CHAPTER SEVEN

LUCE Venfeld carefully studied the file on Dr. Kathleen Sainsbury for a third time, making a few additional notations in the margins of some of the pages. His spacious office was lit by the soft glow of a single desk lamp. It was quiet. Indeed, at this late hour on Saturday night, the only occupied offices in the entire building were those on the eleventh floor belonging to the LHV Group, Venfeld's consulting firm.

Satisfied that he now knew Kathleen Sainsbury better than she knew herself, Venfeld closed the manila folder and placed it neatly atop a foot-high stack of similar folders, each profiling the life and daily habits of a different molecular biologist.

Including Kathleen's, there were nine such files in all. *Although one of them no longer mattered.*

Venfeld pulled the file on Dr. Michael Kim from the bottom of the stack and flipped it open. Across the first page of Dr. Kim's curriculum vitae, a large "X" had been scrawled in black marker. The word "DECEASED," in neat block letters, ran diagonally across the page.

An unfortunate incident.

Venfeld tossed Dr. Kim's file to one side and placed his palm on the remaining stack of eight files, each more than an inch thick. *Eight horses left in the race.*

Venfeld stood and gazed out the window of his K-Street office at the nighttime sky. He stood perfectly still, hands clasped behind his back. The top button of his starched white shirt was undone, his tie loosened slightly. His gaze shifted momentarily to his own reflection in the window. Fifty-four years old. Wealthy. Handsome.

A sly smile crept over his scarred face.

Eight horses in the race; who would win?

That was the beauty of his plan. *It didn't matter.* Whichever horse crossed the finish line first, he stood to earn a fortune. He liked those odds very much.

He turned and strode casually across the plush Turkish rug to the six framed pictures near the door. His gaze fell on the photograph of him and Guillermo Gomez shaking hands at Gomez's sprawling coastal estate in Quintana Roo, Mexico. He vividly recalled the night, five years ago, that he'd crept into Gomez's private villa, intending to kill the man he'd befriended just a few years earlier. It would have been a sanctioned execution, of course. Part of the CIA's secret war on drugs. *Very secret.* Just "Joseph Browning" doing his job, once again.

But, as Venfeld eavesdropped that night via a collapsible antenna no bigger than a cereal bowl, he overheard something quite extraordinary. A secret meeting among seven wealthy men was taking place in the villa's library.

They called themselves the "Olam Foundation," and the topic of their meeting that night had nothing to do with cocaine or marijuana, or even money laundering.

This was something entirely different. Something momentous. Something life changing. *World* changing.

And Venfeld wanted in.

CHAPTER EIGHT

"**How** much do you know about your parents?" asked Dr. Hakeem Abdul Sargon. He was seated in an ornately carved high-back chair a few feet from where Kathleen sat.

Kathleen sipped Turkish black tea from a clear, slender glass and reclined against the couch's oversized pillows. Two hours ago, she'd never heard of Dr. Sargon (at least not that she could remember), and now she was sipping tea on his couch. She felt a little ridiculous, aside from being apprehensive about the entire situation.

"I know they were archeologists," she replied.

"Yes, your *father* was an archeologist," Sargon said with a nod, "and a very good one at that. Your mother, however, was an anthropologist. And also quite an expert on Assyrian mythology."

At that moment, Kathleen reflected on how little she actually knew about her parents, especially her father. Practically everything she knew about them came from her maternal grandfather, and that information had come only in small, pasteurized bits. Through the years, the whole concept of her parents had taken on a synthetic gloss—like a Disney movie. She knew the basic story but few meaningful details. To Kathleen, her parents had never seemed . . . *real*.

"I first met Daniel—your father—in 1972," Dr. Sargon continued. "At that time, my main responsibility as Director of Antiquities was to oversee the Iraqi National Museum in Baghdad, as well as other regional museums throughout the country. I was also in charge of issuing permits for excavation of historical sites in Iraq. Your father had written to me from Harvard University, where he was a professor. He wanted to excavate the Tell-Fara temple."

Kathleen interrupted. "Tell-Fara?" She'd heard that name before but never knew what it meant.

Sargon looked at her with sorrowful eyes, obviously surprised by the question. "Yes, dear, Tell-Fara. That's where your parents were killed."

Kathleen blanched. "You mean where they died in the *accident*?"

Sargon held her gaze for a moment then shook his head slowly from side to side. "There was no accident."

Kathleen suddenly felt lightheaded. For as long as she could remember, she'd been told her parents died in an "accident" while excavating ruins in Iraq.

"Shall I explain?" asked Dr. Sargon delicately.

Kathleen nodded.

"As I said, your father had written for permission to excavate at Tell-Fara, which I initially denied. At that time, the policy was not to allow foreigners to excavate historical sites in Iraq. I assumed I would never hear from Daniel Talbot or Harvard University again. But . . ." He smiled. "I was wrong."

Kathleen sat motionless, absorbing this new information with a mixture of fascination and trepidation.

"Your father wrote to me several more times, urging me to allow just a small exploratory excavation of the Tell-Fara site. He was quite persistent." Sargon chuckled and took a long sip of his tea. "In the summer of 1972, he and your mother, Rebecca, came to visit me in Baghdad. I must say, that was quite a surprise. They had just been married and were on their honeymoon." He raised an eyebrow and added, "Of course, that was before you were born."

Kathleen shook her head in amazement. She vaguely recalled her grandfather once telling her that her parents had spent their honeymoon in the Middle East. Now, that random bit of information suddenly had context. For the first time, she was beginning to visualize them as real people.

Sargon continued. "It was no surprise, of course, that they'd come to ask for permission to explore Tell-Fara. This time, however, when I heard their ideas about the site, I must say I became very intrigued. Your mother, in particular, had some very interesting theories about the temple."

"Like what?"

"Well," said Sargon, holding up his hand politely, "first, there is some history you need to understand." He rose to his feet slowly, his aged body clearly causing him great discomfort. "But before we get to that, may I offer you some more tea?"

Kathleen nodded.

Sargon refilled her tea glass, carefully pouring from two separate containers, a custom he had learned in Turkey. "As a young man, I spent five years near Izmir helping excavate the Temple of Artemis in Sardis, once a mighty city in the late Roman Empire. I became virtually addicted to Turkish black tea."

Kathleen thanked him for the tea and took a small sip, savoring the unusual, spicy flavor.

"Now," said Sargon in a slightly more animated tone, "let's discuss Mesopotamian history." He stooped down and carefully pulled a framed antique map from beneath the oval table in the center of the room. Leaning the map against the table, he spoke as if he were addressing his old Assyriology class at Oxford.

"The name *Mesopotamia* is derived from the Greek," he explained. "It means the land between the rivers. And from this map you can see why—Mesopotamia was situated between the two great rivers of the Middle East, the Tigris and the Euphrates. The land between those rivers was fertile farmland, much sought after in the ancient world. This area of land, which we now call Iraq, has been continuously populated for more than *ten thousand* years. It is, quite literally, the birthplace of modern civilization.

"Starting around thirty-five hundred BC, a great culture arose in Mesopotamia called the Sumerian civilization. It was centered in the cities Ur and Uruk." Dr. Sargon pointed to where those two cities appeared on the map, near modern-day Basra and Warka in southern Iraq. "The name 'Iraq,' by the way, comes from the word *Uruk*. These were the first modern city-states, where government, art, agriculture, and commerce flourished."

"As you can imagine," Sargon continued, "Sumerian civilization was heavily influenced by the Tigris and Euphrates rivers, which provided irrigation for crops and drinking water for people and animals. They also provided a mode of transportation throughout the region. And, of course, they caused periodic floods, which were also an integral part of Sumerian life, much the way they are today along the Nile."

Sargon looked up from the map and met Kathleen's eyes. "But some floods were worse than others."

Kathleen sipped her tea and nodded politely.

"In about twenty-nine hundred BC, a massive flood inundated the entire Sumerian plain. None of the city-states up and down the Tigris and Euphrates rivers was spared. We know from archeological evidence and from written records—clay cuneiform tablets—that the rivers crested anywhere from ten to twenty meters above their normal levels, which would have put nearly every city in the region completely under water. We have to imagine that tens, perhaps *hundreds* of thousands of people died in that flood."

"I guess there's no easy escape route when you live in a plain between two rivers," said Kathleen, pointing to the map.

"That's exactly right. So you might say this was a calamity of *biblical* proportions."

Kathleen considered that comment for a moment, shifting in her seat. "I assume you're referring to *The* flood? As in the Bible and Noah's ark and all that?"

"Yes, indeed."

Kathleen pressed her lips together but said nothing.

"Most scholars agree that the flood of the Old Testament and the historical flood that took place at the beginning of the third millennium BC in Mesopotamia are one and the same event. After all, what *is* the Old Testament but a history of Mesopotamia and Egypt that begins around the time of that great flood?"

Kathleen nodded obligingly but was unable to suppress her doubtful expression.

"I'm sorry, you look puzzled," said Dr. Sargon.

"Sorry . . . it's just that I don't really subscribe to the Bible at all, Old Testament, New Testament, or otherwise. I'm a *scientist*. I seek truth through observation and experimentation, not through divine scripture." She waved her hand at the map. "But, please, continue."

An awkward silence ensued. "Interesting," muttered Sargon after several seconds.

"What is?"

"It's just that . . . Well, your parents, they were *also* committed to seeking the truth. And they, too, believed in the power of observation—archeological evidence, anthropological evidence, pottery fragments, carbon dating, sediment samples. You see, they, too, were scientists. *Like you.*"

Kathleen squirmed uncomfortably in her seat. She didn't like where this was going at all.

"But your parents also studied the Bible," Sargon continued. "They studied the Quran. They studied the Torah. They knew and understood those texts well. Because, you see, there is *truth* in those books that goes beyond carbon dating and sediment samples."

Kathleen felt uneasy and desperately wanted to change the topic. The fact was, she hadn't believed in God or the Bible since she was a teenager. It had marked a major turning point in her life, and one she firmly believed had been for the better. Biology was her religion now.

"So where's Tell-Fara?" she asked, changing the subject.

"Tell-Fara is here, near Babylon." Sargon pointed to the map with his index finger. "In ancient Mesopotamia, before the flood, Tell-Fara was known as Shuruppak, a Sumerian city that was then on the Euphrates River. Many believe it was the birthplace of Noah."

Kathleen ignored the last comment. "What happened to my parents there?"

Sargon drew a deep breath, obviously bracing himself for an unpleasant task. Then, with great delicacy and respect for the memory of the Talbots, he explained the events that he observed at Tell-Fara on a September morning thirty years earlier, just a day after his own family had been ruthlessly murdered on the outskirts of Baghdad.

CHAPTER NINE

Dr. Hakeem Abdul Sargon stepped on the brakes of his black Mercedes. *Why such traffic at midday?* he wondered. He honked impatiently at the rusty Peugeot mini in front of him, but to no avail. Traffic on Bagdad's main artery had slowed to a glacial pace.

Sargon had woken up this morning with a bad feeling about today. The ominous sensation had intensified when he arrived at work. There was a buzz amongst those in his office that a coup d'état was imminent. Not that a coup would have come as a great surprise to anyone. Politically speaking, President Al-Bakr had been growing progressively weaker in the past six months, his political power seeming to slip away with his health. In Iraq, physical weakness invited challenge, and there was no mystery as to who would soon step up to challenge Al-Bakr's authority. Saddam Hussein, Al-Bakr's young cousin from Tikrit, had been amassing power as quickly as

Al-Bakr had been losing it. Though just a cabinet official by title, Hussein had, in recent months, been acting more like president-elect. The unspoken transfer of power between the two was palpable in the governmental corridors of Baghdad.

Change was afoot, Sargon was sure of that. It was only a question of when . . . and how bad things would get.

This morning, he'd decided things were going get *very* bad. There was talk of imprisonment, or worse, for anyone who dared challenge Hussein's accession to power. And that made Sargon particularly uneasy. Years ago, he'd had a run-in with Hussein. Not a big deal at the time, but in hindsight perhaps enough to earn him a spot on Hussein's infamous "enemies list."

The run-in was silly, a mere trifle in the larger scheme of things. As Director of Antiquities, Dr. Sargon had begun an aggressive repatriation program, searching the world over for Iraqi relics that had been spirited away by adventurers and so-called archeologists over the past century. Using the oil revenues that had swelled the governmental coffers thanks to Al-Bakr's nationalization of the oil industry, Sargon had arranged to buy back precious Iraqi artifacts from foreign collectors and museums and repatriate them to the Iraqi National Museum. Occasionally, museums—and more rarely private collectors—were kind enough to return the antiquities without charge. On most occasions, however, the Iraqi government had to pay dearly for the privilege of owning its own historical artifacts. Sargon knew this well, because he was the one who wrote the checks.

The trouble began when Hussein—then just a lowly bureaucrat in the defense ministry—decided he wanted to "repatriate" a precious fifteenth-century mosaic from a private collection in London for his own personal summer residence in Tikrit. It was a beautiful mosaic; there was no doubt about that. It depicted a heroic Persian cavalry officer in full battle regalia. Surely, it would have enhanced the décor of Hussein's summer home. But, as Sargon explained to a fuming Hussein, the National Museum simply could not use government funds to purchase artwork for a private residence. Thus began an unspoken feud between the two that had simmered on low boil for more than five years. The situation intensified when, two years later, Sargon purchased that very mosaic for the National Museum and displayed it prominently in the museum's front gallery.

Things got even worse when Hussein got wind that Sargon had authorized foreign archeologists to excavate a temple in southern Iraq. "*Treasonous!*" Hussein had famously declared in a meeting of interior defense officials.

Sargon was sure he was on Hussein's dreaded "enemies list." Moreover, he was sure Hussein would soon be treating the Iraqi National Museum as his own private art gallery, taking anything that struck his fancy. Undoubtedly, that beautiful fifteenth-century mosaic would be among the first pieces appropriated.

The buzz around Sargon's office this morning made him think that today might be the day. When he tried to call home at 10:00 A.M. and found the phone line dead, that confirmed it beyond all doubt. Cutting off government communications was the first step of any successful coup.

For months, Dr. Sargon had been planning for this exact moment. But now that it was actually here, he suddenly feared his plans were inadequate. He'd planned to drive his family south to Az Zubayr and then into Kuwait. His political credentials would facilitate their safe passage. If not, he had plenty of cash to make it happen. For months, he'd been exchanging modest amounts of Iraqi dinars for British pounds, using his official position as curator of the National Museum so as not to raise any suspicions. He now had nearly £20,000 in British currency in his personal possession—enough to exit Iraq safely, if not comfortably. Hard currency went a long way in this part of the world.

On the other hand, it could also get you killed.

Sargon honked his horn again, which had no effect other than to prompt an obscene gesture from the driver in front of him. *Curse this traffic!*

If he could have called his wife from the office, she would have been packed and ready to go by now. *What if she wasn't even home? What if she'd taken Farhana to the market?* Unthinkable, Sargon concluded. His wife would never go out without checking with him first, and she'd said nothing about going to the market this morning.

His street was now just a block away. Losing patience, he punched the accelerator and veered the Mercedes halfway onto the sidewalk. Vendors and pedestrians yelled at him as he zoomed past the backed-up mess on the Qadisiya Expressway, the main highway that bisected downtown Baghdad. He didn't care. His official tags made him practically invisible to the local police.

He banked right onto Rasheed Street. Now liberated from the traffic-clogged main artery of the city, he pushed the Mercedes hard, reaching fifty miles per hour as he roared down the wide, palm-tree-lined avenue toward his house.

At 110 Rasheed Street, he pulled the car over and jumped out. He rushed through the front door of his luxury apartment and bounded up the stairs to the living quarters on the second floor. "Nisreen!" he called, barely suppressing his panic.

"What is it?" his wife responded from the kitchen. Her fearful tone mirrored Sargon's own anxiety.

"Where's Farhana?"

"Upstairs, sleeping. What's the matter?"

Sargon grabbed his wife firmly by the shoulders and said sternly, "We have to go."

"*Allah have mercy!*" Nisreen whispered. She knew exactly what her husband meant and what they had to do. She ran immediately upstairs to pack her bags.

Thirty minutes later, Sargon, Nisreen, and a sleepy six-year-old Farhana were belted into the Mercedes, Sargon in the front, the girls in the back. The trunk of the car sagged noticeably beneath the weight of clothes, cash, and valuables they intended to take with them. Sargon was careful to drive the speed limit in the city, not wanting to draw any extra attention to the vehicle. When they cleared the Baghdad city limits without incident, however, he breathed an audible sigh of relief and eased the Mercedes up to a more comfortable cruising speed.

With Baghdad safely behind them, Sargon relaxed and tried to engage his nervous wife in conversation. "Is Farhana still sleeping back there?" he asked without taking his eyes off the road.

"Yes, sound asleep."

"Nisreen," said Sargon reassuringly, "everything will be fine. I *promise*." He swiveled his head around and flashed a quick, confident smile.

And that's when he noticed the military van advancing rapidly from behind.

Sargon's heart skipped a beat as he straightened in the driver's seat. He clutched the wheel tightly. "Don't look at them," he warned as he gently slowed the Mercedes to allow the van to pass.

But the van did not pass. Instead, it pulled alongside and slowed to the same speed as the Mercedes. The two vehicles were now driving side by side along the deserted, two-lane highway that led south out of Baghdad. Sargon squeezed the steering wheel tightly with both hands and held his breath. He risked a quick glance at the van and saw a soldier glaring back at him from the driver's side window. He also saw a black object moving inside the van, which he recognized immediately as a weapon.

Dr. Sargon gunned the accelerator, and the Mercedes responded obediently with a roar. Farhana woke up and began to whimper. The Mercedes was now several car lengths ahead of the van and pulling away quickly.

Suddenly, a burst of automatic gunfire erupted from behind them. The Mercedes's back window shattered instantly in a deafening explosion of glass and bullets. Farhana and Nisreen shrieked in horror as shards of glass flew everywhere. Sargon felt tiny bits of glass slam into the back of his head like birdshot. He pushed the accelerator harder, but it was already on the floor. The Mercedes was screaming down the highway at nearly one hundred miles per hour.

More gunfire was now coming from behind them in short, emphatic bursts. Suddenly, there was a loud *pop*, and the steering wheel jerked sharply to the left, nearly escaping Sargon's grasp. He struggled with all his strength to keep the car pointing south, but it was no use. The left rear tire had been blown out, and the car was now skidding into an uncontrollable spin. Nisreen let out a long, sustained shriek as the Mercedes spun around several times and finally came to rest on the soft, sandy shoulder of the desolate highway, facing north toward Baghdad, toward the home they loved but were desperately trying to escape.

"Get down!" Sargon bellowed as the military van skidded to a halt beside them on the road. He pulled his Tariq 9 mm pistol from under his seat.

Seconds later, the driver's side windows exploded in a barrage of bullets from the soldier's automatic weapon.

Sargon felt a stinging pain in his left shoulder and slumped far down into his seat. The onslaught lasted for only a few seconds, though it seemed like forever to Sargon. Then it ceased abruptly.

Sargon was wounded but conscious. He sat motionless and watched, using his peripheral vision, as a soldier approached the Mercedes cautiously. The man wore an Iraqi infantry uniform and had a military-issued AK–47 drawn to his shoulder. *He was coming to finish them off!*

Sargon gripped his pistol tightly and, with his thumb, gently clicked the safety off.

As the soldier neared the driver's side window, Sargon lifted the Tariq and fired twice in rapid succession. The soldier lurched backward and fired a short burst of bullets over the top of the Mercedes as he fell to the ground. Sargon wasn't sure if the soldier was dead but had no time to find out. For, at that exact moment, the driver of the van was getting out of the vehicle. Sargon aimed and fired twice in the man's direction. The first shot missed, but the second landed squarely between the man's eyes, bringing him down instantly. The soldier fell out of the van's open door, his feet catching on the seat belt as he did, so that he ended up dangling awkwardly, upside down over the road.

Frantically, Sargon looked in the backseat, where Farhana and Nisreen were huddled on the floor. Beneath a blanket of broken glass and tattered upholstery, he saw movement. Then he heard Farhana crying softly and Nisreen hushing her. *Thank Allah*, they were alive! He was just about to speak to them when he saw movement out of the corner of his eye.

Time seemed to stand still as Sargon turned to see the first soldier staggering to his feet beside the driver's side window, his torso bloody from the two gunshot wounds Sargon had inflicted. The wounded soldier hoisted his automatic weapon to his hip and, for a split second, locked eyes with Sargon. Reflexively, Sargon lifted the door handle and pushed the door open as hard as he could with his wounded shoulder. He yelped as an excruciating pain surged through his upper body.

The car door connected squarely with the gunman's weapon just as the AK–47 erupted in a burst of fire and bullets. The lethal barrage, meant for Sargon, instead slammed into the vehicle's rear door and quarter panel. Simultaneously, Sargon lifted his pistol and fired through the open door. His first shot caught the soldier in the right shoulder, the second in the neck. The soldier fell to the ground and dropped his weapon.

Fueled with rage, Sargon exited the vehicle and stood over the soldier's prone body, his pistol aimed directly at the man's head. But the soldier was already dead.

There was now only silence, and the acrid smell of gunpowder and burned rubber.

Sargon stepped over the soldier's bloody body

and stuck his head through the Mercedes's shattered rear window. One glance confirmed his deepest horror—Nisreen and Farhana lay in a bloody, lifeless heap, their bodies riddled with bullet holes.

He opened his mouth to scream, but nothing came out.

He couldn't breathe. His knees buckled.

For several seconds, he braced himself awkwardly on the car, desperately gasping for air, until, finally, he lost consciousness and collapsed.

CHAPTER TEN

September 4, 1979. Mishkhab, Iraq.

Sargon couldn't stay long in Mishkhab. By now, Hussein and his cronies almost certainly knew what had happened on the highway south of Baghdad. At the very least, someone had surely reported the abandoned Mercedes and two dead soldiers to the authorities. *They were after him, and they knew he was heading south.*

He had driven four hours in a panic-induced haze, with the bodies of Nisreen and Farhana in the back of the military van, wrapped in green blankets. He'd driven and shifted gears with one hand because his left shoulder was stiff from the gunshot wound. The bullet had nicked the soft, fleshy portion of his upper arm. Whenever he tried to move his injured arm, the searing pain made him feel lightheaded. But, in an odd way, that pain was the only thing that kept him grounded as he drove. Everything else around him seemed like a horrible dream.

He was dressed like an army corporal now,

having removed the military uniform from the body of the van driver. The olive green fatigues were snug at the waist but otherwise fit surprisingly well.

Just after 4:00 P.M., Sargon arrived at the modest house in Mishkhab where Nisreen's sister, Aaliya, lived with her husband, Lutfi. They were not expecting him, so his appearance—in military fatigues and driving a military vehicle no less—caused a tremendous commotion.

Mishkhab was a small farming village about 150 miles southwest of Baghdad. The villagers there were blissfully unaware, of course, of the political upheaval taking place at that very moment in the Iraqi capital. Although Sargon explained as best he could to Aaliya and her husband, he could tell they did not fully grasp the gravity of the situation.

That changed, however, when they saw the bullet-riddled bodies of Nisreen and six-year-old Farhana in the back of the van.

Pandemonium erupted almost immediately. Aaliya howled uncontrollably and was soon joined by other relatives, including Nisreen's aunt and uncle, cousins, second cousins, and dozens of people vaguely related by blood and marriage. The whole village, it seemed, poured out of their houses to share in the family's grief.

Sargon stood silently by, still in shock and unable to mourn.

Once the initial chaos subsided, it was decided that Nisreen and Farhana should be buried before sunset, in accordance with Muslim tradition. Nisreen's brother-in-law, Lutfi, left to take care of the funeral and burial arrangements while Aaliya and several other female relatives carefully washed the bodies with scented water and shrouded each with a *kafan*—a clean, white linen cloth.

An hour later, Lutfi and several men from the village returned and transported the shrouded bodies on crudely constructed stretchers to an open courtyard near the town mosque. There, the local imam led the mourners—more than two hundred men and women—in a traditional funeral prayer.

Following the prayers and a long period of silent reflection, the crude stretchers bearing the shrouded bodies of Nisreen and Farhana were carried by hand to the village cemetery for burial. By Muslim tradition, only the men of the community accompanied the bodies to the gravesites.

Just before sunset, Sargon watched stoically as the shrouded bodies of Nisreen and Farhana were lowered together into a single grave, each lying on her right side, facing Mecca. By tradition, no tombstones, markers, or mementos were left at the gravesite, signifying that all ties to this physical world were now broken. The souls of Nisreen and Farhana were thus humbly submitted to Allah.

It was later that night, as Sargon lay awake on the floor of Lutfi's house, that despair descended upon him like a deluge. He wept and convulsed for several hours in the dark until, finally, he saw that the sky outside had changed from black to gray.

He left Mishkab at dawn, having not slept at all. Although tradition dictated that he should remain near the burial site for at least three days of mourning and prayer, he simply could not stay in Mishkhab any longer. *They were after him, and they knew he was heading south*.

He gave his wife's family ten thousand British pounds, nearly half the money he'd planned to use for his family's escape. In exchange, they gave him their rusty Datsun pickup truck. The military van was accepted in return, destined to be stripped, repainted, and converted into a farm utility vehicle.

Sargon drove south out of Mishkhab with no real plan. He was reasonably certain that Hussein's goons would be waiting for him at the Kuwaiti border. He'd changed into simple clothes, which Lutfi had provided, and had shaved his moustache, but he lacked the proper paperwork to cross into Kuwait.

His original plan had been to bribe a border guard, usually not a difficult task. But if the border guards had already been contacted and intimidated by Husseins's men, Sargon knew that *no* amount of money would get him through safely. He'd killed two soldiers, and, as he well knew, the only price that could be paid for that crime was public execution.

He considered his other options. *West to Jordan? North to Turkey?* He doubted the old Datsun would make it that far. So he continued driving south, nearly certain he was driving toward his own execution.

Then he remembered the Talbots.

Immediately, he pulled over and retrieved a tattered road map from the glove compartment and spread it across the steering wheel. Al Hilla, the town nearest to Tell-Fara, was less than fifty kilometers away. For the first time since the attack outside of Baghdad, Sargon allowed a tiny glimmer of hope to enter his heart as he turned the rickety Datsun around and veered east off of Highway 8 onto the narrow dirt road to al Hilla.

CHAPTER ELEVEN

THE first thing Sargon noticed when he arrived at the excavation site was the Talbots' dusty Land Cruiser parked on the side of the road. He pulled his pickup truck alongside and got out to investigate.

The Land Cruiser was empty but running at idle.

"Strange," he whispered to himself.

From where he stood, Sargon could not see the temple ruins, which were obscured behind a large, rocky berm a few hundred feet away, covered with scraggly vegetation and squat palm trees. A narrow path led through the vegetation up and over the hill, toward the temple ruins on the other side.

Sargon made his way along the path and was nearly at the top of the hill when he suddenly heard gunfire. Instinctively, he dropped to his hands and knees and crawled the rest of the way to where the path crested the berm. From there, he had a clear view of the temple site below.

He saw two gunmen dressed in fatigues, weapons raised, running toward the excavation pit. One wore a black and white headscarf, the other a black ski mask. He watched as they fired their weapons and then tossed a small object into the pit.

Seconds later, a powerful explosion rocked the entire area. Sargon flinched and dropped flat against the ground, his heart pounding furiously. *What in Allah's name was going on here?*

When he looked up again, the gunmen were on the move, walking quickly around the site and periodically looking into the pit, which was now belching thick black smoke. A few moments later—to Sargon's horror—they began walking quickly up the path. *Toward him.*

Sargon scampered away and crouched low behind a small stand of date palms, his gaze fixed on the path. A minute later, the two gunmen crested the hill and passed less than three feet away from where he hid.

They were conversing in low tones, and Sargon distinctly heard one of them say "vehicle" in Arabic. Sargon gasped audibly.

Instantly, the man in the ski mask halted and motioned for the other to be quiet.

Sargon held his breath.

"What is it?" the second gunman asked.

"I thought I heard something," replied the first, squinting and scanning both sides of the path.

Seconds passed in agonizing silence. Sargon

was sure the man in the ski mask would logically retrace his steps and, if he did, would quickly find Sargon's absurd hiding place, just a few feet off the path.

Several more seconds passed in silence, and Sargon became acutely aware of his own breathing. *Had it always been this loud?*

"I didn't hear anything," the second gunman said finally. "Come on, let's get the vehicle."

Those words struck Sargon like a jolt of electricity. His pickup truck was parked right next to the Land Cruiser. As he watched helplessly, the two gunmen turned and started back down the path.

Moments later, there was shouting and the sound of shuffling feet near the road. *They'd spotted his truck.* He could hear them returning, their footsteps growing louder by the second.

Sargon saw the head and shoulders of the first gunman just cresting the hill. He pulled his Tariq pistol from his pocket, unlocked the safety, and took aim. Without a second thought, he pulled the trigger and fired a single 9 mm round into the man's chest, causing him to stumble backward and downhill.

The second gunman, now visible, immediately dove off the path and disappeared into the vegetation.

Sargon's left shoulder ached with pain, and the rest of his body was weak with fatigue and stress. He knew he'd be no match for the second gunman in a hand-to-hand struggle. As he considered his options, he became acutely aware of the silence. For a full minute, there was no sound at all, save for the soft whooshing of the *shamal* through the dry brush and palm trees. Somewhere in that thicket, however, the second gunman was lurking. *What was he doing?*

Another minute passed in silence, and Sargon began to think maybe—*just maybe*—the second gunman had fled.

Suddenly he heard rustling nearby. He peered into the brush but saw nothing. Off to one side, a palm frond moved. *Was that the wind*? A tense moment passed as he strained to hear any sound.

Then, without warning, an explosion of automatic gunfire erupted to Sargon's left, and the tree he was leaning against shook violently as several rounds slammed into its trunk. Splinters and bits of plant material flew all around. Crunching footsteps were now coming toward him.

Sargon had only one option. He rolled left onto his wounded shoulder, raised his pistol in his right hand, and fired two quick shots in the direction of the rustling noise. His bullets whizzed into the palm forest and disappeared.

A split second later, more automatic gunfire erupted from the brush. One of the rounds whizzed so close to Sargon's ear that he could feel the heat and disrupted air. But he didn't flinch. Instead, he remained in his firing position, raised the pistol firmly, and fired repeatedly in the direction of the automatic gunfire. He kept firing until his clip of 9 mm rounds was empty. This would be his last stand.

When the chaos ended, the only sound left

was the whooshing of the *shamal*. Sargon did not hesitate before venturing into the brush. *If he was going to die today, there was no reason to delay the inevitable.* Twenty yards into the thicket, he found the second gunman lying awkwardly on his back, his black-and-white headscarf soaked red with blood. One of Sargon's shots had slammed into the man's head.

Sargon's next thought was about his friends, the Talbots. He rushed down the path and approached the edge of the archeological pit adjacent to the temple ruins. Thick plumes of black smoke were still billowing from the pit. He couldn't see much through the smoke, but he could tell the scaffolding was completely demolished, and some of it was still on fire at the bottom of the pit.

"Daniel!" he screamed into the pit. "Rebecca!" There was no answer. *He had to get down there!*

He ran back to the vehicles, carefully stepping over the body of the dead gunman in the path. He reached the rusty Datsun and searched in the back for something useful. But all he found were old oil cans and greasy automotive parts.

He then searched the Talbots' Land Cruiser, which was still idling on the side of the road.

"Aha!" he exclaimed as he spotted a large coil of high-quality nylon rope in the back compartment. Grabbing the rope and a large flashlight, he rushed back up the path toward the temple.

Sargon worked quickly, believing his friends might still be alive. It had been more than fifteen years since he'd done any actual fieldwork, but his archeological training came back to him quickly. He tied a series of square knots in the nylon rope at intervals of approximately three feet, doing his best to ignore the pain in his left shoulder.

Using a sturdy half-hitch knot, he secured one end of the rope to a nearby palm tree. Then, peering over the edge of the pit, he tossed the other end of the rope into the hole and watched with considerable concern as it disappeared into the swirling cauldron of black smoke. Near the bottom, he noted a few areas of flickering flames where the remains of the wooden scaffolding were still burning. *He had to keep the nylon rope away from those flames.* Carefully, he swung the rope to the far side of the pit, away from the charred and burning remains of the scaffolding. *Would that be far enough to avoid the heat of the flames?* There was only one way to find out.

The climb down was excruciating and terrifying. Sargon slid down the rope with one hand, using the knots to brace his feet as he did. As he descended, the smoke and dust became almost unbearable. He coughed and winced as he dropped, knot by knot, deeper into the pit. Near the bottom, the heavy smoke and dust stung his eyes so badly that he was forced to close them completely. He descended the last fifteen feet with his eyes shut, barely able to breathe.

Finally, his feet touched rubble. With his eyes still shut, he felt his way toward the wall of the temple, stumbling several times over loose stones, broken wood, and twisted metal. After some moments of struggling forward, his hands touched the smooth, glazed bricks of the temple wall. Then, with some effort, he pressed his back flat against the wall and opened his eyes, for the first time assessing the situation around him.

A small amount of sunlight filtered through the smoke and dust, dimly illuminating his surroundings. He could see that part of the temple's north wall had collapsed, creating a huge pile of loose bricks and rubble, upon which he was now standing. With a sinking feeling, he realized that his friends, Daniel and Becky Talbot, were trapped somewhere below.

He fumbled with the flashlight for several seconds before managing to turn it on. Surveying the damage around him, he spotted a tiny opening near his feet. *He might be able to reach the Talbots through that space!* Dropping to his hands and knees, he began removing bricks and debris, widening the hole. When it was big enough to fit his hand through, he shoved the flashlight into it and pressed his face close to take a look. He saw what seemed to be a small cavern beneath him. Encouraged, he quickly removed more debris until the opening was about two feet wide.

"Daniel! Becky!" he screamed into the space below. No reply.

Carefully, and with considerable pain, Sargon inched, feet-first, into the cavity until his entire body was crouched inside. "Daniel!" he screamed. "Becky!" He swept the flashlight beam around the small cavern and gasped at what he saw. Instead of being surrounded by loose rubble as he'd expected, he was instead surrounded by structural mud-brick walls. This was not an accidental space formed by the crumbling wall; *this was a man-made internal chamber of the temple!*

Sargon, at five foot eight, was just barely able to stand up inside the low-ceilinged chamber, which measured about six by eight feet. It appeared to be an anteroom of some sort, with a passageway at the interior end that led farther into the temple. He was just making his way toward that passageway when he heard a noise behind him. He turned with a start and trained his flashlight on a pile of bricks and rubble. In the beam of the flashlight, he saw the head and torso of a man, whom he recognized immediately.

"Daniel!" Sargon shouted incredulously, recognizing his friend Daniel Talbot lying helpless beneath a pile of bricks and debris.

Talbot responded in a series of shallow, wheezy spurts. "How . . . did . . . *you* . . . get . . . in here?"

"I . . . I climbed down on a rope I found in your truck," Sargon sputtered. "Where's Becky? Who were those men? What happened?" He asked these questions in a bewildered staccato.

Talbot, however, did not respond.

Frantically, Sargon began removing the debris that was piled high on Talbot's body. As he did, he repeatedly asked, "Daniel, can you hear me? Are you okay? Daniel?"

But there was no longer any response.

Sargon could not budge the largest of the boulders that lay across Talbot's legs, pinning him tightly to the floor. At this point, however, he was quite sure Talbot was dead.

Exhausted, frustrated, and deeply saddened, he dropped to his knees and said a silent prayer for his friend Daniel Talbot from Harvard University. As he did, he recalled that the Talbots' young daughter, Kathleen, had recently returned to the United States to visit her grandparents and to start first grade. He thanked Allah that at least *she* was safe.

Then, looking up, Sargon turned his attention to the passageway at the far end of the anteroom . . . and the interior chambers of the temple that lay beyond.

He moved cautiously across the anteroom toward the passageway on the other side, concentrating intensely on his surroundings, willfully pushing everything else out of his mind. At this moment, he was simply an archeologist, seeing something incredible and wondrous for the first time—something that had likely not been seen by human eyes for more than *five thousand* years.

His thoughts were everywhere at once. *A chamber inside the Tell-Fara temple?* It was utterly inconceivable and contrary to all conventional wisdom. Tell-Fara, after all, was a ziggurat, not a tomb. Or so most Assyriologists believed.

Everyone, that is, except the Talbots.

Sargon inched forward, awestruck by his surroundings. The walls of the anteroom were bare and formed of flat, baked bricks like those on the exterior of the temple. The room was entirely empty, but for the rubble and debris that had been pushed in by the explosion. Sargon tried not to think about the body of his friend, Daniel

Talbot, lying just a few feet behind him under a massive boulder.

Having crossed the anteroom, he now stood at the entrance to a narrow passageway, which led to what appeared to be another, larger chamber. He trained the flashlight on the corridor and stared in wonder. It, too, was constructed of baked brick, stretching straight before him a length of some twenty or thirty feet.

He focused for a moment on the contours of the passageway's entrance, marveling at its intricate brickwork. The entryway had a horseshoe shape, often seen in later Moorish architecture but hitherto unknown before about the fourth century BC.

Sargon regretted that Daniel and Becky Talbot were not there with him to share in this amazing discovery. After all, it was their dogged persistence and intuition that had made this revelation possible.

He continued farther into the temple, the white beam of his flashlight providing the only source of illumination. The air was stale and musty. The floor was packed earth—firm beneath his feet.

The passage led into a larger chamber. As his flashlight washed over the contours of this room, he gasped aloud. For a long while, he simply stood motionless, awestruck.

The chamber was astonishingly large, its floor measuring at least thirty by forty feet, with a high, arched ceiling. He first surveyed the ceiling with his flashlight. The brickwork was tight and superbly arranged in six adjacent archways, each measuring approximately twelve by twelve feet. Such technology was not known to exist in Mesopotamia for another three thousand years after Tell-Fara was built. Yet, here it was, holding up the roof of a *five-thousand-year-old* temple. Sargon shook his head in disbelief.

He trained the flashlight lower, washing the beam over the room's mud-brick walls. He counted at least thirty small niches arranged at uneven intervals and heights around the room, most containing small figurines or other carved objects.

He approached the nearest niche and shone his flashlight into it. His heart leapt as he found himself gazing upon the stone likeness of a bearded man, approximately life-sized, with translucent opals embedded in its eyes. The alabaster face stared back at him intensely, as stern and commanding a presence today as it had been five thousand years ago.

"My God," Sargon whispered, utterly astonished. He now knew that he was standing inside a tomb, not a ziggurat at all. Tell-Fara was a massive *tomb*—a concept absolutely unique in Mesopotamia in the third millennium BC.

But whose tomb?

Sargon centered the flashlight's beam on the enormous structure in the center of the chamber. As improbable as it seemed, the structure appeared to be a massive sarcophagus. He stared for several seconds before approaching it haltingly.

The dimensions of the sarcophagus were so large that, for a moment, he felt disoriented. It towered more than four feet over his head and measured approximately ten feet long and five feet wide. It sat atop a massive limestone pedestal, about five feet off the hard dirt floor.

The sarcophagus itself was constructed of four large alabaster slabs, the corners of which were secured by thick pillars of Turkish marble. Another slab of alabaster covered the top. The joints of the structure were tight, and the stone surfaces incredibly smooth. This was a work of meticulous craftsmanship and engineering for any era—let alone the third millennium BC.

Slowly and methodically, Sargon began circumnavigating the sarcophagus, inspecting each side carefully for any inscription that might give a clue as to whose tomb this was. He was surprised to find no markings at all on the first side he inspected, which appeared to be either the head or the foot of the sarcophagus. Nor were there any markings on the second and third sides. On the fourth side, facing away from the entrance, he found a marking. There, etched deeply into the limestone base was a large inscription measuring more than a foot high and nearly three feet wide:

Sargon studied the inscription for some time, mystified as to its meaning. After several minutes, he concluded he must have missed something on his first inspection. So, once again, he circled the sarcophagus slowly, carefully inspecting each visible surface with his flashlight, searching for markings. Again, however, he found no other inscription.

There must be additional markings on top, Sargon surmised. The top, however, was more than four feet above his head, and there appeared to be no easy way for him to climb up for a better view. He was still thinking about how to solve that problem when he heard a noise. His heart pounded as he tried to locate its source.

He heard it again. This time there was no mistaking the faint sound of *voices* somewhere outside the chamber.

Sargon immediately clicked off his flashlight and stood motionless in the blackness. For a few minutes, the voices continued wafting through the dark in undulating tones, always too faint to decipher. Then one of the voices began to grow louder.

Whoever it was, was coming into the temple.

CHAPTER TWELVE

"**H**EY American! Are you in there?"

Those words, shouted in Arabic, were the first words Sargon could hear clearly enough to understand. And from the volume and direction of the words, it was clear the shouter was in the excavation pit, not more than thirty or forty feet from where Sargon was now standing.

In the complete darkness of the burial chamber, Sargon performed a quick mental calculus. First, the only way out of the temple was through a small hole that led into the pit, the very space now occupied by the owner of that voice. Second, it had taken considerable effort to squeeze through that hole to get into the temple, and therefore, it would take at least as much time and effort to get out. In other words, there would be no element of surprise if he tried to escape. Third, he was out of ammunition. Fourth, he was far too weak to fight an able-bodied opponent. Considering those facts, Sargon decided his best option was simply to remain still in the darkness. *Perhaps they would go away.*

"Hello, American! Are you in there?" the voice repeated in Arabic.

Sargon swallowed hard and said nothing.

Then the voice said, quieter this time, "Ahmed, come on down!" He heard another voice, much farther away, responding to the first with an answer that was indecipherable.

"Ahmed, be careful!" the first voice yelled a minute later.

"I've got it," the second voice responded, louder this time.

Sargon deduced that a second person—presumably Ahmed—was now descending into the pit. Sargon remained motionless in the blackness of the mysterious tomb, once again awaiting his fate.

"Are they in there?" the second voice asked.

"I don't know, they didn't answer."

"You think they're dead?" the second voice asked after a long pause.

"I don't know. Go in and check."

"Why don't *you* go in and check?"

Another long pause. "It's dark in there!" said the first voice squeamishly.

"So use the flashlight."

"I didn't bring it."

"Honestly, Ahmed! Why was I cursed with such a *stupid brother?*"

Sargon listened to this conversation with bewilderment. These two voices sounded like . . . teenagers.

"Hey!" Sargon bellowed in his most authoritative, masculine voice. "Who are you?"

There was a long pause. Sargon imagined the two brothers miming to each other frantically, deciding how to respond.

Finally, the first voice said timidly, "We are Ahmed and Jabar, from the village."

"Why are you looking for the Americans?" Sargon demanded.

"We heard an explosion. We came to see if they were okay."

"How do you know them?"

"We work for them sometimes. They pay us . . . you know, to fetch things . . . clean their equipment. Stuff like that."

Sargon clicked on his flashlight and made his way quickly toward the anteroom. "Stay right there," he ordered as he walked.

As he approached the hole leading into the pit, he could hear scrambling and muffled voices on the other side. Using his flashlight, he peered through the hole and saw two young boys, perhaps twelve and fourteen years old, frantically trying to climb the nylon rope out of the pit.

"Wait a minute," Sargon called to the boys, using a milder voice this time. These kids clearly were not a threat. "You're not in trouble. It's okay. *Stop!*"

The brothers, however, continued their escape from the pit, furiously ascending the rope.

"Wait, boys, I need your help!"

The brothers continued climbing.

"I can *pay* you!"

The clambering stopped. The older brother, near the top of the rope, looked down at his younger brother below. "How much?" he asked.

"A lot."

Jabar and Ahmed proved quite cooperative after that. Once Sargon explained who he was—curator of the Iraqi National Museum—and that there had been an accident at the excavation site, the brothers were only too eager to help out, for a fee. They agreed on a flat rate of two Iraqi dinars for the day, equivalent to about six U.S. dollars.

First, Sargon constructed a crude hoist system using the nylon rope and a large bucket that one of the boys found topside. Jabar, the older brother, was stationed at the top of the pit and was responsible for manning the rope. Twelve-year-old Ahmed was stationed at the bottom of the pit and was responsible for filling the bucket.

Sargon then spent several hours crawling into the temple, making his way into the burial chamber, and methodically retrieving all the artifacts he found that could be removed. One by one, he brought the five-thousand-year-old artifacts into the pit, where Ahmed carefully placed them in the bucket for Jabar to hoist slowly to the surface.

"Careful with that! Careful!" Sargon warned at least a dozen times throughout this procedure.

As best he could, Sargon kept a mental inventory of where each piece had been retrieved and its position relative to other pieces in the tomb, though he knew he'd never be able to keep it all straight. This was haphazard, slash-and-burn archeology of the type he absolutely abhorred. But it couldn't be helped. Better to recover these precious artifacts than to let them be looted by villagers or, worse, destroyed by religious zealots. There was simply no time to observe proper archeological procedures. No photographs, no sketches, no inventory control numbers—not even notes. What he was doing today was nothing short of sacrilege for a trained archeologist. But it had to be done.

The three took a break in the early afternoon, and Sargon sent the boys into the village for some food. "Don't tell *anyone* about this," he warned as the boys were leaving. Then, thinking better of it, he added, "There's an extra two dinars if you keep this quiet."

Ecstatic, the boys ran off to retrieve lunch. When they had gone, Sargon went to the Land Cruiser and searched it thoroughly. He did not find what he was looking for. On his way back, he dragged the first gunman's body into the brush, so that it could not be seen from the path.

He then returned to the pit and squeezed himself through the small hole into the temple's anteroom. There, as he held the flashlight with one hand, he searched Daniel Talbot's pockets and finally found what he was looking for—the official paperwork granting the Talbots permission to excavate at Tell-Fara. Sargon remembered signing that very paperwork more than two years ago. He flipped through several pages in the bundle and eventually found what he needed. It was a letter of support from Harvard University signed by Dr. Charles Eskridge, dean of the Department of Near East Studies.

A short time later, the boys returned from the village with lunch, which consisted of flat, un-leavened bread and a large pot of *khoresht*—beef-and-vegetable stew. They ate communal-style on the ground, each of them scooping warm stew from the pot with pieces of flatbread. Sargon had a hunch the boys' mother had prepared this stew, which, surprisingly, wasn't half bad.

By mid-afternoon, Sargon had retrieved 127 artifacts from the Tell-Fara tomb, including more than a dozen funerary statues, jewelry, orna-ments, pottery, and a beautiful gold-leafed lyre carved at one end to resemble the head of a ram. The task now was to load these precious artifacts into the Land Cruiser. Sargon had already de-cided that his brother-in-law's open-bed pickup truck was not a suitable option.

It took another hour for Sargon and the boys to load the vehicle. This involved repeated trips up and down the rocky path, which was exhausting for all of them, especially Sargon.

When they were done, Sargon announced, "I have one more job for you boys."

"And then we get paid?" Jabar asked.

"Yes."

"Four dinars total, right?"

"Help me with this last job, boys, and I'll make it *ten*."

The brothers smiled at each other and eagerly followed Sargon back to the temple.

———

"We need more rope!" Sargon yelled to the boys.

"We've looked everywhere," Jabar responded, "We can't find any more rope." He and Amhed had just completed a thorough search of the entire excavation site.

"Why can't we just use this one?" Ahmed asked, pointing to the rope dangling into the pit, which was still tied to a palm tree.

"Because," Sargon explained in an exasperated tone, "we need a rope *down there*." He pointed down into the pit. "If we untie this rope up *here*, we won't be able to get back up."

"Oh."

"Okay, here's the plan," said Sargon. "You—" He pointed to Jabar. "You stay up here and tend the rope."

Jabar nodded.

"Ahmed, you come down with me."

One at a time, Sargon and Ahmed descended into the pit. At the bottom, Sargon pulled out a pocketknife. He picked up the slack end of the nylon rope, which lay loosely coiled at the bottom of the pit, and measured off several arm lengths—about twenty feet in all—until he reached a point in the rope that dangled about four feet above the floor. "Can you reach this high?" he asked Ahmed, pointing to a knot just above his hand.

Ahmed reached up and verified that he could.

With that, Sargon quickly sliced the nylon rope with his knife, just below the knot. He then gathered up the remaining loose rope on the bottom of the pit and said to Ahmed, "Come with me."

"Hey!" Jabar yelled from above, "where are you going?"

"We'll be right back," Sargon responded. "Stay where you are."

Sargon went first through the hole into the anteroom and then helped Ahmed through. He carefully trained the flashlight away from Daniel Talbot's lifeless body to prevent Ahmed from seeing it. "Keep walking . . . not much farther," he said as the two of them traversed the narrow passageway toward the large room at the end.

"Wow!" Ahmed said as he entered the burial chamber.

"Amazing, huh?"

Ahmed nodded in agreement.

"Okay, here's what I need you to do." Sargon tied a knot at one end of the rope and walked to the far side of the sarcophagus. He threw the knotted end over the giant stone structure, so the rope was now draped across the top. Sargon and Ahmed stood on opposite sides.

"Grab that knot and put it between your feet."

Ahmed complied.

"Now, hold on tight. You're going up!" With that, Sargon pulled hard on his end of the rope, using the sarcophagus as a crude pulley. "Can you get on top yet?" he asked, wincing in pain.

"I'm up!"

Sargon tossed the boy the flashlight and instructed him to inspect the top of the sarcophagus for markings. "What do you see?"

Ahmed reported back in a baffled tone, "I see . . . *nothing*."

"Isn't there writing on the stone? Tell me what it looks like."

There was a long pause. "No, there's no writing."

"Are you sure? There must be *something*—symbols, pictures, markings, anything?"

"No, mister, there's nothing. Just a smooth, flat stone, like I said."

Sargon was confused. There *had* to be more markings on this tomb somewhere. The one on the base of the sarcophagus didn't make any sense. "Okay, jump down," he said. "We'll have to think of something else."

They returned to the anteroom, where Sargon instructed Ahmed to crawl back through the hole and into the pit. Sargon stayed inside the anteroom and shouted instructions through the hole. "Grab that metal pole," he yelled, using the flashlight's beam to direct Ahmed to a long metal pipe sticking out of the smoking debris pile. The pipe had once formed part of the scaffolding. "Can you pry it loose?"

"Yes, I've got it."

"Okay, pass it to me." With some effort, the two of them finessed the twelve-foot metal pole through the access hole and into the anteroom and passageway. "Now, tell Jabar to send down one of those flat metal shovels that are lying around up there."

Ahmed nodded.

"And make sure it has a sturdy handle," Sargon added.

After a few minutes, Jabar sent down a suitable shovel to Ahmed, lowering it carefully on the rope.

"Now pass me the shovel," Sargon ordered, "and the bucket, too."

Ahmed complied.

Five minutes later, Sargon and Ahmed were back in the burial chamber with the implements they had just retrieved. Sargon went to work quickly as Ahmed held the flashlight. First, Sargon inserted the wooden handle of the shovel into the metal pipe, making sure that the metal sleeve of the shovel head extended fully into it. He pushed several small wedges of wood, which he had cut using his pocketknife, around the metal sleeve to make the connection tight.

Next, he tied the twenty-foot length of rope tightly to the other end of the pipe, wrapping it around several times to make sure it wouldn't slip off. Finally, he inspected the sarcophagus carefully with the flashlight, slowly running the beam along the crevice where the top and the sides of the sarcophagus met. He eventually found a spot he liked and placed the bucket upside down on the floor about six feet laterally from that spot.

"Stay back," Sargon warned as he picked up the pipe/shovel apparatus and stepped onto the overturned bucket. With a quick spearing motion, he slammed the shovel head into the sarcophagus, aiming for the seam between the lid and walls. The steel shovel head contacted the alabaster slab with a loud, metallic clank, producing a small shower of bright orange sparks. Sargon nearly lost his balance as the pipe vibrated sharply in his hands. Recovering his footing, he repeated the blow again. As before, the shovel head hit the sarcophagus and bounced back, producing noise and sparks.

This process went on for several minutes, with Ahmed watching in bewildered amusement.

Frustrated, Sargon redoubled his effort. With all his strength, he swung the pipe over his head and slammed it hard into the stone sarcophagus. This time, his aim was true. The flat shovel head aligned perfectly with the horizontal seam in the sarcophagus. He slowly released his grip on the pipe and exhaled with relief when he found that it no longer needed his support. The shovel head was now wedged tightly beneath the lid of the sarcophagus, with the pipe extending outward a distance of nine feet.

"Grab the rope," Sargon instructed, "but don't do anything until I say so." He repositioned the bucket to get a better view.

"Now, pull down," he ordered, nodding at Ahmed.

Ahmed pulled down on the rope with both hands. Sargon watched the lid carefully. Nothing happened.

"Pull harder!"

Ahmed groaned as he pulled down with all the weight his scrawny body could provide. This effort was rewarded with the sounds of metal grinding on stone and creaking wood.

"Keep pulling!" Sargon barked, reaching up and grasping the pipe over his head. With one hand, he, too, pulled down using the weight of his body. The sound of grinding metal and creaking wood intensified. *Something was going to give.* He just hoped it wasn't the shovel.

Sargon felt a movement and suddenly heard a new grinding noise. Not metal on stone, but *stone on stone*. With his left hand, he reached up, ignoring the throbbing pain in his shoulder, and ran his fingers along the horizontal seam where the shovel head was lodged. He felt a gap. He quickly shoved small wooden wedges into the gap on either side of the shovel head.

"Ahmed, slacken the rope!" Ahmed complied, and, as he did, the sarcophagus lid gently creaked down onto the wooden wedges. Sargon quickly repositioned the pipe and shovel. This time, the shovel head went a fraction of an inch farther beneath the lid.

Sargon and Ahmed repeated this process several more times until, finally, the entire shovel head was lodged beneath the lid of the sarcophagus, creating a gap of about three inches. At that point, Sargon disconnected the pipe from the shovel head and slid the pipe off of the shovel handle. He maneuvered the end of the pipe through the gap that was now held open by the shovel head. The pipe just barely scraped through.

"Pull down!" Sargon ordered as he, too, pulled down hard on the metal pipe. The massive sarcophagus lid responded by tilting farther upward with a deep, stone-on-stone grinding sound.

"Okay, now, hold that! *And don't let go!*"

"I'll try," Ahmed responded through gritted teeth. He was clearly struggling.

"*Keep holding it!*" Then, with a strength that came from somewhere deep in his soul, Sargon pulled himself up toward the metal pipe and swung his left leg up and over. He wriggled his body over the pipe and positioned himself lengthwise, so that the pipe was now running beneath his torso and through his legs. He was facing the sarcophagus and had a full view of the five-inch gap that had been opened by the leverage of the pipe—the very pipe he was now lying on.

"Ahmed, can you reach the flashlight?"

"No, it's too far," Ahmed grunted. "Mister, I'm getting really tired. How much longer?"

"Just a little longer. *Hold on!*" Slowly, Sargon extended his hand toward the sarcophagus and inserted it through the gap. He blocked out of his mind the distinct possibility that, at any moment, something (including Ahmed's skinny arms) could give way, sending the massive alabaster top slamming down on his arm.

He reached in farther and felt . . . something . . . something cool and dry. It was . . . *sand*. Perplexed, he dug deeper with his hand, shimmying along the pipe to get as close to the lid as possible. As he repositioned his body, however, he felt the sarcophagus lid move slightly, putting pressure on his arm. His own weight, he realized, was helping to keep the lid open.

With his hand, he felt sand in every direction. Cool, dry sand. He dug deeper and stretched his fingers as far as they would go. Again, he felt only sand.

"*My arms hurt!*" Ahmed whined from below.

"A little longer!" Sargon shouted. *"Don't let go!"* He shoved his arm deeper into the gap, ignoring the pain as his elbow scraped tightly through. He now had his entire arm inside the sarcophagus. Still, though, he felt only cool, dry sand.

"Mister . . ."

"Not yet, Ahmed! Keep holding." Sargon was searching frantically now with his hand. He repositioned his body again to get his arm even deeper into the sand—as deep as it would go. As he did, the lid jostled with a grinding noise, and he felt even more pressure on his arm. He began to wonder how he would ever get his elbow back out. But he pushed the thought aside.

"Mister . . . I can't hold on."

Sargon felt something!

"It's slipping!" Ahmed cried.

"Hold on!" Sargon barked, "I'm almost done!" He had the object between his fingers now. Something smooth, something . . . not sand. But he couldn't move it. *It was connected to something else.*

The lid was now moving, coming down perceptibly. The pressure on his arm had turned distinctly to pain. "Hold onto the rope!" Sargon screamed.

"I can't!" Ahmed whimpered. "It's slipping!"

This was it. Sargon grasped the object firmly between his fingers and jerked it hard. It came loose! Frantically, he now attempted to extract his arm from the sarcophagus. But his elbow would not pass, no matter how hard he pulled. He didn't care about the pain anymore. He had to get his arm out of there before that lid came down!

"Ahmed, this is it, I promise! Pull as hard as you can! *Now!*"

Sargon could hear Ahmed struggling behind him, and he felt the pressure on his elbow reduce slightly. But it wasn't enough. His elbow was still stuck. Intuitively, he repositioned his body on the pipe. He knew that his weight, too, was contributing to the lever effect. *If he could shift his weight down the lever arm . . .* Delicately, he slid backward an inch and brought his feet up to the pipe. He was now fully prone and balanced on the pipe, with his outstretched arm wedged tightly beneath the lid of the sarcophagus.

The slight shift in weight on the pipe made the lid jostle slightly, creating just enough room for Sargon to pull his arm out. He nearly dropped the object in his clenched fingers as it passed through the gap.

A split second later, the rope slipped completely through Ahmed's hands, causing an immediate chain reaction. The pipe popped upward—with Sargon on it—and came dislodged from the sarcophagus. Sargon and the pipe tumbled down toward the dirt floor. Simultaneously, the lid of the sarcophagus slammed down hard with a thunderous crash, flattening the shovel head instantly and snapping its handle clean off.

The sarcophagus—which had remained tightly sealed for over five-thousand-years—was sealed once again.

Sargon hit the floor awkwardly on his side, which knocked the wind out of him. He remained motionless for a few moments before finally rolling over and sitting up with a groan.

For a long while, neither of them spoke. Then, finally, Ahmed asked in a timid voice, "Hey, mister, what *is* that thing?" He pointed to the small object still grasped between Dr. Sargon's fingers.

Sargon inspected the object closely in the dim light and responded quietly, "I don't know . . ."

CHAPTER THIRTEEN

Present Day. Washington, D.C.

CARLOS Guiterez double-parked his road-weary Ford Explorer alongside Dr. Sainsbury's Subaru on the 1800 block of U Street and gazed with great concern at the brick townhouse directly to his right. At half past midnight, it was the only house on the block with its interior lights still on.

He double checked the address he had jotted on a scrap of paper. *What the heck is she doing in there?* he wondered.

Carlos cared a great deal about the welfare of Dr. Kathleen Sainsbury. Not only did he like her personally, he depended on her. He needed her to succeed, and that meant she had to stay safe. Of course, until about six months ago, her safety hadn't been a particular concern of his.

But that was before the incident in North Carolina.

He'd first learned about it from Dr. Sainsbury herself, who, in turn, had heard it through the grapevine. Dr. Michael Kim, a molecular biologist and a friend of hers from Johns Hopkins, had been shot and killed in his house in Chapel Hill, North Carolina. The official story was that Dr. Kim had surprised a burglar, who shot him while escaping. But that story never made much sense to Carlos. Dr. Kim lived in a very safe area of Chapel Hill, and there were no other reported burglaries in his neighborhood during that time. Moreover (according to the rumor mill at least) the police found evidence that Dr. Kim's phone had been tampered with—as if someone had been trying to insert a bug. In any event, the police never caught the shooter.

All of this made for fascinating conversation and whispered conspiracy theories at biology conferences in the ensuing months. But what made Carlos particularly nervous was the exact nature of Dr. Kim's research.

Dr. Kim was one of a handful of biologists in the entire world studying the INDY gene.

Since the incident in North Carolina, Carlos had kept a wary eye out for Dr. Sainsbury's safety. He secretly worried about her living alone and her habit of dropping by the lab at odd hours of the night, by herself. He was also vaguely distrustful of Bryce Whittaker, her new acquaintance, although he had no rational reason for that suspicion.

Now, with Dr. Sainsbury inside some stranger's house in the middle of the night—especially after her disconcerting phone call an hour earlier—Carlos was worried to the point of distraction.

He stared unblinkingly at the illuminated foyer window of the townhouse, trying to discern any movement inside. He thought about calling her again but decided against it. *She said she was fine.*

It had been a little over two years since Carlos had first responded to Dr. Sainsbury's online ad for an office manager. At that time, he'd just graduated from Northern Virginia Community College with an accounting degree. He was thirty-nine and had served twenty-one of those years in the Marine Corps. Although he'd used the G.I. bill to defray tuition costs, his wife, Ana, still had to work overtime as a dental technician just to make ends meet. With two young children, a mountain of debt, and an overworked wife, Carlos needed a job. He was therefore thrilled when he received the offer to be QLS's office manager.

But also a little worried.

QLS was a small startup with no revenue, no infrastructure, and no commercial product. In fact, the only thing QLS had going for it was Dr. Kathleen Sainsbury and her promising research.

To her credit, Dr. Sainsbury had always treated Carlos fairly. More than fairly, in fact. He'd always received a decent salary—including bonuses—even when Dr. Sainsbury herself went without pay. Carlos knew this because he kept all of the company's books. And he appreciated Kathleen's generosity more than she would ever know.

He checked his watch and looked up again at the brick townhouse. *What was she doing in there?* His Marine Corps instincts were telling him something wasn't right.

His thoughts raced quickly through the past year at QLS, which had been a tough one. They'd missed two important milestones: isolation of a therapeutic treatment and commencement of Phase I animal studies. Although Dr. Sainsbury had quickly dismissed these stumbling blocks as trivial—a "natural part of science," she'd said—Carlos knew better. He knew these missed milestones were causing great concern among the investors. Indeed, for the past several months, he'd managed to assuage a few of them only with vague promises of something big being "right around the corner." Their patience was wearing thin, and he wondered how much longer QLS could realistically stay afloat.

Something inside the townhouse caught his attention. Two moving figures in the foyer were casting shadows on the curtained window. His muscles tensed.

Kathleen checked her watch. It was past 1:00 A.M., and she was fading quickly. Between the wine at dinner with Bryce Whittaker, the anxiety preceding her meeting with Dr. Sargon, and the unexpected bombshell about her parents' murder, she was drifting into a mental fog. She desperately needed sleep.

Sargon had just finished recounting his escape from Iraq in 1979. How he drove from Tell-Fara to Najaf the night of the shootings and called Charles Eskridge at Harvard from a private phone in the back of a bakery, paying the owner the extortive sum of fifty British pounds for the privilege. How Dr. Eskridge, in turn, had contacted the U.S. Embassy in Turkey and made arrangements for Sargon—now traveling under the assumed name of Tariq Khalid Al-Fulani—to pass safely into Turkey. How Dr. Eskridge, himself, had flown to Turkey to meet Sargon and had eagerly inspected the truckload of artifacts that had been recovered from Tell-Fara.

That had been the deal, after all. More than a hundred priceless relics from Tell-Fara in exchange for Sargon's freedom and safe passage to the United States. Sargon had upheld his end of the bargain by handing over every artifact he'd found at Tell-Fara.

Except one.

Dr. Eskridge had likewise upheld his end of the deal. Twenty months and three political-asylum hearings later, Sargon—now Dr. Tariq Khalid Al-Fulani—became a naturalized citizen of the United States of America. A free man.

"Those pieces from Tell-Fara," Sargon said, concluding his monologue, "are still on display at the Oriental Institute in Cambridge, Massachusetts."

Kathleen yawned, too tired to even pretend to be interested anymore. "I need to go," she announced, rising to her feet.

"Yes, of course. It's been a very long night." Sargon stood and said nothing for several seconds.

Kathleen broke the silence. "Uh . . . you said you had something to give me?"

"Oh, yes, yes, of course." Dr. Sargon shuffled quickly out of the room and returned a short time later holding an ornate silver box, similar to the antique Quran boxes on the table. He handed it to her ceremonially. "This box is from Turkey, eighteenth century."

"Wow," said Kathleen, doing her best to fake enthusiasm. "It's beautiful." She had absolutely no need for an antique Quran box, but maybe she could use it as a makeshift jewelry case or something.

"No, no, the box is not important," Sargon said. "It's what's *inside* the box . . ."

Kathleen took the box and carefully unlatched and lifted the lid. The interior was lined with faded crimson silk embroidered with an intricate gold pattern. A small object, about an inch long, rested in the center of the box, wrapped tightly in cheesecloth. She looked at Sargon, who nodded approvingly for her to unwrap it.

"I believe this artifact is very significant," he explained. "Perhaps one of the most important ever found in Iraq."

Nervously, Kathleen set the box on the table and picked up the clothbound object. It was surprisingly light in her palm. She began to unwrap it slowly.

"This would have been the culmination of your mother and father's professional work," said Sargon. "I am *convinced* it would have been the most important find of their careers."

Kathleen unraveled the object more quickly now, removing layer upon layer of the gauze-like cloth. "What is it?" she asked before she was even done unwrapping.

"It's something I've had it in my possession for a very long time. Since that day at Tell-Fara."

"This is from Tell-Fara?"

"Yes, from the sarcophagus that was inside the temple."

Kathleen removed the final layer of cheese-cloth and recoiled at the small object now resting exposed in the palm of her hand. "Is that what I *think* it is?"

Dr. Sargon nodded slightly.

"But I . . . I don't understand." Kathleen inspected the grotesque object in her hand. It was a human tooth—a front incisor including the conical root—brown with age and well worn at the crown. She quickly replaced it in the box and brushed her hands together with a slight feeling of revulsion.

"It's several thousand years old."

"But . . . why do you want *me* to have it?"

"I've had it for so long," said Sargon. "I never knew what to do with it. I asked Allah for guidance many times. But, for thirty years, I never received an answer. This *secret*"—he pointed to the tooth in the silver box—"has weighed heavy on my heart for many years."

Kathleen stared through bleary eyes, unsure of how to respond.

"And then, just today, I saw the article in the newspaper about your company—*Quantum Life Sciences.*" Dr. Sargon enunciated the words with reverence, as if the company's name itself had some religious significance. "And I saw your picture. You looked so much like your mother that

I knew immediately . . . This is God's will!" He motioned emphatically toward the silver box and the ghoulish artifact it contained.

Kathleen stood dumbfounded. Was Sargon speaking incoherently, or was she just too exhausted to understand? "What am I supposed to do with this?" she asked, gesturing toward the tooth in the silver box.

Sargon shook his head and spoke in a reassuring, almost patronizing tone. "It's late. And you're tired. Let's talk about this tomorrow. Can you come by in the morning?"

Kathleen was taken off guard by the question. "I, uh . . . I have a lot of work to do."

"Just for an hour," said Sargon insistently. "*I promise.*" There was a twinge of desperation in his voice.

"No, really, I can't—"

"Please. I have some important things to tell you about this artifact. You'll understand after I explain, I promise. Just an hour . . . that's all I ask."

Kathleen sighed. She was too tired to argue about it. "Okay, I'll try." In her mind, though, she'd already decided that Sargon was, at the very least, *odd*. All this talk about Allah and God's will was making her uncomfortable, and she had no desire to spend another minute with him, let alone an entire *hour*.

She made her way to the front door, opened it, and bid him good night. She stepped out onto the porch, exhausted both physically and emotionally, and relished the rush of cool, nighttime air.

"Wait," Sargon called after her. "You forgot this." He caught up with her on the porch and held out the silver Quran box.

"I don't want it."

"But you *must* take it. It's important."

"I'll get it when I see you tomorrow."

Sargon thrust the box toward her emphatically. "No. It belongs to you. It's *connected* to you . . . through your parents, through—" He paused. "Through *God*." He held the box inches from her hands. "You must take it. Please."

Kathleen needed sleep, and the path of least resistance was clearly just to take the box. Besides, this man had been her parents' friend. "Fine," she relented, taking the antique box from his hands.

Sargon smiled wanly. "Good. You'll understand tomorrow, I promise."

Kathleen turned quickly and started down the steps. She was surprised to see Carlos's car double-parked beside hers.

"Dr. Sainsbury!" Carlos called, getting out of his car. He waved and hurried over to meet her at the bottom of the steps.

"Carlos, what are you doing here?"

"I was worried about you."

"I *told* you I was fine."

"Well, you didn't sound very convincing to me. I thought you might be in trouble."

"How did you even know where I was?"

Carlos shrugged. "You said you were on U Street. So, I drove up and down until I spotted your car."

Kathleen shook her head in disbelief.

"I would have called, but, uh . . ." Carlos nodded toward the house, where Dr. Sargon was still standing on the front porch, arms folded, watching the two of them intently. Carlos lowered his voice to a whisper. "I didn't know if you might be *with* someone."

"Oh Jeez, no!" Kathleen pointed to the house and tried to explain. "That's . . . he's . . . we . . . it's complicated."

"Are you okay to drive?" Carlos asked.

"Yeah, I'm fine. I just need some sleep. I'm exhausted."

As they spoke, a black Lincoln Navigator with tinted windows glided by, its brake lights flashing momentarily as it passed.

"That's weird," Carlos said.

"What is?"

"I've been here thirty minutes, and that's the third time that same car has passed by."

"Probably a drug dealer."

"Yeah, we should get out of here."

Kathleen unlocked her car door, and Carlos held it open as she got in and fastened her seat belt. "Carlos," she said, as he was about to close the door.

"Hmm?"

"Thanks again for checking up on me. It was really a sweet thing to do. Totally *unnecessary*, but sweet."

"No problem, Dr. S. Just making sure you're okay." He pointed to the antique silver box on the front passenger's seat of the car. "What is that thing, anyway?"

Kathleen had almost forgotten about it. "Oh, this? I guess you'd call it a gift."

"From him?" Carlos nodded at Sargon on the porch.

Kathleen thought about it for a moment. "Actually, it's sort of from my parents."

CHAPTER FOURTEEN

Luce Venfeld inspected the digital image on his computer screen. It was just past 2:00 A.M., and he was sitting in the library of his penthouse condo in Crystal City. Across the Potomac River, the Jefferson Memorial gleamed brightly in the glow of several dozen spotlights. The night was otherwise black and moonless.

"Who's the old man?" Venfeld said into a pre-paid cell phone.

"His name's Tariq Al-Fulani," replied Semion Zafer. His voice was hoarse, with a thick Israeli accent. "Some sort of antiques dealer."

The photograph was a grainy nighttime shot taken through a telephoto lens. It showed Dr. Kathleen Sainsbury receiving a blurry object from an elderly man in a white shirt. They were standing together on the front stoop of a brick row house.

"What's that he's handing her?" Venfeld asked.

"A box."

"What *kind* of box?"

"I couldn't tell. It might have been metal. It was sort of shiny."

"Any idea what was inside?"

"No."

"Okay," said Venfeld calmly, "stay where you are." He pressed a button on the phone, terminating the call. Then, turning his full attention to the photograph on the screen, he zoomed in on the old man.

Venfeld knew a great deal about Dr. Kathleen Sainsbury. He knew she was the only child of Rebecca S. Talbot and Daniel S. Talbot, both deceased. He knew she'd been adopted and raised from the age of seven by her maternal grandparents, John and Abigail Sainsbury of Great Falls, Virginia. He knew she'd attended Langley High School, where she was a straight-A student and a standout soccer player, and that she'd received both a B.S. and M.S. in biology from the University of Virginia, followed by a Ph.D. in microbiology from Johns Hopkins University. And he knew all about her post-doctoral work at NIH, which had terminated abruptly two years ago.

Venfeld also knew a fair amount about Kathleen's parents, who were both killed in 1979 in southern Iraq as a result of some sort of archeological mishap. What he *didn't* know was who this old man was in the photograph . . . and why he was meeting with Dr. Sainsbury in the middle of the night.

Venfeld did not believe in coincidences, something he'd learned in the CIA. Here was an old man with an Arabic surname giving a shiny metal box to a woman whose parents died mysteriously in Iraq in 1979. There was a connection, and Venfeld aimed to find out what it was. The Olam Foundation was now tantalizingly close to its goal, for which he would soon earn a fortune. *Nothing* could be left to chance.

He pushed REDIAL on the prepaid cell phone.

Zafer answered on the first ring. "Yeah?"

"Pay Dr. Al-Fulani a visit and find out what was in that box."

"Now?"

"Yes, *now.*"

CHAPTER FIFTEEN

Bethesda, Maryland.

It was an unusually cold morning for late March—below freezing with a stiff, northwest breeze. A perky brunette "meteorologist" was calling for a 30 percent chance of mixed precipitation.

Kathleen hit the remote and went to the closet for her warmest overcoat. "Oh no," she muttered, seeing that the wooden hanger was empty. She remembered immediately where she'd left her cashmere coat.

She pictured the exact moment when she'd handed the coat to Dr. Sargon at his house last night. She distinctly remembered having the coat on when she finished her date with Bryce Whittaker . . .

Her mind lingered on that thought for a moment. Her date with Whittaker had been . . . *interesting*. No, it had been more than interesting. It had been enjoyable. Pleasant. *Fun*. Surprisingly, she found herself wanting to see him again as soon as possible. *Should I call him? No.* She dismissed the idea. *He'll call if he's interested.*

Her thoughts then shifted back to her Versace coat and to Dr. Sargon, the strange old man who claimed to be a friend of her parents. Kathleen had no reason to doubt his account of events in Iraq decades ago, and she was genuinely glad that he'd told her what really happened to her parents there. But the talk of "God's will" and the Great Flood had been a bit too much for her. Dr. Sargon was apparently obsessed with something biblical and grandiose, and Kathleen simply did not have the time to get involved with such things. Her focus had to stay on QLS, which was having problems of its own.

Nevertheless, she wanted her coat back.

When Kathleen arrived at the 1800 block of U Street Northwest, just after 10:30 A.M., everything was different from the night before.

Two D.C. Metropolitan police cruisers were parked at the curb in front of Dr. Sargon's row house, their red and blue lights flashing insistently. Double-parked beside the police cruisers was a bright yellow ambulance from Sibley Hospital, its emergency lights blinking white and red.

Kathleen drove by slowly, searching for a parking spot.

On the sidewalk, she saw two D.C. police officers and a man in a blue blazer talking to one another. One of the uniformed officers was pointing toward Sargon's house. And that's when Kath-

leen noticed the yellow police tape draped across
the front entrance.

She pulled into the first available space, about
a block and a half away, and walked back toward
the scene. She was slightly out of breath from the
brisk walk when she approached the two officers
and the third man standing in front of Sargon's
house. "What's going on?" she asked.

"Police investigation, ma'am," said one of the
uniformed officers. His tone was polite yet stern.
"Please stay clear of the area for the time being."
He pointed across the street, where a small clutch
of neighbors was gathered, some holding steam-
ing cups of coffee.

"But—" Kathleen hesitated. Her first instinct
was to walk away—*fast*. Nothing good could
come of getting involved. But her coat was in
there. And her car had been parked directly in
front of the townhouse for nearly three hours last
night. Surely, someone had seen it—possibly one
of those neighbors standing across the street at
this very moment.

"Ma'am . . ." The officer was clearly getting annoyed with her.

"I left my coat in there," Kathleen blurted.
"Can I just go in and get it?"

The two uniformed officers exchanged surprised glances.

"You left your coat in *there*?" asked the second
officer. "When?"

Kathleen sighed. *Here it comes.* "Last night."

"You were here last night?" asked the first officer.

"Yes."

"What time?"

Before Kathleen could respond, the man in the blue blazer interrupted. He was thin, African-American, in his late forties with a neatly trimmed mustache and beard. He was impeccably dressed. A photo ID badge pinned to his jacket identified him as Special Agent Anthony Wills of the Federal Bureau of Investigation. "I'll take it from here, guys," he said to the two hulking officers, much to their apparent displeasure. Then, turning to Kathleen, he said politely, "Let's go get your coat."

Relieved to be dealing with someone reasonable, Kathleen followed the FBI man up the walkway and stairs to Sargon's house. They ducked under the police tape and walked through the front door, which was wide open.

"Okay, where's your coat?" said Agent Wills.

Kathleen stood in the foyer, temporarily distracted by all the activity around her. At the front door, an evidence technician in a blue jumpsuit was dusting the brass doorknob for fingerprints. Another evidence technician was taking photographs in the living room adjacent the foyer, where Kathleen and Dr. Sargon had been sitting last night. Two EMTs stood at the top of the front hall steps, apparently waiting for something to be completed in one of the upstairs rooms.

"Ma'am?" said Agent Wills, still waiting for an answer.

"Oh, sorry . . . I think he put it over there somewhere." Kathleen pointed toward a door under the stairs.

"What does it look like?"

"It's long, cream-colored, with three brown buttons down the front."

As Wills disappeared behind the closet door, Kathleen surveyed the scene around her. She felt conspicuous and self-conscious, and more than a little uneasy about the situation. She glanced into the living room and noticed an evidence technician eyeing her curiously. He looked away immediately as she caught his gaze.

Then she saw the table—the same one she'd looked at last night with all the Persian antiques—except, now, something was out of place. It took her a moment, but she finally realized that all of the Q'uran boxes were open, their lids standing erect on their hinges.

"Is this it?" Agent Wills asked, returning from the coat closet and holding up a cream-colored overcoat.

"Yes, thank you! I wouldn't have bothered you, but this is a really expensive coat."

"Yeah, looks like it."

Kathleen watched as Agent Wills—still holding the coat up with one hand—ran his other hand slowly up and down the length of the coat, apparently feeling the softness of the cashmere. Then he felt both sleeves. Then he felt all along the inside of the coat. *He's searching for a weapon*, Kathleen realized. Her stomach began to churn.

Agent Wills handed her the coat, and she thanked him meekly. "So, should I see myself out now?" She nodded toward the police tape across the doorway.

"Actually, I was hoping you could stay and answer a few questions."

Kathleen's heart sank.

Wills's tone had suddenly turned crisp and professional. Gone were the easygoing smile and friendly demeanor of just a few minutes ago. Out of nowhere, a short, stocky woman in a blue FBI windbreaker appeared at his side, holding a notepad and pen. She gave Kathleen a surly glance that seemed to say, *Bitch, I already know you're lying.*

Kathleen swallowed hard. This was not how she'd envisioned spending her Sunday morning. "Am I in trouble?" she asked, her stomach starting to knot.

Wills replied without smiling. "It's possible."

CHAPTER SIXTEEN

THE ride to the FBI's Washington, D.C., field office was not as humiliating as Kathleen had expected. Special Agent Wills drove a dark blue Crown Victoria, unidentifiable as a law-enforcement vehicle except for the shotgun rack and police radio mounted on the center console. More important, there were no sirens, as Kathleen had feared. Nor was she forced to sit in the backseat behind bulletproof glass. Instead, to her surprise, Wills had politely offered her the front passenger's seat and even opened the door for her. His partner with the notepad, Agent Cheryl Hendricks, sat in the back, frowning the entire time.

They arrived at the field office at Judiciary Square just after 11:15 A.M., cleared security, and took the elevator to the fourth floor. The office was spacious and sparsely appointed, and surprisingly quiet. A guard at the front desk greeted Wills and Hendricks familiarly as they entered.

"Before we get started," Wills said to Kathleen

in the reception area, "would you like something to drink? Coffee or soda?"

"Coffee, please."

"Cream and sugar?"

"Black."

Special Agent Wills disappeared and returned a minute later with a small Styrofoam cup of coffee, which he handed to Kathleen. The three then navigated their way around the various desks and cubicles that took up most of the open floor space, eventually arriving at Wills's desk near the back. It was a plain, government-issue desk with a simulated-wood-grain top—like all the others. But, unlike most of the horizontal surfaces in the field office, Wills's desk was clean and organized. Somehow, this didn't surprise Kathleen.

"Have a seat," Wills said, motioning to a chair adjacent his desk.

Kathleen complied, draping her coat across her lap. She sipped the coffee, which was painfully hot—and *awful*. It tasted like it had been brewed sometime yesterday morning.

Hendricks pulled a chair from her cubicle and dragged it conspicuously across the vinyl-tile floor to a spot next to Kathleen's chair. She sat down and flipped open her writing pad.

"Let's start from the beginning," Wills said. "Dr. Al-Fulani called you at some point last night, correct?"

"He called my home phone and left a message."

"When was that?

"I'm not sure of the exact time. I was out at

dinner. I guess somewhere between eight and ten thirty."

Kathleen answered questions of this nature for the next hour and a half. Wills's questions were methodical, meticulous, almost surgical in nature. Each moved the timeline of last night's events forward one small increment. If Kathleen gave an answer that jumped too far ahead in the timeline, Wills carefully looped back with follow-up questions, filling in all the gaps. His interrogation technique was systematic and professional.

For her part, Kathleen answered each question as best she could, holding nothing back. They covered her initial meeting with Al-Fulani at the front door, the room with all the antiques, the revelation of his real name—Hakeem Abdul Sargon. They covered the coat, the Turkish tea, the map of Mesopotamia, and Sargon's story about Kathleen's parents and his own escape from Iraq.

Suddenly, the tenor of Wills's questions changed. "Would you say Dr. Al Fulani was acting strangely last night?" he asked.

"Strangely?"

"Did he do anything unexpected? Out of the ordinary?"

"Well, I didn't know him before last night, so I don't know how he normally acted. But, yeah, I guess I would say he was acting a bit strange."

"How so?"

"He seemed kind of . . . I don't know . . . *obsessed* with something. Or maybe 'frantic' is a better word. He just seemed agitated to me."

"What do you think he was obsessed with?"

Kathleen paused for a moment. "God," she replied.

"God?"

"I think he believed God was . . . *talking* to him, or directing him to do something. He kept talking about God's will and stuff like that. Which I found very strange."

"I see. And at any point last night, did you see him with a weapon?"

"A *weapon*?" Kathleen straightened in her chair. "No."

"Did he say anything that might lead you to believe he was suicidal?"

Then Kathleen suddenly understood. "Is *that* what happened?"

Wills searched Kathleen's eyes. "The police will probably conduct an autopsy before they pronounce an official cause of death, but I've seen enough self-inflicted gunshot wounds to know one when I see one."

Kathleen grimaced.

"Odd circumstances, though."

"How so?"

"Someone set off the house alarm around 4:00 A.M. A rear window was pried open."

Kathleen shook her head, confused.

"That reminds me," said Wills. "Did anyone see you leave Al-Fulani's house?"

Kathleen hesitated. She didn't like where this was going. "Yes," she said finally. "My office manager, Carlos Guiterez. He was waiting for me outside when I left." She hated getting Carlos involved in this mess, but she was glad for the alibi just the same. She wondered, though, *Why do I need an alibi?*

The interview ended just before 1:00 P.M., leaving Kathleen mentally exhausted, hungry, and anxious about the entire situation. Her head was spinning from the events of the past twenty-four hours.

"Cheryl will give you a ride back to your car," Wills said, nodding to Agent Hendricks.

"Thanks," said Kathleen.

"And we may have to call you again if we have more questions. I assume that's okay?"

"Of course."

Agent Hendricks stood up slowly with exaggerated stiffness, making no attempt to hide her annoyance at having to chauffeur Kathleen back to U Street. "Come on," she said.

"Oh, Dr. Sainsbury," said Wills as they were leaving. He rose to his feet. "One last question."

Kathleen turned to face him.

"Did Dr. Sargon give you anything last night?"

The question hit Kathleen unexpectedly, and she reflexively stalled for time. "What do you mean?"

Wills frowned. "Just what I said. Did he *give* you anything while you were at his house? A package, a gift, anything?"

To her recollection, Kathleen Sainsbury had never lied to any person of authority in her entire life. Not to her grandfather, not to her teachers, not to the IRS, and certainly not to the police. Yet, for some inexplicable reason, at that very moment, she felt an unavoidable urge not to tell Agent Wills about the silver box Dr. Sargon had given her. Whether it was simply too hard to explain, or whether it was something Sargon had said about the artifact inside, Kathleen didn't know. Nor did she have time to think about it. *Detective Wills was waiting for an answer.*

"No," she said firmly, trying hard not to blink.

A short pause. Then Wills nodded with apparent satisfaction. "Okay, then. Thank you for your time."

The ride back to U Street was awful. Kathleen sat in the backseat of Hendricks's Crown Victoria, behind a pane of thick bulletproof glass. She felt like a criminal, though she'd done nothing wrong.

Except now she had done something wrong. She'd lied to the FBI. Why had she done that? She could almost picture Special Agent Wills right now, documenting her lie, annotating it, cross-referencing it. He was so meticulous—certainly he'd figure out that she'd lied. *And then what?*

Kathleen wished none of this had ever happened. She wished Dr. Sargon had never called and that she'd never gone to his house.

"Where's your car?" Agent Hendricks asked.

But Kathleen was still absorbed in her thoughts.

"Ma'am, where is your car?" Hendricks repeated, practically yelling at Kathleen.

"Oh, sorry. It's right there. On the left."

The Crown Victoria pulled to an abrupt stop next to Kathleen's silver Subaru. Kathleen went to open the door but realized there were no door handles in the backseat. *Criminals could not be trusted with door handles.*

Hendricks exited the car slowly, obviously relishing the circumstances of the situation. After a long, unnecessary delay, she finally opened the door for Kathleen.

"Thank you," Kathleen mumbled as she alighted from the backseat.

"Mmm-hmm."

The Versace coat was still draped over Kathleen's arm, and she was careful not to drag it on the ground as she exited the car.

"Hey," said Hendricks, pointing to the coat.

"Yes?"

"You may want to get that dry-cleaned."

Kathleen looked down and grimaced. On the side of the cashmere coat was a large, dark coffee stain, which must have leaked from the Styrofoam cup. "Oh no," she moaned.

A smile crept over Hendricks's face. "Well," she said, clucking her tongue, "have a nice day."

CHAPTER SEVENTEEN

"**W**HAT the hell happened?" Venfeld demanded angrily. He was sitting at a red light behind the wheel of his brand-new BMW 645i, a sleek black convertible sports sedan with soft black leather interior. The disposable prepaid cell phone was pressed tightly to his ear.

"I dunno," replied Zafer in his thick Israeli accent, "It was weird . . ."

"Just tell me what happened."

"I went to pay that old man a visit, like you said. I went through a back window, but it must have set off an alarm."

Idiot, Venfeld thought.

"I knew I didn't have much time. So I ran upstairs to his bedroom, and, well . . ."

"And *what*? What happened?"

"The door was locked. I told him to open it, but he just kept mumbling something in Arabic."

"Do you know what he said?"

"Something about Allah, that's all I could tell.

I told him to open the fucking door or I'd, you know, send him straight to Allah myself. But he just kept mumbling. It was weird. So I kicked open the door, and he was, like, just standing there. Waiting for me . . ." Zafer's voice trailed off.

"Damn it, Semion. I don't have all day. Tell me what happened."

"He shot himself! Right there in front of me. I . . . I didn't expect it. Shot himself right in the head."

"Did he say anything before he did? Anything about the box?"

"No. His last words were something about *misery* and *farana* . . . I really couldn't tell. Anyway, after that he was just . . . dead and fucking useless. I checked all the boxes downstairs but didn't find anything. Then I had to go 'cause I heard sirens coming."

"Shit." Venfeld terminated the phone call and waited impatiently for the light to turn green. When it did, he punched the accelerator and made a sharp, squealing U-turn in the intersection.

He had work to do.

CHAPTER EIGHTEEN

Springfield, Virginia.

"**W**HAT'S going on?" Carlos asked in a hushed voice. He and Kathleen were standing on the back deck of his Springfield townhouse. Kathleen clutched a brown paper bag beneath one arm. Carlos's wife, Ana, and six-year-old twin girls were watching TV inside. The late-afternoon sky was mottled with dark gray storm clouds, and a few stray raindrops were already starting to fall. The family cat, Slinky, prowled restlessly back and forth along the railing behind them as they spoke.

"I need to talk to you about last night," Kathleen said in a hushed tone.

"Okay . . ."

An hour earlier, she'd driven straight from U Street to QLS in Rockville and called Carlos from her office. She needed to talk to him immediately about the "situation" and wanted to meet at his house.

Kathleen moved closer to Carlos and spoke nearly in a whisper.

"You know the man I was visiting last night?"

"The old guy?"

"Yes. Something happened to him after I left. They found him dead."

"*Whoa!* Are you serious? Are you okay?"

"I'm fine. But the FBI took me in for questioning."

"*The FBI?*"

"They asked me a lot of questions. It sounds like he committed suicide, but there was also a break-in, apparently. And why would the FBI be involved in a suicide investigation, anyway? Isn't that something routine that the police would normally handle? I don't know; there's something strange going on."

"Well *you* didn't have anything to do with it. I mean, I saw you leave, and that old guy was still out on the stoop. So you've got nothing to worry about, right?"

"Right. But there's something else . . ."

"What?"

"They asked me if he gave me anything."

"And?" A moment later, a wave of recognition spread over Carlos's face. "Oh."

Kathleen looked down, shaking her head remorsefully.

Carlos sighed. "Dr. Sainsbury, you really should've told them about that. I mean, the FBI. That's serious business."

"I know, I just . . . It was a split-second decision, and I blew it."

Carlos's face showed obvious concern, but he said nothing.

"Carlos," Kathleen said quietly, "I gave them your name and your number at work."

Carlos frowned and bobbed his head from side to side, obviously weighing the implication of Kathleen's words.

"I'm sorry to put you in this position. It was just too hard to explain the—"

Carlos cut her off. "It's okay. *Really*. But I think it's time you told me what was in that box."

Kathleen nodded her head and slowly unrolled the paper bag she'd been holding under her arm. She carefully pulled the silver box out of the bag.

Carlos watched closely.

With the silver box firmly in one hand, Kathleen opened the top, revealing the contents. "This is what he gave me."

Carlos took the box cautiously from Kathleen's hand and spent several seconds inspecting its contents. "Is that a *tooth*?"

"Yeah."

Carlos shrugged "I don't understand. What's the big deal?"

"It's from a five-thousand-year-old temple. Or so I'm told."

"Okay . . ."

"It's a long story."

"I've got time."

Kathleen nodded. Of course Carlos was right. Given what she'd gotten him into, he deserved to know everything. She drew a deep breath and summarized the situation as best she could.

"Okay, but I still don't understand," said Carlos after she'd finished. "Why did that old guy give this to *you*?"

"You know, I don't fully understand it either. He said it was very important that I have it and that he'd explain everything to me it later. But now, of course . . ." Kathleen closed her eyes and began rubbing her temples. "I just need some time to figure it out."

"Right."

"So if the FBI calls you—"

Carlos cut her off. "I get it. I won't mention anything about this." He nodded toward the box.

Kathleen bit her lip and summoned the courage for one more request. "I need one more favor."

Carlos raised his eyebrows, as if to say, *There's more?*

Kathleen pointed to the silver box in his hand. "Can you put that somewhere?"

"You want *me* to have it?"

"Carlos, what if the FBI searches my apartment? Or my office? How would I explain it?"

"But—"

"And to tell you the truth, I just don't want that thing around anymore. It gives me the creeps."

"Okay," said Carlos with a sigh. "I'll take care of it."

CHAPTER NINETEEN

BILL McCreary checked his watch. It was Monday morning, 8:00 A.M. Time for his meeting with Director DuBose and the new deputy. *Frank will be precisely on time*, he predicted. Seconds later, as predicted, there was a knock at the door to the "Logistics Analysis" office. McCreary opened the door and greeted the two men standing in the hallway.

"Morning," said Frank DuBose, DARPA's director. He was a thin man of medium height with a ruddy face and a serious, tight-lipped expression. His white hair was cropped short in a buzz cut—tight over the ears and flat on top. He wore a white shirt, narrow tie, and thick, black-rimmed glasses, as if he'd just stepped out of NASA's space program, circa 1968. "This is Gary Sorenson," he said, introducing the younger man next to him, "the new deputy director. He's ready for his SER-RATE read-in."

McCreary ushered both men into the small

front vestibule of the "Logistics Analysis" office. "Sorry about the cramped quarters," he said. "We don't get many visitors here." He introduced the muscular man sitting behind the desk in the center of the room. "This is my assistant, Steve Goodwin."

Sorenson nodded at Goodwin, who nodded back.

McCreary led DuBose and Sorenson into his private office and closed the door behind them. "Please, have a seat." He motioned to two chairs at a small, round table. "I'm sure you have a lot of programs to hear about today, so I'll get right to it." McCreary remained standing as he spoke. "Gentlemen, this program is classified Top Secret, SCI."

Sorenson nodded that he understood. Many programs at DARPA were classified as SCI, or Sensitive Compartmented Information—which meant the program included classified information deemed especially important or sensitive to the national security of the United States or its allies. SCI information was handled via special SCI "channels," each of which was given a unique SCI code word. The code words themselves were classified Top Secret.

McCreary continued. "The SCI designation for this program is SERRATE. Therefore, all information in this program is designated Top Secret SERRATE."

Sorenson nodded again.

"I assume Director DuBose has briefed you generally about the SCI procedures here?"

"Yes," Sorenson replied. DuBose nodded his head in concurrence.

"So you know this entire OSNS wing is a SCIF, right?"

"Yes."

"And no compartmented information ever leaves the SCIF, right?"

"I understand."

"As an added precaution for this program"—McCreary gestured toward the front room—"Steve out there makes sure that *no one*—including me—carries any SERRATE materials out of this office. *Ever.*"

Sorenson nodded that he understood.

"Okay then, all you need to do is sign this paperwork." McCreary placed a small stack of forms on the table and waited patiently as the new deputy read and signed each one. "Good. Now that *that's* out of the way, let me tell you a little about SERRATE." McCreary paused. "By the way, what's your technical background?"

"Electrical engineering," Sorenson replied.

Ugh, this is going to take a while. McCreary took a deep breath and commenced his presentation. "Up until a couple of years ago, I was a researcher at NIH, working on a small offshoot of the Human Genome Project. It was a massive project funded by the U.S. government to decode the entire human genome. The project began in 1990 with a multibillion-dollar grant from the Department of Energy. The research was coordinated by NIH and carried out by a large consortium of U.S. and international laboratories. It was a monumental effort, some would say the most important scientific undertaking since the Manhattan Project."

Sorenson nodded.

"The project was essentially completed—about ninety-five percent of the genome sequenced—in 2004, with the assistance of some very aggressive, venture-backed biotech startups that were competing to see who could finish the sequence first. You might remember the epic battle between GenSystems and Rial?"

"Sure," said Sorenson, nodding his head. "Didn't they both announce completion of the sequence on the same day?"

"Yep. And they've been fighting over the patent rights ever since. GenSystems merged with West-Pharma a couple years ago. And Rial moved into the pharmaceutical business. It's now the largest pharmaceutical company in Israel."

Sorenson shrugged. "So what does this have to do with SERRATE?"

McCreary leaned over the table and replied emphatically, *"Everything."*

CHAPTER TWENTY

Bethesda, Maryland.

KATHLEEN SAINSBURY HELD her grandfather's hand tightly. His hand seemed massive and strong compared to her own tiny, seven-year-old hand. It felt comfortable, like a snug blanket. They stood together in a small, rural cemetery on a warm September afternoon.

Kathleen had lots of questions. *Are Mommy and Daddy in heaven? When will they be back?* But the silence of the small crowd around the open graves and her grandfather's firm, steady grip told her those questions would have to wait. She looked curiously at the two shiny coffins, draped with flowers, and listened as an emaciated preacher in a black suit recited passages from the Bible. His voice was low and melancholy, like a gurgling river. Kathleen liked the scent of the fresh flowers.

Suddenly, there was a loud buzzing noise . . .

Kathleen awoke with a start. It was light outside, which confused her at first. Then she remembered she'd set her alarm for 7:30 A.M, instead of the usual 5:30 A.M. After the hectic past two days, she'd decided she needed an extra couple hours of sleep. She punched the alarm and rolled out of bed with a groan.

Forty minutes later, she was sitting in bumper-to-bumper traffic, regretting having slept in. Shiny luxury cars crawled along Old Georgetown Road in both directions. In the D.C. area, "rush hour" was a misnomer, since it lasted at least three hours in the morning and another three in the afternoon. And, to make matters worse, she still had to drop by the dry cleaners on her way to work.

At about 8:30, Kathleen turned left from Old Georgetown Road into a low-rise shopping center, squeezed her Subaru into a tight parking spot, and hurried into Lee's Cleaners with her stained coat.

"Good morning," said the young woman behind the counter.

"I need to have this dry-cleaned," Kathleen said, presenting the young woman with the Versace coat. "It has a coffee stain right here." She pointed to the dark brown stain on one side of the coat.

The young woman clucked her tongue. "Ooh, that looks bad. But we'll try, okay?"

Kathleen took a receipt for the coat and turned to leave.

"Excuse me!" the young woman called out, just as Kathleen reached the door.

Kathleen turned and returned to the counter. "Hmm?"

The young woman held a small piece of folded paper in her hand. "I found this in the pocket." She nodded toward the coat.

Kathleen took the paper, perplexed. "In the pocket of *this* coat?"

"Yeah, right here." The woman pointed to one of the coat's inside pockets.

Kathleen unfolded the paper and stared at it for a moment, perplexed. It was a small, white sheet of paper—entirely blank except for a hand-drawn sketch in the center, which Kathleen didn't recognize at all:

"Thanks," she mumbled as she turned back toward the door, still studying the mysterious piece of paper.

Kathleen sat in her car for a long time in the strip-mall parking lot, oblivious to the parade of well-dressed professionals hurrying by, some with Starbucks coffee cups, others with gym bags, some with both. One woman in a silver Mercedes SUV waited nearly three minutes for Kathleen's parking space before eventually speeding off in disgust, giving Kathleen a dirty look and a quick honk as she zoomed away. Kathleen didn't care. Her head was spinning. The note in her hand had brought everything suddenly rushing back: the evening with Dr. Sargon, the revelation about her parents' murder, Sargon's apparent suicide, the FBI, the silver box.

Somehow, these things were all connected.

Dr. Hakeem Abdul Sargon—former curator of the Iraqi National Museum, friend of her parents, witness to their deaths—had called her out of the blue to give her something "very important." He'd given her a silver box with a five-thousand-year-old tooth in it, from an ancient tomb in Iraq called Tell-Fara, the very tomb her parents were excavating in 1979 when they were murdered. He'd told her he had something "very important" to explain to her the next morning. *Was it something about the tooth? About Tell-Fara? About her parents? About the tomb?* Kathleen didn't know. But it was apparently something important, and Sargon had said she'd understand everything once she heard it.

One thing was sure: she didn't understand anything now.

What else did she know? Dr. Sargon had apparently committed suicide—or was murdered— just hours after she left his house. Why would he have committed suicide if he wanted to see her the next morning to tell her something "very important"?

And why were the all the Quran boxes in Sargon's living room open? Was someone else looking for what Dr. Sargon had given her?

Kathleen felt confused, scared, and, for some reason, vaguely ashamed. Something Dr. Sargon had said kept coming back to her: "This is connected to you, through your parents, through God."

She thought about her parents, whom she had barely known. They had dedicated their professional lives to something they didn't live to see. Sargon had apparently found what they'd been searching for—a tomb, or something *in* the tomb, or something *about* the tomb. Kathleen didn't know what. But her parents had risked everything to find it. *Why?*

Agent Wills said that Dr. Sargon probably committed suicide. But Dr. Sargon had a secret—a *very important* secret—that he desperately wanted to tell her, and he was prepared to do so the very next morning. He wouldn't have taken his own life, unless . . .

Kathleen looked down at the paper in her hands.

Unless this was the secret.

Kathleen arrived at work at 9:45, three hours later than normal.

"I was about to send out a search party," said Carlos jokingly, greeting her at the front door. "Is everything okay?"

"I'm fine," said Kathleen. "Has anyone collected data in the lab this morning?"

"Julie took care of it."

"Good. Tell her thanks. I'll be in my office." She rushed past Carlos and continued briskly down the hall.

"Dr. Sainsbury?"

Kathleen turned around but continued walking backward toward her office.

"Are you *sure* you're okay?"

"I'm fine."

Carlos looked unconvinced.

"I'm fine." Kathleen slipped into her office and closed the door behind her.

An hour later, Kathleen dialed Carlos's extension.

"Yes?"

"Carlos, I need you to arrange a trip for me."

"Sure. Where to?"

"Boston."

"When do you want to go?"

"Right now."

CHAPTER TWENTY-ONE

LOGAN International Airport was typically crowded for a Monday evening. Travelers trudged in every direction, some arriving, others departing, all moving with weary determination. Moms with strollers, groups of school kids in matching sweatshirts, grandparents arriving from Florida, college students on spring break, businesspeople, immigrants—people of every size, color, and description—all hustling with their carry-on bags, or sitting in chairs at the gates, or standing three deep at the airport bars.

But there was only one person at Logan International Airport that evening with a five-thousand-year-old secret in her pocket.

Kathleen Sainsbury made her way to the main terminal from Gate C12, where the flight from Reagan National had just arrived. She checked her voice mail on the way.

There was a message from Carlos, confirming her hotel reservation at the Kendall Square Marriott. Another from Julie, asking some questions about an experiment Kathleen had left half-completed. It wasn't like Kathleen to take off on such short notice. In the past two years, she'd barely traveled anywhere, other than periodic trips to Annapolis to visit her grandfather at his assisted living home.

There was *another* message from Carlos, wanting to know if she'd arrived safely and whether she was all right. Almost as an afterthought, he added that Agent Wills had called to ask him a few questions about the other night. That was all he said—that the FBI had called him to "ask a few questions." It didn't sound like anything to be concerned about. But, then again, Carlos had a habit of downplaying things. *Twenty years in the Marines would do that to a person*, she figured.

The last message was from Bryce Whittaker. The sound of his voice provided a pleasant distraction.

"Hi, it's me Bryce . . . Whittaker. I just wanted to tell you I had a really great time on Saturday. And uh . . . well, I'd love to see you again if you're up for it. I was thinking maybe drinks tonight after work. What do you say? Give me a call."

The message had been left at 4:22 P.M. Kathleen checked her watch; it was already 6:15. "Not happening tonight," she muttered. Her love life in the past few years had been an absolute disaster—a series of tragic miscues and false starts, mixed signals, misunderstandings, and generally just bad timing. On most days she reassured herself that the problem was QLS; it simply left no time for relationships. In more reflective moments, however, she allowed an alternative possibility: *Maybe the problem was her.*

Kathleen waited in the taxi line for twenty minutes, shivering and impatiently checking her watch. It was bitter cold and windy outside, and she wished she'd brought a pair of gloves. But, in fact, she'd packed nothing at all. She carried only her briefcase with her. Eventually, she made it to the head of the line and climbed into a Bayside cab.

"Where to?" asked the driver in a strong Boston accent.

Kathleen's hotel was in Kendall Square, but that's not where she was heading right now.

"Fifteen Chauncy Street in Cambridge."

It had taken Kathleen less than fifteen minutes to track down Dr. Charles Eskridge via a Google search in her office. Within minutes, she'd learned that Eskridge had been Dean of Near East Studies at Harvard University from 1976 to 1983, and then executive director of the Oriental Institute from 1984 to 1990. A phone call to the Institute revealed that he was no longer the director but that he still worked at the Institute's museum as a docent on Mondays, Wednesdays, and Fridays. Ten minutes later, Kathleen was speaking with him on the phone.

The conversation had been awkward at first. He sounded like a nice-enough man—gruff but amiable. But Kathleen was nervous and unsure of how to explain why she was calling. In fact, she wasn't exactly sure why she was calling.

"My name is Kathleen Sainsbury," she began nervously. "My parents were Daniel and Rebecca Talbot."

"You don't say?" Eskridge replied, with obvious recognition.

"I recently met a man named Dr. Hakeem Abdul Sargon. Do you know him?"

There was a pause. "You mean . . ."

"Yes. Dr. Al-Fulani. Dr. Sargon. Whatever his name is."

"Sure . . . I *knew* him. But it's been a long time."

"Well, he gave me something that he said was very important. Something from Tell-Fara. Are you familiar with Tell-Fara?"

"Yes," Eskridge said after a short pause.

"I think I need your help understanding some things."

"Okay."

"Can we meet?"

To Kathleen's surprise, Eskridge seemed as eager to meet her as she was to meet him. "When were you thinking?" he asked.

"How about tonight?" Kathleen suggested.

"Tonight?" Eskridge seemed a bit surprised. "Are you in Boston?"

"No, but I can be."

"Tonight would be fine."

According to Google, the Oriental Institute Museum was located at 15 Chauncy Street in Cambridge, six blocks from the Harvard campus. As the cab pulled up to that address, however, Kathleen double-checked her Google Maps printout and peered doubtfully through the car window.

"Is this the Oriental Institute Museum?" she asked.

"I don't know, lady," said the driver curtly. "This is Fifteen Chauncy Street, like you asked."

It was a historic-looking three-story brick house, nicely maintained with taupe trim and dark green ivy creeping up the façade. A black wrought-iron fence enclosed the entire property. It was certainly a beautiful house. Kathleen could easily imagine a Harvard professor or a successful doctor or lawyer living in it. But it didn't look like a museum. It looked more like a private residence.

The house was almost entirely dark except for a single window on the second floor, which emanated a pale yellow glow through white curtains.

Kathleen paid the cab driver forty-five dollars and asked him to wait a few minutes until she was sure someone was there.

"It's extra for waiting," said the driver. "Fifty cents per minute."

Kathleen rolled her eyes and handed him a ten-dollar bill. "Will that cover a few minutes?"

"Sure, I'll wait."

Kathleen opened the creaky wrought-iron gate and walked to the front entrance of the house. A sign next to the door indicated that it was, indeed, the Oriental Institute Museum, and that it was open on Mondays, Wednesdays, and Fridays, from 10:00 A.M. to 3:30 P.M. *Not a very popular museum*, Kathleen surmised.

There was no doorbell, so Kathleen knocked on the door—three loud raps with the brass knocker. She waited half a minute and then knocked again.

"Coming!" said a distant voice from inside the museum.

A few seconds later, the door rattled and opened, and a rotund, barrel-chested man stood in the doorway. "Ms. Sainsbury?" he asked in a husky voice.

"Dr. Eskridge?"

The man nodded affirmatively, and Kathleen turned and waved off the cab driver. The Chevy Caprice sped away.

"Come on in," Eskridge said. He was a bull of a man—over six feet tall with a bulky, substantial presence. His tan, leathery face was punctuated—oddly—with a snow white handlebar moustache that drooped down past the corners of his mouth. His head was bald and shiny. Kathleen had deduced from his résumé that he was at least seventy years old, but he certainly didn't look it. He had the vigor and presence of a much younger man. Seeing him in person, Kathleen had the feeling that Eskridge had been a force to be reckoned with in his younger days, and perhaps he still was. Behind a pair of silver wire-rimmed glasses, his eyes were intense—a peculiar shade of pale blue.

"Sorry about the dark," he said. "The lights are on timers. They turn off automatically after eight P.M." He flipped a switch and the entry hall lit up with a warm, yellow glow from an overhead chandelier.

Not like a museum at all, Kathleen thought. "Thanks for staying late to see me," she said.

"No trouble at all. Actually, I live here."

"You do?"

"Second and third floors are mine. First floor's the museum."

"Oh, I didn't realize that. The woman at the Institute said you were a docent of some sort."

"I am. Mondays, Wednesdays, and Fridays. If people come by, I let them in, give them tours, answer questions. Whatever they want. The rest of the time, I just live here."

Kathleen detected an accent. "You from Minnesota?"

"Yah, you betcha," said Eskridge with a quick smile that was barely discernable beneath his moustache. Only his cheeks and the deep creases around his eyes gave it away.

"Truth is," he continued, "we don't get many visitors. A half dozen a week, maybe. The occasional grad student or a visiting professor. A few history buffs here and there. But it's mainly quiet."

"So, it's just you here?"

"Yep. People from the Institute drop by every once in a while to help out, especially if we're expecting a high-profile visitor. But it's usually just me."

"Kind of lonely, isn't it?" Kathleen looked around at the sparsely furnished entry hall. The rooms beyond were still dark.

"Not for me. I kind of like it. Besides, the Institute was gonna shut this museum down a few years ago and sell the building back to the university. They only agreed to keep it open because I volunteered to operate it three days a week without pay. And also because I help keep costs down."

"The lights?"

Eskridge smiled and winked. "I also do all the maintenance around here."

Kathleen was starting to like this guy.

"I know the day I quit, they'll shut this place down faster than a Minnesota heat wave, donate everything in the collection, and sell the house to the university. Official word is, the university wants to turn it into faculty housing. Truth is, the dean of Undergraduate Admissions—Cecil Greenberg—has had his eye on this house for years. I told him myself, though, it'll be over my dead body." Eskridge laughed heartily. "And that's probably just how it'll be."

"That's a terrible thought."

"Not really," said Eskridge with a chuckle. "That son of a bitch Greenberg's gonna be waiting a *long* time. 'Cause I don't plan on dying anytime soon."

Kathleen believed that. Eskridge was built like a Sherman tank. On a hunch, she asked, "You built the museum's collection yourself, didn't you?"

"A lot of it. My students, too. It was the culmination of a lot of work by a lot of people." He paused and glanced around. "Would you like a tour?"

"Sure."

As Kathleen followed Dr. Eskridge into the adjacent room, she had the strangest feeling that he'd been waiting for her. Not just tonight . . . but for a long time. A vague sense of guilt came over her—like she should have come here a long time ago. And, in an odd way, she felt like her parents were in this museum, too. In spirit. And they, too, had been expecting her—*waiting* for her to finally come and visit. She regretted now that it had taken this long.

Eskridge flipped a switch and the white fluorescent lights in the next room flickered and came on.

The room was small, with creaky wooden floors and yellow walls. Two glass display cases sat atop wooden tables in the middle of the room. Three smaller glass cases were mounted on the walls, curio style, along with various engravings and photographs. *Not exactly a world-class museum,* Kathleen thought to herself.

They stopped in front of the first glass display case, which contained a dozen or so small cylindrical objects.

"These are seal stones," Eskridge explained, "from Mesopotamia. The ones on the left are from about eight hundred BC. I found them on my very first expedition to Iran in 1961."

Kathleen inspected them closely. They looked like tiny rolling pins, each intricately carved with a design. Behind each seal stone was an ink print showing what the relief design looked like when it was rolled out. The designs depicted men with swords, galloping horses, rearing lions, and fantastic winged beasts.

"These would have been rolled across clay before it was fired to form an identifiable seal or symbol—a sign of ownership or affiliation."

"They're beautiful."

"The others in this case, and those in the next case over, were found by students of mine over the years."

Kathleen nodded.

The next room had a similar layout, with two large A-frame display cases in the center and several wall-mounted cases along the perimeter.

"Everything in this room is from Egypt," Eskridge said with a subdued flourish. "I spent two years there, in sixty-one and sixty-two, excavating three different tombs in the Valley of the Kings. Of course, they'd pretty much been picked clean by looters, although we still managed to find a few important artifacts there."

"Did you find any mummies?" Kathleen asked, a bit bashfully.

"*Mummies?*" Eskridge laughed. "No, I'm afraid not. I'm sure they'd been there at one time. But, like I said, those tombs had been robbed so many times over the centuries that barely anything remained. See these photographs?" He pointed to a series of enlarged black-and-white photos on the wall behind the display cases. They depicted hieroglyphic writing, presumably from the tombs. "According to those hieroglyphs, one of the tombs belonged to a king named Kyhan, who reigned for forty-two years in the Sixteenth Dynasty, around 1550 BC."

Kathleen nodded politely.

"Anyway, at one time, there was almost certainly a sarcophagus with his mummified remains, not to mention funerary vessels and tools, furniture, weapons, jewelry, and more. But all of that was long gone by the time we got there, probably stolen centuries ago. We did manage to unearth a few things, though." He pointed to the first display case, which contained a menagerie of broken pottery pieces, spear tips, and two tiny, onyx statuettes depicting women with absurdly exaggerated breasts and buttocks.

Fertility charms, Kathleen guessed.

"In this other case are artifacts from Alexandria, Egypt. I led summer expeditions there with grad students in seventy-one, seventy-two, seventy-four, and seventy-five."

Kathleen peered into the glass case, which housed a ragtag collection of coins, cups, daggers, pellets, tools, and a badly dented helmet—all of them pocked, pitted, and generally lackluster in appearance.

"These are from the time of the Roman annexation of Alexandria, around 80 BC.—during the reign of Ptolemy Alexander the Second. Most of these items were found under water in the port of Alexandria. Now *that* was some dirty diving, let me tell ya."

"I'll bet."

Eskridge let out a hearty belly laugh. "Hardest part was dodging the damned freighters coming in and out of the harbor. I'll tell ya—they didn't give a rat's ass about our little diving flags!"

"Sounds dangerous."

"The Russians were the worst. Those bastards would sooner run you over than be late for a port call or a shot of vodka."

Kathleen nodded and smiled, as if she knew all about that particular trait of Russian freighter captains.

"But, I tell ya, it was fun back then. *Real* archeology. Nobody does stuff like that anymore. The schools today aren't willing to take any risks. Nobody will cough up funding, anyway. And frankly, we just don't get the same type of students these days. There's no romance left in archeology. No sense of adventure."

"A bygone era, I guess," said Kathleen, still inspecting the artifacts in the glass case.

"Now your parents—"

Kathleen snapped her head up and met Eskridge's gaze.

"*They* were the last of a breed. They had that fire—that *passion* for what they were doing." His voice trailed off. "Come on, let me show you something."

Kathleen followed Eskridge through a series of rooms like the first two until, finally, he flicked a light switch and revealed a room that was much larger than the others, and very different in appearance. Unlike the previous rooms, this space was *packed* with display cases—eight in all—and adorned with gleaming and interesting objects all along the walls. The artifacts in this room were perceptibly different than those in the others— larger, more stunning, almost . . . *pristine*. Gold and silver details jumped out and glimmered in the overhead light. Without a doubt, this was the heart of the museum's collection.

"These," Eskridge announced proudly, "are from Tell-Fara."

Kathleen looked around, astonished. One display case contained a stunning collection of gold and silver bracelets, necklaces, and what appeared to be a jeweled ceremonial staff.

Another case contained an impressive collection of ancient Sumerian weaponry—curved sabers, a short dagger with a golden sheath, an ornately embossed shield.

On the walls of the room, mounted on sturdy shelves, were a half dozen carved heads, similar to the one she'd seen on the table at Sargon's house. Each depicted the same, fierce-looking man, with jewels in his eye sockets and studding his beard.

"Who is that?" Kathleen asked.

"Good question. I wish I knew."

Kathleen thought about that for a moment and then asked, "Did you get all these things from Dr. Sargon?"

"Well, he was the deliveryman, if you will. But don't forget, it was your parents' fieldwork that led to these incredible finds. They did all the work and deserve all the credit."

"Dr. Sargon told me he gave these things to you in exchange for helping him escape Iraq. Is that true?"

"Yep. And it wasn't easy getting him out, believe me. I don't know who he'd pissed off there, but he was in big trouble. I had to call in some big-time favors for that one. But it was a fair trade. Because we got these." He swept his hand around the room.

"Did Dr. Sargon ever say anything about there being a sarcophagus inside the Tell-Fara temple?"

Eskridge's eyebrows shot up. *"A sarcophagus?* No. Why do you ask?"

Kathleen shrugged.

A hint of frustration entered Eskridge's voice. "Hell, I must have asked him fifty times if he'd seen any sign of a tomb, or a burial pit, or anything like that, and he always said no. But it never made any sense to me. I mean, if it wasn't a tomb, what the hell was it?"

Kathleen drew a deep breath and slowly let it out. "Well . . . he told *me* he saw a sarcophagus."

Eskridge's eyes widened.

Kathleen continued. "He said he saw a large, rectangular sarcophagus made of alabaster and black marble."

"That son of a bitch," Eskridge whispered. "He held out on me." His voice grew louder. "I'm gonna have to pay him a visit."

"I'm afraid it's too late for that."

"Why?"

"Dr. Sargon's dead. He apparently killed himself two nights ago."

Eskridge's expression turned solemn. *"Jesus!"* he whispered, shaking his head slowly. "I'm . . . I'm really sorry to hear that."

"But he left me this." Kathleen pulled the folded paper from her pocket and handed it to Eskridge.

Eskridge unfolded the paper slowly with his fat fingers, glancing at Kathleen as he did. He studied the notation on the page for a long time, rubbing his chin and stroking his moustache absently. Several times, he nodded and grunted quietly. "Mmmm . . . mmm-hmm."

Kathleen watched nervously.

After a long while, Eskridge spoke. "*This* was inscribed on the sarcophagus he told you about?"

"Yes, I think so."

He studied the paper for several more seconds, still shaking his head slowly. Then he mumbled, "Well, I'll be damned. I'll be *goddamned*!"

CHAPTER TWENTY-TWO

Cambridge, Massachusetts.

"Wнат does it say?" Kathleen asked breathlessly as she followed Dr. Eskridge up the stairs. He was climbing them two at a time—an impressive feat for a man his age and size.

"Could mean several different things," Eskridge said over his shoulder. He held the folded sheet of paper Kathleen had given him in his hand.

They reached the landing on the second floor. Eskridge turned right and hurried down the darkened hallway toward the only lighted room on the floor.

A few moments later, they entered a spacious study with dark-stained oak bookshelves on two walls and an antique mahogany library table in the middle. A threadbare Persian rug covered most of the wooden floor, its red-and-blue geometric pattern largely scoured away by decades of foot traffic. Four antique-brass sconces on the walls and a cloisonné lamp on the table bathed the room in soft, incandescent light. The air smelled like old paper.

Eskridge was already busy pulling books from the shelves and stacking them, one by one, on the mahogany table.

"What do you think it means?" Kathleen said anxiously.

Eskridge ignored her. He was now standing on a small stepladder, reaching for more books. "Here grab this," he said, handing Kathleen a dusty volume from the top shelf.

She added it to the stack on the table.

Several minutes later, Eskridge pulled up a chair, unfolded the paper Kathleen had given him, and laid it flat on the table in front of him. Kathleen stood beside him.

"Now, are you *sure* this was something Dr. Sargon saw at Tell-Fara?" Eskridge asked.

"Yeah. Pretty sure."

"These symbols are Sumerian pictographs. Technically, they're called *proto-cuneiform* symbols."

"What does that mean?"

"It means they were probably inscribed sometime before twenty-eight hundred BC—about five thousand years ago."

"Can you tell what they say?"

Eskridge drew a deep breath and inspected the paper. "All right. See this here?" He pointed to the symbol on the upper left of the inscription.

"Yes."

"That's the proto-cuneiform symbol for Orion,

the Hunter, also associated with Gilgamesh in Sumerian epics. The Orion symbol was used to express many different meanings, depending on the context. It could mean strength, for instance. Or power. Or victory. It could also mean a person of great size, or wealth, or good fortune. And, of course, it could refer to the actual god himself, Orion."

"Okay . . ."

"See the symbol below it, the one that looks like a rain cloud?"

"Yes."

"The rain cloud was used to indicate rain, of course."

"Makes sense."

"But also the concept of falling, or dropping, or descending."

Kathleen nodded.

"Now, you see these two symbols?" He pointed to the right-hand side of the inscription.

"Uh-huh."

Eskridge flipped open a book on Sumerian symbology and thumbed through it quickly, finding the correct page after several seconds. He laid the book flat and scrolled down the page with his index finger, obviously looking up the meaning of the two symbols. "In combination like this, they could mean broken or finished, or the end of something. Something that's depleted or exhausted. Like the end of a dynasty or the destruction of a city, for instance."

"Uh-huh." But Kathleen wasn't exactly following. There were too many combinations of possible meanings for her to draw any logical conclusions.

Eskridge seemed to agree. "When you put those all together, it doesn't really make much sense, does it? The end of falling strength? The depletion of descending wealth or good fortune? It could be *anything*."

"How about a fallen hero?"

"Sure. Could be. But that would be a fairly vague epitaph to put on someone's tomb, don't you think?"

"I guess so," Kathleen mumbled.

"Actually, I think it's something entirely different." Eskridge pulled another book from the stack and flipped through its pages. He eventually found the page he was looking for and began reading quietly to himself, periodically bobbing his head and mumbling indecipherable comments.

Kathleen watched with growing anticipation.

After a long time, Eskridge suddenly sat up straight in his chair. "Yep!" He tapped a particular place in the book with his index finger and exclaimed, "Just what I thought!"

"What is it?" Kathleen asked, unable to contain her excitement any longer.

"This combination of symbols"—he held up the piece of paper and pointed to Orion and the rain cloud—"had a very peculiar meaning in ancient Sumerian culture."

"Okay . . ."

Eskridge paused and stroked his moustache lightly, the wrinkles around his eyes revealing a faint smile. "They symbolized . . . the Nephilim."

"The *what*?"

Eskridge arched his eyebrows. "You've never heard of the Nephilim?"

"No . . . can't say that I have."

Eskridge looked astonished but said nothing for a long time, apparently lost in thought. Finally, after nearly a minute, he pushed back abruptly from the table. "Put that on," he said, pointing to Kathleen's coat. "We're going for a walk."

PART II

It was he who opened the mountain passes,
who dug wells on the flank of the mountain.
It was he who crossed the ocean,
the vast seas, to the rising sun,
who explored the world regions, seeking life.
It was he who reached by his own sheer strength
  Utanapishtim, the Faraway Land,
who restored the cities that the Flood had destroyed!
. . . for teeming mankind.
Who can compare with him in kingliness?
Who can say like Gilgamesh: "I am King!"?
Whose name, from the day of his birth, was called
  "Gilgamesh"?
Two-thirds of him is god, one-third of him is human.
The Great Goddess Aruru designed the model for his
  body,
she prepared his form . . .
. . . beautiful, handsomest of men,
. . . perfect.

> —EPIC OF GILGAMESH (TABLET I OF TWELVE CUNEIFORM
>   TABLETS FOUND IN THE RUINS OF THE LIBRARY OF
> ASHURBANIPAL, KING OF ASSYRIA 668–627, AT NINEVEH)

CHAPTER TWENTY-THREE

ELIAS Rubin took in the stunning view of the Red Sea from the balcony of his hillside mansion. Below him, the resort town of Eilat—Israel's southernmost city—bustled with activity, as tourists, shoppers, and sun seekers strolled up and down the palm-lined streets of this quaint seaside city of 55,000. A gleaming white cruise ship was moored alongside one of the commercial piers in the harbor.

Rubin was a distinguished-looking man. Late seventies, white hair, with a clean-shaven, wrinkled face and intelligent, dark eyes. He wore a fashionable golf shirt tucked neatly into pressed khaki slacks. A pair of steel-rimmed glasses completed the look of an intelligent, successful man. Which he was.

It was a warm, pleasant day in the biblical city of Elath—now Eilat—home to the oldest copper mines in the world. Yet Elias Rubin was not happy. He stood, arms folded tightly over his chest, brooding over one of the rare goals that, thus far, he'd been unable to achieve in his life—a goal that loomed increasingly more important with each passing day.

Past achievements meant little to Rubin. Twenty years earlier, he'd founded Rial Laboratories, now the largest pharmaceutical company in Israel. Under his inspired management, Rial had gained worldwide notoriety by successfully mapping the complete human genome years ahead of schedule. Rubin, himself, was not a scientist. But his ability to raise massive amounts of cash and overcome countless business and governmental obstacles had been crucial to the success of the gene-mapping project and the emergence of Rial as a pharmaceutical powerhouse. It had also made him incredibly wealthy. Five years ago, he'd risen as high as number fifteen on *Forbes* magazine's World's Richest People list, before settling down to his current position in the low forties.

All of these successes, however, were in the past, and of little interest to Rubin now. Five years ago, he'd stepped down as Rial's CEO, citing health concerns. He still bristled at that term. "Health concerns," a generic whitewash that Rial's communications people came up with in order to calm the market. Rubin was dying, and he knew it.

He could feel it.

Since stepping down from Rial, his sole endeavor and his only real passion—which he shared with just a handful of like-minded individuals—had been something he termed *olam*, a nuanced Hebrew word meaning something akin to "perpetual" or "forever." The word had jumped out at him twice as he read the following passage from First Book of Moses in the Torah:

> And the Lord said, My spirit shall not always strive with man forever [*olam*], because he also is flesh; nevertheless his days shall be a hundred and twenty years. The Nephilim were on the earth in those days, and also afterward, when the sons of God came in to the daughters of men, and they bore children to them. Those were the mighty men who were of old [*olam*], men of renown.

Rubin called his new endeavor the Olam Foundation, a highly secretive organization with immense financial resources but just seven members. The foundation's work was carried out by several "facilitators"—mainly ex-intelligence officers—one each in Europe, Japan, China, Russia, Israel, Africa, Australia, and North America. The Olam Foundation paid these facilitators handsomely for their specialized and highly discreet services. In addition, Rubin—the consummate businessman—had established a hefty bonus for whichever facilitator successfully delivered to the foundation the prize that it sought.

Currently, that bonus stood at 100 million dollars. And Luce Venfeld—the North American facilitator—was closest to earning it. *But time was running out.*

"Elias, come inside," said his wife, calling from the living room. "It's time to take your medicine."

Rubin walked back inside. His wife handed him a glass of water and the first of six pills that had been prescribed for his various ailments. He downed the tablet and grimaced. He despised this process, which he was required to repeat twice a day. "I believe these pills are killing me," he said with a scowl. He coughed, straightened his posture, then choked down the second pill.

"Please don't say that," said his wife. "The doctors say you need these. They know what they're doing."

"They know nothing!" Rubin snapped, pushing away the third pill.

His wife of forty-eight years looked at him with a hurt expression. "Elias . . ."

Rubin's eyes softened. "I'm sorry," he said, touching his wife's face. "Give me the pill." She handed it to him, and he swallowed it quickly with a gulp of water.

His thoughts soon turned back, as they always did, to the Olam Foundation and its goal. Five years of his life had been spent on this project, and tens of millions of dollars. He'd even sent his own ne'er-do-well grand-nephew, Semion, to help out in North America, although he wasn't sure if that was such a good idea. *What was taking so long?*

Elias Rubin had never failed at anything in life that he'd sought to achieve. He had no intention of doing so now.

CHAPTER TWENTY-FOUR

Cambridge, Massachusetts.

"WHERE are we going?" Kathleen asked, struggling to keep up with Dr. Eskridge. They had already walked six blocks from the Oriental Institute Museum and were now almost halfway across the Harvard campus. It was cold and damp outside, and the campus was not particularly well lit.

"Just a bit farther," Eskridge replied.

Eventually, they reached a series of intersecting walkways at the center of the Harvard Yard, and Kathleen followed Dr. Eskridge as he strode quickly along one of the dimly lit paths. Two minutes later, they arrived at the steps of the Harvard Memorial Church, a classic New England redbrick structure with four prominent columns supporting a Greek-style pediment, and a tall spire above.

"A church?" asked Kathleen incredulously.

"Yep. Come this way." Eskridge made his way around the side of the church to an unlit service entrance in the back.

"Is it even open?"

Eskridge smiled and retrieved a large bundle of keys from his pocket. "The rector is a former student of mine." Moments later, they were inside.

Without turning on any lights, Eskridge made his way along a short corridor and up a narrow flight of stairs to the clergy offices on the second floor. Kathleen followed close behind.

"This way," Eskridge said quietly as he entered a small, windowless room on the left. When they were both inside, he shut the door softly and flicked on the lights.

They stood inside a small, high-ceilinged library with parquet floors and five rows of bookshelves on each wall. Above the bookshelves were twelve dark oil paintings mounted on the yellow walls, each depicting a black-roped clergyman. To varying degrees, the twelve men bore serious, almost angry expressions, some bordering on downright scorn. The library smelled of oil soap and furniture polish. A solitary square table occupied the middle of the room, situated beneath a dull bronze chandelier.

Eskridge was already busy pulling books from the shelves and stacking them on the table in front of Kathleen. "People have written entire *books* about the Nephilim," he said as he scanned the shelves for additional volumes. "It's one of the oldest, most enduring mysteries in all recorded history."

"Hard to believe I've never heard of it," Kathleen said quietly.

"Well, don't feel bad. Unless you're a divinity major or an Assyriologist, the Nephilim aren't exactly a topic of dinner conversation." He reached up and pulled another book off the shelf.

Eskridge ran his fingers down the large stack of books he'd just assembled on the table, drawing a deep breath and exhaling loudly as he did. "Okay, let's start . . . *here.*" He pulled a large black leatherbound volume from the middle of the stack. The words HOLY BIBLE were embossed in gold letters on the front cover and the spine.

Kathleen took a seat at the table.

Eskridge flipped the book open, thumbed to a certain page, and began reading aloud. "The original King James version of the Bible, Genesis chapter six, verses one through four." He read the verses slowly, heavily emphasizing certain words and phrases as he went:

And it came to pass, when men began to multiply on the face of the earth, and daughters were born unto them, that the *sons of God* saw the daughters of men that they were fair; and they took them wives of all which they chose. And the Lord said, My spirit shall not always strive with man, for that he also is flesh: *yet his days shall be a hundred and twenty years.* There were *giants in the earth in those days*; and also after that, when the *sons of God* came in unto the daughters of men, and they bare children to them, the same became *mighty men which were of old, men of renown.*

"Now," Eskridge said, looking searchingly at Kathleen, "what do you think that passage means?"

Kathleen laughed dryly. "Honestly? It means nothing to me. It's a fable . . . folklore . . . a work of fiction. As a scientist, I don't find any meaning in it."

"I see." Eskridge looked away for a moment and then quickly turned back to Kathleen. "Well, let's assume it *is* a work of fiction. What would you say the *plot* is?"

Kathleen was surprised by the question. She hesitated and then slowly pulled the Bible toward her. She read verses one through four silently to herself and then looked up. "The plot is . . . a group of men—chosen men, sons of God, if you will—marry a bunch of beautiful women and have children who grow up to become famous and powerful. Half the soap operas on TV have the same plot."

Eskridge smiled, but he kept his eyes locked on Kathleen's. "And what about the part about the giants?"

"Metaphor," Kathleen said with a shrug. "Perhaps giants of industry. Political giants. Giants of culture, arts, athletics. Could be anything."

"And the part about man's days being one hundred and twenty years?"

Kathleen was stumped by that one. She read the passage again and thought for a while. "I have no idea," she admitted finally.

By then, Eskridge had retrieved another

book—also black and embossed in gold. "Now, here are the same four verses from the Revised Standard Version of the Bible. Listen for the differences." He once again read aloud, carefully emphasizing certain words and phrases:

When men began to increase on earth and daughters were born to them, the *divine beings* saw how beautiful the daughters of men were and took wives from among those that pleased them. The Lord said, "My breath shall not abide in man forever, since he too is flesh; *let the days allowed him be one hundred and twenty years.*" It was then, and later too, that the *Nephilim* appeared on earth—when the *divine beings* cohabited with the daughters of men, who bore them offspring. They were the *heroes of old*, the men of renown.

"Notice how giants became Nephilim in the Revised Version?" Eskridge asked.

"Uh-huh."

"And how the sons of God became divine beings?"

"Sure."

"So, according to these versions of the Bible, the Nephilim were the offspring of divine beings and human women. And they were renowned men of old. Not ordinary men of flesh, mind you, whom God had limited to a hundred and twenty years. Do you follow so far?"

"I *guess* so."

"Now, since you have that Bible already open

in front of you, go ahead and look at the next few verses in Genesis chapter six and tell me what happens next . . . you know, in the *plot*."

Kathleen skimmed the next few verses. "Well, it says that God saw that man was wicked, so he decided to destroy all of mankind and every creeping thing on earth."

"What else?"

"It says that Noah had found grace in the eyes of God, so God decided to spare him. Told him to build a big ark—one hundred cubits long, fifty cubits wide, and thirty cubits high—load a male and female of every animal on board, and then get ready for a big flood."

"Right," Eskridge said, "the *Great* Flood."

Kathleen shot him a curious look. "You know, Dr. Sargon mentioned the flood, too, the other night. He said it corresponded to an actual flood that took place in Mesopotamia several thousand years ago."

"And he was right about that. The great flood in the twenty-ninth century BC was a singular event in the ancient world. We find it recounted again and again in ancient Sumerian texts, in the epic tales of Gilgamesh, which were handed down from generation to generation, in ziggurat carvings, in cuneiform symbology, and, of course, in the Old Testament of the Bible, as well as in the Quran."

"All the same flood?"

"Well, that's what many scholars believe . . . including me." He inched closer to Kathleen.

"You see, folklore is almost always based, at some level, on *fact*."

Kathleen pursed her lips and weighed that idea in her mind, tilting her head equivocally from side to side.

"Take one of my favorite folk heroes," Eskridge continued, "Paul Bunyan. A giant lumberjack from the Northwest. Legend has it he was so big that his footprints created ten thousand lakes in Minnesota. And he dug the Grand Canyon by dragging his axe handle behind his giant blue ox, Babe."

"Mm-hmm."

"Now, did such a giant lumberjack ever exist?"

"No."

"Of course not! *But* . . ." Eskridge held her gaze for a moment. "There *are* ten thousand lakes in Minnesota. Eleven thousand to be exact. And there *is* a Grand Canyon."

Kathleen smiled slightly.

"Do you see my point?"

Kathleen nodded halfheartedly.

"Paul Bunyan is folklore, but he was created to explain true facts."

"Okay," said Kathleen begrudgingly. "But the ark? The animals?"

"Maybe it happened that way, maybe it didn't. That's the thing about folklore—you have to decide what's real and what's fiction. The flood—in my opinion—was real."

Kathleen turned the idea over in her mind. It did make a certain amount of sense that the story of the Great Flood could have emanated from real events in Mesopotamia. And, if so, it seemed reasonable to assume that certain facts had been embellished over the centuries by storytellers and eventually spun into religious folklore, namely the story of Noah and the ark. Kathleen could at least accept that possibility without abandoning all notions of logic and reason.

"Now," Eskridge continued, "let's talk about the Nephilim. What do you think: fact . . . or fiction?"

"Fiction," Kathleen said quickly.

"Are you sure?"

Kathleen rolled her eyes. "C'mon, Dr. Eskridge. *Divine beings* breeding with humans? What are we talking about? Angels? Demigods? Aliens? I'm sorry, I just can't accept it."

Eskridge shook his head and sighed. "I think you're missing the point. The question is not whether angels actually came down from heaven and bred with humans. The question is whether that story was created to explain something *real*. Something that people in ancient Mesopotamia actually observed but were unable to explain . . . at least not without resort to mythology." He paused for a few seconds. "Think about the Grand Canyon. Think about the ten thousand lakes in Minnesota. Those were *real things* that people observed, and then invented myths to explain."

Kathleen sat motionless in her chair as the wheels in her head began to spin. New thoughts were forming quickly, bridging to old thoughts, connecting previously disjointed ideas together.

"Okay," she said slowly. "So what you're asking is . . . *Why* was the Nephilim story created in the first place?"

"Precisely."

Kathleen became aware of a new idea percolating just below the surface of her consciousness. Every time she tried to grasp it, however, it evaporated. It was as if this new idea could not break through the thick barriers of logic and reason she'd constructed in her mind through years of dogged scientific inquiry.

"Before you answer," Eskridge said, standing up, "let me show you something else you might find interesting." He repositioned the stepladder to the other side of the room and climbed all the way to the top rung. Then, stretching his arm to the highest shelf, he pulled down a bound academic paper, two inches of yellowed typewriter paper sandwiched between two brown covers. "Your mother, Becky, wrote her Ph.D. thesis on this *exact* question." He descended the ladder and returned to his seat.

"What question?"

"The meaning of the Nephilim story. Who created it, and why."

"You're kidding, right?"

"Nope. It's right here." Eskridge held up the binder momentarily, then opened it and read aloud. " 'An Anthropological Study of the Origins of the Nephilim in Sumerian Mythology. Rebecca A. Sainsbury, Department of Anthropology, Harvard University. Presented May 12, 1971.' "

Kathleen stared blankly. It was strange to hear

her mother's name spoken aloud. "Sainsbury," just like her own.

"I was her thesis advisor," Eskridge added.

Kathleen was suddenly lost in thought. Her mother—an expert on . . . Nephilim? It seemed beyond coincidence, beyond serendipity. It seemed downright inconceivable. *Did fate bring her here tonight? No.* She rejected the idea instantly. *There's no such thing as fate.* She cleared her throat—which had begun to tighten involuntarily—and gestured toward the thesis. "What does it say?"

"A lot, actually," said Eskridge, jabbing the bound volume with his finger. "This thesis was really groundbreaking stuff at the time."

"How so?"

Eskridge drew a deep breath and put the thesis aside. He picked up the Bible again. "Let's start with some biblical ages. Remember our friend Noah?"

"Uh-huh."

"I'm reading now from Genesis, chapter seven, verse six. It says here that Noah was *six hundred years old* when the flood of waters came on the earth." He glanced at Kathleen over his glasses. "Pretty old, huh?"

"Sure, if you take it literally."

He flipped back a few pages. "Noah's father, Lamech, was *one hundred and eighty-two years old* when Noah was born, according to chapter five, verse twenty-eight. Pretty virile guy, wouldn't you say?"

Kathleen shrugged.

"Here's Genesis chapter five, verses thirty and thirty-one. 'Lamech lived after he begat Noah five hundred ninety and five years, and begat sons and daughters. And all the days of Lamech were *seven hundred seventy and seven years*: and he died.'" He looked evocatively at Kathleen.

"Those aren't literal," she said, already sensing where he was going.

But Eskridge ignored her; he was on a roll. "Lamech's father, Methuselah . . . *nine hundred sixty-nine years*. Methuselah's father, Enoch . . . *three hundred sixty-five years*."

"Okay, I get the picture. They were old."

"Yeah, really old. Now let's talk about Noah." He thumbed forward a few pages. "According to Genesis nine, Noah was *nine hundred and fifty years old* when he died. He had three sons before the flood, all of whom survived the flood with him. Shem, Ham, and Japheth."

Where's he going with this? Kathleen wondered.

"According to Genesis ten, those three sons divided the land after the flood and spread out to rule their respective kingdoms." He scanned the page, apparently looking for a particular verse. "Ah, here it is, Genesis ten, verse thirty-two. 'These are the families of the sons of Noah, after their generations, in their nations: and by these were the nations divided in the earth after the flood.'"

Kathleen shrugged and held out her palms. "Sorry, I'm not following."

"Shem survived the flood and lived a total of six hundred years. But if you look at Genesis chapter eleven, none of his progeny after the flood lived anywhere near that long. Over eight generations, their life spans dropped steadily from about four hundred years to about two hundred years." He paused. "Now, that's not bad, mind you . . . but nothing compared to Shem . . . and Noah . . . and Lamech . . . and Methuselah." He peered over the top of his glasses. "You know, all those *pre-flood* guys."

Ahhhh! Now Kathleen got it. He was comparing the pre-flood life spans in the Bible with those after the flood. She remembered seeing something about this on the History Channel. She nodded her head emphatically, indicating her understanding.

Eskridge continued. "In fact, by the time you get to the ninth generation after Shem—a fellow named Haran—he up and died before his own father. Genesis eleven, verse twenty-eight."

"Okay . . ."

"In Genesis twenty-five, the Bible says Abraham lived to be one hundred and seventy-five years old. His son Isaac died at one hundred and eighty. Then there's Jacob, one hundred forty-seven; Joseph, one hundred ten; Levi, one hundred thirty-seven; Kohath, one hundred thirty-three; and Amram—Moses' father—one hundred thirty-seven. Moses, himself, died at *exactly* one hundred and twenty. See a trend?"

"They're going down."

Eskridge fanned through a series of pages, quickly finding a different section of the Bible. "By the fifteenth century BC, when Psalm Ninety was written, we have this account of the prevailing human life span at the time:

> The days of our years are *threescore and ten*;
> and if by reason of strength they be *fourscore
>   years*,
> yet is their strength labor and sorrow;
> for it is soon cut off, and we fly away.

"Three score and ten—that's only a seventy-year life span, eighty if you have good strength. Not much different from what we have today, right?"

"Right . . ."

"So, by the fifteenth century BC—fourteen hundred years after the Great Flood—it seems the longevity gene had plumb petered out."

Kathleen's eyes widened. "The longevity gene?"

"Sure. Your mother laid it all out in here." Eskridge held up the thesis and shook it slightly. "She said the Nephilim myth was created to explain an actual phenomenon that people of that era observed, or at least had heard about from their recent ancestors."

"The long life spans."

"Yep. A small group of people—perhaps just a few families—who seemed to live for centuries while the rest of the population lived and died in just a span of decades. At that time, there would have been no logical explanation for such a phenomenon. So, as people often do, they attributed it to the supernatural—the *Nephilim*. The author of Genesis simply incorporated that mythology, borrowing it from common Sumerian folklore." He arched his eyebrows and peered deeply into Kathleen's eyes. "Remember, folklore is almost always used to explain something real, which is otherwise inexplicable."

Once again, a vague notion was swirling around in the recesses of Kathleen's mind, just below the surface, just out of reach.

"And by the way," Eskridge continued, "it's not just the Bible where you find this marked decrease in life span after the Great Flood. Have you ever heard of the Sumerian king list?"

"No."

"It's an ancient Sumerian text, recorded on clay cuneiform tablets, which lists all of the kings of Sumer in chronological order, practically from the beginning of recorded history." Eskridge flipped open the thesis, scanned the table of contents, and then turned quickly to a particular page. "The Sumerian king list records about twenty-five anteduluvian kings."

"Antediluvian?"

"Pre-flood." He placed his finger on the opened page and read aloud. "Now, here are some examples of kings from the First Dynasty of Kish, along with the length of their reigns. Jushur of Kish—twelve hundred years; Kullassina-bel of Kish—nine hundred and sixty years; Nang-ishlishma of Kish—six hundred and seventy years; En-Tarah-Ana of Kish—four hundred and twenty years; Tizqar of Kish—three hundred and five years. The last king of that dynasty was Aga of Kish, who reigned six hundred and twenty-five years. Pretty long time, huh?"

"Yeah."

"After that, the Sumerian king list indicates that Kish was defeated and the kingship taken to E-anna, a rival city in ancient Sumer. Thus began the First Dynasty of Uruk."

"Uruk was in Iraq, right?" Kathleen remembered that from her conversation with Dr. Sargon the other night.

"That's correct. The first king of Uruk was Mesh-ki-ang-gasher, who ruled for three hundred and twenty-four years . . . until something very interesting happened."

"What?"

Eskridge turned to the next page in the thesis. "This is a direct translation from the Weld-Blundell Prism. It's a baked-clay four-sided cuneiform prism, the most comprehensive Sumerian king list ever found. It was discovered in 1922 near Babylon in Iraq. Today it's on display at the Ashmolean Museum in Oxford."

"Okay."

Eskridge read aloud from the thesis, moving his finger along as he did. " 'Mesh-ki-ang-gasher of E-ana, son of Utu, went into the Sea and disappeared.' " He paused. "Sound familiar?"

"The Great Flood?"

"That would be my guess. And now, look carefully at the reigns of kings after that event." He spun the thesis around and pushed it across the table toward Kathleen.

Kathleen studied the page carefully, tingling

slightly at the idea that she was looking at her mother's writing from nearly four decades ago:

```
Enmerkar, who built Unug: 420 years
Lugalbanda of Unug, the shepherd:
   1200 years
Dumuzid of Unug, the fisherman: 100
   years. Captured En-Men-Barage-Si
   of Kish.
Gilgamesh, whose father was a phantom,
   lord of Kulaba: 126 years
Ur-Nungal of Unug: 30 years
Udul-Kalama of Unug: 15 years
La-Ba'shum of Unug: 9 years
En-Nun-Tarah-Ana of Unug: 8 years
Mesh-He of Unug: 36 years
Melem-Ana of Unug: 6 years
Lugal-Kitun of Unug: 36 years
Then Uruk was defeated and the
   kingship was taken to Semionm.
```

"Notice any similarities between that account and the biblical account we read a little while ago?" Eskridge asked.

"The life spans . . ."

"Yeah, they petered out a couple generations after the flood, didn't they?"

"Uh-huh."

"And who was the last recorded king with an abnormally long life span?"

Kathleen looked down at the thesis. "Gilgamesh."

"Son of a *phantom*, right?"

"Uh-huh."

"Sound familiar?"

"The Nephilim?"

Eskridge stood up, leaned over the table toward Kathleen, and then spread Sargon's sheet of paper on the table between them. "Now, let's look at this epitaph again."

They both studied it for several seconds, and then Eskridge spoke—slowly, deliberately. "Okay. Putting all these symbols together, here's what I think they mean . . ."

Kathleen waited anxiously as Eskridge considered the paper in silence, apparently collecting his final thoughts.

"My best translation is . . . 'The Last Nephilim.'"

As those words sunk in, Kathleen's mind exploded with a dozen thoughts at once.

"Or," Eskridge continued, "using a slightly different vernacular of the time . . . 'The Last Giant.'"

"Gilgamesh," said Kathleen quietly.

"So it would seem."

CHAPTER TWENTY-FIVE

Rockville, Maryland.

"SORRY I'm late," Kathleen said as she entered the QLS conference room. "Reagan National was an absolute madhouse this morning."

Kathleen, Carlos, Julie, and Jeremy—the staff of QLS—took their seats around the conference table just before noon. Office supplies were stacked high at one end of the table, and boxes of glassware and other laboratory supplies were lined up along the walls.

"The reason I wanted to get everyone together," Kathleen said, "is to discuss a new project that I'd like to get started on right away." She nodded toward Carlos.

Carlos acknowledged her signal and quickly retrieved from his briefcase the clear Ziploc bag containing the tooth. She had called him from Boston last night and asked him to bring it to the meeting, though she hadn't explained why.

"This," Kathleen announced, holding up the Ziploc bag for everyone to see, "is an artifact from

Iraq. As I understand it, it came from the tomb of a very important figure in Mesopotamian history. I won't bore you with the details, but suffice it to say that it may be important to our research."

"How?" Jeremy Fisher asked skeptically. He was a lanky guy in his late twenties, with black, unkempt hair and two days of stubble on his face. He wore ripped, faded jeans and a long-sleeve T-shirt with the words AIM SHOOT DELIVER on the back, and the logo of the U.S. Paintball Association on the front. Aside from being a first-rate slacker, Jeremy Fisher was also a brilliant molecular biologist. He'd graduated near the top of his undergraduate class at Berkeley and then completed an impressive Ph.D. program at Stanford. He'd been a much sought-after post-doc at NIH when Kathleen discovered him and quickly recruited him away to QLS two years earlier.

"Well," Kathleen said, answering Jeremy's question, "it's possible this artifact may contain some useful DNA."

"DNA?" blurted Jeremy. "What is that thing, anyway?" He craned over the table and brought his face to within inches of the Ziploc bag. There was a momentary pause, and then—"Is that a . . . *tooth*?"

"Yes," Kathleen replied flatly. "It's a tooth. From a mummy."

There was immediate commotion in the room as Julie, too, stood up to inspect the relic. "Gross!" she whispered as the details of the discolored tooth became apparent.

Julie Haas was the opposite of Jeremy in many

ways. Most notably, she was an optimist, who (unlike Jeremy) naturally assumed things would always work out for the best. She was pretty—short blond hair; sparkling blue eyes; round, smooth face; and an easy smile. And she had a breezy personality that made her a pleasure to be around. That was one reason Kathleen had brought her over from NIH two years ago, where she'd been Kathleen's lab assistant since graduating from college three years earlier.

But Julie was more than just pleasant and pretty. She was also a very competent biologist. Perhaps not as brilliant or inspired as Jeremy, but a solid researcher nonetheless. Indeed, Julie and Jeremy seemed to complement each other nicely in the lab. What Julie lacked in raw talent, she more than made up for with determination, perseverance, and plain hard work, qualities that Jeremy did not always exhibit.

The commotion over the artifact eventually died down, and Kathleen gestured for everyone to take his seat. "Like I said," she continued, "I'd like to conduct some tests—"

"On *that?*" Jeremy interrupted.

"Yes. On this."

"What kinds of tests?" asked Julie. "I mean, how does this relate to our core research?"

Kathleen hesitated. "Well, to tell you the truth, it's kind of complicated. And I'm not even sure I understand it myself. So let's just take things one step at a time, okay? This may turn out to be nothing at all . . . or it may be huge. I just don't know at this point. So let's start with a few simple tests."

The room fell silent, and Kathleen noticed Jeremy and Julie exchanging disbelieving glances. *They think I'm crazy*, she thought to herself. *Maybe they're right.*

Suddenly, Carlos spoke up in his typical, authoritative voice. "Absolutely, Dr. Sainsbury. Just tell us what tests you want run, and we'll make sure they get done."

Kathleen smiled appreciatively at him. *Sergeant Guiterez to the rescue!*

"Let's first see if we can extract some usable DNA from this thing." She placed the bag on the table in front of Jeremy and gave him a nod. "I was hoping you could take care of that."

Jeremy picked up the bag with his thumb and index finger and inspected its contents. He was already shaking his head doubtfully. "I'd be amazed if there's any intact DNA in here," he said dismissively. "I mean, look at this thing. It's degraded. It's discolored. Who knows what kinds of conditions this thing's been exposed to. Not to mention contamination. I mean, you've probably got viral DNA, insect DNA, bacteria . . . all sorts of garbage in there." He shrugged his bony shoulders. "I mean, you might get a few *fragments* of DNA, but an intact sample? I don't see it happening."

"Well, please try," said Kathleen.

"Sure, okay," Jeremy said, adding under his breath, "just don't expect much."

Kathleen ignored his last comment and turned to Julie. "Now, assuming Jeremy is successful in extracting some usable DNA, can you be in charge of sequencing it?"

"Okay. Are we looking for anything in particular, or—"

Kathleen cut her off. "For starters, let's just verify it's human."

There were confused looks all around the table.

"What else would it be, Dr. S?" asked Julie.

"Uh, what I mean is, let's just verify that we have a complete human sequence, okay?"

"Sure," said Julie, a bit hesitantly.

"Hey, Dr. Sainsbury?" Jeremy interjected. "Like, when do you want all of this done?"

Kathleen turned to Carlos. "When's the next shareholders' meeting?"

"Teleconference next Friday."

Kathleen winced. The quarterly shareholders' meeting was only ten days away. Those meetings were always an uncomfortable experience for her, and this one—coming at the end of Year Two with funding nearly depleted—promised to be a doozy. "Okay," she said, "if possible, I want the results by then."

Julie and Jeremy looked at each other with wide eyes.

"I know that's asking a lot," Kathleen continued, sensing their uneasiness. "And I know Sunday is Easter. But this is really important. You know, our funding is getting low. At our current burn rate, we're going to be out of cash in a few months, and the investors are getting nervous. It's been two years, and—let's be honest—we've really got nothing to show for it. We need to give them some results or . . ." She paused and looked around the room. "Well, I don't know what will happen." She pointed at the Ziploc bag on the table. "Let's just give this a try, okay? I have a hunch about it."

"Don't worry," said Carlos. "We'll get it done."

Bryce Whittaker called a little after 3:00 P.M., and Kathleen took the call in her office. "How was Boston?" he asked.

"It was . . . Hey, how'd you know I was in Boston?"

"I called your office this morning. Your colleague, Carlos, told me you were flying in from Boston."

"Oh."

"Were you up there for business?"

"Yeah . . . sort of. It was an unexpected trip. By the way, I'm sorry I missed your call last night. My meeting went pretty late."

"No problem. That's what I figured. So anyway . . . you up for dinner tonight?"

Kathleen smiled, relieved that Whittaker apparently wasn't angry about being blown off last night. "Sure."

"How do you feel about sushi?"

"Love it."

"Great. I know a wonderful little sushi place in Bethesda, not too far from your apartment."

"You must be talking about Hake, I *love* that pla—" Kathleen stopped short. "How'd you know where my apartment is?"

"I looked it up."

"You did?"

"Hey, I'm a reporter, remember? I get paid to be nosey."

Kathleen said nothing.

"So, can I pick you up around eight?"

"Better make it nine. I've got a lot to catch up on here."

"Nine it is."

"And I'll meet you at the restaurant."

"Okay. I'll see you there."

Late in the afternoon, Jeremy and Julie stood alone in the QLS laboratory, on opposite sides of a long soapstone workbench. Julie had just completed the last batch of data for the day on the fruit flies, and Jeremy was preparing materials and glassware for his new project—the artifact.

"Check it out," Jeremy said jokingly, holding the Ziploc bag in front of his mouth. "Think I ought to see a dentist?"

Julie grimaced. "Very funny. Will you please put that thing down. It is *so* gross!"

Jeremy complied.

"So, have you figured out what you're going to do with it yet?" Julie asked.

"Yeah, I called a friend of mine who does forensics analysis for the San Francisco PD. He sent me a procedure they use for degraded specimens like this. You know, like when they find human remains buried in some psycho's basement."

"What's the procedure?"

Jeremy picked up a sheet of paper and skimmed it. "Let's see . . . sterilize in phosphate balanced salt solution, stabilize in polyester resin. Hmmm . . . then I need a drill."

"What, are you building a birdhouse?"

"No, seriously. According to this, I've gotta drill into the tooth to extract the dental pulp, if there still is any."

"Can't you just grind up the whole specimen and extract the DNA?"

"Nah. Too many contaminants in the outer surface. We've got to get to the pulp and hope this guy's dental hygiene was pretty good. Otherwise, *bacteria-ville*."

"Yeah, I guess that makes sense. No telling where that thing's been in the past few thousand years."

"Exactly."

"What do you do after you extract the pulp? PCR amplification?"

"Yep. Of course, most likely, I'll just be amplifying garbage."

Julie smirked. *Faux pessimism*—classic Jeremy. "Hey, do you think you can handle this yourself this weekend? I'd like to drive up to Philly to see my folks for Easter."

"Yeah, no problem. I'm just gonna UV sterilize all the tools and glassware tonight. I'll go shopping for a dental drill tomorrow."

"Good luck."

"Thanks, I'll need it."

Two hours later, Jeremy was alone in the QLS laboratory. Julie and Kathleen were gone for the day. Carlos was in his office, working on some paperwork for the upcoming shareholders' meeting. A small collection of glassware sat assembled on the workbench, awaiting sterilization. Jeremy surveyed this collection carefully, mentally going through each of the steps of the procedure he intended to follow. As he stood there with his arms crossed, the artifact caught his eye.

The brownish tooth was clearly visible through the plastic Ziploc bag, resting a few feet away on the soapstone workbench. Jeremy walked over, leaned down, and inspected it closely.

Something about it was strangely mesmerizing.

Who had it belonged to? He moved closer and studied the minute details: the way the crown was worn down smooth, the texture of the enamel. Soon, his imagination was off and running, the tooth seemingly taking on a life of its own.

CHAPTER TWENTY-SIX

"TRY the Unagi Maki," Whittaker said, placing a cylindrical sushi roll on Kathleen's plate. "Freshwater eel. It's delicious."

They were seated by the front window of Hake, a trendy Japanese restaurant on Cordell Avenue in Bethesda. Outside, fashionable people bustled by: young, beautiful women in impossibly tight miniskirts, men in casual sport coats, and gaggles of twenty-somethings gearing up for the clubs.

"Any special plans for the weekend?" Whittaker asked as he ate.

Kathleen shrugged. "Just driving to Annapolis to see my grandfather."

"Oh, I thought he lived in Great Falls."

"He used to. But he moved to a retirement home in Annapolis a few years ago."

"Hmmm. I've never been to Annapolis," said Whittaker. "I hear it's nice."

"It's beautiful. Especially in the spring. He really loves sailing, so I thought it'd be nice for him to be in a place where he could see sailboats every day."

"Sounds perfect."

"Mm-hmm." Kathleen watched as Whittaker transported a piece of sushi from his plate to his mouth with a pair of chopsticks.

"So," Whittaker said after devouring the morsel, "would you like some company?"

"What, for Easter?"

"Sure. I don't have any plans, so I thought, you know . . . maybe I could go to Annapolis with you."

Kathleen didn't respond.

"Like I said, I've never been there."

Kathleen was consciously debating the idea in her head. Her instincts, however, were already screaming, "*No!*" A dozen logistical and personal issues came to mind all at once. Her grandfather . . . the travel arrangements . . . dinner at the nursing home? It all seemed so *awkward*.

Seconds passed, and Whittaker suddenly began to look embarrassed.

Decision time, Kathleen realized. She liked Whitaker and definitely wanted to get to know him better. He was really a sweet guy, and she enjoyed being around him. *But a whole day in Annapolis?* She was just about to politely decline the offer when something stopped her. A tiny voice in the back of her mind was whispering: "Book smart, man dumb." *Not this time*, she decided. She would not let this relationship fizzle like all the others before it.

By now, Whittaker was already backtracking. "If you've got other plans—"

"No, no, no," Kathleen said. "That sounds great. Let's go together."

Whittaker looked doubtful. "Are you sure?"

"Absolutely. I could use the company."

Whittaker smiled broadly. "Great," he said. "I'm really looking forward to it." Then he devoured another piece of raw fish.

CHAPTER TWENTY-SEVEN

Easter Sunday. Sunset Knoll, Maryland.

THE Garrison Manor Assisted Living Center could easily be mistaken for an upscale hotel and conference center. Located on twenty acres of manicured lawns and gardens in Sunset Knoll, ten miles north of Annapolis, it consisted of two long wings adjoining a large, two-story entry hall with a buff-colored limestone façade and a high, red-tiled roof. The wheelchair-accessible front entrance led to a Southern-style covered porch, painted light gray, with white wooden columns and a white turned-spindle railing. At the back of the porch was a wide automatic sliding-glass door, flanked by two stylishly etched sidelight windows and a semicircular transom-and-window unit above.

"Very nice," said Whittaker as he and Kathleen pulled up to the front entrance in her Subaru.

"It's one of the best assisted living homes in the area," Kathleen remarked as she eased into the first available parking space. "The staff's really great. They do a lot of fun stuff with the residents. Music nights, and different themes for meals on weekends. Every Wednesday in the spring and summer they take a bus down to the harbor to watch the regattas. That's my grandfather's favorite."

"Yeah, you mentioned he likes sailing."

"Uh-huh. I come out here to watch the races with him sometimes . . . when I get can get away from work, that is." She frowned as she surveyed the parking lot, which was less than half full. "Sad that more people don't visit on holidays. It means a lot to the residents when their families show up."

"I bet."

They made their way toward the front entrance, where Kathleen stopped just short of the steps. "Bryce?"

"Hmmm?"

"There's something I need to explain about my grandfather before we go in."

"Okay . . ."

Kathleen took a deep breath and braced herself. "My grandfather has Alzheimer's disease. Stage five, which is a fairly advanced stage of the disease."

"I'm sorry to hear that."

"He has good days and bad days. And lately, more bad than good. I just wanted to let you know in case . . . well, in case he's having a bad day."

Whittaker smiled compassionately and said, "I understand."

They walked up the steps together and entered the building through the automatic glass door. The main hall was nicely furnished, though far from luxurious. It smelled strongly of disinfectant—like a hospital. There were garish Easter decorations pinned here and there on the walls. A paper cutout of a cartoon bunny on one wall, paper Easter eggs on another. A banner across the front desk read "Happy Easter!" in bright pastel colors. It reminded Kathleen of the décor of a second-grade classroom.

"Well *hello*, Ms. Sainsbury!" boomed a middle-aged woman behind the front desk. She was cheerful, overweight, and loud. Her dark hair was pulled back tightly in a bun, and she wore purple nurse's scrubs over a white, wide-collared blouse.

"Hi Ellie," Kathleen replied. "Happy Easter."

"Same to you! Oh, your grandfather will be so glad to see you. He asked about you the other day."

"He did?" Kathleen was surprised to hear that.

"Well . . . sort of. He asked when that girl with the Oreo cookies was coming back." Ellie McDougal let out a boisterous laugh, obviously finding the comment utterly hilarious.

Kathleen, on the other hand, managed only a melancholy smile. She turned to Whittaker to explain. "Sometimes, I bring him Oreo cookies. He likes them."

Whittaker nodded.

"Okay," said Nurse McDougal, several decibels too loud, "I've got you all checked in. You can go on back now. Dinner starts at two."

Kathleen made her way around the front desk and through a set of double doors that led to the north wing. Whittaker followed behind and quickly caught up with her in the corridor. "How long's your grandfather had Alzheimer's?" he asked as they walked.

"First signs were about six years ago. Forgetfulness, trouble concentrating. I thought it was just a passing thing, but it kept getting worse and worse. Pretty soon, he was getting lost coming back from the store or the library, even from the neighbors'. Then he starting forgetting simple words, like 'toothbrush' and 'dishwasher.' That's when I realized he needed full-time care."

They stepped into an elevator, and Kathleen pushed the button for the third floor.

"So that's why you're working on a cure for Alzheimer's, isn't it?"

"Well, it's certainly part of it." Kathleen turned to face him. "Bryce, it's an awful disease. It robs people of some of the best years of their lives. I mean, you should have seen my grandfather before—" She stopped short, feeling herself getting choked up. *No need for that right now*, she reminded herself.

"You okay?" Whittaker asked.

"Yeah, I'm fine."

A monotonal voice announced, "Third floor," and the elevator doors slid open. Kathleen and Whittaker exited, turned left, and made their way to Room 308.

"Here it is," said Kathleen nervously. She rang the doorbell and gave Whittaker a wilting smile.

More than thirty seconds passed in silence with no apparent activity inside.

Finally, Kathleen unlocked the door with her own key and poked her head inside. "Grandpa?" she said. "It's me, Kathleen." She swung the door fully open and walked in.

Whittaker followed.

The most prominent piece of furniture in the small room was an adjustable bed opposite the door. It sat lengthwise beneath a large picture window overlooking the lawn. The bed was neatly made up with a floral-pattern bedspread and a slipcover over the pillow, but it was still, unmistakably, a hospital bed, with its collapsible side rails and painted footboard. The room was carpeted with a light taupe Berber, and the walls were painted nearly the identical color. A framed print of the 1983 America's Cup champion—Dennis Connor's *Stars and Strips*—adorned the wall above the bed.

John Sainsbury—Kathleen's grandfather—sat in an upholstered armchair, watching TV. He looked at Kathleen and Whittaker with demonstrable surprise as they walked in.

"Hi, Grandpa," said Kathleen sweetly.

"Oh, hello . . ." replied the elder Sainsbury without the slightest sign of recognition. He could just as easily have been speaking to a nurse or a janitor.

Kathleen pointed to Whittaker. "This is my friend, Bryce. He's a newspaper reporter."

"Uh-huh," said her grandfather shakily, obviously still confused as to why these two people were entering his room in the middle of *Family Feud*.

John Sainsbury was eighty-five years old and looked every day of it. His face was deeply creased and craggy. Across his forehead were four deep parallel lines, like two sets of railroad tracks running temple to temple. The wrinkles around his eyes extended halfway down his face and blended into the wrinkles around his mouth. His white hair was neatly combed, yet swept awkwardly to one side, as if someone else had combed it. He had a gentle, almost bemused expression on his face that somehow conveyed both intelligence and an utter absence of recognition or command of the events around him. His light blue eyes were hazy and distant.

"You look nice, Grandpa," Kathleen said. "Are you dressed for dinner?"

The elder Sainsbury was dressed in a sky blue checkered shirt, a navy blue button-down sweater, and tan corduroy pants. "Is it time for dinner?" he asked uncertainly.

"Not yet," Kathleen replied. "We thought we'd visit with you for a while before dinner. Is that okay?"

"Okay."

Kathleen walked over and gave her grandfather a big hug and a kiss on the cheek. He smiled and nodded.

Does he recognize me? Kathleen wondered. "Grandpa, I brought you something."

"Huh?"

Kathleen reached into her purse and pulled

out a small package of cookies. "Oreo cookies—your favorite." She smiled and whispered, "Don't tell the nurses I gave these to you, okay?"

Mr. Sainsbury took the package of cookies and slipped them, fumblingly, into his sweater pocket. "Is it time for dinner?" he asked again.

"Not yet, Grandpa." Kathleen stepped in front of him and bent down so that her face was directly in front of his. "Grandpa, do you know who I am?" Kathleen hated asking this question, and she hated even more the response she usually got. But she forced herself to do it each time she saw him because she had to keep track of the progression of the disease.

Mr. Sainsbury studied her face for several seconds, clearly trying to remember—struggling to make a connection. He grimaced for a moment and then replied in a shaky, confused voice. "Becky?"

Kathleen closed her eyes and turned her head away. "My mother," she whispered to Whittaker in a choked-up voice. Then, despite her best effort, she began to cry.

Dinner was pleasant enough. Yet, for Kathleen, it was just one more heartbreaking episode in a long string of heartaches involving her grandfather's Alzheimer's disease. She watched in dismay as he pushed food around his plate, barely eating anything. "You need to eat, Grandpa," she admonished several times. Yet, he barely ate five bites. He was wasting away before her eyes, and it was agonizing for her to watch.

For Kathleen, the only bright spot at dinner was Whittaker's valiant, albeit clumsy, efforts to engage her grandfather in conversation. Whittaker talked to him endlessly about sailboats, about how much he liked Virginia, and, after Kathleen explained to him that her grandfather had been an engineer for NASA, about airplanes and spaceships and the moon landing. For the most part, Mr. Sainsbury responded with a series of indistinct grunts, offering nothing in the way of return conversation. At one point, though, when Whittaker asked about his experience with the space program in the 1960s, Mr. Sainsbury started to say something that sounded meaningful. "Yeah," he began, "we were working on . . . uh . . . the Apollo . . . that, uh . . . Apollo . . ."

Kathleen leaned in expectantly. "Go ahead, Grandpa," she said encouragingly, "You were working on the Apollo project?"

But the moment had passed. Whatever thought John Sainsbury had managed to seize upon had already slipped away.

"Sometimes, he remembers things from way back then," Kathleen explained quietly to Whittaker. "That's one of the strange things about Alzheimer's. It leaves some memories intact but erases others."

"It must be very frustrating," Whittaker said.

"Very frightening is more like it."

After dinner, they walked with Grandpa Sainsbury around the grounds of Garrison Manor. It was a cool spring afternoon with almost no wind at all. The giant pin oaks and sycamores that dotted the manicured grounds were still bare from the cold Maryland winter. But the crocuses and tulips in the raised flower beds were already beginning to bloom, providing a cheerful, if sparse, backdrop of lavender and yellow.

Easter—a time of loss and renewal.

They returned Mr. Sainsbury to his room around 4:00 P.M. and said good-bye. Kathleen watched with lingering sadness as an orderly helped her grandfather into bed and administered his medication. He was asleep in less than a minute.

"Bye, Grandpa," she said quietly as they left his room.

Leaving the nursing home after a visit like this was always difficult for Kathleen. She walked slowly down the hall, lost in her thoughts, wondering, as she always did, if she'd see him again.

Whittaker walked silently beside her.

They reached the main entry hall without saying a word, and Kathleen signed them both out. Then, willing herself into a better mood, she said to Whittaker, "How about a tour of Annapolis?"

"Sure," said Whittaker with a smile. "I think we still have a little daylight left."

They parked near the old market square at the Annapolis harbor, which was nearly deserted. Only a handful of people were strolling about.

They spent an hour touring the grounds of the U.S. Naval Academy, making it as far as Bancroft Hall—the massive dormitory that housed the entire Brigade of Midshipmen—before finally turning back. It was nearly dark, and noticeably colder, when they returned to the market square. After some searching, they found an open pub—McGarvey's. They entered and ordered drinks at the bar.

"Here's to my first visit to Annapolis," Whittaker said, hoisting a mug of Aviator Lager, McGarvey's specialty.

"Cheers," Kathleen said, touching her glass to his.

Whittaker took a long swig of his beer. "You know, your grandfather seems like a really nice guy."

Kathleen smiled. She knew he was just being polite. "I wish you could have met him before. He really was a wonderful man. Even in his seventies, he was energetic and full of life." Kathleen sipped her beer and thought about how lively her grandfather had been just five years ago. "We used to go sailing together."

"Really?"

"Oh yeah. We'd come here to Annapolis, or go up to Delaware, and rent out a thirty or thirty-five-foot boat. Take it out for the day. He was a really great sailor."

"You guys were close, then, huh?"

"He basically raised me. And after my grandmother died, he raised me by himself."

"Must have been tough."

"Yeah, but you know what? In a way it was nice. All my friends' dads were lawyers or doctors or businessmen. Always traveling, always working. They never had time for their kids. But Grandpa . . . he was always home. Always there . . . for me."

Whittaker nodded.

"And now, I intend to be there for him."

Whittaker was about to say something when Kathleen's cell phone rang. She fished it out of her purse. "Hello?"

"Dr. S, it's me, Jeremy."

"Jeremy, where are you?"

"At work."

"At work? I thought I told you not to come in today. It's a holiday, remember?"

"Actually, I didn't come in today . . . I came in yesterday."

Kathleen mulled that fact for a second. "You've been there since *yesterday?*"

"Yeah, I've been working on that mummy tooth you gave me."

"Jeremy—"

"And you're not going believe what I found!"

CHAPTER TWENTY-EIGHT

Bill McCreary sat alone in the study of his modest suburban home, deep in thought, a bound collection of Einstein's essays open in his lap. He flinched when his secure phone line rang unexpectedly. That could be one of only a handful of people. "McCreary," he said quietly, answering on the first ring.

"It's me," said Steve Goodwin. "I'm sending you an audio file you should listen to. The guy speaking is Jeremy Fisher, a QLS scientist. The woman is Dr. Sainsbury."

At that moment, an encrypted e-mail popped onto McCreary's computer screen, with the subject line, "HERE IT IS."

"Okay, I see it," McCreary said. "I'll call you back."

McCreary sat down at his desk, opened the e-mail, and double-clicked on the attached audio file. He leaned back in his chair and closed his eyes as a crackly, intercepted phone conversation played over his speakers:

"Jeremy, where are you?"

"At work."

"At *work?* I thought I told you not to come in today. It's a holiday, remember?"

"Actually, I didn't come in today . . . I came in yesterday."

"You've been there since *yesterday?*"

"Yeah, I've been working on that mummy tooth you gave me."

"Jeremy—"

"And you're not going believe what I found!"

There was a pause. "I'm listening . . ."

"Well, first of all, I extracted the dental pulp from the tooth. I was surprised there was any left, but there was."

"Okay."

"Dissolved the extract in a CTAB buffer solution, let it sit at room temperature for about six hours, then centrifuged it to separate the DNA. I extracted with isoamyl alcohol and chloroform.

"Not phenol?"

"Nope. I used a new workup protocol from a friend of mine at the SFPD. Really cutting-edge stuff."

"Okay . . ."

"Anyway, I wasn't expecting much because the sample was so degraded. I did the workup protocol that my friend sent me. Removed the PCR inhibitors using a Qiagen spin column . . ."

"Wow, you've been a busy beaver."

"Like I said, I really wasn't expecting much, but . . . Dr. S, I got a clean sample."

There was an audible gasp. "Intact?"

"Yep. I just did a quick sequence, and it hit, like, *ninety-eight* percent of the base pairs. It's totally intact."

"You're kidding."

"Nope. It's weird. I didn't want to use the whole sample at once, so I split it into eight aliquots. The first few I tested were absolute garbage—nothing identifying at all. Then on four, five, and six, I got bacterial DNA."

"Totally contaminated, huh?"

"Yep. I figured it was a lost cause, so I just kept going. Seven was a bust. And then, *bam*, on number eight—the *last aliquot I had*—I pulled this perfect strand of human DNA—like it was the last one remaining. I mean, a complete strand from *that* thing. Who would've figured?"

McCreary shifted in his chair and frowned as the recorded conversation continued over his speakers:

"Jeremy, that's wonderful! I mean, truly . . . truly amazing. You've really outdone yourself."

"Yeah, I couldn't believe it myself."

"Now, *go home.*"

"Yeah, yeah, I will."

"No, I mean it. Go home. You need sleep. I know you. You must be completely exhausted."

"I am pretty tired."

"Julie will be in tomorrow morning to finish the sequencing. Go home and get some rest."

"All right, I will."

"And Jeremy?"

"Yeah?"

"I'm really proud of you."

"Thanks, Dr. S."

As the audio file ended, McCreary leaned forward in his chair and ruminated over the conversation he'd just heard. "Damn it," he whispered under his breath, shaking his head. Things were getting out of control. He *hated* when things got out of his control.

And what was this "mummy tooth" they were talking about? His thoughts immediately turned to Kathleen's parents. *Archeologists.*

He slid his wireless mouse around on the mouse pad and began navigating through a series of screens on the computer. On a hunch, he logged on to a special DARPA search engine that retrieved academic papers from all around the world. He typed in the name of Kathleen's father, "Daniel Talbot," and waited impatiently. Fifteen seconds later, a list of several dozen titles appeared on the screen. He scanned the list quickly, focusing on one almost immediately:

Talbot, Daniel J., The Ruins at Tell-Fara—Ziggurat or Not?, Ph.D. Diss., U. Chicago, Defended June 12, 1968. Hardcopy only—Near East Studies Lib., U. Chicago.

He clucked his tongue, perturbed that an online copy wasn't available.

Next, he typed in "Rebecca Talbot" and pressed enter. "0 Records Found" was the result several seconds later. Dismayed, he leaned back in his chair and thought for a while, hands behind his head, eyes closed. Then, in a burst of energy, he quickly typed in a new search term: "Rebecca Sainsbury."

Five seconds later, a half dozen results popped onto the screen. McCreary arched his eyebrows as he quickly skimmed the list and found one in particular that caught his interest. "What's this?" he said quietly.

Sainsbury, Rebecca A., An Anthropological Study of the Origins of the Nephilim in Sumerian Mythology, Ph. D. Diss, Harvard U., Defended May 12, 1971. *Available online.*

He clicked the hyperlink for the online version, entered his DARPA user name and password, and began printing out Rebecca Sainsbury's 1971 dissertation on the Nephilim.

An hour later, McCreary put down Rebecca Sainsbury's dissertation, immediately picked up the secure phone and punched in ten digits.

"Yeah?" answered Secretary Stonewell in a raspy voice.

"Sorry to bother you at home, sir. It's Bill McCreary."

"Uh-huh."

"I need authorization for a special operation."

"Military or—?"

"Military."

There was a pause. "Hold on. Let me patch in Defense . . ."

CHAPTER TWENTY-NINE

Route 50 West, Maryland.

"SOMETHING exciting going on at work?" asked Bryce Whittaker, trying in vain to start a conversation. He was sitting in the front passenger seat of Kathleen's Subaru, which was traveling westbound on Route 50 toward D.C. Kathleen had been lost in thought ever since leaving Annapolis. It was dark outside, and the highway was relatively empty.

Whittaker's question interrupted Kathleen's private reverie. "What? Oh sorry. Yeah, something really exciting."

"Care to share it?"

Kathleen glanced at Whittaker and reflected on how things had changed between them tonight. The trip to Garrison Manor, it turned out, had been a revealing experience. She'd discovered something unexpected in Whittaker, something she liked very much—a sensitive, compassionate side she hadn't noticed before. She loved how kind he'd been to her grandfather, so understanding of his condition. "Can you keep a secret?" she asked.

"Are you kidding? I keep secrets for a living."

"Oh really?" She shot him a disbelieving look. "And here I thought you were a reporter."

"Ouch, that hurts."

"Bryce, I'm serious. This is big. You can't tell anyone."

"My lips are sealed."

Kathleen sighed heavily and braced herself for what was going to be an awkward conversation. "Have you ever heard of the Epic of Gilgamesh?" she asked finally.

"Gilgamesh? No, can't say that I have."

For the next twenty-five minutes, Kathleen told Whittaker everything that had happened to her in the past week. She began with her meeting with Dr. Sargon. She explained what she'd learned about her parents. She explained about the Tell-Fara temple, where they were killed. She told him about the silver box and its bizarre contents.

"Wow!" Whittaker exclaimed.

"Wait, it gets weirder." Kathleen continued outlining the details of Sargon's apparent suicide, her trip to Boston to meet with Dr. Eskridge, and finally her decision to test the tooth for DNA. The only thing she left out was her meeting with the FBI. *Bryce doesn't need to know that*, she decided.

For the most part, Whittaker remained silent during her long narrative, interjecting only the occasional "uh-huh" or "wow" at appropriate intervals.

Kathleen glanced over occasionally to gauge his expression. This was a lot to lay on him all at once, she realized. But it felt great to get it off her chest. "I know it sounds crazy," she said, "but this could really be huge."

"Do you think it's true?" Whittaker asked. "I mean, the stuff about the Nephilim and the super-long life spans and all?"

"Well, it's not as crazy as you might think. We already know there's a gene in fruit flies that controls their life span. That's the INDY gene I told you about at the lab. So it's not inconceivable that a similar gene exists in humans—or at least did exist at some point."

"Yeah, but what happened to that gene? I mean, nobody's lived more than about a hundred and twenty years in modern history. At least not that I'm aware of."

"You're right. The longest known life span in modern recorded history was a woman in France who lived to be one hundred and twenty-two. She died in 1997. The oldest person currently alive is about a hundred and fourteen."

"Okay, so that's my point," said Whittaker. "I mean, if there was this Nephilim gene floating around somewhere in the human gene pool, wouldn't it have surfaced by now?"

"Not necessarily. I've been thinking about this a lot in the last couple of days, and I have a theory."

"What's that?"

"I'm thinking it could have been a virus."

"*What* could have been a virus?"

"The source of the DNA that gave those Nephilim such long life spans."

"A virus?"

"Sure. There's been a lot of research lately showing that a good percentage of our DNA is actually made up viral DNA that entered the human genome millions of years ago and has simply come along for the ride all these years."

"Really?"

"Uh-huh. For instance, researchers have found precursors to the HIV virus that exist in all of our DNA. Every single one of us. They've been there for millions of years, passed on from generation to generation."

"So how come we don't all get sick?"

"Well, what happens is, over time the viral DNA becomes neutralized. It becomes what some biologists call junk DNA, which means it doesn't do anything at all. It just comes along for the ride, generation after generation, slowly deteriorating into randomness."

"Seems strange that our DNA would be loaded down with junk like that."

"I know. But our DNA is actually chock full of these viral remnants, most of which entered the human genome tens of millions of years ago, literally while we were still monkeys."

"How come I've never heard of this before?"

"I guess it's not something people like to think about. I mean, there's this misconception that our DNA is a perfectly engineered blueprint for human life. Concise and well tailored in every way. In fact, nothing could be further from the truth. Our DNA is patchwork quilt of all sorts of stuff. Parts of it work, of course, but a lot of it's just filler."

"Like spaghetti code."

"Exactly! The system works, but it's not elegant."

"Okay, but how does this relate to these . . . Nephilim you were talking about?"

"Well, like I said, when viral DNA enters the human genome and begins to be passed down from generation to generation, it may start out being pathogenic."

"Meaning?"

"Meaning it causes some perceptible symptoms. AIDS, for instance. Or leukemia."

"Okay . . ."

"But over a period of time, the viral DNA begins to lose its effectiveness. It might take one generation; or it might take many. Scientists aren't quite sure how this happens, but it appears that, somehow, the rest of the genome is able to neutralize the invading species . . . contain it, so it becomes progressively non-pathogenic."

"All right . . ."

"So, I've been thinking . . . what if these Nephilim were infected with a virus that injected the INDY sequence into their DNA? The symptom of that virus would be an abnormally long life span—just like the fruit flies in my lab."

"Uh-huh . . ."

"But over many generations, the pathogenic effect of that virus would fade as the viral DNA became progressively neutralized. The INDY sequence itself would degrade to the point where it was no longer functional. After thousands of years, it wouldn't even be recognizable—just random, junk DNA."

Whittaker thought for a moment. "Like what happened to the Nephilim . . ."

"Yes. Their life spans became progressively shorter over a period of several hundred years until, finally, they became entirely asymptomatic."

"You know," Whittaker said with a crooked smile, "that actually makes some sense to me."

"Yeah . . ." Kathleen's voice trailed off. "Anyway, now you understand why I'm so excited about this DNA sample. We may have found an actual sample of human DNA with an intact INDY gene!"

Whittaker was silent for a long while, obviously lost in thought. "So . . . when will you know? I mean, how long will it take to confirm that you've actually found the INDY gene?"

"We have to sequence the sample and compare it against a modern reference sample. That could take a few days . . . or weeks. It really depends on luck."

"Then you'll know?"

"We should."

"Wow," said Whittaker, rubbing his chin.

After that, they both became lost in their respective thoughts.

Whittaker was the first to break the silence. His tone was academic and deliberative. "You know, there's a real religious angle here. Have you given any thought to that?"

"Frankly, no. Religion's not really my thing."

"Okay, but I'm just thinking out loud here. You mentioned some passage in the Bible that talked about these Nephilim, where God said that man was just flesh and would be confined to live no more than one hundred and twenty years, right?"

"Something like that. I think it was in the Book of Genesis."

"And didn't you say that, even with all our modern medicine, the longest any person's been able to live is one hundred and twenty-two years?"

"Yeah."

"Almost like there's a limit to our life span or something?"

"Okay, I see where you're going, but—"

"Hold on, just think about it for a moment. For the devout . . . they might see this as a violation of, I don't know . . . God's will or something."

Those words hit a sharp chord in Kathleen's mind. Dr. Sargon had used that exact phrase the other night. "God's will." *Why does it keep coming back to that?*

"Do you see what I mean?" Whittaker asked.

"I guess so. But you could use that same argument to challenge just about every scientific advance. For instance, you could say that cancer is God's will. AIDS is God's will. Leukemia. Diabetes. Gallstones. You could chalk up every conceivable human ailment to God's will and oppose any form of treatment. And you know what? There are people who believe exactly that. They'll sit there and refuse medical treatment as their children suffer painful illnesses that are totally treatable. Well, I just don't subscribe to that nonsense. Frankly, I think it's bullshit!"

Kathleen rarely cursed, and she was surprised by her vitriol on this topic. But this was something she believed in strongly. Science could not be handcuffed by outdated superstitions about "God's will" and biblical fairytales. "I can't accept it," she declared firmly.

"All I'm saying is, there's a debate there. And even if you don't agree with it, there are millions of people out there who might see this as an affront to their most closely held beliefs."

"Well," said Kathleen with a shrug, "they're wrong."

Whittaker laughed. "Maybe so. But I'm telling you, you could really be opening Pandora's Box here."

CHAPTER THIRTY

Rockville, Maryland.

JEREMY Fisher was thoroughly exhausted. He'd been awake since early Saturday morning— nearly forty hours ago. His hair was a mess, he had the beginnings of a full beard on his face, and his clothes were badly wrinkled and ripe. Earlier in the day, he'd driven to McDonald's for a Big Mac and fries—his only meal of the day.

In his entire life, Jeremy could not remember being as tired as he was right now. Still, despite Kathleen's admonition to go home, there were a few important things he needed to finish up in the lab before he could leave. Most important, he needed to transfer the purified DNA sample into a half dozen sterilized neoprene sample bottles for retention. After a lucky success like today's, the last thing he wanted to do was leave his DNA sample sitting overnight at room temperature where it could decay, or worse, get contaminated.

He knew that if any bit of stray DNA got into

the sample at this point—even a tiny bead of sweat from his fingers or a microscopic cell of airborne yeast—all would be lost. If any polymerase chain reaction ("PCR") solution remained unquenched in the sample, it could amplify the invading DNA and quickly turn the entire sample into an ambiguous, multi-species DNA soup. In other words, useless. At this stage of the process, more so than at any other, contamination was the enemy. And he wasn't about to be robbed of his breakthrough success.

Jeremy's plan was to divide the bulk sample into six equal aliquots, each sealed in a sterilized sample bottle. He then planned to freeze five of the aliquots with liquid nitrogen for long-term storage. The remaining sample bottle would go in the laboratory's refrigerator for Julie's sequencing work.

He rubbed his bloodshot eyes, which were burning badly. He'd left his contact lenses in far too long, and he desperately needed to take them out. Fumbling through his tattered canvas backpack, he found his "geek glasses" and slipped them into his pants pocket. He exited the lab, being sure to close the airtight door behind him, and lumbered slowly down the hallway toward QLS's small unisex bathroom. He entered the bathroom, flipped on the light, and closed the door with a soft *ka-chunk*.

Groggily, he removed his contacts and splashed cold water on his eyes, which felt great. He washed his unshaven face with soap and water and, for nearly a minute, savored the feeling of having his eyes closed. Finally, reluctantly, he dried his face with a paper towel and put his glasses on.

It took a long time for his bloodshot eyes to adjust to their new corrective lenses. As they came into focus, he stared at himself in the mirror with amazement. He looked like hell. He poked the dark, puffy circles under his eyes and wondered what, exactly, caused them. At some point, he became aware of the monotonous electrical buzz of the overhead fluorescent light . . . *and something else.*

Straining to hear, he detected something metallic and irregular—a rattling noise somewhere just outside the building. It lasted a few seconds—*tat tat tat*—then stopped. A few seconds later, it resumed—*tat tat tat tat*—then stopped again. Jeremy stood motionless, straining to listen. But, as before, the buzz of the bathroom's fluorescent light was the only audible sound.

He exited the bathroom and started back toward the lab, stopping momentarily at the emergency door at the back of the building. "Hello?" he said tentatively.

Silence.

"Hmph." He shook his head. He *really* needed some sleep. Rubbing his eyes beneath his glasses, he continued on.

Halfway down the hallway, he heard the same noise again—a soft, metallic clicking sound. This time, though, it came from the other end of the hallway, near the lab. It was just a brief, isolated noise, but this time, he was *sure* he'd heard it.

He picked up his pace. The hallway was dim

and his vision still slightly blurred from rubbing his eyes. He entered the anteroom to the lab and stopped short.

Something was out of place.

He spotted it immediately. The door to the lab was open—just a faction of an inch, but open nonetheless. He was sure he'd closed it. It was something Dr. S had drilled into his head since Day One at QLS. The airtight door to the lab must always remain shut because slight temperature fluctuations can affect the breeding cycle of *Drosophila*. He was positive he'd closed that door.

Hadn't he?

"Hello? Julie? Dr. S?"

No reply.

He approached the door and reached for the doorknob but quickly withdrew his hand. The light was on inside, just as he'd left it. *But how did the door get open?* A fleeting image of the discolored tooth crossed his mind. Two days ago, he had extracted human dental pulp from it. The process had repulsed him somewhat, but he'd gotten through it. Now, the image of that tooth returned to his mind—strange and grotesque.

His hand hovered just inches from the doorknob. His pulse was racing wildly. "Hello?" After a long period of silence, he laughed to himself nervously. *Don't be ridiculous*, he thought. Obviously, he'd left the door open by mistake. It was late, and he *seriously* needed some sleep.

He cracked the door open farther and poked his head through. "Hello?" he said again. "Julie? Dr. S?" He stepped through the door and scanned the lab quickly with his blurry, bloodshot eyes. Everything looked normal.

He walked farther into the room. Nothing appeared to be out of place—

Bam! The lab door slammed shut behind him and latched with a reverberating clank.

Jeremy spun and immediately found himself staring down the barrel of an enormous black handgun, inches from his face. The man holding the gun was tall and lanky. He wore black jeans, a grimy white T-shirt, and a thin, partially zipped black leather jacket. His face was boney and angular, his eyes dark and ruthless.

"Don't move," said Semion Zafer.

The order was entirely unnecessary. Jeremy was already frozen in place, speechless. *Am I imagining this? Is this really happening?*

"Where's the sample?" Zafer croaked.

"The what?"

Zafer frowned and thrust the barrel of his SP–21 Barak pistol directly into Jeremy's forehead. "Don't fuck with me, asshole! I want that DNA sample you told Dr. Sainsbury about tonight. Where is it?"

The feeling of the cold steel barrel on Jeremy's forehead acted like an eraser, making his mind go entirely blank. He struggled for words but managed only to open and close his mouth like a beached fish.

"Where . . . the *fuck* . . . is it!" Zafer brought his face within inches of Jeremy's, the Barak pressed firmly against Jeremy's skull.

"Th . . . there." Jeremy motioned with his eyes toward the black soapstone bench behind him.

"Get it."

Jeremy backed away from the pistol, unable to take his eyes off the barrel. Slowly, unsteadily, he inched backward toward the bench. When he got within arm's reach of the sample flask, he picked it up with a trembling hand. "This is it," he said.

Zafer lowered the pistol and held out his hand. "Bring it here."

"What do you want with it?" Jeremy asked, immediately regretting the question.

"Hey!" Zafer bellowed. "I didn't say talk. I said bring it here . . . *Now!*"

"Okay, okay." Jeremy handed the flask to Zafer, who snatched it away.

"Now," Zafer said, "get on the floor."

Jeremy's heart was pounding against his ribcage. A single thought was reverberating in his head. *He's going to kill me. Right now! Right this very second! He's going to kill me!*

"On the *floor!*" Zafer shouted.

Slowly, Jeremy complied. His mind was spinning chaotically, every synapse firing at once. He had to think! He was on his knees now.

"Lie down!" Zafer ordered. "On your stomach."

Think! Jeremy commanded his brain. *Think!*

Zafer was stepping toward him now, standing over him.

Think, think, think! was the shrill refrain in Jeremy's head. He was fully prone now with his nose on the cool vinyl-tile floor. He could almost feel the barrel of the gun above his skull. Then he heard a click. *The gun safety?* It had to be. *Come on, think!*

"The sample's not quenched!" Jeremy blurted.

"What?"

"It's not quenched," Jeremy repeated, his nose still pressed to the floor. "There's a polymerase chain reaction going on in the flask. You have to quench it or the sample will be ruined in a matter of minutes."

That was not true, but Jeremy wasn't exactly concerned with scientific accuracy right now. He was trying to avoid a bullet in the back of his head.

"You're lying!" Zafer snarled.

"No, I swear! Look at the workbench. I was just about to add the quench solution. I . . . I just went to the bathroom to take out my contacts before I got started. If you don't quench it, the sample will be ruined. I'm telling the truth!"

There was a long pause as Zafer apparently mulled over this new information. "Okay, get up."

Jeremy stood up, grateful for the reprieve but still shaking uncontrollably. "If you want, I can—"

"Shut up!" Zafer moved close to Jeremy and put his mouth next to his ear. Jeremy could smell alcohol on his breath. "If you try anything stupid," Zafer whispered in a heavy accent, "I'm gonna blow your *fucking head* off. Understand?"

Jeremy nodded clumsily.

"Now. Quench it." Zafer placed the flask on the

benchtop next to the titration setup that Jeremy had referred to.

Jeremy approached the bench cautiously and slowly slid the flask under one of the pipettes. Out of the corner of his eye, he could see Zafer glaring at him, scrutinizing every move he made. Carefully, Jeremy pulled the neoprene stopper from the mouth of the flask. He glanced nervously over his shoulder at Zafer, recalling his whispered promise: *I'm gonna blow your fucking head off* . . .

"It's a five-hundred milliliter sample," Jeremy said nervously over his shoulder, "so I'll have to add two point five milliliters of the quench solution." He nodded toward the sheet of paper on the bench next to the titration setup. "I'm following the protocol on that paper. You can check if you want."

"Just do it," Zafer said.

Jeremy exhaled loudly. "Okay . . ." He reached up to adjust the stopcock and noticed that his hand was shaking badly. *Calm down*, he told himself. *Relax. You can do this.*

"Hurry up!" Zafer bellowed. "I don't have all night!"

Jeremy grasped the frosted-glass handle of the stopcock with this thumb and forefinger and twisted it open. A thin stream of liquid began to dispense from the bottom of the pipette into the flask. The liquid was not quench solution as he'd said. In fact, it was PCR solution. It would have the *opposite* effect of actually accelerating the polymerase chain reaction in the flask. Jeremy watched the calibrated markings on the pipette carefully, keeping track of how much liquid had been dispensed. 0.5 ml . . . 1.0 ml . . . 1.5 ml . . . 1.7 ml . . . 1.9 ml . . . 2.0 ml . . .

He shut the stopcock. "I'll add the rest drop-wise," he said over his shoulder. "Ten drops should take it to exactly 2.5 milliliters."

He eased the stopcock open a tiny bit, causing a single drop of liquid to form at the tip of the pipette. The drop grew larger until it eventually fell into the flask. "One," Jeremy said aloud. *I need a plan*, he thought to himself.

Another drop formed at the bottom of the pipette and fell into the flask. "Two . . ." *He's got a gun. He's blocking the door!* Another drop. "Three . . ." *He's going to kill me!* "Four . . ."

Suddenly, an entirely different thought entered Jeremy's mind. "Five . . ." *Who is this asshole, anyway?* "Six . . ." *Why does he want our DNA sample?* "Seven . . ." *This sample must be it.* "Eight . . ." *The INDY gene!* "Nine . . ." *That's why he wants it!* "Ten."

Well . . . screw him.

Jeremy closed the stopcock and replaced the neoprene stopper on the flask. "I've got to mix it now," he announced, picking up the flask with both hands. He turned to face Zafer and nodded toward the paper on the bench. "The protocol says so."

"Just do it."

Jeremy began gently swirling the flask around in the air at about chest level. The cloudy liquid inside the flask sloshed around in uneven circles.

Zafer watched for several seconds with increasing impatience. "Okay, that's enough!"

"Wait," said Jeremy. "Just a few more seconds." Then, without warning, he tossed the flask high in the air behind him, away from Zafer.

"*No!*" Zafer shouted, diving for the flask.

At the same moment, Jeremy darted past Zafer and lunged toward the door. He opened it quickly and ran out of the lab, pulling the door shut behind him. As he passed through the anteroom and into the hallway, he heard the distinct sound of breaking glass and Zafer cursing loudly back in the lab. He turned left and raced toward the front doors. Seconds later, he heard the laboratory door slam open. The gunman was after him.

Jeremy ran past the QLS conference room, through the small lobby, and straight to the glass double doors at the front entrance of the building. He pushed hard on the doors.

Locked!

"C'mon," Jeremy pleaded as he fumbled with the deadbolt, trying—unsuccessfully—to unlock it. "*C'mon!*" He could hear Zafer coming down the hallway toward him.

"You're a fucking dead man!" Zafer yelled from the hallway.

Finally, the deadbolt slid into its recess and Jeremy shoved open the glass double doors and ran out into the cool night air. It was pitch-black outside, save for a few security lights.

He sprinted down the short walkway leading away from QLS's front entrance until it intersected with the sidewalk running the length of the five-unit building. There, for a split second, he hesitated, trying to decide which way to turn.

That proved to be a terrible mistake.

Instantaneously, the glass doors to QLS shattered with two successive blasts of gunfire from inside the building.

Jeremy's back exploded with a searing, white-hot pain. He'd been shot. He fell face forward onto the cold cement sidewalk. Unable to breathe. Unable to scream. But still alive.

Seconds later, he heard something behind him, near the front door. Shards of glass were falling and breaking. A scraping noise. *The gunman was coming through the front door!* The crunching of broken glass beneath the gunman's shoes. *He's coming toward me!* There was a loud, metallic *ka-chunk* of a round being chambered in the gunman's pistol. *He's coming to finish me off!*

"You messed with the wrong guy today!" Zafer said.

Jeremy was already losing consciousness. But just before everything went black, he heard an unexpected noise.

CHAPTER THIRTY-ONE

First Lieutenant Stacey Choi pulled back on the joystick of her PPO console and studied the display on the console's video screen as it changed perceptibly. She was sitting in the air-conditioned Predator control room of the heavily fortified OP–12 building on Tallil Airbase, a combined U.S. and British command in central Iraq, about 150 miles south of Baghdad. It was 5:30 A.M. and quite dark inside the control space, except for the greenish glow of the six PPO video screens positioned strategically throughout the room.

The end of "major combat operations" in Iraq may have been announced back at home, but one would never know it at Tallil Airbase. Flight ops continued around the clock, just like always.

Seventy miles to the southeast, at an altitude of ten thousand feet, an unmanned MQ–1 Predator aerial reconnaissance vehicle responded obediently to Lieutenant Choi's command. Its airspeed dropped and its altitude began steadily decreasing. The long, spindly wings of the black reconnaissance drone sliced gracefully through the predawn sky, virtually invisible against the canopy of bright stars that stretched across the desert from one horizon to the other.

Back at the airbase, Lieutenant Choi watched unblinkingly as the monochromatic digital image of the sparse desert floor scrolled slowly down her screen like a waterfall. The image was digitally constructed using real-time information gathered by the Predator's downward-looking infrared sensors.

As a member of the 361st Expeditionary Reconnaissance Squadron, Choi was used to missions like this. Maneuver her MQ–1 Predator to spot X, fire up all the sensors and collect data for twenty or thirty minutes, then kill the sensors and guide the unmanned vehicle safely back home for recovery and preparation for its next mission. Sometimes she knew the purpose of the mission; other times she didn't.

Here, all she'd been told was that the mission was classified "Top Secret SCI—SERRATE" and that the real-time video feed was to be sent directly to a secure receiver in Arlington, Virginia, via encrypted Ku band satellite link.

Major "Hutch" Hutchinson, the squadron's operations officer, hovered just over Choi's shoulder, closely monitoring the Predator's video display with equal interest. Hutchinson was already on his third cup of coffee for the night. As ops officer, he rarely took the "mid-watch"—the stretch between midnight and 6:00 A.M. That unpopular duty was instead relegated mostly to junior officers. But, then again, the squadron didn't often get SCI missions assigned directly from Washington. Although he had no idea what "SERRATE" was all about, he knew it must be pretty damned important. To make sure everything went smoothly, he personally took the mid-watch and assigned the squadron's best PPO operator to the MQ–1 console. "How we doing?" he asked Lieutenant Choi.

"Fine, sir. I've got her heading two-two-zero true, one hundred knots, altitude coming down from one zero thousand feet. It should be on target in approximately twelve minutes."

Hutchinson compared the digital readout of the Predator's latitude and longitude to the coordinates he'd received via Top Secret SCI message earlier that evening. 32.0593 N, 45.2966 E. It was almost on target. "Nice job," he said, patting Choi lightly on the shoulder.

Several minutes later, Choi quietly announced, "Two minutes to target, sir."

"Okay, start the uplink."

Bill McCreary sat alone at the Criticom console in the small clean room of the Logistics Analysis office, carefully inspecting the greenish imagery now cascading down the video screen in front of him. He was uncomfortable with "military-speak," but he knew enough to understand that he was "zulu six delta" according to today's daily key codes. "Uh . . . foxtrot seven bravo, this is zulu six delta," he said tentatively into the bright red handset, "I'm receiving the video feed now."

McCreary stared at the monochromatic imagery for more than a minute, trying to figure out exactly what he was looking at. He was almost too embarrassed to admit that he couldn't make heads or tails of it. "Is that the ground I'm seeing?" he asked finally, forgetting entirely to use proper radio protocol.

"Zulu six delta, that's affirmative. You're looking at a live infrared video of the coordinates you requested. We can stay on station for approximately seventeen more minutes. Over."

"Can you widen the angle?" McCreary asked, again ignoring radio protocol.

"Affirmative. Stand by, over."

Thirty seconds later, the image on McCreary's video screen began to change noticeably, beginning at the top and cascading down the screen like a waterfall. As the screen became nearly filled with the new imagery, McCreary could now see recognizable features on the desert floor. He saw the distinct appearance of a road running down the left-hand side of the screen, with a small ridge or hill running alongside of it on the right. He quickly consulted his map and compared the coordinates on the screen to those he'd previously jotted down. "Can you widen the angle just a little more and look more to the right of that road?" he said into the handset.

"Zulu six delta, this is foxtrot seven bravo. Stand by. Over."

After a short delay, the imagery on the screen

once again began to change, cascading slowly from top to bottom. As it filled the screen, McCreary continued checking frenetically between the displayed coordinates on the screen and the coordinates scrawled on his map next to the site of the Tell-Fara temple.

Almost there . . . almost . . .

"There!" McCreary shouted into the red handset. "Stay on that spot. Can you get any closer and get some better resolution?" He waited impatiently as the screen became a swirl of unrecognizable spaghetti. The Predator was now changing course and altitude, circling around for another pass.

Several minutes later, the voice of Major Hutchinson came back over the secure telephone. "Zulu six delta, this is foxtrot seven bravo. We're at two thousand feet. You should get better resolution on this pass. Over."

McCreary watched with great anticipation as aerial footage of the Tell-Fara temple site began cascading down his screen. Major Hutchinson was right; the resolution was much better this time. Individual rocks and vegetation were now clearly visible. Ninety seconds later, the Tell-Fara archeological site filled the entire screen in superb detail.

But McCreary was confused. "Freeze the picture!" he barked into the handset. The picture froze. He studied it carefully, baffled. *Where was the temple? And what was that big, dark circle in the middle?* "Can you tell me what we're looking at?" he said into the handset.

There was a long pause. Finally, Major Hutchinson's voice came back on the line. "Zulu six delta, this is foxtrot seven bravo. It looks to us like a bomb crater . . . a pretty big one."

McCreary put his hands behind his head and exhaled as he finally recognized what he was seeing on the screen. The entire temple site now consisted of one, gigantic crater. Rocks and debris were scattered in every direction.

Tell-Fara was gone.

CHAPTER THIRTY-TWO

Rockville, Maryland.

KATHLEEN leaned on the horn of her Subaru for several seconds. As she did, she accelerated across the Gateway parking lot toward QLS's front entrance, skidding to a halt just shy of the curb.

It was just before midnight. She had dropped Whittaker off at his apartment in DuPont Circle half an hour earlier and had been heading home when she decided, on a whim, to drop by the office to check on things. Mainly, she wanted to make sure Jeremy had actually gone home, like she'd told him to.

As her car's headlights washed over the front entrance of the building, however, her heart nearly stopped. The glass doors had been smashed, and a man in a black leather jacket was walking out at that very moment. *A burglar!*

Several months before, one of the other units in the Gateway Office Park had been burglarized, and the police had never found the culprit.

Screeching to a halt in front of the curb, Kathleen didn't notice the body of Jeremy Fisher lying facedown on the sidewalk, just inches from her car. Nor did she notice the loaded Barak pistol in the right hand of the man exiting the building.

Simeon Zafer stopped in his tracks, evidently caught by surprise. Kathleen flipped on her high beams, shining them directly in Zafer's face. He shielded his eyes for a second, then quickly bolted to his right. Seconds later, he disappeared around the corner into a wooded area behind the building.

For a moment, Kathleen considered chasing him but immediately thought better of it. *He might have a gun.* Instead, she pulled her phone from her purse and quickly dialed 911. "There's been a burglary," she said. "Please hurry!"

She waited in her car for several minutes, scanning the dark wooded area where the man had disappeared. Finally, she decided it was safe to get out. Stepping from her car, she nearly tripped over the body of Jeremy Fisher lying facedown on the sidewalk in a pool of blood.

"Oh my God!" she screamed, gazing in horror at Jeremy's limp, bloody body. "Jeremy!" She knelt down beside him and touched his shirt, which was soaked with blood. In the bright glow of her car's headlights, she could tell he was badly wounded. A crimson pool was still spreading out along the sidewalk. "Jeremy, can you hear me?" she said frantically.

Jeremy let out a weak, barely perceptible groan and moved his legs slightly.

"Jeremy," she said, relieved that he was alive. "What happened?"

This time, there was no response.

She was afraid to move him because of the injury to his back. Her heart was beating furiously, her breathing shallow and constricted. *Who could have done this? What kind of sick bastard would do this?* She was bewildered and terrified all at once.

Frantically, she flipped open her phone and dialed 911 again. "I need an ambulance!" she screamed. "Hurry!" She gave the address and hung up.

Ten minutes later, the parking lot in front of QLS looked like a scene from a TV police drama. Three Montgomery County squad cars and an ambulance were parked at skewed angles, lights flashing. Three policemen with flashlights were combing the area, looking for signs of the shooter in the woods behind the building. Two other uniformed officers were inspecting the smashed double doors at the entrance to QLS.

Kathleen stayed by Jeremy's side as two EMTs carefully lifted him onto a stretcher— still lying on his stomach—and transferred him into the ambulance. One of the EMTs was a young pimply-faced kid with red hair who looked no older than nineteen. The other was a chunky man in his late forties with gray whiskers and tattoos on both arms.

"I'm coming with him," Kathleen announced as the EMTs were about to close the ambulance doors. Before they could respond, she climbed in. The two EMTs looked at each other and shrugged.

Seconds later, the ambulance pulled away from the crime scene, sirens blaring, with Kathleen, Jeremy, and the two EMTs in the back.

The EMTs went to work quickly on Jeremy's wounds. He'd been shot twice, once in the back of the ribs, a few inches from his spine, and once in the small of his back, just above his right buttocks.

"Get the IV bag set up," said the older EMT to the younger one. "A thousand cc's of saline." Seconds later, a bag of saline solution was draining into Jeremy's arm. The two EMTs busied themselves cutting away Jeremy's bloody shirt and dressing the wounds with white compresses as the ambulance raced through the empty streets of Rockville.

Kathleen watched anxiously as the EMTs struggled to keep Jeremy alive. "He's lost a lot of blood," she heard the older EMT say under his breath. The man's tone was distressingly pessimistic.

Jeremy was lying facedown on the stretcher, his head turned awkwardly toward Kathleen. His eyes were open but glassy and dilated—almost lifeless. Kathleen wondered whether he was even conscious.

"Jeremy?" she said softly, leaning toward his face, which was partially obscured by an oxygen mask that lay loosely by his nose and mouth.

"Ma'am, please," said the tattooed EMT gruffly, stepping in front of her.

A few seconds passed in silence as the EMTs continued applying compresses to Jeremy's wounds.

Then Jeremy made a gurgling sound.

"What?" Kathleen said excitedly. "What is it?" She put her ear close to his mouth.

"Sam . . ." Jeremy whispered slowly, laboring hard to speak, "pull . . ."

"Sam . . . pull? Sample? The DNA sample?"

"Uh . . . huh . . ."

"What about it?"

The tattooed EMT pushed Kathleen away. "Ma'am, *please*. We need some room here."

A few seconds later, Jeremy spoke again in a whisper. His voice was weak and raspy. "Bro . . . kkkk . . . ."

"Broke? Broken? The sample is broken?" Kathleen was doing her best to decipher Jeremy's garbled utterances. "It broke?"

"Uh . . . huh." Jeremy's voice was barely audible now. His eyelids were beginning to close.

"Blood pressure's below ninety palpable," shouted the redheaded kid excitedly. "Heart rate one twenty."

"Shit," panted the older EMT. "We're losing him!"

"Jeremy!" Kathleen screamed. "Stay with us! We're almost there!"

Jeremy's eyes widened a bit as he tried once again to speak.

"Don't talk," Kathleen said. "Just hold on!"

But Jeremy continued, forcing a series of gurgled, whispered syllables out of his mouth. "I . . . dint . . ." He paused, wheezing. "Clee . . . n . . ."

Kathleen cupped her mouth and shook her head in disbelief. Jeremy was dying in the back of an ambulance, and he was worried about *cleanup*? "Jeremy," she said reassuringly, "it's okay. Don't worry about it. Just stay with us! We're almost there!"

But Jeremy had lost consciousness.

"Cardiac arrest!" bellowed the tattooed EMT.

"We're here!" announced the redheaded kid simultaneously, as the ambulance came to an abrupt halt.

"Please stay clear, ma'am," said the older EMT. "We need to get him out of here."

Kathleen pressed herself against the side of the van. There was a flurry of activity as the ambulance doors flew open and a team of people in light blue scrubs slid the stretcher out of the ambulance and attached it to a wheeled gurney. An exhausted resident took one look at Jeremy and shouted, "Multiple gunshot wounds to the back! Code! E.R. three, *stat!*"

Kathleen watched helplessly as Jeremy's bloody, shirtless body was wheeled down a short hallway and through a set of double swinging doors. Seconds later, he was completely out of sight. Her mind went numb. *This can't be happening.*

"Ma'am?" said a deep voice from outside the ambulance.

Kathleen looked down and saw a uniformed police officer approaching.

"We didn't realize you were leaving the scene," he said. "I'm going to have to ask you to come back with me."

Kathleen nodded compliantly and exited the ambulance. She followed the police officer to his squad car.

Fifteen minutes later, they were back in the parking lot in front of QLS. She got out of the police cruiser and gazed in disbelief at the smashed glass doors, the flashing police lights, and the general chaos swirling all around her. *What the hell was happening?* Six hours earlier, she'd been enjoying a beer with Bryce Whittaker in Annapolis. Now she was standing in the middle of a bloody crime scene. She had no idea whether Jeremy was alive or dead.

Suddenly, she heard a familiar voice behind her.

"Dr. Sainsbury?"

Kathleen turned to see Special Agent Wills standing nearby. He was well dressed, like before. Khaki pants, light pink shirt, fashionable tie, navy blue blazer, overcoat. Everything pressed, buttoned, and polished.

"I'm working with MCPD on this one," Wills said.

Kathleen had no idea what that meant and didn't care. "I'm going inside," she announced, turning her back on Wills and starting toward the building.

"Hold on a sec," Wills said, grabbing her arm, "We're still—"

"I don't care," Kathleen snapped, pulling her arm from his grasp. "This is my company. That was my colleague. And I'm going in there. If you want to stop me, arrest me."

Kathleen marched up the walkway to the front door with Wills trailing close behind. "Dr. Sainsbury!" he called after her.

Kathleen ignored him.

A policeman was standing in front of the smashed door. Kathleen locked eyes with him. "Excuse me," she said resolutely.

The policeman hesitated, glanced behind her at Special Agent Wills, and then slowly pushed open the broken door. Bits of broken glass beneath the door made a shrill, grinding noise as the door swung open, like nails on a chalkboard. The cop stepped aside to let Kathleen and Agent Wills through.

Kathleen proceeded directly to the lab, where two evidence technicians were busy taking pictures and picking up small objects from the floor and placing them in bags. The distinctive odor of ethyl alcohol was heavy in the air. She stood in the doorway and watched in disbelief.

"Hey," said one of the technicians, "is this your lab?"

Kathleen nodded.

"Anything hazardous in here we should know about?"

Kathleen shook her head slowly, her mind still in a fog. "Some hydrochloric acid in those flasks over there," she muttered. "Phenol, sulfuric acid, ethyl acetate, chloroform, butyl alcohol . . . that's about it."

"How about this liquid on the floor," said the technician. "Any idea what this is?"

Kathleen looked despairingly at the floor,

where the remnants of a glass flask were scattered in a circle of shards near the grated floor drain. "Yeah," she said despondently. "I do." She stared in anguish at the mess on the floor. *Totally gone! Possibly the most important discovery of the century.* She felt like screaming and crying and punching the air all at the same time. Instead, she stood motionless, dumbfounded, shaking her head from side to side.

"And . . ." said the technician impatiently, "what is it?"

"It *was* a DNA sample," she said with a heavy sigh. "Probably in ethyl alcohol and chloroform. Just wear rubber gloves and try not to inhale the fumes, and you'll be fine."

"Thanks." The evidence technician bent down and plucked several of the larger pieces of glass from the grated drain and dropped them into an evidence bag.

"They're going to run those for fingerprints," said Agent Wills behind her, almost in a baiting tone. "Any idea whose they'll find?"

Anger flashed on Kathleen's face. "What, exactly, are you implying?"

"I'm not implying anything. It's just a question."

Kathleen took a deep breath and exhaled, a bit ashamed of her outburst.

"Look, Dr. Sainsbury," continued Wills soothingly, "I'm not here to harass you. I want to solve this crime as much as you do, okay?"

Kathleen nodded. "Sorry."

"Now, is it possible that whoever broke in here

was after what was in that flask?" He pointed to the shards on the floor.

Kathleen nodded that, yes, that was possible.

"You want to tell me what was in there?"

Kathleen stared at the remnants of the flask and rubbed her temples. Then she said quietly: "Mummy DNA."

CHAPTER THIRTY-THREE

Arlington, Virginia.

BILL McCreary entered the Logistics Analysis office at DARPA and said good morning to his assistant. "Anything going on?"

Steve Goodwin held up a single sheet of paper. "Yeah, this."

McCreary took the classified memo and read it quickly:

<u>**TOP SECRET SCI—SERRATE**</u>
Re: EVENT SUMMARY, MARCH 22–23
2353 EST—911 call received by Montgomery County central dispatch. Suspected burglary reported at 201E Gateway Drive, Rockville, MD [QLS]
0002 EST—911 call received by Montgomery County central dispatch. Gunshot victim reported at 201E Gateway Drive, Rockville, MD [QLS]
0005 EST—Dispatcher broadcast to Montgomery County Police and Fire & Rescue.
0016 EST—Montgomery County Police and Fire & Rescue on scene at 201E Gateway Drive, Rockville, MD.

0033 EST—Dr. Jeremy Fisher [QLS] admitted to Montgomery County Hospital, multiple gunshot wounds. Current status unknown.

ADDITIONAL INFORMATION: Suspect reportedly fled on foot into adjacent woods, remains at large. Dr. Kathleen Sainsbury [QLS] questioned at scene and released.

McCreary frowned and folded the paper in half. "You should've called me immediately."

"Sorry, boss. I just got this information twenty minutes ago."

"Then you should've called me *twenty minutes* ago!" He brushed past Goodwin and made his way toward his office. He was already thinking about how to break this news to Secretary Stonewell.

"Uh, boss. There's something else."

McCreary sighed and turned. "What is it?"

"I've been listening to the audio of the police radio runs . . ."

"Yeah?"

"And . . . well, I could've sworn I heard one of the cops say something about 'mummy DNA.'"

"Dear God," McCreary muttered.

"Just thought you should know."

CHAPTER THIRTY-FOUR

Rockville, Maryland.

"I JUST got off the phone with the hospital," Kathleen said as she entered the QLS conference room. Julie and Carlos were already seated at the conference table. It was a little after 10:00 A.M. on Tuesday morning, and they were assembled for their first formal meeting since the shooting Sunday night. "Jeremy's in critical but stable condition."

"What does that mean?" asked Julie.

"They've stopped the bleeding, but he has some very severe nerve damage. They're not sure what effect that may have on his—" Kathleen drew a deep breath. "On his ability to walk."

Julie gasped.

"He also has a significant amount of swelling in his brain, which is a very dangerous situation. They've put him in a medically induced coma to try to reduce the swelling."

Carlos shook his head.

Kathleen continued. "His family is with him now. So all we can do is wait."

"And pray," Julie added.

"Sure. That, too."

The last forty-eight hours had been a chaotic whirlwind at QLS. Julie had arrived at work Monday morning to find the front door smashed, yellow police tape across the entrance, and a hideous bloodstain on the sidewalk. Carlos had tried to call her in advance to warn her not to come in, but her cell phone had been turned off. As expected, she took it hard. "I should've been here!" she kept repeating over and over. It took Carlos and Kathleen the better part of the day just to calm her down.

The Montgomery County police didn't finish their crime-scene investigation until late Monday afternoon, after which Carlos immediately boarded up the broken doors and arranged for replacements to be delivered.

Kathleen had spent nearly all day shuttling back and forth to the hospital, talking to Jeremy's family, dealing with the police, and fielding calls from worried investors. One particularly nasty investor—a broker from the Aurora Venture Capital Fund in New York City—even mentioned the word "lawsuit," just to make matters worse.

Now it was Tuesday, and, whether they liked it or not, QLS had to get back to business.

"Julie, are you sure you're okay to work today?" Kathleen asked with genuine concern. "You can take a few days off if you want. Maybe go back to be with your parents."

"I'm fine," Julie said. "I want to finish what Jeremy started. I owe him that."

Kathleen nodded and smiled compassionately. "All right. Okay." She glanced at Carlos. "Carlos is going to be with you here at all times. Right, Carlos?"

"Absolutely. In fact, from now on, I don't want anyone here alone. We'll use the buddy system just like we did in the Marines."

"Julie," said Kathleen. "Any luck recovering an uncontaminated DNA sample from that spill on the floor? I realize it's a long shot."

"I wiped up what I could from the drain grate with Chem-wipes, washed them with chloroform into a 500 milliliter beaker, and looked for DNA." She shrugged. "It was a mess."

"I figured," Kathleen said glumly. "But it was worth a try."

For a fleeting moment, Kathleen's thoughts flashed back to what Jeremy had said in the ambulance. He could barely speak and was in unbelievable pain, yet, for some reason, he'd made a point of telling her that he hadn't cleaned up. It was such a strange thing for him to say, given the circumstances. She dismissed the thought. *She needed to focus!* The annual shareholders' meeting was less than a week away, and the events of the past two days were likely to shake many of the investors. If they didn't have some positive news to report by next week, QLS was almost certainly doomed.

"I'll keep trying," Julie said. "I'll add some PCR solution and put it in the thermocycler. Who knows, maybe we'll get something."

Something clicked in Kathleen's mind. "Wait a second," she exclaimed, straightening in her chair. "The thermocycler!" She was referring to the piece of equipment used to cycle PCR samples through the rapid temperature fluctuations needed to achieve PCR amplification of a DNA sample.

"What about it?" said Julie, obviously confused.

Kathleen stood and began pacing quickly beside the table. "Jeremy said something strange to me in the ambulance. He said he hadn't *cleaned up*."

"Well, of course not," Julie said, scrunching her eyebrows together. "I mean, he got shot!"

"Right. It didn't make any sense to me either. It was such a trivial thing for him to say given the situation. Unless—" She froze in mid-sentence.

Julie's eyes widened too, recognition passing over her face. "He didn't clean the *thermocycler!*"

"Uh, you guys want to fill me in here?" said Carlos, looking back and forth between the two women.

"Julie!" said Kathleen. "Refill the comb wells with PCR solution and run it through thirty cycles. No, wait . . . make it sixty. I've got to go downtown this morning, but don't wait for me. Get started right away."

Julie was already getting up from her chair. "I'm on it."

CHAPTER THIRTY-FIVE

Rockville, Maryland.

"**You'll** need to leave that cell phone at the security window over there," said the guard at the X-ray machine.

Kathleen nodded and collected her personal items from the X-ray belt at the front entrance to the Montgomery County Municipal Center. Her mission this morning was to look at suspect photographs, as requested by the police detective investigating Jeremy's shooting.

"Stupid rule," she muttered, making her way to the security window adjacent the elevators. Behind a thick pane of bulletproof glass, a skinny young man in a security uniform was reading a hardcover book, his head resting heavily on his hand. Kathleen surrendered her cell phone to him and received, in exchange, a yellow plastic tag with the number 33 on it.

"Dr. Sainsbury?"

Kathleen turned to see a tall, clean-cut man by the elevators. She recognized him as one of the Montgomery County police detectives she'd talked to the night of the shooting. He had thin blond hair and a long, pale face. He shook her hand and re-introduced himself as Detective Philip Andersen of the Montgomery County Police Department.

Kathleen and Detective Andersen took the elevator to the second floor, where they exited and proceeded to Room 202. It was a small, un-adorned room containing four chairs lined up on one side of a rectangular table. A computer and a nineteen-inch flat-screen monitor sat atop the table, facing the chairs.

One chair was already occupied.

"Good morning, Dr. Sainsbury," said Special Agent Wills politely, standing up to face Kathleen as she entered the room. He was impeccably dressed, as always.

"I thought you were with the FBI," Kathleen said.

"I am. As I said the other night, we're working this case together with the Montgomery County police." He gestured toward Detective Andersen. "On account of it being related to the incident on U Street last week."

"Related? How?"

"Through *you*," said Wills matter-of-factly.

Kathleen was sorry she'd asked.

Detective Andersen directed Kathleen to one of the chairs at the center of the table, and he and Wills sat down on either side of her. "Dr. Sains-bury," Detective Andersen began, "I'm going to be showing you pictures of possible suspects we have on file. We've narrowed these down based on your description of the shooter and the type of weapon that was used. Stop me if any of them look like the man you saw the other night, okay?"

Kathleen nodded that she would.

Using the mouse and keyboard, Andersen navigated through a series of windows on the computer screen, entering passwords and bits of information until, finally, a digital photograph appeared on the screen of a scowling man with angry eyes and wild hair.

"Look familiar?"

Kathleen shook her head. "No."

"How about this one?"

"No."

This process dragged on for more than an hour, with face after face of rough-looking men flashing onto the screen, none of whom Kathleen recognized in the least. *When will this end?* she wondered. She had a mountain of work to do—

"Wait!" she exclaimed suddenly.

"This guy?" Andersen inquired.

"No, not him . . . back up . . . *there!* That's the guy I saw."

"Are you sure?" asked Special Agent Wills.

Kathleen studied the picture carefully. It showed a man with a bony, angular face, dark, deep-set eyes, and a menacing frown. "I'm positive. He stared right at me for more than a second. That's definitely the guy I saw."

Andersen picked up the phone and dialed four digits. "Cooper, bring me the file on Ida 140943."

A minute later, a young police corporal

knocked and entered the small room carrying a thin manila folder. Andersen flipped through the file while Wills stood behind him, looking over his shoulder.

"It's from Interpol," Andersen said quietly to Wills.

"Mm-hmmm."

Kathleen watched anxiously.

"Are you *sure* he's the guy you saw?" Andersen asked after a while.

"Yes, I'm sure. Why, who is it?"

"His name's Semion Zafer."

Wills piped in. "Looks like you've gotten yourself mixed up with a pretty nasty character."

"I've never heard of him in my life," Kathleen protested. "How could I be *mixed up* with him?"

"I don't know," said Wills, crossing his arms. "Who do you know in the Israeli Mafia?"

"The Israeli *what?*"

Wills leaned closer to Kathleen. "Care to tell us more about the DNA sample that was in that broken flask?"

Kathleen flinched.

"Where'd you get it?"

Kathleen's heart was racing. If she told the truth, they'd know she lied earlier to Agent Wills. And that would make her look guilty. She felt her throat tightening.

"Dr. Sainsbury?" Wills prodded.

Kathleen panicked. "I don't know."

"You don't know what?"

"I don't know where it came from. I mean, Jeremy Fisher was working on it after hours . . .

some sort of project he was interested in. I . . . I'm not sure where he got it." Kathleen's heart was beating furiously. She'd just lied *again* to the FBI. And this time, it was *a big, fat, whopping lie.* She was going to regret this. She was absolutely sure she was going to regret this for the rest of her life. It was only a question of when.

An uncomfortable silence descended upon the room. Finally, Detective Andersen stood up and announced, "All right then, I guess we're done."

Kathleen presented tag 33 to the young man at the security window and asked for her cell phone back.

"Wow," said the security guard as he handed the phone to her, "your phone feels hot."

"Yeah, it gets that way sometimes." Kathleen thought nothing of it.

The young security guard looked intrigued, though. He adjusted his wire-frame glasses and straightened in his chair. "Let me ask you something. Does the battery drain down a lot, even when you're not using it?"

"Yeah, I guess so. But it's an old phone. I think the battery's going bad."

"Maybe," said the guard. He held up the hardcover book he was reading, which was titled *Technology, Crime, and Law Enforcement*. "I'm studying criminal justice at Montgomery College at night. I just got through reading all about cell-phone bugs and different ways your phone can be hijacked and turned into a listening device. You'd be amazed how easy it is to do. One telltale sign is a phone that stays hot even after you turn it off."

Kathleen eyed her phone suspiciously. *Could it really be bugged?*

"You should take out your battery when you're not using that phone," said the guard. "Or, better yet, get a new phone and don't let it out of your control."

"Thanks," Kathleen said.

As she exited the building, Kathleen touched the phone to her cheek. It *did* feel hot. *But could it actually be bugged? Who would do that?* She turned the phone on and noted that the battery was, indeed, nearly depleted, even though she'd charged it just last night. Navigating the call list, she was surprised to see four incoming calls in the past hour, one from Julie and three from Carlos.

She pushed redial for Carlos's number.

Carlos answered on the first ring. "Dr. Sainsbury," he exclaimed, obviously recognizing her incoming number. "I've been trying to reach you all morn—"

"Carlos! Don't say anything else."

"Why?"

"I'll explain later."

"All right. But you should get down here right away."

"I'll be there in twenty minutes."

Special agent Wills sat hunched over the interview table in Room 202 of the Montgomery County Municipal Center, his chin resting on a clenched fist. He was reviewing the Interpol rap sheet on Semion Zafer for the umpteenth time.

Detective Andersen entered the room. "You still here, Tony?"

"Yeah, still trying to figure out what to make of this guy." Wills thumped the thin file on Semion Zafer. The first page contained a photocopy of a booking photo from the Tel Aviv police department, which showed a frowning Zafer—a few years younger than he was now, but with the same dark eyes and skeletal facial features. "What do you think?"

Andersen leaned over and skimmed the file. "Small-time operator. Street punk."

"Yeah, that's what I thought, too. He got busted in Tel Aviv when he was nineteen for roughing up a jeweler. They pegged him as being part of the Israeli Mafia, but it sounds like a shakedown racket to me, kid stuff."

"Mm-hmmm."

"Certainly not *international* caliber . . ."

Andersen shrugged.

"I mean, what's an Israeli street thug like Semion Zafer doing breaking into a high-tech biology lab in the United States and shooting a scientist in the back?"

"Looking for drugs? Could be an addict."

Wills was unconvinced. "Seems like an odd place to look for drugs."

"Loan sharking? Could be that QLS was funding its operations with easy money, and Zafer came looking for his first installment."

Wills shook his head doubtfully. "Doesn't

sound right to me. QLS had millions of dollars in venture capital."

"Well, *I'm* out of ideas," said Andersen, shrugging his shoulders.

Wills was still rubbing his chin, deep in thought. "Did you hear what Dr. Sainsbury said the other night about *mummy* DNA?"

"Yeah, that was weird."

"Then today, she tried to back away from it. Said it was something her colleague Jeremy Fisher was working on." Wills leaned back in his chair, his fingers laced tightly behind his head. "There's something I'm missing here . . ." His voice trailed off as he turned his attention back to Zafer's Interpol file.

"Well," said Andersen, starting back to his office, "I'm sure you FBI boys will figure it out."

CHAPTER THIRTY-SIX

"Wʜᴀᴛ's going on?" Kathleen asked as she stepped through the boarded-up front doors of QLS's headquarters.

Carlos and Julie were standing in the lobby, and both began speaking at once.

"One at a time," Kathleen admonished.

Julie started over in an excited, high-pitched voice. "Dr. S., you were right! The thermocycler still had uncontaminated residue from Jeremy's sample. I was able to increase the concentration by running it through, like, three *hundred* cycles. It took all morning, but I consolidated the samples and quenched it and . . ." She stopped to take a deep breath and broke into a broad smile. "Dr. S, we got it!"

"An intact DNA sample?"

Julie nodded.

"My God," Kathleen said, "that's *great*!" She gave Julie a tight hug. "I knew you could do it."

"I've already started sequencing it," Julie continued, "and so far it looks really good. I mean, really clean."

Kathleen was still beaming over the good news when she turned to Carlos. "And what news do you have?"

Carlos looked down. "Nothing good, I'm afraid."

The smile faded quickly from Kathleen's lips. "What's wrong? Is it Jeremy?"

"No. I haven't heard anything about Jeremy. I got a call from an attorney at Tillman, Feldstein and Roth. They represent Crescent Venture Group and Aurora Capital, two of our investors."

"Yeah?"

"Seems they've given us five days' notice for a cash call."

"A *what*?"

"They're pulling their investments out. We've got five days to buy back all their shares at half par value or they can force us to roll up the company and sell off all the assets."

"How much do we owe them?"

"At this point, about eight hundred thousand. And that's just for their cash calls."

"Carlos, that's impossible!" Kathleen's face was flush. "We don't have that kind of money sitting around."

"I know."

"How can they do that?"

"It's in the contract. You know, we've missed two milestones . . . it's all completely legit."

"We have the shareholders' meeting coming

up. I thought everyone was going to hold tight 'til then."

"I did too. But it looks like Crescent and Aurora got cold feet and decided to head us off at the pass."

"Why *now?*"

Kathleen's question was still hovering in the air when there was a loud knock on the plywood panels covering the front doors. Carlos opened the doors to reveal Bryce Whittaker standing just outside.

"Bryce," said Kathleen with unchecked surprise. "What're you doing here?"

Whittaker stepped into the lobby and gave Carlos and Julie a perfunctory nod. Then, moving closer to Kathleen, he spoke in a low voice. "I tried to call you a couple times, but you didn't answer your cell phone."

"Yeah, I turned it off. I thought it might be . . . well, never mind. What's up?"

"I heard what happened and just came by to make sure you're okay." Whittaker's tone was earnest. "*Are* you okay?"

"I'm fine, Bryce. But, actually, I've got a lot going on right now." Kathleen tilted her head toward Carlos and Julie. "Can I give you a call later?"

"Sure . . . of course." There was an awkward pause as Whittaker searched for a graceful exit. "Okay, so . . . just give me a call when you get a chance."

"I will," said Kathleen with a nod. "And, Bryce,

thanks for coming by. Really. I'll call you later, okay?"

Whittaker made his way to the door but stopped short. "By the way." He turned to face Kathleen. "Were you ever able to recover anything from that DNA sample? You know, the one we talked about the other night."

Carlos and Julie shot inquisitorial glances at Kathleen, as if to say, you *told* him about that?

Kathleen avoided their looks. "We're working on it," she said.

"That's good," said Whittaker. "I mean, it would be a real shame to lose something that important."

"Yeah, it sure would. I'll call you later tonight, okay?"

"Sure. Talk to you then." Whittaker nodded politely to Julie and Carlos. "It was nice seeing everyone." Then he turned and exited.

Carlos shut the door behind Whittaker and was just about to say something when Kathleen cut him off.

"Julie," she said urgently, "we don't have much time. How quickly can you finish sequencing that sample?"

"I guess I can work on it tonight. Maybe have it finished by tomorrow afternoon."

"Okay, I'll help you. Carlos, can you stay here tonight too?"

"Sure, of course."

"Okay, guys . . . this is it." Kathleen was doing her best to channel Knute Rockne. "It's do-or-die time. We need to have something big to announce by the end of this week, or I'm afraid we're all going to be looking for new jobs. Julie, I hate to put all this pressure on you, but we need that sample sequenced ASAP. We need to find that INDY gene."

Julie looked perplexed. "I'll try Dr. S, but . . . what *exactly* am I supposed to be looking for?"

Good question. "Start with the INDY sequence from *D.* Melanogaster and look for something similar in the sample. If you find a close match, bounce it off the NCBI library and see if it matches any known human sequences. Remember, we're looking something that's *not* supposed to be there. Something that sticks out like a sore thumb. Possibly viral in nature. That's all I can tell you for now. Just use your instincts."

Julie looked unconvinced.

"Julie, the INDY gene is in there. *Trust me.* We just need to find it."

When Kathleen returned to her office, the phone was already ringing. She raced to pick it up, thinking it might be news about Jeremy. "Hello?" she said.

"Hi Dr. Sainsbury, it's Charles Eskridge. I hope I'm not catching you at a bad time."

"No, it's fine," she lied.

"Listen, I'm in D.C. today, and I was wondering if I could stop by your office for a few minutes."

"Uh, sure. What brings you to town?"

"Actually, I came to help settle Dr. Sargon's estate. Seems he named me as the executor of his will."

"Really?"

"Yep. His attorney called the day after you left Boston. To be honest, it didn't surprise me. Poor guy had no family. He left everything to Harvard University, which I guess makes sense. Given the circumstances."

"Yeah, I guess so," said Kathleen.

"Anyway, my flight doesn't leave for a few hours, and I was hoping I could drop by to give you some things. Would you mind?"

Kathleen told him that would be fine and gave him the address.

Dr. Eskridge arrived at QLS by cab an hour later, looking uncomfortable in a dark blue suit and black wingtip shoes. He carried a leather portfolio under one arm. Kathleen met him at the door and invited him in.

"Sorry I'm overdressed," said Eskridge, looking genuinely embarrassed. "I was meeting with lawyers downtown." He rolled his eyes. "You know how *they* are."

They made their way to the QLS conference room and took seats at the table. For a few minutes, they exchanged small talk, chatting about his trip to D.C., the weather, and Quantum Life Sciences. He asked about the boarded-up front doors, and Kathleen explained about the shooting several nights before. Eskridge was visibly shocked to hear the news and had many questions about what had happened and who might have done it.

Kathleen cut him off. "I'd rather not talk about it," she said.

Eskridge quickly changed the subject. He opened his portfolio and retrieved a two-inch stack of postcards, letters and photographs bound with a rubber band. "I found these while rummaging through my office last week after you left. I thought you might want to have them."

Kathleen took the stack, removed the band, and inspected the top item. It was a picture postcard showing a wide river running through an unimpressive cityscape of dilapidated, 1960s-era buildings. The riverbanks were steep and dirty and devoid of trees. To Kathleen, the scene hardly seemed worthy of a souvenir postcard. She flipped it over and read the caption: "The Tigris River in Baghdad, Iraq."

"Your mother was in the habit of sending me postcards from her travels," said Eskridge. "This one was from her honeymoon, 1972."

Kathleen read the handwritten note on the back: "Dear Dr. Eskridge, Iraq is wonderful, and we are really enjoying our honeymoon. Mixing work with pleasure, of course. Still trying to get permission for a dig in Tell-Fara. Hope all is well. Love, Becky."

Mesmerized, Kathleen inspected and read each of the other postcards and letters in the stack. Like the first, they had all been sent to Dr. Eskridge by Kathleen's mother from places throughout the Middle East.

Near the bottom of the stack was a black-and-white photograph of a group of sixteen archeology graduate students, obviously taken in the early 1970s. In the middle of the group was a tall, muscular man with a handlebar moustache and a cowboy hat, smiling broadly. Kathleen recognized him as a younger version of Dr. Eskridge. On the far right side of the group was a pretty woman in her mid-twenties, wearing a sleeveless blouse and cutoff jeans. "My mother," she said quietly, pointing to the smiling woman.

"Yes. That was our summer trip to Alexandria in 1971."

The last item was a faded color photograph of Kathleen's parents, pressed shoulder to shoulder and holding up an infant girl between them. They were smiling proudly.

"Is that me?" Kathleen asked. She flipped the photo over and read the cursive notation: "Kathleen Mary Talbot, age 3 months."

"That's you," said Eskridge. "By the way, do you know who you're named after?"

Kathleen searched her memory and came up blank. "No."

"You were named after Kathleen Mary Kenyon, a famous British archeologist. She was best known for excavations in Jericho and the City of David in Jerusalem in the 1950s. Your mother was a big fan."

"I didn't know that," said Kathleen.

"And you can thank *me* for not being named Gertrude."

"Huh?"

"Your mom wanted to name you after Gertrude Caton-Thompson, another famous female archeologist. I talked her out of it."

Kathleen laughed. "*Thank you.*"

Eskridge reached into his portfolio and retrieved another object. "Here, I thought you also might enjoy this." He handed Kathleen a thin book with a soft, glossy cover.

Kathleen studied the dark nineteenth-century painting on the cover of the book. *Fallen Angel* by Alexander Calabral.

"It's an introductory text about the Nephilim," said Eskridge.

Kathleen was still considering the sepulchral scene on the cover, which depicted a sullen angel sitting awkwardly on the ground, head turned away, wings drooping down, a brooding sky above. "Why such dark imagery?" she asked.

"In most accounts, the Nephilim story is a cautionary tale, a dark chapter in the relationship between God and man. The Nephilim represented a corruption of both. So God responded by destroying nearly every living thing on earth. A do-over, if you will."

"You mean the flood?"

"Yes. In Genesis, the presence of the Nephilim immediately precedes the Great Flood."

Kathleen considered that fact for a few moments. "You said folklore usually has some element of truth to it, right?"

"That's right."

Kathleen looked again at the fallen angel on the book cover. "So if there really were Nephilim in ancient times, why would they be blamed for the flood?"

Eskridge stroked his moustache and smiled. "Well, that's a good question, isn't it?"

Kathleen stared inquisitively.

"What I mean is, we don't really know what these Nephilim were like, do we? Maybe the rest of civilization was glad to see them destroyed because they thought they deserved it. That would certainly explain why Genesis identifies the Nephilim, specifically, as invoking God's wrath."

That was not the answer Kathleen had expected. She shifted uncomfortably in her seat.

"In fact, other accounts are even less kind to the Nephilim. Have you heard of the Book of Enoch?"

Kathleen shook her head.

"It's an ancient Jewish text, dating back to the time of the Dead Sea Scrolls, probably around three hundred BC. It recounts the story of Genesis but with some additional details. It's been highly controversial throughout the history of Judaism and Christianity. May I?" He gently took the book from Kathleen's hands and opened it to a particular page. "The Book of Enoch is broken into five parts. The first is called the Book of Watchers, which is the name given to the group of angels who came to earth to intermingle with humans. Here's a passage from chapter seven."

Then they took wives, each choosing for himself; whom they began to approach, and with whom they cohabited; teaching them sorcery, incantations, and the dividing of roots and trees.

And the women conceiving brought forth giants, whose stature was each three hundred cubits. These devoured all which the labor of men produced; until it became impossible to feed them;

When they turned themselves against men, in order to devour them;

And began to injure birds, beasts, reptiles, and fishes, to eat their flesh one after another, and to drink their blood.

Then the earth reproved the unrighteous.

Eskridge looked up. "Sounds like the Nephilim weren't very popular with the town folk."

"I guess not," Kathleen mumbled.

Eskridge flipped a few pages forward in the book. "And listen to this passage from the Book of Giants, another Jewish text found among the Dead Sea Scrolls in Qumran."

"Giants . . . as in Nephilim?"

"That's right. The Book of Giants is all about the Nephilim before the flood. At one point, according to the book, Enoch presents a stone table to Shenihaza, the leader of the angels who descended to earth to marry human women. The tablet contained a warning from God." Eskridge read aloud from the book.

Let it be known to you that you will not escape judgment for all the things that you have done, and that your wives, their sons, and the wives of their sons will not escape, and that by your licentiousness on the earth, there has been visited upon you a heavenly judgment. The land is crying out and complaining about you and the deeds of your children and about the harm you have done to it. Until the heavenly angel Raphael arrives, behold, destruction is coming by a great flood which will destroy all living things, whatever is in the deserts and the seas.

"Does this answer your question about the dark imagery?" Eskridge asked.

"Yes," said Kathleen absently. Her thoughts were already drifting to the tooth Sargon had given her, and to the DNA sample that Julie was sequencing at this very moment.

CHAPTER THIRTY-SEVEN

Bethesda, Maryland.

KATHLEEN was on her third cup of coffee, trying in vain to kick-start her brain following yet another night of almost no sleep. She sat in silence in the tiny breakfast nook of her kitchen, staring out the window at Sandalwood Street, six floors below, replaying the events of the last three days in her head.

She and Julie had continued sequencing the remainder of the Tell-Fara sample, working straight through the night and into yesterday morning. The breakthrough had come late in the afternoon.

On chromosome 14, Julie discovered a lengthy sequence containing more than eighty thousand base pairs that matched passably well with the *D. Melanogaster* INDY gene. Yet it correlated only about 40 percent to any known sample in the NCBI human genome database. In other words, nobody living today had anything like that long sequence in their DNA.

When Kathleen discovered that that same sequence of base pairs correlated more than 96 percent to a class of retroviruses found only in the subfamily Cercopithecinae of "Old World" monkeys, that confirmed it beyond all doubt.

They'd found it.

The phone rang. Instinctively, Kathleen checked the digital clock above the oven and noted that it was only 7:17 A.M. "Hello?" she answered.

"Dr. Sainsbury, it's Carlos. Have you seen it?"

"Seen what?"

"The newspaper. There's a story about us in the Local section of the *Post*!"

Kathleen laughed nervously. "You're kidding, right?"

"Nope. It's on TV, too. You'd better get down here Dr. S; it's a madhouse outside."

"I'll be right there."

Kathleen hung up the phone and quickly retrieved the *Washington Post* from outside her front door. As she unfolded the Local section on the kitchen counter, her eyes were immediately drawn to a color photograph below the fold. It was a close-up of the embossed sign at the front entrance to her building, which read, "Quantum Life Sciences, Inc." Her heart sank as she read the accompanying headline and lead paragraph.

"Oh no," she whispered. "No, no, no . . ."

AREA COMPANY FINDS LONGEVITY
GENE IN MUMMY
Discovery May Triple Human Life Expectancy
By BRYCE WHITTAKER
Washington Post Staff Writer

ROCKVILLE, Md.—The key to near immortality may have been found in a 5,000-year-old tomb near the ancient city of Babylon in southern Iraq. Quantum Life Sciences, Inc., a small biotech company based in Rockville, has reportedly recovered human DNA from mummified remains that were found in the tomb in 1979. The tomb was discovered deep below a mud-brick structure in southern Iraq known as the Tell-Fara temple.

The article went on to explain, in great detail, the entire saga of the Tell-Fara remains, revealing virtually everything Kathleen had confided in Whittaker over the past few weeks.

Kathleen raised her hand to her forehead. *How could he have done this?* After she'd confided in him? After she'd implored him to keep this information confidential? This didn't even seem legal, let alone ethical. And how long had he been planning this? Was their relationship nothing but a premeditated sham? Kathleen couldn't help but to think so.

"Guess he got his *big break*," she muttered.

She continued skimming the article, which she had to admit was mostly accurate. She noted, in particular, that Whittaker had done a passable job explaining the concept of junk DNA:

Genes are often closely associated with particular attributes, such as eye color, height, or the predisposition to certain diseases. While scientists have learned a great deal about which genes control various attributes in the human genome,

the exact function of most of the genes in the genome—and, indeed, the vast majority of the human genome itself—remains a mystery.

For instance, scientists believe that more than
half of the human genome consists of non-coding
or so-called junk DNA. The reason for this non-
coding DNA has long been a mystery, often dubbed
the "C-value enigma."

In recent years, however, scientists have discovered that some of this junk DNA may actually
consist of "pseudogenes," or copies of genes or viral
species that were long ago disabled by mutations.
These pseudogenes are like genetic fossils, no longer
functional yet instructive about what used to be.

Kathleen was also surprised to note that Whittaker had already solicited the opinions of ex-
perts in biomedical ethics and religion:

"It would be very difficult to control this particular technology," said Dr. Sylvia Matherson, an ethics professor at Stanford University who teaches a
course called The Ethics of Technology. "Ideally, we
would want to take years, perhaps decades, to study
such a profound technology before unleashing it
on the world population. But, in reality, it would
be nearly impossible to restrain such a technology
for any significant period of time." Matherson explained that some technologies, like the Internet,
are so compelling that they take on a life of their
own, seemingly resistant to any centralized attempt
to control them. "With some technologies, you just
can't put the genie back in the bottle," she said.

In addition to ethical issues, manipulation of the INDY gene in humans will likely raise many thorny religious issues.

In the Bible, Noah and his progenitors are described as having abnormally long life spans, some covering many centuries. While many in the Judeo-Christian faiths—including some serious students of the Bible—dismiss these ages as erroneous or as reflecting an alternative measure of time (perhaps months or seasons), fundamentalists steadfastly adhere to the notion that the ages in the Old Testament are literal. And now, it seems, science may actually be confirming that belief.

To date, no major religious organization has specifically taken a stand on the INDY gene technology.

"As far as I know, the Catholic Church does not have an official position on this particular technology," said Father Michael Prendergast of Georgetown University. "However, the church has made clear that engaging in genetic engineering that alters the human DNA is a sin. And that would certainly include altering the human genome to extend life spans."

Kathleen refolded the paper and tried to sort out the tangle of emotions competing for attention in her mind. The one that kept rising to the surface was an overwhelming sense of betrayal by the man she had foolishly trusted—Bryce Whittaker.

Then she suddenly remembered Carlos's words: *"You'd better get down here."* She grabbed her coat and hustled out the door.

CHAPTER THIRTY-EIGHT

Bᴉʟʟ McCreary burst through the door of the Logistics Analysis office, short of breath and sweating. "You seen this?" he asked Goodwin, holding up a copy of the *Washington Post*.

Goodwin nodded.

"Shit!" McCreary hissed. "This is the worst possible thing that could've happened right now. The *worst*! We're not ready for this yet. The new deputy . . . Sorenson, he's clueless about this stuff." McCreary shook his head in frustration as he read the byline of the article for the fourth time. "Bryce Whittaker," he said contemptuously under his breath. Turning back to Goodwin, he asked, "Anything from Stonewell yet?"

"Not yet. Should I call his office and set up a secure video link?"

"Yeah. And tell them it's urgent."

"Will do."

McCreary once again held up the newspaper and thumped the front page with his fingers.

"Steve, did we pick up *anything* about this? I mean, anything indicating they'd actually isolated the INDY gene in that sample?"

"No. Last we heard, they were still trying to isolate a DNA sample from the mess that was left after the break-in the other night. But, then again, Dr. Sainsbury hasn't been using her cell phone since then."

"Not at all?"

"Nope. It's been off. Totally off."

McCreary shook his head. "Stonewell's not going to like this."

Just then, the phone in McCreary's office rang, and he rushed to pick it up. "Hello?"

"Have you read this goddamned article in the *Post*?" boomed the voice of Secretary Stonewell.

"Yes, sir. I've read it."

"Well . . . what the hell's going on, Bill? How did this happen?"

McCreary swallowed hard. *Choose your words carefully.* "Uh, Mr. Secretary . . . we have no confirmation that the story is even true—"

"God damn it, Bill! You're supposed to be on top of this stuff!"

"Yes, sir, but—"

"But nothing! This is serious business. Hell, you know that."

"Yes, sir, I do. And I think we should go on the secure—"

"Screw that! Jesus Christ, we don't have time for that anymore. You need to clean up this mess *right now*, right this very minute, before it gets out of control. God almighty, you of all people should know what'll happen if we lose control of this thing!"

"Yes, sir. So what are you proposing we do?"

"I'm not proposing anything, Bill. That's your job. Figure it out, and *do it*. Hell, do the Pons-Fleischmann thing if you have to, I don't care. Just nip this thing in the bud right now! Do you understand me?"

"Yes, sir. I understand."

The phone went dead in McCreary's ear, and he hung up the receiver gingerly. He cradled his forehead in his hands and closed his eyes for several seconds, massaging his temples in slow circles with the pads of his fingertips as he struggled to straighten everything out in his mind. *The story was out already. It'd be all over TV in an hour, if it wasn't already. But the technology, itself . . . that was still a question mark. It hadn't been confirmed.*

Which left only one option.

"Steve," said McCreary, emerging from his private office, "grab your coat. We're going to Rockville."

CHAPTER THIRTY-NINE

KATHLEEN merged her Subaru onto Rockville Pike, nearly oblivious to the traffic around her. She was still lost in thought when something on the radio caught her attention. She turned up the volume of WTTL, a local talk-radio station. The segue music—The Who's "My Generation"—was just fading out.

"Welcome back," said the voice of Michael Roland of the *Michael Roland Morning Show*. "This morning, we're talking about a fascinating story in the *Washington Post*."

"Yeah, this is really something," intoned the bubbly voice of his co-host, Cindy Trudeau. "Imagine living for two or three hundred years!"

Roland's voice weaved back in. "Well, that's what researchers at Quantum Life Sciences in Rockville are saying may be possible using a new gene therapy. It seems they've found a longevity gene that can be manipulated to double, or even triple, peoples' life spans."

"This is really an amazing story, Mike."

"It sure is. But the question for our listeners today is, would you *want* to live that long? Is this is a good thing, or do you foresee problems? We'd like to hear from you. Let's first go to Gary in Manassas. Good morning, Gary, you're on WTTL."

"Good morning, guys," said the crackly voice of Gary in Manassas. "Great show today."

"Thank you," said Roland. "So, Gary, what do you think about this story in the *Post*? Pretty amazing stuff, huh?"

"Absolutely. I read it twice, and I was just . . . blown away. But here's what I want to know. What happens if you start taking this gene therapy when you're already in your sixties or seventies? I mean, will you stay that age for the next hundred years, or will you, like . . . grow younger?"

"That's a great question," said Trudeau. "I was wondering the same thing myself. Because, you know, there's a big difference between being twenty-five years old for a century and being ninety-five years old for a century."

"Exactly," said Gary.

"Well, that's something we just don't know yet," said Roland. "We've tried contacting the folks at Quantum Life Sciences, but so far we haven't been able to reach them for comment."

"I bet they've got their hands full today," said Trudeau chirpily.

"Yeah, I imagine you're right," said Roland. "So, anyway, Gary, do you think this is a good thing, or do you foresee problems with this technology?"

"Personally, I think it's a good thing. In fact, I'm wondering where I can sign up! I mean, we all want to live longer, right? Of course, I'd want to make sure this therapy is safe and all, but . . . I mean, assuming it's safe, I don't see any downside at all."

"Okay," said Roland. "So we have at least one listener who thinks this is a good thing. Thanks for the call, Gary."

"You know," Trudeau interjected, "I've got to agree with that last caller. We have to make sure this therapy is safe. But, assuming it is, I see this as a really good thing. Just imagine how much you could accomplish in two or three hundred years."

"Okay," said Roland, "next we have Evelyn from McLean. Good morning, Evelyn, you're on WTTL."

"Good morning," said the raspy voice of Evelyn from McLean.

"What do you think about all this, Evelyn . . . good thing or a bad thing?"

"Well, personally, I don't want to live that long. I mean, I'm worried as it is about having enough retirement savings to last another twenty or thirty years. What would I do if I lived another hundred? I'd be out of money!"

"Well that's certainly something to think about," said Trudeau empathetically. "Would people have to go back to work? *Could* they go back to work?"

"And would they *want* to?" added Roland.

"Yeah," said Evelyn from McLean, "that's my

point. I wouldn't want to go back to work at this point in my life. And can I make another point, too?"

"Sure, very quickly," prodded Roland.

"Well, has anyone given any thought to the population explosion this would cause? I mean, I'm worried about overcrowding and depletion of our natural resources as it *is*. If everyone suddenly starts living another hundred years, I think that would be disastrous for the environment and society in general."

"Well, *Florida* certainly would get crowded," quipped Roland, "what with all those retirees heading down there. But, seriously, you do raise some very important issues, Evelyn. Thank you for the call."

Trudeau interjected. "You know, she raised some very good points that we should all think about. Maybe the government should study these things in detail before this technology is implemented."

"That would probably be a good idea," said Roland. "Okay, it looks like we have time for one more call. So let's go to . . . John in Damascus. Good morning John, you're on WTTL."

"Hello?" said John in a deep, Texas drawl.

"Yes John, you're on the air. What do you think about this breaking story in the *Post*?"

"Personally, I think it's a sin."

"Okay, that's interesting—you've got a slightly different perspective than our last two callers. So tell us, John, why do you believe it's a sin?"

"Sir, the Bible states that all things were created *by* God and *for* God." John's voice rose and fell in the style of a revivalist preacher. "We were made in God's image and are subject to *his* plan. Read Genesis one, verses twenty-six and twenty-seven. When you alter the genetic code, sir, you're destroying God's image and you're deviating from his plan. This longevity-gene business is nothing more than an attempt to steal immortality from God. And sir, there *is* no greater sin!"

"Okay, but—"

"In Genesis," the caller continued, ignoring Roland, "God took immortality away from man because man had sinned. Read Genesis chapter three. It's all in there."

"Okay, but let me ask you—"

"And God inserted death into the world *because* of man's sin. He did so by putting death right into our genetic makeup. Right in our DNA! So those people at . . . Quantum Life Sciences . . ." He said the company's name in a snide tone. "What they're trying to do is undo what God has done. What they're trying to do is provide a path *around* death. But God has already said that only he has the remedy for death." The caller's voice was growing more emphatic, almost wild.

"Okay, John, thank you for your—"

But John from Damascus wasn't finished. "Genetic engineering is a direct defiance of God!" he exclaimed, practically yelling now. "If you want to see what happens to those who attempt to exalt man above the creator, sir, read Genesis eleven! Read Romans one! God destroyed them for their arrogance—"

"John, I'm afraid we're out of—"

" . . . and He'll do the same to Quantum Life Sciences! God will smite—"

Suddenly, the radio went silent as the three-second delay went into effect. When the show resumed, Michael Roland was apologizing.

"I'm sorry about that folks. Boy, this is certainly an emotional issue for some people."

"It sure is," added Trudeau.

"Well, I'm sure we haven't heard the end of that debate. But, right now, it's time for an update on the traffic out on the roadways . . ."

Kathleen turned the volume down and tried to mentally digest what she'd just heard. Her stomach felt queasy.

Did he just say God was going to smite me?

CHAPTER FORTY

Luce Venfeld was nervous. He refolded the Local section of the *Washington Post* and placed it on his desk, having reread the QLS article for the third time. *It wasn't supposed to happen this way. That damned reporter was screwing everything up!*

To say the least, Elias Rubin and the Olam Foundation were not going be pleased about this. Which was why he was nervous. He'd never disappointed this client before, nor did he want to. He exhaled loudly and tapped his fingers on the exquisitely burled surface of his walnut desk.

There was something else troubling him about the article, too. The FBI was involved. And a "source close to the investigation" had already drawn a link between the QLS break-in and "organized crime."

"God damn Zafer," he muttered under his breath. Semion Zafer was sloppy. And cocky. And stupid. And now the FBI was on his trail. *What if he got caught? Could he be expected to keep his mouth shut?*

Venfeld put that thought aside and returned his focus to the QLS story in the *Post. What could be done about this situation?* He thought about QLS's facility in Rockville. Somewhere in that lab was a DNA sample and some sort of computerized analysis that contained all the information the Olam Foundation wanted. If no one else had that data yet, then maybe, just maybe, it wasn't too late.

He stood up and straightened his tie. Zafer was probably still asleep at this hour. No matter. It was time for Plan B.

Venfeld retrieved his Berluti briefcase from beneath his desk and set it softly on the desktop. He clicked the latch and lifted the front flap. The contents of the briefcase were mundane: newspapers, several manila folders, some bills. Venfeld slid his hand behind the stack of papers until it found its way into a special silk-lined pocket on the backside of the briefcase. There, he felt the hard, cold contours of the object he wanted.

He hadn't used it in a while, but he certainly remembered how. He pulled the custom-tooled Beretta 90-TWO pistol from its hiding place and felt its weight in his hand. Reaching in again, he pulled out a cylindrical Trinity suppressor and attached it to the gun's barrel.

Plan B.

CHAPTER FORTY-ONE

For a moment, Kathleen thought she'd pulled into the wrong parking lot. Looking around, she barely recognized the small paved area in front of QLS's building. It was teeming with people. Every parking space was occupied, and about a dozen other vehicles were parked haphazardly along the edges of the lot and in the median strip.

She parked her silver Subaru at the edge of the lot with two wheels on the grass. She stepped out of her car and hugged her coat tightly against her body as she surveyed the surreal scene around her. A raw northeast wind swept through the parking lot in long, sustained gusts. Overhead, dark clouds were accumulating.

Two white news vans were parked side by side at the back of the lot, one from Channel 5 News, the other from Channel 7. Atop each van was a long, telescoping satellite antenna that extended high into in the air.

Directly in front of the building, two television cameras were set up on tripods about fifteen feet apart, each accompanied by portable lights and white reflective screens. In front of one of the cameras was an attractive woman in a bright red dress, whom Kathleen recognized immediately as Tina Chang from Channel 5 News. She appeared to be just beginning a live report. Kathleen inched closer to hear her speak.

"Thank you, Terry," said Ms. Chang into a microphone emblazoned with the NEWS 5 logo. "I'm here in front of the offices of Quantum Life Sciences in Rockville, where there's an incredible report out this morning about the discovery of a gene in the human DNA that many are calling the longevity gene. According to a story in the *Washington Post* this morning, this small biotech company behind me may have successfully isolated a gene in the human body that apparently controls our life span and can be manipulated to actually double or triple human life expectancy. Details are still sketchy at this time, but some are saying that when this particular gene is triggered using gene therapy, we could expect to live *hundreds* of years, perhaps even longer. So, as you can imagine, this news is causing quite a stir.

"As you can see behind me, a small crowd has gathered here at the front entrance to the Quantum Life Sciences building. Some of them have been here since as early as five thirty this morning. I spoke with some of these folks a little earlier to find out why they decided to come down here today. And some of their answers were surprising.

"I talked to one man whose wife is in the hospital with terminal cancer. He said he came here to see if he could enroll her as a test candidate for this new gene-therapy treatment. Another elderly man I spoke to said that he wanted to volunteer to try the treatment himself. In fact, that was the case for a lot of the people in this crowd. Not everyone, though, is happy about this news. I spoke to several people who are worried about the effect this technology might have on the environment, on the economy, and on the general fabric of our society. A couple folks here were also very vocal about their belief that this technology is a violation of what they consider to be God's will. So it appears there's a wide variety of strong feelings about this technology."

Chang paused momentarily and put her finger to her left ear, apparently listening to a question posed by the Channel 5 news anchor. She resumed a few seconds later.

"Yes, Terry, I've been told that there are some people inside the building. Now, remember, this is a very small company, with only a few employees, but I believe there is someone inside the building right now. So far, there's been no official word from the company about this news. But I imagine at some point a representative of the company will have to come out to address this growing crowd.

"Terry, I should also mention one other thing. As you can see, the front doors to the building are covered with plywood. This was the result of a break-in here on Easter Sunday, in which one of the employees of this company was shot, just outside the building here. I understand he is still in critical condition at this time, and it's not clear whether that shooting has anything to do with the discovery of this new longevity gene. Of course, we'll be following this story very closely, and we'll let you know if anything develops.

"Reporting live from Rockville, Tina Chang, Channel 5 News."

Kathleen checked her watch; it was 8:35. She had to get inside the building. She quickly weighed her options. She could just walk up to the plywood-clad front door and unlock it with her key. But then, of course, she'd have to walk past TV cameras and reporters, and cut through a phalanx of at least thirty people standing directly in front of the doors—some of whom looked quite agitated. *She'd never make it.*

The only other option was to go through the emergency door in the back, for which, unfortunately, she had no key. If she'd had her cell phone, she could have called Carlos and asked him to open the back door. But, of course, she didn't have her cell phone. She'd left it at home with the battery removed.

She made up her mind.

Glancing discreetly in all directions to make sure she hadn't been spotted, she slowly walked away from the chaos in the parking lot. She strolled, in no apparent hurry, to the side of the five-unit building and slipped quickly around the corner. Now out of view of the TV cameras and the crowd, she walked briskly in the grass alongside the building, glancing behind her several times to make sure she hadn't been followed. Rounding the corner at the rear of the building, she quickened her pace to a jog.

She navigated through the mulched area that separated the back of the building from the thick pine forest behind it, weaving around unkempt clusters of ornamental shrubs and plants until, finally, she reached QLS's back door. She knocked softly.

There was no answer.

She knocked again—louder this time—glancing left and right to make sure she was still alone behind the building. Again, there was no answer. "C'mon, Carlos," she whispered. She put her ear to the cold metal door and could hear the muffled voices of Carlos and Julie inside.

She pounded hard on the metal door—ten times. The noise seemed to reverberate everywhere. She was sure the people in the parking lot would hear it. "C'mon, c'mon, c'mon," she whispered anxiously.

Finally, she heard Carlos's voice on the other side of the door. "Who is it?" he asked suspiciously.

"Carlos, it's me, Kathleen! Open up, please."

After a momentary pause, the door opened with a clank, and Carlos Guiterez stood on the other side with an exasperated look on his face. He pulled her inside and closed the door. "Dr. Sainsbury," he said as he reset the door's alarm, "I've been trying to call you—"

"I know, I know. My cell phone's dead. Tell me what's been going on here."

"It's been crazy all morning. It started about three hours ago. I was sacked out in my office and Julie was asleep in the conference room. You know she stayed here all night after you left, right?"

Kathleen nodded.

"Anyway, about six in the morning, we heard someone banging on the front door. Given everything that's happened lately, I wasn't about to open up. I asked who it was through the door. It was some old guy asking if he could sign up for the "longevity gene therapy." I asked him what the hell he was talking about, and he told me it was in the *Post*. I told him to come back during business hours. Then I went and found the article online, and I was, like . . . *Whoa! How do they know already?* Then I saw the byline."

Kathleen felt ashamed. "He said he'd keep it confidential."

"Don't worry about it, Dr. S. That guy's an asshole. Turns out, though, it's not all bad."

"What do you mean?"

"Guess who called me at seven o'clock this morning."

Kathleen shrugged.

"Remember our friends at Crescent?"

"Let me guess: They rescinded their cash call?"

"Yep. Now they're behind us 'one hundred percent.'" Carlos mocked the thick New York accent and pushy mannerisms of the young broker at Crescent whom they both loathed.

Kathleen rolled her eyes. "Anything else?"

"Yeah, a lot. The phone's been ringing off the

hook for three straight hours. People calling for interviews, people wanting confirmation of the newspaper story, people wanting to volunteer for the 'treatment,' people wanting it for their wife, their father, their mother, you name it. One lady wanted to know if it would work for her *cats*. Another guy started screaming at me about usurping God's role as the divine creator . . . Jeez, I don't even remember what he said. Sounded like a nut job. After a while, I just stopped answering the phone. Julie's pretty upset—you may want to talk to her."

Kathleen drew a deep breath. "All right. Grab Julie. Let's meet in the conference room in five minutes."

A low, sustained rumble permeated the entire building for several seconds, shaking it ominously.

"Sounds like we're in for a storm," said Carlos.

CHAPTER FORTY-TWO

LUCE Venfeld parked his gleaming, black BMW on 6th Street in Southeast D.C., on the edge of Congress Heights. This was easily the worst neighborhood in the District—a twelve-block cluster of city-owned apartment buildings and dilapidated row houses that was practically run by drug dealers. Shootings were a nightly occurrence.

Venfeld, however, wasn't worried about parking his brand-new BMW here. He'd been in this neighborhood before, and he knew that most of the thugs in this neighborhood would be hibernating at this hour. Daylight in Congress Heights was a reprieve, a time when normal working-class folks could get out of their apartments and go about their daily lives in relative safety. Besides, driving a shiny expensive car in this neighborhood was so audacious and conspicuous that anyone who did so was presumed to be someone important—a corrupt alderman perhaps, or a drug kingpin. People like that generally got a pass in this neighborhood. At least for a while.

Venfeld walked two blocks north on 6th until he reached Savannah Street, where he turned right. He walked casually, comfortably—like he belonged here. Half a block down Savannah on the right, he stopped at a set of crumbling, rust-stained cement steps that led to the front door of the Trenton Terrace Apartments. His destination.

Venfeld's Burberry raincoat nearly covered his dark blue suit and red silk tie. He wore a pair of thin black leather gloves and a black fedora. A pair of dark sunglasses obscured his eyes. With the brim of his fedora pulled down nearly to his eyebrows and the collar of his raincoat flipped up, you could barely see his face at all, even at a close distance. The most anyone could tell about him was that he was white, and well dressed.

Not that Venfeld was particularly worried about people noticing him around here. In this neighborhood, people didn't usually "notice" things. "Noticing" things could get you killed. As a popular saying around the neighborhood went, "Don't trouble trouble." You didn't ask questions, and you didn't "notice" things.

Venfeld climbed the cement steps and typed a four-digit security code into the call box. A buzzer alerted him that the door was now unlocked. He pulled it open and stepped into the dingy elevator lobby. It was poorly lit and smelled like stale cigarette butts and urine. In one corner, a large collection of beer and liquor bottles was assembled next to an overturned laundry basket—apparently someone's nightly perch.

The building had just one elevator. A tattered cardboard placard taped to the elevator door proclaimed in scrawled handwriting that it was "BROKE." Venfeld rolled his eyes and walked to the back of the lobby, where a dented metal door led to the stairwell. He opened it and stepped inside. The stairwell was dimly lit and adorned with gang graffiti. It, too, smelled like urine. *Jesus,* he thought, *don't they have bathrooms around here?*

For a moment, he stood motionless at the bottom of the stairwell—just listening. Somewhere, a television was on. But, otherwise, the building was quiet. It was 8:30 on a Thursday morning, yet no one was rushing off to work; no one was getting kids ready for school; no one was going out for coffee. This was Congress Heights. Morning here was like nighttime elsewhere. People in this building were sleeping.

Venfeld pulled his Beretta pistol from the pocket of his raincoat and ascended the steps slowly. A few minutes later, he exited on the seventh floor and made his way to Apartment 7E.

There was no need to knock; Venfeld had a key. He carefully unlocked the door and swung it open, waiting a full ten seconds for any possible noise or reaction inside. Hearing nothing, he slipped quietly through the open door, leaving it slightly ajar behind him. With his right hand, he squeezed the handle of his 9 mm tightly, releasing the grip safety. His index finger rested lightly on the trigger. He was ready for anything.

Jesus, what a fucking slob, he thought to himself as he stepped around half-eaten fast-food meals, dirty dishes, and crumpled clothes on the floor. The living room smelled like pizza, booze, and old socks. Porno magazines were stacked high on the floor next to the only legitimate piece of furniture in the room—a tattered lime green couch with a pizza box occupying the central cushion.

Venfeld quietly made his way across the carpeted living area, past the greasy kitchenette, and into the short hallway adjoining the apartment's two bedrooms and one bathroom. He generally knew the layout of the apartment. What he didn't know was which bedroom Semion Zafer slept in.

He approached the first bedroom door, twisted the doorknob carefully to avoid a click, then pushed the door open quietly, just enough to poke his head through. The room was dark. A thick shade covered the only window in the room, blocking out what little sunlight would have been available from the adjacent alleyway on this overcast morning. Venfeld could see that the floor of the room was covered wall-to-wall with boxes, clothes, and a vast collection of junk. There was no bed—no furniture at all—and nobody in the room.

He proceeded down the hallway to the next door—the bathroom—which was wide open. Leaning backward against the hallway wall, he craned his head ninety degrees around the corner and peered inside. The bathroom was dark—and empty.

Which left just one more room . . .

Venfeld was just starting toward the last door in the hallway, when suddenly, the doorknob rattled and the door began to open.

"Shit!" he mouthed silently. He quickly retreated a few steps and slipped into the bathroom. It smelled like mouthwash and mildew. He climbed into the shower and pulled the shower curtain closed ever so slowly, coaxing each metal curtain ring across the steel curtain rod so that it barely made a sound. He positioned his body like a statue—feet planted on the bottom of the shower, right arm outstretched, finger on the trigger. He could hear Zafer's footsteps in the hallway.

The bathroom light clicked on.

Through the opaque shower curtain, Venfeld could see Zafer yawning and rubbing his face, coming closer.

Venfeld decided not to wait any longer. With a rapid sweep of his left hand, he ripped open the shower curtain. Zafer was standing less than four feet away, fully nude, directly facing him. He'd obviously been heading for the toilet.

They locked eyes for a fraction of a second. Then Venfeld raised his firing arm, took aim, and fired his pistol. The suppressor emitted a muffled pop.

The 9 mm round caught Zafer in the chest. A thin circle of blood splattered on the yellow tiles behind him as the bullet passed through his flesh and exited between his shoulder blade and his spine. "*Lech!*" he grunted in Hebrew, staggering backward. He hit the yellow-tiled wall and slid down, leaving a slimy trail of blood.

Venfeld quickly aimed and fired again—the CIA's "double tap" technique. *Pop!*

Zafer's eyes widened as the bullet hit him square in the forehead. A small, dark circle formed just below his hairline, and his head snapped back violently. Simultaneously, the back of his skull exploded, splattering blood and brain matter all over the tiled wall behind him. Zafer slumped down into a lifeless heap, his eyes frozen in an expression of disbelief.

Venfeld could be sure of one thing now: Zafer wouldn't be talking to the FBI.

He stepped out of the shower, still clad in his raincoat, gloves, and Fedora, and carefully navigated around the body of Semion Zafer, deftly avoiding any blood spatter. He made his way to the front door but, before exiting the apartment, paused to listen carefully.

Silence.

Don't trouble trouble.

Venfeld exited Apartment 7E, locked the door behind him, and strode leisurely back to his BMW on 6th Street. He found it parked just where he'd left it, untouched.

Seven minutes later, Venfeld merged his BMW into the morning rush on the Southeast Expressway. He typed the address of Quantum Life Sciences into his navigation system and sat back and relaxed to the sounds of Mozart's Symphony no. 40 in G Minor, one of that composer's darkest works.

CHAPTER FORTY-THREE

Rockville, Maryland.

"**How's** everyone holding up?" Kathleen asked as she walked into the QLS conference room. Carlos and Julie were already seated at the table.

"Fine," said Carlos. He was an ex-Marine. Resilient, unflappable. *Of course he was fine.*

Julie Haas, on the other hand, looked disheveled and frazzled. Her clothes were uncharacteristically wrinkled, her lipstick and makeup worn away, and her hair a tangled mess. "I'm okay," she said unconvincingly.

"Are you sure?" Kathleen prodded.

Julie looked as if she might cry at any moment. "It's just—" She exhaled loudly. "It's just that everything's happening so fast! People are screaming out there . . . Jeremy's in the hospital . . ." Her chin began to quiver as she fixed her eyes on Kathleen's. "And we never really talked about whether this was, you know, the right thing to do."

"What do you mean?"

"I don't know. It's just that this is really big, you know . . . much bigger than I realized. And now that it's actually happening, I—" She looked down at her fidgeting hands. "Well . . . I guess I'm having second thoughts."

"Julie," Kathleen said soothingly. "This treatment could help millions of people. How could you have second thoughts about that?"

"I can't explain it Dr. S. It's just this weird feeling I get when I see all those people out there, arguing and yelling at one another. When I think about Jeremy getting *shot* because of this. It just makes me wonder."

"Wonder what?"

"Whether we're opening up Pandora's box. Like, maybe we weren't supposed to discover this gene in the first place."

Kathleen mulled those words over in her head. She liked Julie and valued her opinion. *Could she be right? Have we unknowingly violated some sort of natural barrier in the human genome?* It was true they were about to reintroduce a virus that had been eliminated by natural selection thousands of years ago. *Had it been eliminated for a reason?* That thought was still percolating through her mind when Carlos suddenly changed the topic.

"Dr. S, I think we need to talk about some business issues here."

"Right," said Kathleen firmly. But her mind was still lingering on Julie's comment about Pandora's box, the same comment Bryce Whittaker had made last week. And another thought had suddenly popped up, something else Whittaker had said. Why would natural selection *eliminate* a gene that increased life expectancy? She still had not arrived at an answer to that riddle.

"Dr. S?" said Carlos impatiently.

"Oh, sorry. Yes, business issues, I'm listening."

"We need to talk about getting patent protection for this gene sequence."

Kathleen nodded in agreement.

"In fact, that was the first thing that jerk from Crescent asked me this morning, after he rescinded their cash call. He wanted to know if we'd filed a patent application yet."

"I guess we need to do that ASAP, huh?" Kathleen's mind was now shifting back to the pragmatic aspects of managing this new discovery.

"Already on it," Carlos replied. "I started drafting a disclosure this morning using the data Julie gave me." He pulled a small jump drive from his shirt pocket and slid it across the table to Kathleen. "Can you take a look at what I've got so far and let me know if anything else needs to be added?"

"Sure," said Kathleen, slipping the jump drive into the pocket of her jeans. "I'll do it this morning."

"When you're done, I'll forward the disclosure to our patent attorney at Coulter and Meyers. If I recall, I think we also have to deposit a biological sample at the Patent Office along with the application. So let's make sure to preserve the DNA sample that you guys sequenced last night."

"It's in a neoprene sample container in the

fridge," said Julie, rubbing her eyes. "Second shelf."

Kathleen looked at Julie empathetically. "You must be exhausted. Why don't you go home and get some rest. Carlos and I can hold the fort today." She nodded toward the parking lot, where the sound of shouting voices made the "fort" analogy seem oddly appropriate.

Julie smiled appreciatively. "Thanks Dr. S."

Carlos pushed back from the table and stood up. "I'll walk you to your car."

"Go out the back," Kathleen instructed. "Walk around casually to your car. If anyone asks you any questions, just say, 'No comment.'"

Carlos nodded and left with Julie.

Meanwhile, Kathleen returned to her office. There were a thousand things to do today: the patent application, the agenda for the upcoming shareholders' meeting, a whole new research plan. But her most immediate concern was what to tell the press. *Should she deny the story in the* Post*?* She considered it for a moment, relishing the idea of denying Whittaker's story. That would certainly make him look like an ass—which he deserved. But, in the end, she decided she couldn't do that. The story was basically true, and, besides, there were shareholders to consider. She decided "no comment" was the best approach for now, until they could sort everything out.

She began typing a short press release but was quickly distracted by something outside. The crowd noise had intensified. Something was happening. She ran to the conference room and pulled the shade up just enough to peek through the window. She was surprised to see the crowd had grown significantly. There were now at least fifty people outside the door, and they seemed to be forming an unorganized circle around something . . . or someone.

Carlos! She realized with a start. A crowd of people, about six deep, surrounded him on the walkway, shouting and screaming. Kathleen saw Tina Chang in her bright red dress, pushing her way through the crowd, microphone in hand, cameraman following close behind.

Carlos needed help. Instinctively, Kathleen rushed to the lobby, unlocked the front door, and stepped outside into the cold.

From where Kathleen now stood, the crowd was about thirty feet away, on the walkway connecting the QLS entrance to the sidewalk that ran along the front of the building. Tina Chang was still trying to squeeze her way through the writhing throng of people. The other news reporter, however, was standing at the fringes, and he spotted Kathleen right away. "Dr. Sainsbury!" he called out, jogging toward her, his cameraman in tow.

Someone in the crowd looked up and pointed at Kathleen. Then, suddenly, the entire crowd began stampeding down the walkway toward her.

The reporter from Channel 7 reached her first. "Dr. Sainsbury," he shouted excitedly. "Can you confirm the report in the *Washington Post*?" He shoved a microphone in her face.

Before she could answer, the crowd swarmed around her, grabbing at her arms and shoulders, everyone trying to get her attention at once. "Please help my wife!" an elderly man shouted. "I'm ready to volunteer," said another. A shrill female voice screeched above it all: "Sinner!"

Kathleen made eye contact with Carlos, who was still standing about twenty feet away on the walkway. She mouthed the words, "Where's Julie?"

Carlos pointed toward the edge of the parking lot, where Julie's car was just leaving.

"Can you confirm the story?" the Channel 7 reporter repeated.

Kathleen spoke into the microphone. "We have no comment at this time."

At that, the crowd went crazy. "Will you be holding a press conference?" the reporter shouted above the frenzy.

"We'll issue a press release later today," Kathleen replied.

As the crowd activity reached a feverish pitch—more questions, more shouting, more pushing and jostling—a loud crack of thunder boomed overhead, momentarily drowning out the cacophony of voices.

Then it began to rain.

Carlos managed to break through the crowd and position himself next to Kathleen. "That's it, folks," he shouted above the roar, mainly in the direction of the Channel 7 reporter. He gently nudged Kathleen toward the front doors, pushing several people out of the way. He muscled open one of the boarded doors and pushed Kathleen through the opening. Then he stepped into the building and closed and locked the door behind him.

"This is getting out of control," Kathleen said breathlessly, dripping and shaking from the rain.

Seconds later, a deafening crack of thunder shook the entire building, and the sky outside turned white. Lightning nearby. Kathleen and Carlos watched nervously as the lights in the QLS lobby flickered several times, then went out completely.

They returned to the darkened conference room and stared through the window at the chaos outside. The crowd was dispersing quickly in the pouring rain. Both news vans were lowering their antennas.

The lights came on about five minutes later, accompanied by an unexpected sound.

The fire alarm!

Kathleen and Carlos both jumped at the shrill, pulsating siren and ran immediately to the laboratory. They stopped just short of the door.

"Look!" Kathleen said, pointing to the digital temperature display above the door. It read "99.1°C."

Carlos's eyes grew wide and his Marine Corps instincts took over. "Get back! Get back!" he screamed, grabbing Kathleen's arm and pulling her down the hallway.

"What?" Kathleen shouted.

But Carlos didn't have time to answer. There

was a deafening crash behind them as the lab's airtight door blew wide open and fire and smoke exploded into the hallway.

The last thing Kathleen remembered was the sensation of her feet leaving the floor.

Then everything went black.

PART III

He saw the great Mystery, he knew the Hidden:
He recovered the knowledge of all the times before the
*   Flood.*
He journeyed beyond the merely distant; he struggled
*   beyond mere exhaustion,*
And then he carved his story on stone.

— EPIC OF GILGAMESH (TABLET I)

CHAPTER FORTY-FOUR

WHEN Kathleen regained consciousness, everything was dark. The force of the explosion had knocked her off her feet and sent her tumbling down the hallway until she'd hit the back wall—hard. She had no idea how long she'd been out.

Now, struggling to orient herself, she felt nauseated and confused. *Which way was up? Was she standing or lying down?* Within seconds, she realized with a terrifying jolt that she was having trouble breathing; an acrid stench was causing her to choke. Noxious gas stung her windpipe and burned her lungs as she began to cough. Through the darkness, she saw something flickering nearby, just inches away—something bright and orange. It took several seconds before she realized: *it was fire.*

She was lying on her stomach against a wall, flames and smoke swirling all around her. Panicking, she scrambled to her feet and searched frantically for a way out—an open door, a lighted exit sign, *anything!* But the smoke stung her eyes, and she was forced to shut them almost immediately.

Temporarily blinded and still coughing uncontrollably, Kathleen stumbled forward with her arms outstretched, away from the heat of the flames. She felt something snag her arm. *Something was grabbing her tightly, tugging her, dragging her backward!* In a panic, she fought against the unknown force. As she did, she inhaled another breath of thick smoke. Her mind was beginning to go numb from the lack of oxygen. And, still, she was being dragged . . .

Suddenly, she felt the soothing sensation of cold air on her face, filling her lungs, salving her skin. Desperate for oxygen, she sucked in the air greedily, coughing and sputtering as she exhaled. Her eyes were still shut tightly and stinging badly. Soon, she became aware of another sensation: cold rain.

"Dr. Sainsbury, are you okay?" said a man's voice. It was Carlos.

She rubbed her watering eyes and cracked them open slowly, struggling to focus. Everything was blurry at first, but gradually, Carlos's face came into view. She now saw that they were standing just outside the emergency door at the back of the building. Carlos had saved her life! "I . . . I'm fine," she sputtered between violent coughs. She held up her hands and inspected them—they were black but not burned. She felt her head and face and then checked her hands again, whimpering when she saw a bright smear of blood.

"You've got a nasty cut on your forehead," Carlos explained. "But I think you'll be okay."

"What happened?"

"Fire in the lab. Something must have exploded."

Those words triggered an awful realization. "The sample!" she exclaimed. Without hesitation, she yanked open the emergency door, intending to enter. A thick plume of black smoke billowed out of the open doorway, forcing her backward, coughing.

"No!" Carlos said, grabbing her arm just as she lurched forward again to enter.

She met Carlos's eyes pleadingly.

"I know where it is," said Carlos after a moment's hesitation. "Wait here." In an instant, he disappeared through the open doorway and into the swirling darkness.

"Carlos!" Kathleen screamed after him. But he was gone.

Her head was spinning. *This can't be happening.*

Moments later, she heard sirens in the distance. They grew closer until finally, they reached the parking lot on the other side of the building.

"Come on, Carlos," she whispered. "Come on . . ." Her heart was beating heavily, her entire body fidgety. She felt helpless waiting by the door, soaked with rain, wondering with each passing second whether Carlos would make it out alive. Black smoke was still pouring out of the open

emergency door. As seconds turned into minutes, she could no longer ignore the agonizing
realization creeping into her mind.

He isn't going to make it.

Carlos couldn't hold his breath much longer. It
had taken him nearly a minute—much longer
than he'd expected—just to make it down the
hallway to the lab. The problem was, he couldn't
see *anything*. The smoke and intense heat inside
the building stung his eyes so badly that he
could only keep them open for a split second at a
time. And even then—squinting through watery
eyes—he could only make out rough shapes.

Finally, he reached the lab, where, thankfully,
the smoke was not as intense. A gaping hole in
the north wall was allowing most of the smoke
to escape to the outside. Carlos drew a quick
breath and winced in pain. The air was hot, and
it burned painfully as it went down his windpipe
and into his lungs. He knew he wouldn't last long
in here. Through bleary eyes, he spied the lab's
main workstation in the center of the room, engulfed in flames. His heart sank. The refrigerator
was directly behind the flames. He wondered how
he could get there without being burned to a crisp.

On hands and knees, he crawled toward the
back of the lab, away from the north wall, hoping
to find a clear pathway around the flames. The
fire, however, had already spread to the back of
the lab, consuming the computers and monitors,
the spectroscopy machine, the micro-injection
microscope, a bookshelf crammed with equip-

ment manuals and notebooks, and, most troubling, a storage cabinet full of chemicals. Carlos no sooner realized the danger of the chemical locker when an explosion erupted inside the metal cabinet, blowing its doors clear off their hinges. Carlos ducked low as one of the locker doors flew over his head, banging into the wall behind him. Looking up, he observed with horror that dozens of bulk chemical containers were now directly exposed to the flames. *He had to get out of there!*

Scampering backward toward the north wall, he just barely escaped the spray of glass and caustic liquid as one after another of the chemical containers exploded with a series of fiery pops. He shielded his eyes and searched frantically for a clear path to the far side of the lab where the refrigerator was located. Finally, he spotted it: a tunnel of sorts between two soapstone workbenches that looked just wide enough for him to crawl through.

He hadn't gotten very far when he heard a loud, crackling noise above him. He looked up just in time to see that the ceiling was coming down. Instinctively, he tucked himself into a tight ball as a maelstrom of flaming rafters and construction debris fell all around him. When it subsided, he looked up and saw that the tunnel was still clear. Behind him, however, there was a wall of flames where there had once been a doorway. *Only one way to go now.*

He crawled forward to the narrow tunnel, flattening himself to the ground as he approached it.

Snaking his way on his belly and his elbows, he blocked out of his mind the intense heat that was blistering his exposed skin. *Five more feet . . . three more feet . . . two more feet!* Suddenly, there was a loud crash behind him as another huge section of the roof caved in, nearly crushing him beneath several hundred pounds of burning debris. He ignored it. *One more foot . . . six inches . . . he was out!*

He felt woozy, his vision blurry. But his goal was in sight. He saw the refrigerator through the haze of smoke and scrambled toward it. Rising to his feet and staggering to the fridge, he pulled on the handle, barely managing to open it with the remaining strength in his arms. He could hardly make out the objects inside the darkened refrigerator. To his dismay, there were dozens of cylindrical vials, canisters, and flasks. "Second shelf," he recalled Julie saying. *But was that from the top or the bottom?*

A loud crackling sound above caught his attention. In the same instant, he spotted a single cylindrical container on the second shelf from the bottom. *That must be it!* He reached for it . . . felt the hard plastic cylinder between his fingers. Then he heard another loud crack above him. Suddenly, everything around him exploded in a barrage of debris and fire as a huge section of the burning roof came crashing down.

His vision dimmed, then went completely dark.

Kathleen couldn't wait by the back door any longer. Ignoring the tight feeling in her lungs, she sprinted along the back of the building, sloshing through wet grass and mud puddles. She rounded the corner to the side of the building, then rounded the corner to the front. As the parking lot came into view, she stopped for a moment and gawked in disbelief.

It was pandemonium.

A hook-and-ladder truck was parked parallel to the curb just in front of the building, with at least half a dozen firefighters in full protective gear scurrying around it. Two hoses were already trained on the blazing building, pumping powerful streams of water into the flames and onto the partially collapsed roof. Two other firefighters were busily stretching a third hose from a smaller pumper truck parked on Gateway Drive, adjacent to the parking lot. At the back of the lot, an unorganized crowd of people stared and pointed, some holding their hands over their mouths in apparent disbelief. A policewoman was trying, with little success, to push the crowd farther back toward the tree line.

"I need help!" Kathleen screamed as she approached the nearest firefighter, a stocky man with a ruddy face and strong Irish features. He wore full protective turnout gear—thick fireproof jacket and pants, gloves, boots, and a yellow fire helmet with a clear Plexiglas visor. "There's someone inside there!" she shouted over the roar of the fire, pointing toward the building.

"Where?"

"I don't know. He went in about five minutes ago to get—"

"Is that him?" shouted the fireman, cutting her off. He was pointing to the front of the building, where two firefighters were just emerging through a curtain of smoke. They were covered with black soot and breathing through masks connected to compressed air tanks. One of them was carrying the limp body of Carlos Guiterez.

"Oh my God!" Kathleen screamed, taking a step in their direction.

"Whoa!" The ruddy-faced fireman held up his arm to restrain her. "You need to wait over th—"

Kathleen ducked under the fireman's arm and raced to Carlos, who was slung like a sack of potatoes over a firefighter's shoulder. "Carlos!" she shouted as she approached him.

"Hey, lady!" yelled the ruddy-faced fireman, catching up to Kathleen and seizing her roughly by the arm. "You can't be here!" He escorted her across the parking lot and Gateway Drive to another parking lot, where two ambulances and several other emergency vehicles were parked, their flashing lights glinting off the wet asphalt in a disorienting collage of blue, yellow, and red. "Stay here!" he instructed sternly.

Kathleen nodded. She waited anxiously for Carlos to arrive, pacing back and forth in front of the two ambulances. Finally, she spotted him being carried across the street on a stretcher by two EMTs. She ran to him and walked beside the stretcher as the EMTs ferried him to the nearest of the two ambulances. He was conscious now—coughing hoarsely and rubbing his eyes. His face was covered with soot, his clothes ripped and burned. Kathleen could see charred, bloody skin through one of the large holes in his shirt.

"Carlos! Are you okay?"

He nodded slightly, still coughing and wheezing loudly.

"You shouldn't have gone in there . . . it's my fault! I'm sorry—"

"Ma'am, I need you to step back," said one of the EMTs as they prepared to lift Carlos's stretcher into the ambulance.

Carlos managed a weak smile and stretched out a clenched fist, as if to give her something. Instinctively, Kathleen extended her palm, and Carlos dropped a small, cylindrical object into it.

Holding up the object in the rain, Kathleen observed that it was a dark gray plastic sample container—about the size of a film canister—with a screw-on lid sealed with yellow Teflon tape. She smiled and touched his cheek. "Thank you, Carlos . . . Thank you."

Carlos closed his eyes and seemed to drift off as the EMTs hoisted him into the back of the ambulance. Seconds later, the ambulance doors closed, and Kathleen watched as it pulled out of the parking lot and accelerated down Gateway Drive toward the highway, sirens blaring. The two EMTs turned their attention to Kathleen, who was still bleeding from her forehead. They quickly dressed the wound with a square adhesive bandage and insisted that she let an ambulance take her to the hospital for further treatment. She steadfastly refused. Eventually, they relented.

"Just wait here," one of the EMTs instructed,

wrapping a thermal blanket around her shoulders.

Kathleen nodded, and the two EMTs trotted back across the street to the scene of the fire, leaving her alone in the parking lot, freezing and soaking wet.

She looked across the street at the charred, burning mess that had once been Quantum Life Sciences—her company, her dreams, her . . . everything. It was all gone now. *Except* . . . She glanced down at the small container in her hand and wiped soot and rainwater from the lid. The handwritten label was now an unreadable smudge of black ink. She pursed her lips and shook her head pensively.

"Dr. Sainsbury?" said a deep voice behind her.

Kathleen turned to see a well-dressed man in a khaki raincoat approaching. He was handsome in every respect, except for a long, purplish scar that ran diagonally down the left side of his face. "I'm with the fire department," he explained in an official tone. "I need to ask you a few questions. Follow me, please."

Kathleen nodded numbly and followed the man south on Gateway Drive, away from the fire trucks, away from the police cars and ambulances, away from the TV cameras and the gawking crowd. It was beginning to rain harder now, and she was getting thoroughly soaked. She struggled to keep up with the man, who was walking very quickly, several paces ahead of her.

"Where are we going?" she said, as they rounded a corner and began walking toward a cluster of newly constructed suites at the far perimeter of the office park. The vacant units were situated at the very back of a newly cleared parcel of land, which jutted lengthwise several hundred yards into the surrounding forest.

"Just over here," said the man in the raincoat. "Where it's quieter."

CHAPTER FORTY-FIVE

Eilat, Israel.

ELIAS Rubin paced slowly across the terra-cotta floor of his living room as a dozen logistical problems churned in his head. The seven members of the Olam Foundation were to meet in less than forty-eight hours. Guillermo Gomez had agreed to play host at his estate on Andros Island. Easy enough.

Getting seven of the most important people on the planet to change their schedules for this meeting had been no simple task, especially on such short notice. But he'd managed to get it done. He, himself, would board a private jet tomorrow afternoon for the seven-hour flight to the Bahamas. The other members had all made similar arrangements.

But now there was a much larger problem causing him concern.

Something very important was missing—indeed, the entire reason for the meeting. The DNA sample from Quantum Life Sciences. The

Nephilim gene. Without it, the meeting would
have to be cancelled.

He shook his head and exhaled angrily.

Time to give Venfeld another call.

CHAPTER FORTY-SIX

"**WHY** do we have to go way over here?" Kathleen asked, still following a few paces behind the man in the raincoat.

"Just some routine questions," said Luce Venfeld. He pointed toward a sleek black BMW at the edge of the otherwise empty parking lot. "I'm parked right over there." The only other vehicle in the parking lot was a rusty bulldozer.

Nice car for a fire inspector, Kathleen was just thinking to herself when Venfeld suddenly turned and jabbed his Beretta pistol hard into her ribs. Simultaneously, he clamped his hand around her arm so tightly that it nearly cut off her circulation. She could feel the barrel of the gun poking painfully into her rib cage.

"Let go of me!" she demanded angrily, trying unsuccessfully to free her arm from Venfeld's ruthless grip.

"Shut up!"

Kathleen looked around frantically for help, but to her dismay, she realized they were alone in the rainy, windswept parking lot, hidden behind a cluster of unoccupied buildings. She could still hear the faint commotion from the fire down the street, but everyone there was out of sight now, and well out of earshot.

She tried again to wriggle her arm free from Venfeld's grasp, grunting and wincing with pain. But it was no use. "What do you want?" she said through gritted teeth.

"I want that sample," said Venfeld, his tone cool and measured.

"What sample?"

Venfeld pulled her close and poked the gun harder into her ribs. "Don't play dumb, Dr. Sainsbury. I just saw your colleague give you something back there, a small vial of some sort. I know it's the DNA sample—the Nephilim gene. And I want it."

Kathleen felt heat rising in her face. Her eyes burned with anger. *You son of a bitch,* she thought to herself. *You're the one!*

"Oh, I know all about that sample," said Venfeld, reading her anger. "And I know about your mother's Ph.D. thesis on the Nephilim, too. I think you'll find I'm quite informed about the whole situation." He pulled her tighter, bruising her arm. "And I know you're a gifted scientist. Which is why I'm confident you'll make the logical decision here."

"What decision?"

"Hand the DNA sample over to me and everything will be fine." He paused to let that notion sink in, then he jabbed the gun harder into her ribs. "Otherwise, you're going to die. Right here, right now. It's your choice, doctor. But either way, I'm going to get that sample."

Kathleen felt the blood draining from her head. The neoprene sample container was in the right pocket of her jeans, pressing tightly against her leg. "All right," she said resignedly, nodding toward her pocket. "Let go of my arm."

Venfeld stared at her intently, apparently sizing up her intentions. Then, raising his pistol to within inches of her forehead, he released his grip on her arm. "Don't try anything stupid."

Kathleen's heart was beating like a drum, reverberating in her ears, pumping adrenaline throughout her body. She was terrified and confused and furious all at once. "Who are you?" she said bitterly, digging through her pocket in no particular hurry.

"You don't need to know that. Suffice it to say I'm a businessman with a very demanding client."

"A client who steals other peoples' research?"

Venfeld frowned and planted the barrel of the 9 mm pistol directly on her forehead. "I suggest you stop asking questions and give me that sample. Now!"

Kathleen swallowed hard. She'd pushed her luck far enough with this psychopath. She retrieved the dark gray container from her pocket and held it tight in her hand.

Venfeld watched her every move, keeping the barrel of the gun trained precisely on the center of her forehead. "Good girl," he said with a crooked smile, extending his open palm toward her. "Now, hand it over."

Kathleen sighed heavily as a series of thoughts flashed through her head. *Carlos had risked his life to retrieve this sample. Sargon had died mysteriously. Jeremy had nearly been shot to death. And my parents . . .*

"C'mon, let's go!" Venfeld said, wiggling his fingers expectantly.

Kathleen made a move to hand the small container to him, then chaos suddenly erupted behind her.

There was a loud screech of tires as a dark blue sedan careened around the corner and skidded to a halt about twenty feet away. The driver's side door swung open and a familiar voice shouted, "Freeze!"

Venfeld lunged for the plastic container, smacking Kathleen's hand just as she tried to pull it away. The small cylinder flew through the air and hit the ground several feet away, skittering across the wet asphalt surface.

"I said freeze!" shouted the man who had now jumped out of the dark blue sedan. It was Agent Wills, holding a SIG P229 pistol in a Weaver stance, his shooting arm extended straight, left hand supporting the weight of the gun, body at a 45 degree angle. The gun was trained directly on Venfeld.

Venfeld reacted instantly. He stepped behind Kathleen and wrapped his left arm tightly around her torso, squeezing her so hard she could barely breathe. With his right hand, he pressed the barrel of his pistol tightly against her right temple. Together, they walked backward, slowly toward his car, the gun pressed tightly against her head.

"Let her go!" Wills called out, still frozen in his firing stance.

Kathleen locked eyes with Wills, as if to say, "What should I do?" But there was nothing she could do. She was simply a prop now, a human shield. She was walking backward with Venfeld, following his lead as if they were paired in some sort of bizarre dance. Out of the corner of her eye, she spotted the sample container on the ground, still rolling slowly toward the curb.

"You're making a big mistake," said Wills.

The backward dance stopped. They were at the car. Kathleen felt the pressure on her temple release, and, a split second later, she heard the car door opening. Her body was still positioned directly in Wills's line of fire—providing the perfect shield for Venfeld. She felt some jostling as Venfeld maneuvered himself around the car door. Then, suddenly, she was shoved hard from behind.

Gunfire erupted all around. The force of the fall knocked the wind out of Kathleen's lungs, and for a moment, she wondered if she'd been shot. Seconds later, the BMW's engine roared to life and its rear tires spun out on the wet asphalt, producing an ear-piercing squeal and a cloud of bluish smoke.

More gunfire.

Kathleen looked up to see the BMW accelerating straight toward Agent Wills, who was still positioned near his vehicle, gun trained on the charging sports car. He fired one last shot through the BMW's windshield before leaping out of the way. A split second later, the BMW whizzed through the spot where Wills had been standing, ripping the Crown Victoria's open door clear off its hinges. The severed car door sailed through the air and skidded across the pavement some twenty feet away with a loud scrape of metal and breaking glass.

The BMW braked hard as it reached Gateway Drive, spun ninety degrees to the left, and accelerated again with another loud squeal of tires. By now, Wills had picked himself off the ground and jumped into the blue Crown Vic. He threw the car in reverse and whipped the wheel around, spinning the car 180 degrees. "Stay here!" he shouted to Kathleen through the opening in the driver's side of the car. Then he punched the accelerator and peeled out of the parking lot. Kathleen watched incredulously as the Crown Vic veered sharply onto Gateway Drive and sped north after the fleeing BMW.

For a few moments, she remained prone on the wet asphalt, stunned, her heart racing wildly. Until just a few minutes ago, she'd never even seen a handgun up close, let alone had one pressed to her head. Haltingly, she stood and scanned the parking lot behind her, vaguely worried that someone else might be lurking in the woods.

Then she remembered the sample container. Quickly, she scanned the pavement where she'd seen it a few moments ago, but it was gone.

Then she noticed the storm drain.

"Oh no!" she cried, sprinting toward the metal grate.

She reached the gutter and immediately

dropped to her knees and peered inside. A small river of rainwater was pouring in, making a soft gurgling sound at the surface and a deeper, splashing sound somewhere far below, presumably in the sewer. A thick, muddy tangle of leaves, twigs, and construction debris clogged the gutter, forming a dam that forced the rainwater to snake its way over.

Flattening herself on the asphalt, she stuck her face directly into the gutter, scanning its dark, mucky interior. As her eyes adjusted to the darkness, she spotted something gray and yellow wedged between a pair of twigs. The sample container was perched precariously above the chute that led down into the sewer.

Kathleen held her breath and extended her hand carefully into the storm drain, stretching until her shoulder was pressed tightly against the cast iron lip that lined its opening. Ignoring the pain, she pushed her arm in as far as it would go, extending her fingertips toward the sample bottle. *Almost there . . . almost . . .* She felt the plastic container brush momentarily against the tip of her middle finger and gasped in horror as it tipped away and fell downward, out of sight.

Grimacing, she shoved her arm even farther into the storm drain, stretching every tendon as she maneuvered her hand down the chute where the container had just fallen. With one last effort, she plunged her hand downward and grasped a huge handful of slithery leaves and twigs. Then slowly, carefully, she extracted the fistful of muck from the sewer.

With her arm now free, she opened her clenched fist. There, amongst the tangle of debris in her palm, was the sample bottle—dirty and wet, but with its yellow Teflon seal still intact. Breathing a sigh of relief, she plucked it out of the muck, carefully wiped off the grime and dirt, and slipped it back into the pocket of her soaking-wet jeans.

She was just gaining her feet when she heard someone shout behind her, "Dr. Sainsbury!" Her nerves twitched; the last time someone said that, she'd wound up with a gun to her head.

She spun and saw the Channel 7 reporter trotting toward her from Gateway Drive, an umbrella in one hand, a microphone in the other. A cameraman and a small crowd of people followed close behind. "Dr. Sainsbury!" he shouted again, quickly approaching her. Seconds later, the microphone was in her face. "Can you tell us what just happened?" he asked breathlessly.

"Uh . . ."

More people were now entering the parking lot, pressing all around her.

"Are you okay?" someone in the crowd asked. "We heard shots!"

"Step aside, folks!" shouted a security guard who'd just arrived on the scene. He was trying, unsuccessfully, to push his way through the growing crowd.

A woman screamed at Kathleen in a shrill, grating voice, "This is what happens when you try to steal God's divine powers!"

Kathleen wanted them all to leave. *Why*

wouldn't they just leave her alone? Her business was burning down, for God's sake!

"Do you know who fired the shots?" asked the reporter, still jostling for a position at the front of the crowd. He shoved the microphone close to her mouth. "Who was in those cars?"

Kathleen's head was spinning. "Uh . . ."

Still more people were joining the crowd, pressing closer, elbowing for position. The security guard bellowed for everyone to back up, but the crowd ignored him, pressing ever closer to Kathleen. The lady with the shrill voice shouted again—something about "sin." To which a male voice in the crowd replied, "Shut the hell up, lady!"

Kathleen was starting to feel claustrophobic and panicky. Suddenly, above the crowd noise, she heard the rumble of an automobile engine coming closer, growing louder.

"Look out!" someone in the crowd shouted. "He's not stopping!" The crowd began to disperse.

It was not the BMW as Kathleen had feared, but instead, a white Chevy Suburban driving toward her, allowing just enough time for the crowd to part as it approached. Kathleen could see the driver but did not recognize him. *The man in the front passenger's seat, however . . .*

"Watch it!" someone yelled as the white Suburban pressed forward, revving its engine in warning. Kathleen held her breath and stood in frozen amazement as the vehicle approached.

At the last second, the Suburban swerved left and pulled up alongside Kathleen, stopping abruptly. Kathleen watched anxiously as the tinted, passenger-side window descended with a soft, motorized whirring sound. As the man in the passenger's seat came into view, she gasped in disbelief. "*Bill?*"

"Yeah, it's me," replied Bill McCreary. "Get in the back . . . hurry!"

"But . . . where are we going?" Kathleen was still trying to get over the shock of seeing Bill McCreary . . . *here* . . . after all this time.

"I'll explain on the way. Hurry! Before these people eat you alive!" McCreary nodded at the crowd that was now inching back toward her.

Confused and bewildered, Kathleen opened the rear door and climbed into the Suburban, the crowd quickly converging behind her. "What about my wife?" someone screamed. "It's Satan!" shrieked the woman with the shrill voice, pointing at the Suburban. "It's Satan in there!"

Kathleen shut the door, and the Suburban immediately lurched forward, honking and revving its engine as it pushed through the crowd once again. Seconds later, the driver made an abrupt right turn and drove up and over the grassy median strip, bouncing down onto Gateway Drive on the other side. He then straightened the wheel and accelerated smoothly away.

Once they'd cleared the Gateway Office Park and made a right turn onto Enterprise Drive, McCreary looked back from the front seat and flashed Kathleen a quick smile. "Bet you're surprised to see me," he said.

CHAPTER FORTY-SEVEN

AGENT Wills spotted the black BMW several hundred yards ahead, making a sharp left turn onto Middleton Road and cutting across two lanes of oncoming traffic in the process. Wills gunned the Crown Vic's 235-horsepower engine and squinted as cold wind and rain blew through the hole in the side of the car, pelting his face and making it nearly impossible to see. As the Crown Vic topped 60 miles per hour, it became obvious he couldn't continue the pursuit any longer.

"Son of a bitch," he muttered as he hit the brakes and pulled the damaged sedan to the side of the road. He picked up the radio and selected Channel One for the Montgomery County police dispatcher. "Montgomery County Base One, this is FBI unit seven frank nine, in pursuit of a code twenty-six, northbound Middleton Road at Route Three fifty-five. Suspect is armed. Request APB, code three."

A crackly female voice responded. "Roger seven frank nine. What's the vehicle description?"

"Black late-model BMW," Wills responded.

"Virginia tags . . . zebra . . . victor . . . mary . . . five . . . five . . . two."

"Roger, seven frank nine."

Seconds later, Wills listened as the dispatcher passed the same message to a Rockville police patrol unit in the area.

A crackly male voice responded: "Base One, one five six, we're on our way."

Satisfied with the response, Wills switched to the FBI frequency and called in his situation, requesting vehicle assistance. Then he dialed Agent Hendricks on his cell phone.

Hendricks answered on the first ring. "Hey," she protested, "you left without me!"

"Yeah, sorry about that. I couldn't find you."

"Well, did you check the ladies' room?"

"Oops," said Wills with a hint of sarcasm. "I must've missed that one."

"What do you want, anyway?" said Hendricks, obviously not amused.

"I need you to run down a set of Virginia tags for me. Zebra victor mary five five two."

"Who do those belong to?"

"That's what I want *you* to find out."

CHAPTER FORTY-EIGHT

KATHLEEN Sainsbury was feeling anxious, to say the least. She was sitting in the backseat of a Chevy Suburban traveling east on I–270. She didn't know where she was going. And, more perplexingly, she didn't know why Bill Mc-Creary, her former NIH colleague and research partner—a man she hadn't seen for more than two years—was sitting in the front passenger's seat. "You want to tell me what's going on here?" she asked finally.

"It's complicated," said McCreary over his shoulder.

"Complicated?" Kathleen laughed bitterly. "Ten minutes ago, someone was holding a gun to my head. My employees have been shot at . . . my building's been torched, my research sabotaged. Bill, trust me, complicated doesn't even come close!"

"Okay, fair enough. But it's . . . well, it's hard to know where to start."

"Start from the beginning."

"Right." McCreary paused and then pointed to

the man driving the Suburban. "First of all, this is my assistant, Steve Goodwin."

Goodwin raised an arm and waved backward, glancing at Kathleen in the rearview mirror.

A half minute passed in silence as McCreary stared out the window at the road, apparently gathering his thoughts. Finally, he turned to Kathleen and met her eyes. "How long's it been since we've seen each other?"

Kathleen ran a quick calculation in her head. "A little over two years. In fact, if I recall correctly, it was exactly two years ago this past Saturday that we both got fired . . . uh, sorry . . . the day our program was terminated . . . without cause." Kathleen was still bitter that their research project at NIH had ended so abruptly, seemingly without explanation or warning. To her, it had always seemed like they'd been summarily fired—and unfairly at that.

"Yeah . . ." said McCreary sheepishly. "I guess *that* would be the beginning."

Kathleen shifted in her seat.

McCreary lowered his voice and cast his eyes downward. "Kathleen, the reason our project was terminated . . . is that I recommended it be terminated."

"You *what*?"

"Now, hear me out on this—"

"You recommended—" The word got caught in her throat. Her thoughts were suddenly a jumble of anger, resentment, and disbelief. "What do you mean you *recommended* it be terminated?"

"Okay, now, remember we were working on

a tiny offshoot of the Human Genome Project. Hardly anyone even knew what we were doing."

"Of course I remember, Bill. I was there. I remember it like it was yesterday. It was a skunk works project. Tiny budget. Small staff. Barely any oversight. That's the way we wanted it, right? I mean, even if no one else was paying attention, we knew the significance of it."

"Right," McCreary interjected. "We knew the significance of what we were working on. We were searching for the secret to aging . . . the secret to life."

Kathleen said nothing. *Where's he going with this?*

"We were trying to pinpoint exactly where aging is programmed into the human genome and, more important, how to reprogram it. That was our goal, right? Team Methuselah."

Kathleen rolled her eyes at the stupid moniker. It was a slang term McCreary had coined early in the project, and she'd always hated it. "That's right," she said. "And we were close to finding it, too."

"Actually," said McCreary, arching his eyebrows high above his glasses, "we were closer than you think."

His words lingered in the air as Kathleen pondered their import. She cocked her head back and shot him a suspicious look. "What are you talking about?"

McCreary drew a deep breath. "Remember when you took a couple weeks off in March, just before our project was, uh . . . terminated?"

"Sure, I took my grandfather down to Sarasota. But why——" Then it suddenly hit her. "Oh, don't tell me."

McCreary nodded affirmatively.

"You found it?"

McCreary continued nodding. "I found its location. A couple of days after you left."

Kathleen was stunned. "I . . . I . . . don't believe it." She was still shaking her head slowly from side to side."

"Middle of chromosome fourteen. About eighty-thousand base pairs, retroviral in nature. Sound about right?"

Unbelievable, Kathleen thought to herself. *McCreary had found the location of the INDY gene more than two years ago.* "But how?" she asked.

"Dumb luck. I stumbled across it one afternoon just doing a routine screening for extinct viral fragments. As soon as I saw it, I knew there was something odd about that sequence, something really unique. It was heavily degraded but still distinguishable from the rest of the junk around it. I did a bit of reverse engineering and figured out what the original virus probably looked like, a retrovirus almost entirely unique to the Cercopithecinae subfamily of Old World monkeys. After a few days of research, I knew it had to be . . . it just *had* to be the INDY gene." He paused. "You know, it's weird. We always thought the INDY gene would be something elegant and special. Turns out, the brass ring we'd been looking for all that time was just a random clump of viral DNA on chromosome fourteen, hidden among a bunch of other junk DNA. Right there in plain sight."

Kathleen nodded clumsily. She knew everything he was saying was true. Her research had confirmed the exact same thing.

"Of course, the INDY sequence is heavily degraded in the human genome. That's why it was so hard to find and why it's no longer functional. But, with enough research, I knew we could eventually reverse-engineer the original sequence."

"But . . . why didn't you tell me? I was your research partner."

"I wanted to, Kathleen. I swear. I almost called you that week. But I just kept thinking . . ." His voice trailed off.

"You kept thinking what?"

"I kept thinking about the consequences."

"What consequences? The INDY gene was exactly what we were looking for. It was the whole goal of our project! What was the problem?"

"Kathleen, no offense, but my concerns were much bigger than you and me. These were national security concerns . . . human race concerns. I needed to bring them to a higher level."

"Who, Brinard?" Kathleen was referring to Jean Brinard, the head of their research group at NIH at the time, whom neither she nor McCreary respected very much.

"No, not Brinard. Higher."

"Dr. D'Angelo?"

"Higher."

"Higher than the director of NIH?"

"Yeah," said McCreary, arching his eyebrows. "I called Peter Stonewell."

"Secretary Stonewell? You went straight to HHS?"

"Kathleen, I needed someone with the appropriate perspective. Not Jean, not D'Angelo. I needed someone who could look past the scientific thrill of it all and see the bigger picture. I figured Stonewell was the right guy. And I was right."

Kathleen was still shaking her head in disbelief. "I can't believe you've known about chromosome fourteen for two years and haven't published a single paper or breathed a word about it to anyone, including me. That's not how science works, Bill, and you know it." Kathleen could barely control her anger. It wasn't right to sit on this type of discovery. Not something this important—a technology that could potentially save millions of lives, a technology that people needed now. She pictured her grandfather, sitting alone at Garrison Manor, lost in the dark and terrifying world of Alzheimer's disease, while McCreary—Mr. Big Picture—pondered "concerns."

"So what were these *concerns* you had about our research?" said Kathleen coldly.

"Hold that thought," said McCreary, raising his index finger. "We're almost there."

"Almost where?"

"DARPA. It's where I work now."

Kathleen knew the acronym but couldn't remember exactly what it stood for. She gave it her best shot: "Defense . . . Acquisition . . . Readiness . . . ?"

"No," McCreary corrected her. "Defense Advanced Research Projects Agency. I'm a program manager there now."

Kathleen detected a ring of pride in McCreary's voice. And now she was starting to understand. *McCreary had scuttled their research for a promotion. He'd sacrificed all their work for a sexy job title!* She could really feel the heat rising in her face now.

Five minutes later, the three of them were walking up the sidewalk to the glass-enclosed headquarters of the Defense Advanced Research Projects Agency. There were a few minutes of administrative protocol—mainly involving McCreary vouching for Kathleen—then they headed back to his office.

Kathleen was amazed by the phalanx of security measures, which seemed to get more intense as they approached McCreary's area, OSNS. "Jeez, what do you do back here?" she asked half jokingly.

"You wouldn't believe it if I told you. Which I can't."

Finally, they arrived at the door to the "Logistics Analysis" office. Kathleen read the placard on the door aloud, unimpressed.

"Don't let the name fool you," said McCreary, unlocking the door with a simple metal key. Considering all the security measures they'd just passed through, the key seemed downright quaint. The three of them entered the room, and

McCreary closed and locked the door behind them.

"Okay," said Kathleen in an exasperated tone, "*now* can you tell me what this is all about?"

McCreary spoke in a serious, emphatic voice. "Kathleen, what I'm about to tell you is highly classified. It's considered Special Compartmented Information, which means this information is deemed extremely sensitive and vital to the security of the United States. Do you understand?"

Kathleen nodded, though she really didn't appreciate the preachy tone.

"The SCI code name for this program is SER-RATE, and only a handful of people in the entire government know about it. Even the director here at DARPA isn't fully read into the program."

Why all the drama? Kathleen was wondering.

McCreary nodded to Goodwin, who responded by handing Kathleen a small stack of papers. "So, before I begin, I have to ask you to sign these forms, acknowledging that disclosure of this information is a felony, punishable by up to ten years in prison and a fine of up to fifty thousand dollars, or both."

"Whoa! Hold it right there!" Kathleen held up her hand in protest. She'd lost patience with all of this nonsense. "I'm not signing anything, okay? I mean, if you want to play super-spy and call your program 'SERRATE' or 'Team Methuselah' or whatever, that's your business. But don't try to drag me into it, okay? I'm a private citizen. I run a private company, engaged in private-sector research. I'm not affiliated with NIH or the government anymore. *Thanks to you.*" She couldn't resist taking another dig at McCreary. "So either tell me what's going on here . . . or take me back to Rockville." She glared at her former colleague, beaming her displeasure. "Do *you* understand?"

McCreary and Goodwin exchanged troubled glances. Finally, McCreary tossed the paperwork onto Goodwin's desk and reluctantly motioned for Kathleen to have a seat. "Fine," he said with a sigh. "Have it your way."

CHAPTER FORTY-NINE

Interstate 270 East, Maryland.

LUCE Venfeld threaded his car aggressively through eastbound traffic on I–270, thankful that the afternoon exodus from Washington was not yet in full swing. In any event, he was heading in the opposite direction. With luck, he'd be in Bethesda in twenty minutes. As he zipped from lane to lane, he listened intently to the deep, accented voice broadcasting over the car's speakerphone.

"When will I have it?" asked Elias Rubin. His voice was guttural and croaky.

"Soon," Venfeld replied. "I'm on my way to get it now."

"We must have it by tomorrow morning," Rubin said. "Is that clear?"

"You'll have it."

There was a long, uncomfortable pause. "I trust you understand just how much money's at stake."

Venfeld tightened his grip on the steering

wheel. *Of course he knew how much money was at stake! Hundreds of millions of dollars, perhaps billions.* "Yes," he said stoically, "I understand."

"Then you'll understand why I'm very concerned about this situation. You told me three days ago I'd have that sample. And I still don't have it."

"I told you, I hit a snag. But it's been taken care of."

"I don't want to hear about snags, Mr. Venfeld." Rubin's dictum was precise and slow. Deadly serious. "A meeting of the foundation has been convened based on your representation that the sample would be delivered three days ago. The members are on their way as we speak. If I don't have that sample by tomorrow morning—"

"You'll have it," said Venfeld assuredly. "I'm on my way to get it right now."

"Very well, then. You know where the meeting is."

"Yes."

There was another long stretch of silence. "Mr. Venfeld, I'm also very concerned about that newspaper article."

Venfeld sighed. "Yeah, me, too."

"This technology only has value to us if it's exclusive. If the sequence becomes publicly disclosed, the deal's off. Is that clear?"

"Yes."

"I expect to have that sample tomorrow morning," said Rubin, hanging up abruptly.

Venfeld frowned. He'd almost had that sample in his hands an hour ago, but that stupid cop screwed it all up. He punched the accelerator and swerved sharply around a lumbering FedEx truck in the left lane.

As Venfeld merged his BMW onto the inner loop of the Capital Beltway, his thoughts drifted back—as they always did—to the money. Yachts and villas and airplanes suddenly materialized in his mind. He wanted that money. He needed it, like an alcoholic needs a drink.

Nobody was going to stand between him and a hundred million dollars. Least of all some idiot cop.

CHAPTER FIFTY

BILL McCreary paced back and forth in front of the conference table in his office, where Kathleen was seated. "When I started at NIH," he said, "I was working directly under Dr. Andrew Wilson, one of the first scientists to study DNA. A certifiable genius. A legend . . ."

"Yeah, I've heard of him," said Kathleen sarcastically.

"Of course. But do you know why Dr. Wilson left NIH?"

"I remember it had something to do with patent rights."

"Well, that was part of it. Dr. Wilson was concerned about what was happening with the Human Genome Project. He was concerned about private companies being allowed to obtain patents for human gene sequences. He was also concerned about the sheer amount of data NIH was publishing about the human genome. He perceived certain dangers inherent in making such a huge amount of data widely available to the public, particularly to other researchers. In confidence, he once likened it to publishing the blueprints for the atomic bomb. Some things, he said, are just better kept secret—even at the expense of scientific progress."

"That's ridiculous," Kathleen interrupted. "The human genome is nothing like the atomic bomb."

"And that's exactly what Dr. D'Angelo and the other higher-ups at NIH said. So, eventually, Dr. Wilson left NIH in protest. And you'll recall that he died just a few months later."

"Sure, I remember. But what does this have to do with the . . . SERRATE program, or whatever you call it?"

"Just think about it for a second. The man who practically discovered DNA—arguably the most renowned geneticist in the world, an undisputed genius—was gravely concerned about disseminating the sequenced human code to other researchers. Why? Why would Dr. Wilson, of all people, be concerned about disseminating that knowledge?"

Kathleen shrugged. She didn't care why. She didn't like the idea of anyone standing in the way of scientific progress, certifiable genius or not. "Bill, stop with the riddles, and just get to the point."

"The point," said McCreary curtly, "is that science can sometimes be its own worst enemy."

Kathleen rolled her eyes. This was typical McCreary nonsense. "Bill, what the hell does that even mean?"

"It means," said McCreary, leaning over the

conference table toward Kathleen, "that science is relentless. It moves in one direction, and that's forward . . . relentlessly, unwaveringly forward. It never slows down; only speeds up. It's an uncontainable, uncontrollable, unstoppable force. And the more enticing the goal—the shinier the brass ring, if you will—the more unstoppable it is." McCreary pushed himself away from the table and stared at Kathleen intensely, arms crossed, apparently trying to gauge her reaction.

"Sorry, Bill, you lost me. Science is . . . *science*. And everything you've just said is a complete abstraction without context or meaning. Can you give me an example of how science has ever been 'its own worst enemy,' as you say?"

"Nuclear weaponry," said McCreary without missing a beat.

"Ah."

"Arguably the most important scientific achievement of the twentieth century," McCreary continued, pacing again. "Yet the United States has spent the past sixty years, and untold billions of dollars, trying to contain it. Simply trying to control it. Not just the technology itself, mind you, but the *science* behind it. But how do you control science? How do you dissuade scientists in other countries, for instance, from researching atomic weapons? From improving them? From making them better, faster, cheaper, more powerful? The answer is: you can't. At least not peacefully. So, instead, we destroy foreign weapons programs that pose a threat—sometimes overtly, sometimes covertly. We impose economic leverage, political leverage, military leverage to thwart civilian nuclear research programs. We overthrow unfriendly governments that show too keen an interest in nuclear technology. Whatever it takes to stem the tide of nuclear knowledge—channel it, confine it, contain its spread as best we can. And that's just one example of how difficult it is to control the progress of science. Are you following me?"

"I understand the dangers posed by nuclear proliferation, Bill," said Kathleen flatly, annoyed by McCreary's condescending tone. "What I don't see is any link between that and human genetics. So, no, I'm not following you at all."

McCreary rocked back on his heels and pondered her reply for a moment. "Kathleen, you and I both know there's a genetic key to longevity and that, given the pace of research into the human genome, it's just a matter of time before someone else discovers it."

"Sure. You already did . . . two years ago."

McCreary placed both hands on the table again and leaned toward Kathleen. "I'm going to put it bluntly. A rapid and widespread change in human life expectancy would create catastrophic problems around the world. It will destroy this country and maybe even humanity itself."

Kathleen stared blankly at McCreary, who had just said perhaps the most ridiculous thing she'd ever heard in her life. "Bill, you have *got* to be kidding!"

"No, I'm dead serious. And I should know. The SERRATE program is all about the study of dangerously disruptive technologies. I've been studying the potential impact of the INDY gene technology for two years now, and there is absolutely no doubt in my mind that its effect would be devastating . . . and irreversible."

"That's ridiculous. How could extending people's lives be devastating?"

McCreary threw up his hands and shook his head. "It's hard to know where to begin. Let's start with something easy. Take Social Security."

"Okay, I'm listening."

"Since the 1930s, Social Security has provided an important safety net for senior citizens. Millions of seniors depend on it for their monthly expenses—basic needs like food and shelter. Problem is, Social Security is built on a 'PAYGO' model, which means pay as you go. Are you familiar with that?"

"Sure. Current workers pay social security taxes to support current retirees. A dollar in payroll taxes goes immediately to pay a dollar in benefits to a retiree."

"Exactly," said McCreary. "And the system works fine as long as the demographics remain constant, which, of course, they don't. For instance, even the modest increase in life expectancy we've experienced in the U.S. since World War II has placed an incredible strain on the social security system. Not to mention the whole baby boom phenomenon."

"Yeah, I'm aware of that."

McCreary continued, picking up steam. "When social security was originally created in the 1930s, there were more than forty workers for every retiree. Today, there are just over three workers per retiree. As a result, payroll taxes have gone up considerably, benefits have declined, and the entire system is in danger of collapsing within the next fifteen to thirty years. The culprit, Kathleen, is demographics, pure and simple."

"Okay, but—"

McCreary cut her off. "More people are retiring each year than are entering the workforce. And those who are retiring are living longer than originally projected. Which puts a huge strain on the PAYGO system."

"I see where you're going, but—"

"So just imagine what would happen if life expectancy in this country were to suddenly increase by ten years, twenty years, fifty years. Overnight. Thanks to a new wonder drug, a new gene therapy . . ."

"I get it," Kathleen conceded with a shrug. "The system would implode. But that's only one example . . ."

"Exactly!" McCreary exclaimed, thrusting a finger at Kathleen. "That's just one example of the devastating impact the INDY gene would have on this country. And, by the way, this isn't just a U.S. phenomenon. Most of our European allies depend far more heavily on government-funded retirement than we do here in the U.S. Think about France, Germany, Sweden, Great Britain . . ."

"That's true," said Kathleen.

"And social security is just the tip of the iceberg. Medicaid and Medicare would be overrun almost immediately." McCreary nodded toward Goodwin. "We've designed some very sophisticated computer models here to study the impact of the INDY gene technology. And even using the most conservative of assumptions, every projection shows that those two programs alone would quickly balloon to more than ninety percent of GDP—clearly an unsustainable situation."

"Okay, I get it," Kathleen said. "But we'd simply adjust, right? I mean, people would work a few years longer; some retirees would go back to work, whatever it took. Congress could change the law, revamp the whole program, whatever. Things would work out."

"Yes, things would eventually work out with Social Security and healthcare," McCreary conceded, "but not before a period of tremendous social upheaval, perhaps lasting decades. Our models consistently indicate escalating unrest, political turmoil, massive economic depression, and, in many parts of the world, widespread violence. All the ingredients for revolution. And remember, we're not talking about only the U.S. This would be a worldwide phenomenon."

"But those are just models, Bill. You can't—"

McCreary cut her off again. "The strain on the economy isn't the only problem. Imagine if access to this life-extension technology were controlled by one particular person, or one particular group or country."

Kathleen resorted to nodding. It was obvious McCreary wasn't going to let her get a word in edgewise.

"Imagine North Korea, or Al-Qaeda, or some religious cult—pick your villain—having exclusive control of this technology, picking and choosing who got the treatment and who didn't. How much do you think people would pay to extend their lives or the lives of their loved ones?"

"A lot," said Kathleen, thinking about her own grandfather.

"You'd better believe it. So, as you can imagine, the transfer of wealth in such a scenario would be massive and instantaneous. And our models indicate that it would be nearly impossible to regulate. The flow of money would transcend national borders, bypass every conceivable law, skirt around every obstacle. Sales of a life-extension drug would make the cocaine trade look like a bake sale. And with all that money would come a dangerous concentration of power."

"Okay, Bill. But this is all just supposition. Computer models can't predict the future, you know that."

McCreary ignored her. "There's more. What happens if some people have access to the technology while others don't? What kind of society would we have, for instance, if only the wealthiest people could afford to have their lives extended by forty or fifty years? Our projections show something like a serfdom society arising in many parts of the world—particularly in underdeveloped parts of Africa and Asia—with wealthy people living longer and acquiring more and more wealth and power, while the short-lived class toils for day-to-day subsistence, unable to live long enough to accumulate any significant long-term wealth."

"Okay, I get the picture," Kathleen announced. "There are concerns . . ."

"And I haven't even touched on the environmental impact of this technology. Did you know there are nearly seven billion people living on earth today? And that number is growing by more than one percent a year. What do you think the global effect of the INDY gene technology would be on those numbers?"

Kathleen shrugged. "The population would go up."

"Yeah, a lot. The crude death rate would go down, at least for a period of thirty to fifty years. And, at the same time, birth rates would go up because the human fertility window would increase—people would be having babies well into their sixties and seventies. Even using conservative estimates, we've calculated an explosion in the human population of anywhere from ten to forty billion people in the next fifty years. That's clearly an unsustainable population for this planet, even assuming vigorous advances in food and resource management. In fact, our models consistently indicate widespread starvation, a subsistence standard of living throughout most of the world, including in the U.S. and Europe, and, toward the end, all-out war as desperate nations vie for dwindling resources. Kathleen, I'm not making this up. This is the consistent outcome of every simulation we've run using the most sophisticated modeling programs and computers in the world, which happen to be located right here at DARPA. It's not a pretty picture."

Kathleen didn't know what to say. It certainly wasn't a "pretty picture," at least not the way Mc-Creary had painted it. Her mind momentarily flashed back to the passage Dr. Eskridge had read the other day from the Book of Enoch, which described the Nephilim as having "devoured all which the labor of men produced; until it became impossible to feed them." Similar to McCreary's prediction of dwindling resources and mass starvation. But, on the other hand, there seemed to be a lot of guesswork involved in his predictions. How could anyone really know the outcome of this technology on a global scale? There were far too many unknowns . . . too many variables. Still, she had to admit, McCreary had raised some legitimate concerns—issues she hadn't really considered before.

"There's one more thing," McCreary added.

Kathleen wasn't sure she wanted to hear any more.

"And this may sound a little strange . . ."

Kathleen laughed dryly. "Trust me, Bill, at this point, nothing sounds strange to me." A series of thoughts flashed quickly through her mind: Dr. Sargon and the tooth, her mother's Ph.D. thesis on the Nephilim, the Tell-Fara temple, Dr. Eskridge and the Epic of Gilgamesh, the FBI, the fire. . .

"Now, this is just a personal concern, mind you," said McCreary, "not anything we've tested or modeled."

"Uh-huh."

McCreary drew a deep breath and released it. "I'm worried that this technology might actually make us, for lack of a better word, *nonhuman*."

"What?"

"Think about it. What is it, exactly, that makes us human? An easy answer, of course, is that our DNA makes us human. But we all have slightly different DNA, and our DNA differs only slightly from that of other primates, like apes and chimpanzees. So it can't just be the sum total of our DNA that makes us human. There must be some particular part of our DNA that makes us quintessentially human, something that separates us from apes yet links us all together with one unique and invariable human element. The question is, which part?"

"You think it's something on that region of chromosome fourteen?"

"Yes, I do. Mind you, I don't have any evidence to back this up. It's just a hunch. But I'm very worried that a gene therapy that activates the INDY gene might actually turn us into, well, a different species. To what effect, I don't know. Maybe for the better, maybe for the worse. But I'm concerned that this INDY technology could literally signify the end of the human race as we know it."

Kathleen thought about the book Dr. Eskridge had given her and the dark image of a fallen angel on its cover.

McCreary was about to say something else when Kathleen cut him off. "So does all of this give you the right to bury this technology forever?" Her tone was defiant and acerbic. "Why do you get to decide, on behalf of the entire scientific community, that this area of research is off-limits? *Verboten*."

"Like I said," McCreary countered, "it's complicated. HHS is simply trying to control this information as long as we can. To give us—the government, that is—more time to prepare."

"Control it? I thought you said science is unstoppable. How do you propose to control access to the entire human genome?"

McCreary adjusted his glasses. "Well, uh . . . that's where SERRATE comes in."

Kathleen stared blankly.

McCreary took a deep breath and exhaled loudly. "SERRATE was created and funded by HHS to monitor and influence the pace of private-sector research in areas that are likely to become dangerously disruptive, meaning they could pose a serious threat to the security of this country, its allies, and democracy in general. Life-extension technology is currently at the top of that list, mainly because private-sector researchers—like yourself—are already so close to it. But we are also monitoring several other technologies, including human cloning and embryonic engineering."

Kathleen was thoroughly confused. "I'm sorry, Bill, I still don't understand. How can you influence the pace of private-sector research?"

McCreary glanced at Goodwin, who shook his head subtly. "Unfortunately," he said, "that requires access to a different SCI channel, which I'm afraid I can't reveal to you at this time."

"Can't rev—?" Kathleen stopped short. A troubling thought suddenly popped into her mind. She stood up abruptly and stepped around the table to where McCreary was standing. He was a good five inches taller than she, but she locked eyes with him and fixed him with her gaze. "Bill," she said slowly, "did you have anything to do with Jeremy Fisher's shooting?"

"No!" McCreary exclaimed, shaking his head emphatically. "Absolutely not!"

Kathleen continued to press. "How about the explosion at my lab?"

"No. Kathleen, trust me, we don't do that. We don't shoot people, okay? And we don't blow up buildings."

Kathleen held his gaze and jabbed a finger at him angrily. "Bill, if you had anything to do with those things, so help me . . ."

"We didn't, Kathleen. I swear!"

Kathleen relaxed her gaze, but only slightly. "Well, do you know who did those things?"

McCreary pursed his lips tightly.

"Bill?"

"I don't know who did it, okay?" said McCreary. "But I do have a couple of hunches."

"I'm listening."

McCreary put his hand on Kathleen's shoulder. "Kathleen, I don't think you realize the danger you're in. There are people . . . organizations . . . hell, entire governments that would kill you and everyone at QLS in a heartbeat to get their hands on this technology. Do you realize that?"

Kathleen swallowed hard and nodded. *Yes, she was starting to realize that.*

"This isn't your run-of-the-mill economic es-
pionage," he continued. "This INDY technology
has the potential to affect the entire balance of
power in the world. There are national interests
at stake here . . . and likely some very bad people
involved."

Kathleen suddenly pictured the man with the
scar on his face.

"Kathleen, these things that have been happening to you in the past few days . . . well,
they're going to keep happening as long as people
think you have access to the INDY gene technology. There are organizations that want to exploit
that technology for political, economic, and even
military purposes. There are other groups who
want to destroy the technology because of their
religious or environmental beliefs. Are you familiar with Genesis six in the Bible?"

"You mean the part about man's mortal exis-
tence being limited to one hundred and twenty
years and all that?"

"Uh-huh. Some folks consider that to be a commandment, a judgment from God if you will—a
punishment even. They will not look kindly
upon this INDY gene technology, which arguably
undoes God's judgment in that respect—at least
in their view."

"Yes," Kathleen said. "So I'm told."

"Our goal with the SERRATE program is
simply to control the INDY gene technology, slow
down its progress until we—the government—
can come to grips with how to handle it."

"But Bill, what about all the people who need

this technology now, for themselves and their loved ones? Don't they deserve the opportunity to live longer, healthier, more meaningful lives? I mean, this technology isn't *evil*. It has a lot of promise to improve the lives of millions of people."

"Absolutely," said McCreary in a conciliatory tone. "But for how long, and at what cost?"

Kathleen said nothing. At this point, she really wasn't sure anymore. She needed to work some things out in her mind.

"The point is," said McCreary, his voice softening, "there are powerful forces beyond your control that are vying for this technology. Some want to exploit it—perhaps for good, perhaps for evil. Some want to destroy it. And some—and I include the U.S. government in that category—just want to slow it down. Unfortunately, at this exact moment, you're in the crosshairs of all of those forces. And that's why, in my opinion, you're in more danger than you can possibly imagine."

Kathleen felt a lump in her throat. She hadn't asked for any of this. All she'd wanted was to make a contribution to science, advance the vanguard of human knowledge, and maybe—just maybe—help a lot of people in the process. She didn't want to be in the "crosshairs" of anything, particularly something that could get her killed. She sighed heavily and looked at McCreary. "What should I do?"

"Well, that depends," said McCreary, a perceptible tone of self-satisfaction creeping into his voice. "Do you still have an intact sample from that tooth?"

"Well, I—" Kathleen stopped short. "How did you know it was a *tooth*?"

"Huh?" McCreary seemed genuinely surprised. "Well, I . . . I guess I read it in the paper. There was all that stuff about Tell-Fara—" He glanced at Goodwin.

"No," said Kathleen, shaking her head resolutely. "The newspaper used the term 'mummified remains.' I remember that specifically." She inched forward. "Bill?"

McCreary held out his open palms but said nothing further.

Which told Kathleen everything she needed to know. "You bugged my phone, didn't you?"

McCreary was backpedaling slightly, hands outstretched.

"You son of a bitch! You've been listening to my phone conversations, haven't you?"

Still McCreary said nothing.

Kathleen crossed her arms and glowered at McCreary with an expression of disgust and disbelief. "How long, Bill?"

"Kathleen—"

"How long have you been tapping my phone?"

McCreary sighed loudly and glanced again at Goodwin. "Two years. Ever since you left NIH."

Kathleen opened her mouth to say something, but nothing came out. She was simply too angry to speak. *All those private conversations!* She felt sick to her stomach.

"Kathleen, I know you're angry, and I don't blame you—"

"Screw you, Bill."

"But you have to believe me—this was a national security issue. We had authorization to do this from the very highest levels. This INDY gene technology is a serious concern, and the government isn't taking any chances." McCreary reached out to touch her arm.

"I wouldn't do that," Kathleen warned, yanking her arm away.

"Kathleen," McCreary pleaded. "I hope you understand how sorry I am."

Kathleen frowned. She certainly wasn't going to accept any apologies from McCreary—not now, *not ever*! In fact, given this new information, she was starting to wonder again about Jeremy's shooting.

McCreary inched closer. "But, Kathleen, I do need to know whether you still have that DNA sample."

Kathleen flinched. She could feel the sample container in her jeans pocket, pressing against her leg. She made a conscious effort not to glance down at it.

"Because, if you do," continued McCreary, still inching closer, "the best thing to do would be to turn it over to us. The longer you're out there walking around with it, the more danger you'll be in. Trust me when I say this. There are people out there who will stop at nothing to get their hands on that sample."

"Well," said Kathleen with a shrug, "I don't have it."

McCreary studied her face, his brow wrinkled with doubt. "Where is it?"

"Back at the lab. Probably burnt to a crisp."

"*Where* in the lab?"

Kathleen hesitated, considering her answer carefully. "In the fridge, in a canister on the second shelf, labeled 'JH–328.'"

McCreary immediately turned to Goodwin. "Call Agent Wills. Have him pull that sample from the fridge right away!"

Goodwin already had the receiver in his hand. "I'm on it."

"Special Agent Wills?" said Kathleen incredulously. "From the FBI?"

McCreary nodded affirmatively.

"He works for *you*?"

"Well, technically, he works for the FBI. But, yeah, he's sort of on loan to the SERRATE program."

Kathleen sat back down in the chair, feeling utterly overwhelmed and lightheaded. It was as if everything around her for the past two years had been an orchestrated charade. Nothing was as it seemed. Nobody was who she thought. Now, suddenly, she found herself wondering about other people who'd come into her life recently. *Bryce Whittaker? Was he on the SERRATE payroll? Dr. Eskridge? Carlos?* Her mind was racing now, trying desperately to make sense of it all.

"You okay?" asked McCreary.

Kathleen was rubbing her temples. "I'd like to go home now."

CHAPTER FIFTY-ONE

Rockville, Maryland.

AGENT Wills hung up with Steve Goodwin and immediately pushed speed dial "2" on his cell phone.

"Yeah?" answered Agent Hendricks.

"Cheryl, cancel the tow truck. I'm going back to QLS."

Wills turned his car around and started back toward Enterprise Drive. The rain had subsided a bit, but stray droplets still flew through the gaping hole where the driver's-side door used to be, pelting his face and dampening his already-wet suit. "Anything on that tag number yet?" he shouted into the phone.

"Yeah. It wasn't easy, but I think we finally figured it out. The tags didn't match the vehicle description you gave us at all. Turns out they belong to a Ford Taurus registered to a Veronica Campos in Herndon."

"Stolen tags?"

"Mm-hmm. But that's not all. Turns out there *is* no Veronica Campos, at least not anymore. She died four years ago in Costa Rica, while visiting her family. My guess is her daughter's been cashing her social security checks for the last four years."

"Any idea how her tags got on that beemer?"

"Not really. I just got off the phone with the daughter, who claims to know nothing about a BMW. Her mom did have a Ford Taurus, but her daughter sold it a couple years ago to a used car dealer. So that didn't leave us with much to go on."

"Okay . . ."

"But you said the car you were chasing was a black BMW 645i convertible, right? Late model?"

"Uh-huh."

"So, it turns out there aren't too many of those around. I went ahead and checked all the black ones that've been sold in the D.C. area in the past two years. One hundred and forty-nine. I just got through running all the names through the system—"

"And . . . ?"

"We had three possibles, two of which didn't pan out. But the last one is kind of interesting. A guy named Luce Venfeld of Arlington."

"What's so interesting about him?"

Hendricks paused. "He's ex-CIA."

Wills's eyes widened, and his grip tightened on the steering wheel.

"I couldn't access any details 'cause his file's

redacted like crazy. But he was definitely employed there for about twenty years. He left five years ago."

"What's he doing now?"

"He runs some sort of consulting firm downtown called the LHV Group."

"What do they do?"

"That's as far as I've gotten—Oh, wait, I just got something else." There was a muffled conversation that Wills couldn't quite make out and then the sound of ruffling papers. "Hey, check this out," said Hendricks, coming back on the line.

"Hmm?"

"Venfeld's registered under the Foreign Agents Registration Act."

"The what?"

"It means his firm does political lobbying on behalf of foreign companies or governments."

"Like who?"

"Hold on," said Hendricks, followed by another stretch of silence. "As far as I can tell, there's just one. Rial Laboratories of Tel Aviv, Israel."

Rial Laboratories? Wills's mind immediately began churning through ideas as he listened to Hendricks typing furiously on her computer keyboard.

"This is interesting," said Hendricks after nearly a minute.

"What's that?"

"The founder of Rial—Elias Rubin—is apparently a real character. Nothing specific on him in our files, but there's a bunch of stuff about him on the Internet."

"Like what?"

"Mainly rantings about what an asshole he is. Brilliant, apparently, but an asshole. And strange. I'm looking at a collection of all the crazy things he's said to the Israeli press over the years. A bunch of tirades about the U.S. pharmaceutical industry. He's accused them of being anti-Semitic . . . run by ex-Nazis . . . corrupt, et cetera. He's also accused the FDA of discriminating against foreign companies." She paused for several seconds. "Oh, and here's a blog about what he does with all his money. He's worth billions. He bought an entire luxury hotel in some resort town in southern Israel, and then *leveled* it so he could get a clear view of the Red Sea from his villa. Sounds like a nut job."

"Sure does," Wills mumbled. He thanked Agent Hendricks for the update, then hung up the phone. A dozen questions popped to mind at once. *Rial was involved . . . no surprise there. But who was this Venfeld character? How did he fit into the puzzle?*

Those questions would have to wait. Right now, Wills owed another visit to QLS.

CHAPTER FIFTY-TWO

THE Fire Department was just finishing up on the scene when Steve Goodwin pulled his white Suburban into the QLS parking lot. McCreary sat in the front passenger's seat. Kathleen sat in the back, surveying the mess through the Suburban's dark tinted windows. The TV news vans were gone now, as were the ambulances and most of the crowd. Kathleen's heart sank as the QLS office suite came into view. It was a charred, smoking hulk—more of a *hole* than an office suite. The adjacent units had also sustained serious damage, but they looked salvageable. QLS, on the other hand, was completely gone.

"You gonna be okay?" said McCreary with passable concern.

"Yeah," Kathleen said. "Just fine."

"Again, we can put you up somewhere safe. A hotel in the city, if you'd like . . ."

"No, I think you guys have done enough." Kathleen's tone was bitter. Deep down, she'd accepted that Bill McCreary and the SERRATE program were probably not to blame for all of this. Still, she couldn't help feeling betrayed by him, by DARPA . . . hell, by the whole United States government. Eavesdropping? Deception? Spying? *And these were supposed to be the good guys?* As much as she wanted some protection right now, she simply didn't know whom to trust.

Kathleen got out of the Suburban without saying a word and made her way straight to the front of the building. An exiting fireman tried to stop her, but she easily sidestepped him and continued marching up the walkway to the front door, or at least what *used* to be the front door.

The pungent smell of wet, charred wood and burned plastic nearly overwhelmed her as she stepped through the gaping hole. She walked carefully over small mountains of smoldering debris, gingerly avoiding twisted metal, protruding nails, and broken glass, and eventually made her way to the blackened remains of the laboratory refrigerator. The door was partially torn off, hanging awkwardly by just the bottom hinge. Kathleen forced it open farther and peered inside. The glass shelves were all broken and lying in a pile of shards at the bottom of the fridge, intermixed with wet ash and globs of black goop. The neoprene sample bottles had all melted in the fire. *Everything was gone.*

"Not much left in there, huh?" said a voice behind her.

Kathleen recognized the voice of Agent Wills. She shook her head despondently without turning around.

Wills stepped closer. "I know this won't be

much of a consolation," he said, "but we think we know what caused this."

Kathleen turned and saw that Wills wasn't alone. Bill McCreary was standing next to him. "What's that?" she asked.

Wills pointed to the smoking remains of the hazardous waste area in one corner of the lab. "The fire started over there, near that electrical outlet. A utility pole a couple blocks from here got hit by lightning just before the fire broke out. So my guess would be that outlet shorted."

Lightning. Kathleen absorbed that information with a sense of irony. *God strikes again.*

"Also, you'll be glad to know your colleague, Carlos Guiterez, is doing fine. He's at Montgomery County Hospital being treated for smoke inhalation and burns. They'll probably keep him there overnight, but he'll be fine."

Kathleen closed her eyes and sighed with relief. "Thank you," she said with genuine appreciation.

"Dr. Sainsbury," said Wills earnestly, "is there *anything* else we can do for you? Do you need a ride somewhere?"

"No, I'll be okay." Right now, all she wanted was to be left alone. She had a lot of thinking to do and desperately needed a shower, a change of clothes, and—most important—some sleep.

"Okay then," said Wills, handing her his card. "If anyone tries to contact you, or if you see anything suspicious—*anything at all*—call that number right away, okay?"

Kathleen nodded that she would.

"Now if you'll excuse me." Wills flashed a wry

smile. "I've got to go explain to my supervisor how I lost the front door of my car." With that, he turned and made his way carefully through the burned-out lab and out the front entrance, leaving Kathleen and McCreary alone together.

"I'm sorry about your lab," said McCreary after Wills left.

"Yeah, me, too," Kathleen said.

"Looks like that sample's totally gone, though, huh?"

"Yep," Kathleen lied.

"You know, if I were you, I'd let people know that right away."

"Huh?"

"What I mean is, the next reporter who calls you, be sure to tell them that everything was lost in the fire—absolutely everything. Otherwise . . . well, you know."

"Otherwise, people will keep coming after me?"

McCreary nodded. "Look, it's for your own safety. Let everyone know there's nothing left of the INDY gene." McCreary paused pensively and clasped his hands together, pressing both index fingers against his pursed lips. "In fact . . ." His voice trailed off.

"In fact, what?"

"Well, remember when you asked how SER-RATE could control the pace of private-sector research?"

"Yeah."

McCreary looked around the ruined lab and confirmed they were still alone. He moved closer and spoke in a low, barely audible voice. "One of the techniques we're authorized to use is *disinformation*."

Kathleen didn't know where he was going with this, but she didn't like it. She immediately began shaking her head no.

"Scientists are herd animals, Kathleen," he said in a low voice. "You know that."

Kathleen continued shaking her head emphatically.

"They live and die by research grants, university sponsorship, venture funding . . . It's a patronage system, pure and simple. And to get that patronage, they have to sell their research. You've been through all of that. You know what I'm talking about."

Kathleen was still shaking her head. She did not like where this was going.

"To sell their research, it has to be sexy. It has to be promising. It has to offer the allure of prestige, acclaim, prizes, honors, and, most importantly, profit. That's what patrons of science are interested in these days . . ."

"Forget it Bill," said Kathleen firmly, already sensing what was coming.

"Kathleen, the one thing that can stop scientific research in its tracks—faster than anything the government could ever do—"

Kathleen was shaking her head emphatically.

"—is the whiff of a hoax."

There was a long silence, interrupted only by the intermittent squawking of distant radio transmissions from the firemen outside.

Finally, Kathleen spoke. "You want me to say this was all a hoax?"

"Shhhh!" McCreary looked around nervously. "Yes, in a nutshell, that's exactly what we want. And we can compensate you—"

"Compensate me? How?"

McCreary looked around again and spoke in a hushed tone. "Money. A new house. Even a new identity if you want. We can negotiate a nice package for you."

"I don't believe this," Kathleen mumbled incredulously. "You're joking, right?"

"No, this isn't a joke. The government is prepared to pay you to disavow this research. And they can pay you a lot. Think about it, Kathleen. You would never have to work again . . . you could be set for life."

"It wouldn't work, Bill. People would figure it out."

"Oh, you'd be surprised." McCreary arched his eyebrows knowingly. "Kathleen, nobody in the scientific community wants to be associated with a hoax. It's the ultimate form of humiliation for a university or a private foundation. And, of course, venture capitalists won't touch a concept with a ten-foot pole once there's talk of a hoax. Trust me, this has been done before. *And it works.*"

Kathleen pinched her eyebrows together. "What do you mean, it's been done before?"

McCreary looked around again and lowered his voice even further. "I can't tell you the details because it's covered by another SCI channel. But this exact technique was used about twenty years ago to stem the rising tide of research into a particular area of technology that the government felt was . . . let's just say *problematic*. The two scientists involved are both living very comfortably today on the French Riviera. And there hasn't been any serious research into that technology since they publicly declared it to be a hoax more than *twenty years* ago. So, trust me, this can work."

"No way," said Kathleen firmly. "I can't do that."

"There's got to be something that could make you change your mind."

Kathleen stared deeply into McCreary's eyes. She was thinking about her grandfather. "There isn't. Forget it."

McCreary sighed heavily and handed her his card. "Think about it and give me a call."

Kathleen slipped McCreary's card in her pocket, next to Wills's card and watched with a twinge of contempt as McCreary turned and made his way out of the lab.

A few feet shy of the exit, McCreary turned to face her. He had a gloomy, deflated expression on his face. "This is Pandora's box, Kathleen. You know that, right? If this technology falls into the wrong hands . . ." He shook his head slowly. "Well, let's just say we'll be regretting it for a long time."

He turned and disappeared around the corner.

CHAPTER FIFTY-THREE

SPECIAL Agent Wills sat alone at his desk in the FBI's Washington field office in Judiciary Square. It was just after 9:30 P.M. The only other occupants of the second floor were a small cleaning crew busily making its rounds, emptying trash cans, vacuuming, and conversing in Spanish.

The overhead lights were dimmed for the evening. Wills's neatly organized desk, however, was brightly illuminated by a sleek brushed-nickel desk lamp.

Agent Hendricks had left two hours earlier. She'd left abruptly without asking if there was anything else she could do. That was fine with Wills. He preferred to be alone. Besides, Hendricks wasn't part of the SERRATE program, so there were limits to what she could do.

Wills sat motionless at his desk, oblivious to the rhythmic droning of the vacuum cleaners and the clanking of metal trash cans in the background. He was deep in thought, struggling to organize a dozen seemingly unconnected bits of information into some sort of logical explanation.

Something was missing . . .

He glanced down at the four tidy stacks of papers that Hendricks had assembled on his desk at his request. Each was labeled with a yellow sticky note: LHV GROUP, LUCE VENFELD, RIAL, and ELIAS RUBIN. He picked up the half-inch thick stack labeled ELIAS RUBIN.

According to his bio, Rubin was a seventy-six-year-old man from Haifa, Israel, a serial entrepreneur and financier. He was listed by *Forbes* magazine as one of the hundred richest people in the world. Rough estimates put his net worth at anywhere from 3 to 5 billion dollars, depending on Rial's daily stock price.

And he was *eccentric.*

Turning to his computer, Wills quickly typed "Elias Rubin" and "Venfeld" into the Google search engine. There were no hits.

Undeterred, he double clicked the icon for the FBI's intranet, typed in his user name and password, and then clicked on a link to the National Security Analysis Center. This was a new and highly controversial system—developed jointly by the FBI and CIA—that employed sophisticated data-mining techniques and relational software to detect patterns of communications and interaction between people or groups, sometimes four or five removed from an original target. With proper authorization, the NSAC system could

access phone records, ISP records, credit-card records, and a host of other electronic information
floating around the digisphere.

Because of the intrusive nature of the system
and the controversy surrounding it, its use by the
FBI was strictly limited to investigations relating
to counter-terrorism and other certified national-
defense concerns.

But Wills had a way in . . .

On the NSAC login page, he typed in "SER-
RATE" and a nine-digit security code. Seconds
later, the system opened up, and he found himself presented with a start page with more than a
dozen input fields. For the better part of five minutes, he filled in each field, providing numerous
search parameters and field restrictions and entering detailed information about the people and
topics for which he hoped to find a link. These included: "Elias Rubin," "Rial Laboratories," "LHV
Group," "Luce Venfeld," "longevity gene," "INDY
gene," and, finally, "immortality."

He pressed ENTER.

And waited.

Nearly ten minutes elapsed before NSAC returned its first set of results. When the SEARCH
COMPLETE icon finally appeared, Wills briefly re-
viewed the available data-presentation formats
and opted for a simple list of names in order of
relevance. He clicked the appropriate link, and
a total of nine names appeared with relevance
scores above the noise threshold of 250 that he'd
selected. They were

812   Elias S. Rubin
571   Luce H. Venfeld
478   Jin Shan Wu
471   Guillermo J. I. Gomez
462   Eswara Haryadi
414   Aleksei Nazarov
378   Roger C. Glick
320   Leonidas Diakos
270   Wilhelm F. Van der Giesen

Wills leaned forward and studied the list with acute interest. He immediately recognized the names of Elias Rubin and Luce Venfeld at the top of the list. He also recognized Roger Glick, CEO of WestPharma Corporation.

But he was surprised to see another name on the list that he recognized.

Guillermo Gomez. The Mexican drug smuggler turned real-estate mogul.

Wills knew him well.

CHAPTER FIFTY-FOUR

Bethesda, Maryland.

IT was dark by the time Kathleen pulled into the garage of her apartment building, weary and defeated. Her mind was numb, her clothes and skin covered with soot and grime. There was dried blood in her hair and on her face from the cut on her forehead.

Kathleen guided her Subaru into her assigned space on Level P4, parked, locked up, and made her way groggily to the elevator. Every muscle in her body was stiff and aching. She was already thinking about the hot bath she would take when she got upstairs. She would unplug her phone, turn off the TV, pour a glass of Chardonnay, and just sink into the tub. There, she could finally do some thinking. She needed to sort everything out in her head and figure out what to do next.

A good night's sleep wouldn't hurt either.

She arrived at the sixth floor, stepped into the landing, and began making her way toward her apartment at the end of the hallway. She was a few steps shy of her door when a terrifying thought suddenly occurred to her.

She wheeled around and walked quickly to the other end of the hallway, where a small window overlooked the visitors' parking lot. She stood on tiptoe and peered out the grimy window.

She recognized the canary-yellow Mustang that had been parked at the front of the lot for nearly three months. How someone had managed to keep that rust-bucket there for so long without it being towed away was a mystery to her. She also saw a red Toyota pickup truck that belonged to one of her neighbors and a black Corvette that belonged to the current boyfriend of the blond bombshell on seven.

But what about that one?

Kathleen's heart skipped a beat as she spied a shiny black BMW double-parked at the back of the lot. Without question, it was the same make and model she'd seen this morning. The one driven by the man who'd threatened to kill her. She looked around frantically, half-expecting the man to be behind her at that very moment. But the hallway was quiet and empty.

Was he in her apartment?

Kathleen raced to the elevator and pushed the DOWN button. She nervously eyed her apartment door, just twenty feet away, fully expecting it to swing open at any moment to reveal the man with the purplish scar.

"Come on!" she whispered, pressing the down button several more times.

The elevator arrived with a loud *ding*, and she

winced at the noise. As soon as the doors opened, she slipped inside and jabbed the P4 button several times.

Thirty seconds later, the elevator reached her parking level. Looking both directions and seeing no one, Kathleen tentatively stepped out and hurried to her car. She buckled herself in, started the engine, and lurched out of her parking space. She maneuvered quickly through the garage, braking hard at each turn with a squeal of tires as she spiraled up three levels to P1.

With a wave of her electronic pass, the unmanned entrance gate to the garage automatically lifted. She pulled out and turned right onto Sandalwood Street, slowing down momentarily to glance up at the living-room window of her apartment.

A man's face was staring down at her.

Then he was gone.

Kathleen gasped and floored the accelerator, sending her Subaru peeling wildly down Sandalwood Street.

CHAPTER FIFTY-FIVE

"**T**HERE she goes!" Bill McCreary exclaimed, pointing at Kathleen Sainsbury's car as it made a sharp right turn onto Old Georgetown Road about two blocks away.

"I'm on it," replied Goodwin, punching the accelerator of the Suburban.

"Where's she going?" McCreary muttered under his breath.

"I dunno, boss. But we'll find out." Goodwin made a hard right onto Old Georgetown Road and maneuvered his vehicle skillfully through traffic until it was approximately ten car lengths behind the silver Subaru.

"God *damn* it!" barked Venfeld as he turned away from the window and rushed to the door of Kathleen Sainsbury's apartment. He barreled out into the hallway, slammed the door hard behind him, and bounded quickly to the elevator. When the elevator failed to arrive within ten seconds, he cursed again and sprinted to the end of the hallway, toward the fire stairs.

He took the steps two at a time, nearly losing his balance as he flew down six flights to the lobby level. He burst through the stairwell door, banked hard left, and rushed out the back door into the visitors' lot behind the building. The unexpected presence of a brightly painted red-and-yellow tow truck struck him immediately. It took a moment for him to realize what was happening. "Hey!" he screamed at the man standing beside the tow truck. "What the hell are you doing?"

The tow operator remained unfazed and continued pressing up on the hydraulic lever on the side of the tow truck until it had finished lifting the front end of Venfeld's BMW off the ground.

Venfeld raced over and got directly in the man's face. "I said, what the hell are you doing?"

The tow truck driver didn't flinch. Without removing the lit cigarette that dangled from the side of his mouth, he replied in a slow, backcountry drawl, "You're parked illegally."

"I don't give a damn!" Venfeld snapped. "Put my car down."

"Towing fee's two hundred dollars. *Cash.*"

Venfeld's eyes hardened. He reached into this coat pocket, pulled out his Beretta, and aimed it at the man's chest. "How about this instead?"

The man's expression barely changed. Apparently, he'd been through this before. "All right, fella, take it easy." He pressed the hydraulic lever down without saying another word.

Venfeld watched anxiously as his BMW slowly leveled out and the harnesses were unhooked.

"Now, get your truck out of my way!" Venfeld said as he slipped into the driver's seat of his BMW, slamming the door shut.

Venfeld gunned the beemer and squealed out of the visitors' lot. He'd lost a lot of time, and he knew Dr. Sainsbury's car would be long gone by now. But it didn't matter; he knew exactly where she was going.

As he drove, Venfeld plugged a small electronic device into his navigation system and pushed a button on the portable unit. Seconds later, a bright red dot appeared on the street map on the BMW's navigation console.

Venfeld smiled. As it turned out, Zafer had managed to do something right after all. The small GPS tracker that he'd placed inside the wheel well of Dr. Sainsbury's car was still working like a charm.

CHAPTER FIFTY-SIX

Sunset Knoll, Maryland.

"SORRY, visiting hours are over," said Ellie McDougal, the evening shift supervisor at Garrison Manor. Her deep, booming voice reverberated throughout the cavernous lobby and down the long corridors leading to the residents' rooms.

Kathleen Sainsbury stepped closer to the front desk and removed her dark glasses. "Hi, Ellie," she said.

"Ms. Sainsbury, is that you?" Ellie exclaimed, finally recognizing her.

Kathleen nodded sheepishly. She knew she looked awful.

"Oh my word! Are you okay? What happened?"

"Let's just say it's been a rough day," said Kathleen, forcing a smile.

"My goodness! Let me get you a wet towel." Ellie began lifting her large frame out of her chair with considerable effort.

Kathleen held out her hand to stop her. "No, it's fine, Ellie. Really."

Ellie sat back down slowly without taking her eyes off Kathleen.

"I was actually hoping I could sleep in my grandfather's room tonight. You think that would be okay?"

"Well, you're supposed to get overnight stays approved in advance, but . . ." Ellie tilted her head to one side and pressed her lips together, weighing the situation. "I guess it would be okay. I'll send the orderly with some extra sheets and a blanket."

"Thanks," said Kathleen with a relieved smile.

Kathleen made her way to her grandfather's room on the third floor and unlocked the door. The room was entirely dark, save for several bright stripes of moonlight streaming through the Venetian blinds. Her grandfather was sound asleep in his bed, mouth open, snoring loudly. Kathleen approached him, put her hand lightly on his shoulder, and smiled. He'd always been a heavy sleeper. Alzheimer's hadn't changed that. She wondered what he was dreaming about and whether his dreams were more lucid than his memory.

Checking her watch, she was surprised to find it was already past eleven o'clock. She desperately needed a shower and some sleep. She fished her car keys out of her pants pocket and placed them quietly on the glass coffee table in front of the sofa. She was just about to slip off her grungy jeans when the lump in her other pocket jogged her memory.

She pulled out the contents of her right pocket then plopped down onto the couch to study each object carefully in the moonlight. There was Agent Wills's business card, which she placed on the left-hand side of the coffee table. There was Bill McCreary's business card, which she positioned beneath Wills's card. There was the small, neoprene sample bottle with the smudged label, which she positioned upright next to the two business cards. And there was the tiny jump drive—no larger than her thumb—that Carlos had given her this morning, just before the explosion.

She held up the jump drive in the moonlight and considered it for a moment. *What did Carlos say was on here?* It took a while for her to remember—this morning seemed like an eternity ago. Then, it came to her. Carlos had said something about drafting a patent application, which he'd saved to the jump drive. Kathleen twisted the jump drive slowly between her thumb and forefinger, pondering that fact for a few seconds.

Suddenly, she sprang into action. Picking up her grandfather's phone, she dialed extension 1000.

"Front desk," answered Ellie McDougal in a quick, professional manner.

"Ellie, it's Kathleen Sainsbury. Do you guys have a computer I could use?"

"A computer? Uh . . . well, there's one in the rec room on the first floor, but it's locked right now."

"Ellie, I know I'm pushing my luck here, but

could you unlock it for a few minutes? I need to check something really important."

There was a moment of silence followed by a heavy sigh on Ellie's end.

"Please," Kathleen said plaintively, "I know I'm asking a lot . . ."

"Okay," Ellie relented. "Meet me down there and I'll unlock it for you."

Five minutes later, Kathleen and Ellie McDougal were standing outside the Garrison Manor recreation room. "I really shouldn't be doing this," Ellie grumbled as she unlocked the door using one of several dozen keys attached to an enormous key ring.

"I know. Thank you very much. I *promise* I won't be long."

"Just make sure to lock it behind you when you're done, okay?" said Ellie, making no effort to conceal her discomfort with the whole situation.

"I will."

Ellie McDougal walked away, and Kathleen entered the darkened rec room. She quickly found the light switch and flipped it on. At one end of the large room, several rows of couches and chairs were arranged in concentric semicircles around a massive, flat-screen television set. The walls at that end were adorned with old movie posters—*Gone With the Wind*, *Casablanca*, and the like.

In the center of the room were a number of game tables, each surrounded by four folding chairs. A few of the tabletops had preprinted checkerboards; others were covered with green felt.

At Kathleen's end of the room, approximately fifteen upholstered chairs were arranged in groups of two and three, each group centered around a small, round coffee table. Magazine racks and several bookcases lined the walls. In one corner was a small wooden table holding a slightly outdated desktop computer and CRT monitor. Kathleen made her way to the computer and turned it on.

It seemed to take forever for the machine to boot up. But, eventually, it whirred to life and a version of Windows appeared on the screen, apparently functional and ready for use. Kathleen slipped the jump drive into a USB port on the back of the computer, and, seconds later, a small window popped onto the screen showing a single file named "patent_app.doc." She double clicked and opened it.

The document was much larger than she'd expected—eighty-four pages in total. A smile crept across her face. "Carlos, you outdid yourself," she whispered. She quickly scrolled down through the document and saw page after page of text like the following:

GCG GCG GCC GTG CCG CTG CTG GTG ATC TTA AAG

1   5   10

GAA CAG CCT TGC AGC ACG CCC CTC CAG TTC CAA

                     15   20

GGC TAC AAT CTG TCT GGG GGC CTG CTG CAG ACG

                     25   30

CCC CTC TTC CAA GGC TAC AAT CTG TCT GCC AAC
                         35   40
CTG GGC ATC ATC CTC TCA CTG GCC CTG GCT GGC
ATT
45   50   55
CTT GGC ATC TGT ATT GTG TGT TCC ATT TGG CTT
TTC
                         60   65

She'd seen enough. She sat back, crossed her arms, and thought about Carlos lying in a hospital bed somewhere.

"Left turn ahead in . . . two hundred feet," announced the monotone female voice of Luce Venfeld's navigation system. Venfeld slowed his BMW and spotted the red roof of the Garrison Manor retirement home ahead on the left. He was just about to make the left turn into the driveway when he changed his mind. *Better to drive by*, he decided. He straightened the wheel and cruised slowly by, taking note of Kathleen Sainsbury's silver Subaru parked at the front entrance. *Bull's-eye.*

Then something else caught his eye . . .

Immediately next door to Garrison Manor, in a bank parking lot, Venfeld spotted a white Chevy Suburban with dark tinted windows parked lengthwise along the hedge dividing the two properties. "Damn it," he muttered as he drove by, being careful not to tap his brakes or speed up too rapidly.

A quarter mile down the road, well out of

sight of Garrison Manor and the white Suburban, Venfeld doused the BMW's headlights and pulled into the driveway of the Daniel J. Hicks Funeral Home, a small, white brick building with black shutters and a gray roof. He parked behind the building, out of view of the main road. He cut the engine and waited in silence for several minutes before finally emerging quietly from his car. He carefully inspected the chain-link fence at the back of the funeral-home property, beyond which lay the forty-seven manicured acres of Mount Hope Memorial Gardens.

After confirming that no one was looking, Venfeld scaled the chain-link fence and dropped down onto the cemetery grounds on the other side. He walked swiftly along the fence line, guided by the light of the waxing quarter moon, dodging tree trunks, prickly rosebushes, and the occasional stray burial marker, until he reached the back of the Garrison Manor grounds. Through the fence, he gazed at the facility's two residential wings, stretching toward him like open arms. The building was nearly entirely dark, except for the flickering blue luminescence of TV sets in some of the rooms. As quietly as he could, he scaled the fence again and landed on the Garrison Manor lawn with a soft thud. Stooping low, he scurried to the nearest tree—a massive white oak—and crouched behind its trunk.

From his new vantage point some fifty feet behind the building, Venfeld scanned the ground floor, looking for an obvious way in. Almost immediately, his eyes came to rest on an orange pinpoint of light in a dark recess near the back door of the central hall. He stared at it for several seconds, trying to figure out what it was.

Suddenly, it moved.

Reggie Jones took a deep drag from his joint, held it in his lungs for several seconds, then slowly exhaled a thin stream of marijuana smoke into the darkness. This was how he started almost every night shift at Garrison Manor, same as he had for the past two years. He didn't do it to get high, necessarily. It was just a way to relax and put him in the right mood for a long night of cleaning up bathroom accidents, delivering linens and medications to residents' rooms, helping old folks to bed, and—most draining on his psyche—dealing with Nurse McDougal. One "bammy" at the beginning of the shift and another halfway through usually did the trick.

Reggie reclined in a lawn chair and propped his feet up on the picnic table located just outside the back door of the main hall in a little patio nook that was mainly used as a smoking area by residents and staff. He took another drag of his bammy and cranked the volume on his iPod earphones, bopping his head and shoulders to his new favorite rap song, "2 Alive 2 Die."

He did not notice the dark figure creeping up slowly behind him.

Venfeld plodded silently across the grass, arcing his path so that he approached directly behind the man in the blue scrubs. He was close enough now that he could smell marijuana smoke wafting through the air and could hear muffled drum beats from the man's earphones. *This was almost too easy.*

At the edge of the patio was a rack of croquet mallets. Venfeld quietly eased one of them out of the rack and continued approaching the half-stoned orderly from behind, checking in all directions, one last time, to ensure no one was watching.

No one was.

At a distance of about three feet, Venfeld raised the croquet mallet high over his right shoulder and, in one swift motion, swung it hard like a baseball bat. It connected directly on the side of the Reggie Jones's head with a sickening, wooden *thunk*. Jones fell sideways off his chair and let out a loud grunt. As Jones scrambled to regain his footing, Venfeld delivered another powerful blow to the top of his head with the mallet. This time, Jones's body went completely limp, flattening to the ground.

Venfeld stood over the motionless body for several seconds with the mallet poised for yet another blow. After observing no motion for more than five seconds, however, he tossed the mallet onto the grass and crouched close beside Reggie Jones's unconscious body.

He plucked Jones's earbuds, still emitting the muffled strains of rap music, from Jones's ears and unplugged them from the iPod. He wrapped one end of the earphone cord around each of his hands until about one foot of the cord remained slack between his clenched fists. Then, looping the cord around Jones's neck and pressing his knee into the young man's back, he pulled up hard with all his strength.

Even unconscious, Jones emitted an involuntary groan as the cord instantly cut off blood and oxygen to his brain. After that, he was silent. A minute later, his body began twitching involuntarily, legs kicking wildly, torso contorting in spasms. Thirty seconds later, it was all over.

"Reggie?" squawked the voice of Ellie McDougal.

Venfeld was startled for a moment, until he realized the voice had come from a two-way radio clipped to Jones's belt. He unclipped the walkie-talkie and inspected it carefully.

"Reggie, you there?" McDougal repeated.

Venfeld pressed the talk button and mumbled, "Mmm-hmm."

"Have you taken those linens up to Three-oh-eight yet?"

Venfeld thought for a moment, then muttered in a low, guttural voice, "Unh-uh."

"Well hurry up and do it! Ms. Sainsbury is waiting for you."

Kathleen made her way back to her grandfather's room and let herself in quietly with her key. She tiptoed to the couch, placed the jump drive on the glass coffee table beside the sample bottle, and eased herself into the couch's soft, over-stuffed cushions. *A shower could wait*, she thought to herself. *This felt too good.*

Glancing over at her sleeping grandfather, she yawned and spoke in a quiet voice, mostly to herself. "I wish you could help me with this, Grandpa. You were always good with big decisions." She yawned again. "And this one's a doozy." She closed her eyes and leaned back against the cushions, fingers interlaced behind her head, wondering what she should do. She alone held the INDY gene . . . and the power to change humanity forever. *And she had no idea what to do with it.*

It felt so good to have her eyes closed that before long she began to succumb to the powerful urge to sleep. Her thoughts were soon drifting, to the ocean . . . to the beach . . . to the French Riviera. What would life be like there? Could her grandfather live with her? How was the sailing there?

Then, darker questions began intruding into her thoughts. Why were her parents killed all those years ago? Why were Dr. Sargon's wife and daughter killed? And Sargon, himself, why did he take his own life? There seemed to be something about this INDY gene that wreaked death and destruction everywhere it went.

At some point in her semiconscious state, Kathleen began indulging even more irrational thoughts—ideas that otherwise never would have been allowed into the conscious mind of Dr. Kathleen Sainsbury, Scientist. What if there *was* a larger force in the universe—something supernatural, or at least beyond her capacity to understand—that was causing all these events to happen? What if that force was trying stop the

INDY gene technology from being exploited? Who was *she* to defy such a force? And what would happen to her if she did? What would happen to the human race?

Somewhere amongst this tangle of irrational thoughts, Bill McCreary's words crept into the mix. "Sometimes science can be its own worst enemy."

With that, Kathleen snapped her eyes open wide. She was no longer sleepy. Her thoughts had become too absurd, too irrational, and she was afraid of where they were leading.

She picked up the remote and clicked on the TV, turning the volume down to a barely audible level. Hoping for nothing more than a distraction, she flipped randomly through dozens of channels, frowning as she surfed through a depressing morass of home-shopping networks, infomercials, reality shows, and B-grade movies. She was starting to understand why some folks might not want to live an extra forty or fifty years.

Suddenly, something on the TV caught her eye. She flipped back one channel to CNN.

Bryce Whittaker.

His head and shoulders appeared in a square box in the top right-hand corner of the screen, sporting an electric blue shirt, unbuttoned—Hollywood style—to the middle of his chest, and a stylish black blazer. His face was ruggedly unshaven. Below him, a man with a thick white beard and moustache appeared in another square box of equal size. Kathleen immediately recognized him as Frank Fitzgerald, a well-known bi-

ologist and a member of the U. Conn. team that
had originally discovered the INDY gene in fruit
flies. The moderator, who filled the remainder
of the screen, was Randi Rice, the annoying yet
wildly popular host of *Randi Rice Tonight*, a one-
hour topical show with a quasi-judicial theme. A
text banner at the bottom of the screen asked, in
bold red letters, IMMORTALITY GENE DISCOVERED?

"You have *got* to be kidding," Kathleen muttered as she turned up the volume.

Rice was talking. "I'd like to turn to you now,
Dr. Fitzgerald. Can you tell us a little bit more
about this so-called INDY gene?"

"Well, first of all, let me point out that this
is not an 'immortality' gene. In our studies, we
have found that fruit flies with the activated INDY
gene can live two or three times their normal life
spans. But certainly not forever."

Rice frowned, clearly unhappy about being
corrected on her own show. "Well, Dr. Fitzgerald, you'd have to admit that living two hundred
years is getting pretty close to immortality."

"Well, I . . ."

"Actually, hold that thought," said Rice. "Mr.
Whittaker, I'd like to get your thoughts on the
spectacular fire that happened earlier today at
the QLS headquarters in Rockville, Maryland."
As she spoke, the screen switched to a helicopter shot of the QLS building engulfed in flames.
It made Kathleen sick to her stomach to watch.
"What can you tell us about this remarkable turn
of events?"

Whittaker spoke in a deep studio voice, as if

he'd been doing this for years. "Randi, we still don't know what caused the fire and explosion at QLS this morning. We do know that one employee was taken to the hospital for non–life-threatening injuries."

"Were any bystanders injured?" Rice asked.

"My understanding is that no one else suffered any serious injuries."

The screen switched back to the talking heads.

"Well, that's good news," said Rice. "Now, Mr. Whittaker, you're the reporter who originally broke this story, correct?"

Whittaker smiled and nodded with faux modesty. "That's right, Randi."

"And how did you uncover this truly remarkable story?"

Kathleen wanted to scream: *He betrayed me! That's how he 'uncovered' this story!*

But Whittaker just shrugged and flashed a toothy smile. "Just good old-fashioned leg work," he said. "Following leads, picking up on clues . . ."

Kathleen wanted to puke. On the other hand, she had to admit he *did* look good on TV.

"Now, I understand that you've spoken with Dr. Sainsbury, the CEO of Quantum Life Sciences, in the past few days," Rice said. "Have you had any contact with her since the explosion this morning?"

"No, I haven't," Whittaker replied. "She was last seen getting into a vehicle at the scene of the fire. I understand there were reports of gunfire being exchanged, but the facts are still very sketchy."

"Remarkable," said Rice, shaking her head dramatically. "Now, Dr. Fitzgerald, I'd like to get your thoughts on something, very quickly. What do you believe are the implications of this INDY gene technology in humans?"

"Well, assuming it's genuine," said Fitzgerald, "and again, we don't have any confirmation of that, I believe the discovery of this gene in humans could be one of the most important breakthroughs in genetics since the discovery of DNA itself."

"Do you personally see this as a good thing or a bad thing?"

"Oh, a good thing, of course," said Fitzgerald assuredly. "This technology has the potential to improve all of our lives."

"Well," said Rice provocatively, "it seems not everyone agrees with you on that point. Joining us now are two people who have very different opinions on the subject." As Rice spoke, two more squares appeared on the screen, leaving her face in the middle of four remote guests. "Joining us now by satellite are Dr. Sylvia Matherson, a bio-ethics expert from Stanford University, and the Reverend Jeffrey Kline, senior pastor at Freedom Baptist Church in Clarksville, Tennessee. Good evening to both of you."

The two new guests nodded and smiled.

"Reverend Kline, I'd like to begin with you," said Rice. "I understand you have some reservations about this technology based on your religious beliefs. Can you briefly explain those?"

"Yes I can," responded Reverend Kline in a

charming, Tennessee drawl. "In Genesis six, verse three, God commanded Noah and Methuselah that His spirit would not abide with man forever, but instead, being mortal, man's days would be limited to one hundred twenty years. Now, that is a *commandment* from God, no different from 'Thou shalt not kill' or 'Thou shalt not steal.' And anyone who attempts to circumvent that commandment, through genetics or otherwise, will be guilty of a very grave sin. I, for one, will instruct my congregation not to partake of any sort of genetic treatment that offers to extend their lives beyond the number of years allotted by God. Now, Randi, don't get me wrong. Science is wonderful. It has given us many important and useful things. But science should *not* be used to circumvent God's will."

"Very interesting," said Rice, nodding. "And Dr. Matherson, you also have some concerns about this technology . . ."

"Yes, indeed, Randi," said Dr. Matherson. "I am very concerned about the socioeconomic impact this technology could have on our country, and really, around the world. Who will have access to this life-extension technology? Only the very wealthy? Or will it be made freely available to everyone? I fear that if only the wealthy have access to it, it will further widen the gap between rich and poor, with possibly devastating consequences. I'm also very worried about what impact this technology might have on our healthcare system and social security, as well as the environment. These systems are highly sensitive to changes in demographics, so introducing an abrupt change like this could have a far-reaching and insurmountable negative impact. Those are just some of my concerns."

"Thank you. When we come back . . ."

Kathleen turned off the TV and shook her head, wondering in silent anguish what in the world she should do. Her thoughts were interrupted by a quiet knock on the door. *The bedding*, she remembered. She stood to answer it.

CHAPTER FIFTY-SEVEN

SPECIAL Agent Wills clicked "relational time-line" on the NASC screen and anxiously awaited the results. On the screen, a complex, multicolor scatter plot suddenly appeared, showing the degree of interrelation of the nine people he'd just identified, plotted as a function of time. With a few clicks of his mouse, he adjusted the X-axis to focus only on the past thirty days.

As the adjusted plot appeared on his screen, his pulse quickened.

At the far left of the plot—representing about thirty days ago—each of the nine colored lines zigzagged up and down in saw-tooth fashion, generally running parallel to the baseline—a rainbow tangle of lines that was nearly indistinguishable from the baseline noise. But, about two-thirds of the way to the right on the X-axis, or about ten days ago, the colored lines suddenly began ramping up noticeably. The increase in their interrelated activity was gradual at first but spiked significantly about three days ago.

Something was happening.

Then, at the far right of the plot—roughly corresponding to when the QLS article first appeared in the *Washington Post*—the colored lines shot up nearly vertically. Whoever these people were, that article had them buzzing like a swarm of bees. Which told Wills all he needed to know.

Wills next turned his attention to Guillermo de Juan Iglacio Gomez, one of the members of the group. That name brought back a flood of memories. With a few strategic strokes of his keyboard, he retrieved Gomez's old FBI file, which was now prominently annotated at the top, in red letters, CASE CLOSED.

"Like hell," Wills muttered.

Wills studied the grainy black-and-white picture of Gomez and recalled the day, roughly five years ago, when he was ordered to close the case on him. It still burned him up to think about.

Five years ago, Wills had been in charge of a special FBI taskforce called "SUNSHINE," whose sole mission was to track, apprehend, and arrest the elusive mastermind behind one of the biggest drug distribution networks in North America. Guillermo de Juan Iglacio Gomez.

They'd received intelligence—most likely filtering in from the CIA (but nobody really knew)—that Gomez wanted to get out of the drug business altogether. He was allegedly trying to go legit and had already cut deals with the Mexican government, or at least paid off enough people in the government to escape prosecution there. But he wanted more. He wanted the freedom to travel, conduct business, and own property, not just in Mexico and South America, but all around the world. Even in the United States.

In short, he wanted to be reborn.

Of course, there would be no such deals with the U.S. government. Quite the contrary: the FBI was eagerly awaiting the day when Gomez would inevitably misstep and wander into the jurisdiction of U.S. law enforcement. The FBI field offices in Miami, Fort Lauderdale, San Juan, Saint Croix, Dallas, and San Diego were already on high alert for that event, as were other cooperative agencies in the Bahamas, Jamaica, and the British Virgin Islands. It was suspected that Gomez was seeking to acquire real estate in the Caribbean. So, the thinking went, it was only a matter of time before he showed his face on one of those islands.

That all changed, however, when the director of the FBI received a phone call one day from the director of the CIA, who reported that they'd worked out a deal with Gomez. He was now a CIA "asset." He was not to be arrested or bothered in any way in any U.S. territory. His file was to be closed.

The FBI director nearly blew a gasket.

But, in the end, the FBI backed off, having lost yet another turf war to the CIA. And, with that, Gomez was officially "reborn"—free to roam the world, the Caribbean, even the United States, without fear of incarceration, extradition, or prosecution.

Wills *personally* had to close the file on Gomez and fold up the SUNSHINE taskforce, which, needless to say, left him bitter and more than a little disillusioned.

Staring at Gomez's picture on the computer screen now, a strange thought was bouncing around Wills's mind. It had started as a subtle twinge and had grown progressively until the idea was now pounding in his head like a bass drum.

Luce Venfeld had worked for the CIA.

Wills snatched up the stack of papers labeled LUCE VENFELD from his desk and quickly thumbed to Venfeld's government employment history, which—as Hendricks had warned—was almost entirely blacked out with redactions. Frustrated, Wills entered Venfeld's identification number into an interagency database and called up his employment history on the screen. It, too, was mottled with black squares and rectangles, obscuring all but the most mundane information.

But Wills knew how to make those redactions disappear.

He pressed *Alt-F3* on his keyboard, and a small dialog box appeared on the screen, atop Venfeld's employment record. Wills quickly tapped in the nine-digit code for SERRATE and pressed enter. Instantly, most of the black redactions disappeared.

Wills scrolled down, skimming with great interest Venfeld's twenty-year career as a CIA analyst and operative. He stopped just short of the last entry—Venfeld's retirement—and read the second-to-last description with unchecked surprise. It read:

SERRATE—Cont. Surv.; Cont. Ops. (DFA);
Quintana Roo, MX.

Wills shook his head in disbelief. *He should have known*. Venfeld had been part of the SERRATE program . . . *five years ago!*

Staring at the entry, another item jumped off the screen at Wills. The letters "DFA." Deadly Force Authorized. Venfeld was a trained killer.

The puzzle pieces were now coming together. Wills stroked his chin, deep in thought. A twenty-year veteran of the federal government didn't make that much money—a fact Wills knew all too well. He, too, was coming up on the twenty-year point. Retirement was right around the corner, and he was already starting to worry about his savings.

Venfeld, however, had managed to leave the CIA and immediately begin living large—a fancy car, a luxury apartment, top-dollar office space on K Street.

He'd cut a deal with Gomez.

That thought lingered in his mind for a long while as Wills stared blankly across the dim expanse of the FBI field office. The whirring of the vacuum cleaners had ceased long ago; the cleaning crew had moved upstairs. The entire second floor was dark and eerily quiet.

Wills's thoughts seemed to float above the vacant cubicles and government-issued desks of the field office. *What, exactly, did Venfeld get out of the deal?*

Wills once again brought up the file on Guillermo Gomez and stared at his picture for a long time, shaking his head slowly from side to side.

CHAPTER FIFTY-EIGHT

KATHLEEN pressed her eye against the peephole of her grandfather's door and peered out into the hallway. Seeing nobody, she asked, "Who is it?"

"I'm here with sheets and pillows," said a man's muffled voice, indistinct and oddly garbled.

Kathleen didn't recognize the voice, but, then again, she didn't know everyone at Garrison Manor. She wondered briefly why she couldn't see the man's face through the peephole but decided not to let paranoia get the better of her. Drawing a deep breath, she carefully engaged the security chain above the doorknob and slowly cracked open the door.

Which was all Luce Venfeld needed.

In an instant, he smashed the door open with a vicious kick of his foot, tearing the security chain clear out of its bracket and sending the door slamming hard into Kathleen's shoulder.

Kathleen let out a terrified yelp and stumbled backward into the room, managing to regain her balance before nearly smashing into the glass-top coffee table behind her. Before she could do anything else, Venfeld was practically on top of her, pointing his 9 mm pistol directly at her face.

"Where is it?" he demanded angrily.

Kathleen knew better than to play dumb this time. "There," she sputtered, nodding at the coffee table behind her.

"Hand it to me."

Kathleen slowly turned and bent down to retrieve the neoprene sample bottle from the coffee table. Venfeld kept the barrel of the pistol hovering an inch from her head the whole time.

"That's it," he cooed nastily, extending his left palm. "Hand it over. Nice and easy . . ."

John Sainsbury awoke to a raucous commotion in his room. It took him the better part of a minute to figure out exactly what was happening. These days, it wasn't unusual for him to be awakened by nurses or orderlies in the middle of the night to give him his pills or to change his linens. But this was different. Someone had just broken down the door. And there was a man with a gun in his room!

John Sainsbury's life at Garrison Manor was largely a blur of medications, changes of clothes, nurses and orderlies, bland meals, and television—hours and hours of mindless television. He knew he was ill—seriously ill. He knew something was terribly wrong with his mind, although he had no idea what it was. He just . . . couldn't

. . . remember . . . anything. In fact, most days, it took all his mental energy just to remember who he was, let alone anyone else.

But there was one person in particular (although he couldn't remember her name) who was especially nice to him.

She brought him Oreo cookies.

And, right now, someone was pointing a gun at her head.

That's all John Sainsbury needed to know.

He kicked off his covers and clumsily rolled himself out bed. The gunman had his back turned and didn't seem to notice. Without a second thought, John Sainsbury—eighty-five years old and feeble—grabbed the metal clipboard from the foot of his bed, raised it high over his head with two trembling hands, and brought it crashing down on the gunman's head.

"Jesus fucking Christ!" Venfeld screamed as he was struck. He spun angrily and smacked John Sainsbury across the cheek with the handle of his pistol. Sainsbury grunted and fell backward to the floor like a sack of potatoes.

"Grandpa!" Kathleen shrieked.

Venfeld quickly shifted his attention back to Kathleen.

This time, however, she was prepared. Just as Venfeld turned to face her, she brought up her knee forcefully, summoning all the power of her days as a high-school soccer player, and landed it squarely in the center of his crotch.

Venfeld groaned loudly and doubled over,

wincing in pain. "Fucking bitch!" he hissed through gritted teeth.

But Kathleen wasn't done. She answered Venfeld's insult with a roundhouse kick to the side of his head. The powerful blow landed flat on his left temple and sent him sprawling across the floor in agony.

Kathleen wasted no time. She scooped up the remaining items from the coffee table and shoved them all into her pocket.

Venfeld was already struggling to his feet. "Give me that sample!" he demanded, scrambling for his gun.

Kathleen ignored him and stole a look at her grandfather, who was still lying motionless on the floor. Her heart sank. She desperately wanted to help him, but Venfeld was already on his feet, stumbling awkwardly toward her with the gun in his hand. She realized that her grandfather was safer wherever she wasn't.

She had to go.

Kathleen turned and bolted through the open doorway. No time to wait for an elevator, she sprinted full speed toward the central marble staircase. Seconds later, she heard Venfeld's voice in the hallway behind her.

"You stupid bitch!" he screamed. "You don't know who you're dealing with!" A split second later, two deafening gunshots exploded behind her.

The first shot whizzed past her left ear and shattered a porcelain vase on a console table several yards ahead of her. She never broke her stride. The second shot splintered the top of the newel post on the staircase banister, just as she was reaching out to grab it. She retracted her hand but did not slow down. Hooking a hard right at the top of the marble stairs, she began descending the steps two at a time. Seconds later, she heard Venfeld's footsteps above her, in hard pursuit.

Kathleen reached the ground floor and darted into the lobby, where Ellie McDougal was frantically punching buttons on the reception desk phone, a terrified expression on her face. "What's going on?" she screamed.

"Ellie, get down!" Kathleen shouted.

Just then, another shot rang out. The bullet ricocheted off the marble floor near Kathleen's feet and slammed hard into an adjacent wall.

Ellie screamed and ducked behind the front desk. Kathleen sprinted for the front doors and ran out into the parking lot.

She reached her car parked near the front entrance and frantically fumbled her keys from her pocket, which seemed to take forever. Panting and shaking with fear, she unlocked the car and slipped into the driver's seat. She was just cranking the ignition when she saw Venfeld barreling out through the front entrance. "Oh no," she whispered.

Venfeld took a few steps toward her car, stopped, took careful aim with his pistol, and fired.

Instinctively, Kathleen ducked her head. At the same instant, both the passenger's side and the driver's side windows shattered as Venfeld's bullet passed just inches above her head. Still low in the driver's seat and unable to see above the dash, she threw the car into reverse and floored the accelerator. The Subaru squealed backward across two rows of empty parking spaces until it crashed into Nurse McDougal's lime green VW Beetle. The force of the impact snapped Kathleen's head back awkwardly, and, for a few seconds, left her dizzy and disoriented.

Another 9 mm ACP round shattered a rear passenger window and tore through the driver's headrest, just millimeters above Kathleen's head. Realizing she had to get out of there immediately, Kathleen sat up, put the car in gear, and sped through the parking lot toward the exit.

As she made a hard left onto Route 2, she glanced back and saw Venfeld running through the parking lot in the opposite direction.

CHAPTER FIFTY-NINE

THE white Chevy Suburban squealed out of the bank parking lot next door to Garrison Manor and pulled up quickly behind Kathleen's southbound Subaru. Within seconds, it was less than a car's length away.

Kathleen glanced in her rearview mirror and winced. *McCreary.*

She floored the accelerator and braced herself as her damaged car shook and shimmied its way up to 80 miles per hour. To her dismay, however, the 350-horsepower Suburban pulled into the passing lane and drew alongside. Kathleen glanced over and saw Goodwin driving and McCreary in the front passenger's seat of the Suburban. He was signaling to her, pointing emphatically to the side of the road.

"Forget it!" she screamed at him through the Subaru's broken window. "You're all in this together!" She didn't trust McCreary. In fact, she didn't trust anyone anymore. *Why couldn't they just leave her alone?* She saw an exit sign. Without hesitation, she banked sharply to the right, barely managing to keep her car on the road as she skidded into the tight cloverleaf turn onto Route 50 West.

The Suburban slammed on its brakes and skidded seventy-five feet down the emergency lane of Route 2, well beyond the exit Kathleen had taken.

She'd lost them . . . for now.

Kathleen continued west on Route 50 at top speed. Less than three minutes later, however, the Suburban was back on her tail, honking and flashing its lights. Once again, she veered unexpectedly onto an exit ramp, this time onto Route 70. Again, she managed to lose the less nimble Suburban in the process.

The road was deserted at this hour, with virtually no traffic in either direction. After several minutes with no sign of her pursuers, Kathleen breathed a sigh of relief and slowed down.

She seemed to have lost them.

Route 70 terminated at College Avenue. Kathleen turned right toward the historic district of Annapolis, still with no real plan in mind, other than getting away. She entered Church Circle, a roundabout in the center of town, and circumnavigated it slowly, trying to figure out which of the eight roads to take.

The irony did not escape her. Her own life was now at a crossroads—a bewildering intersection of dimly lit paths, each leading to an unknown destiny. Literally and figuratively, she had no idea which way to go.

Without warning, Venfeld's black BMW ca-

reened into the roundabout at high speed, causing Kathleen to swerve sharply to the left. The
BMW slowed and maneuvered alongside her car,
so that both vehicles were now traveling side by
side around Church Circle, with Kathleen's car
trapped on the inside.

She glanced over at the BMW and saw Venfeld glaring at her, his eyes hard with anger. Suddenly, he cut his steering wheel sharply to the
left.

The BMW slammed violently into the passenger's side of Kathleen's car, causing her to lose
control and bounce up over the inner curb of
the traffic circle. The Subaru crashed through a
wrought-iron fence into the grounds of St. Anne's
Church, where it stopped dead.

She punched the accelerator, anyway.

To her surprise, the Subaru lurched forward
across the grass. Kathleen coaxed the damaged
vehicle back onto the roadway, barely able to
control the steering wheel as it yanked wildly
left and right, nearly escaping her grasp in both
directions. The Subaru wobbled around Church
Circle, squealing like a wounded animal.

Out of the corner of her eye, Kathleen could
see Venfeld coming at her again from the right,
approaching fast at an oblique angle, obviously
trying to sideswipe her. Instinctively, she stepped
hard on the brakes and simultaneously cut the
wheel sharply to the right. A half second later,
the BMW whizzed in front of her car, missing
it by inches and plowing into the curb ahead of
her. Without hesitation, she floored the accel-

erator and veered right, guiding the squealing Subaru with great effort down the first available side street, a narrow cobblestone alley lined with brick buildings.

To Kathleen's dismay, the street soon terminated at College Creek. There was nowhere left to go. She stepped hard on the brakes, and the crippled Subaru shuddered to a halt.

The wash of headlights from a vehicle was already approaching from behind. Kathleen's heart skipped a beat. She opened the driver's side door, wrangled herself free of the seat belt, and jumped out of the car. With the rumble of the approaching vehicle growing louder, she sprinted toward a high wrought-iron fence that ran along the side of the road. She approached it, looked up and groaned. *Too high.*

She looked right. *Nowhere to run.* She looked left.

Set into the fence a few yards away was a black wrought-iron gate that led into the darkened expanse beyond. Kathleen reached it just as the headlights of the approaching vehicle flicked across the vertical fence balusters, casting strange linear shadows. She pressed down hard on the latch and was amazed when it clicked open.

Slipping through the gate, Kathleen found herself in a large, manicured courtyard. In the moonlight, she could see a maze of waist-high boxwoods, perfectly trimmed and squared, stretching out before her in the fashion of an English garden. She glanced at the red brick building to her left and realized she was standing behind the caretaker's house at Saint Anne's Cedar Bluff Cemetery.

A car door slammed out on the street.

Terrified, Kathleen darted down a narrow gravel path that led into the boxwood labyrinth, ducking low so she couldn't be seen. As quietly as possible, she navigated her way through the maze, the stones crunching softly beneath her shoes. As she exited the other side, she heard the garden gate screech open and clank quietly shut.

Kathleen froze in place. Breathing became more difficult as panic set in.

Ahead in the moonlight, she saw a white wooden gate between two stone pillars. Leaving the boxwoods behind, she scurried across the lawn to the white gate. Behind her, she could hear the sound of shuffling feet in the boxwood garden. *He was searching for her.*

The painted wooden sign beside the white gate read:

St. Anne's Cemetery
Founded 1783

Kathleen opened the gate slowly about a quarter of the way, cringing at the slight squeak it emitted. She slipped stealthily through the opening and closed the gate quietly behind her.

Spread before her in the moonlight were hundreds of headstones, monuments, statues, and crosses, some grouped together, others standing alone in the manicured grass, all stained dark with age.

She drew a deep breath and headed toward the largest marker she could see, which stood alone in the middle of the cemetery. It was a towering granite memorial crowned with a thick stone cross.

CHAPTER SIXTY

Annapolis, Maryland.

KATHLEEN crouched behind the largest burial marker in Saint Anne's Cemetery, a massive cruciform tombstone marking the final resting place of Sarah Davis Clagett. Kathleen's eyes remained fixed on the churchyard gate, some twenty-five yards away. It had been nearly five minutes since she'd heard any shuffling noise from the garden. Perhaps her pursuer had given up.

She seriously doubted it.

Digging into her pocket, she pulled out the neoprene sample container and stared at it in the moonlight.

She realized now, of course, that McCreary was right. As long as she had this in her possession, bad things would keep happening to her. Whoever—or whatever—was after her, they would never stop until they had what they wanted . . . or until she was dead. *Or both.*

A panicky, desperate emotion swept through her. How would she ever get out of this alive?

Where could she go? Whom could she trust? To
her surprise, she found herself thinking about
McCreary's offer. Cowering behind the cold,
damp tomb in the dead of night, the sunny
French Riviera was starting to seem mighty attractive.

Suddenly, something about the sample container caught her eye. She held it up for a closer
look. In the moonlight, she could just barely
make out the first letter of the smudged label.
Was that an E*?*

"Don't move!" said a deep voice behind her.

Kathleen gasped and froze in place.

"Stand up slowly," Luce Venfeld ordered.

She complied.

"Now, turn around. Slowly!"

Kathleen turned slowly to find herself face-
to-face with Luce Venfeld, his arm outstretched,
his 9 mm pistol aimed squarely at her head. His
scarred face was resolute, his dark eyes cold with
anger, *vengeance.*

"End of the line," he said flatly, arm already
outstretched. He snatched the neoprene sample
container from Kathleen's grasp. As he inspected
the vial in the moonlight, the corners of his
mouth curled up into a sinister smile. He tucked
the container quickly into the breast pocket of
his overcoat.

He took a step backward, keeping the pistol
trained unwaveringly on Kathleen's forehead.
"Now, Dr. Sainsbury, it's time."

Every muscle in Kathleen's body tensed as she
prepared for the inevitable. A thousand thoughts

flooded her mind at once. Her grandfather and grandmother, her parents, Carlos, Julie, and Jeremy, all the QLS investors, cash calls, NIH, Dr. Sargon and the relic, the FBI, and—above it all—the words of Bill McCreary: "Sometimes science can be its own worst enemy."

She met Venfeld's vengeful gaze and studied the cold expression on his face. As she did, she noticed something strange. A bright red dot had suddenly appeared on his forehead. It bounced around for a split second, then stabilized just above his eyebrows . . .

A shot rang out, and Kathleen flinched, closing her eyes tightly.

Had she been shot? Where was the pain? She opened her eyes and immediately observed that Venfeld's face had changed dramatically. His angry eyes were now open wide with surprise. His mouth was agape. And, where the red dot had been a second before, there was now a dark circle with blood oozing out of it.

Venfeld stumbled backward and collapsed on the ground, a .40-caliber bullet lodged deep in his brain.

Kathleen could barely breathe. *What the hell just happened?* She heard footsteps coming up quickly behind her.

"Are you okay?" asked the familiar voice of Agent Wills as he trotted out of the shadows and into the moonlight before her, impeccably dressed as always, a SIG laser-sight pistol in his hand.

Kathleen shook her head in disbelief. "How did you . . ."

"I heard the call come in from Goodwin and McCreary and got down here as fast as I could." Wills stepped cautiously toward the motionless body of Luce Venfeld, pistol at the ready. "I picked up this guy's trail back on Route 2." He was advancing slowly toward the body.

"Who *is* that?" Kathleen asked.

"Name's Luce Venfeld. He's a lobbyist . . . of sorts." Wills knelt down and felt Venfeld's neck for a pulse, apparently finding none. Then he patted Venfeld's overcoat until he found what he was looking for. He removed the neoprene sample bottle from Venfeld's overcoat, inspected it momentarily, then slipped it into his own coat pocket.

Kathleen was just about to say something when she heard another voice behind her.

"Wills? Is that you?"

Kathleen turned to see Bill McCreary and Steve Goodwin bursting through the wooden cemetery gate. They jogged over to where Wills and Kathleen stood, out of breath and obviously confused by the situation.

McCreary positioned himself between Kathleen and Wills. Goodwin stood next to him. "Is that Venfeld?" McCreary asked, nodding at the dead body.

"Yep," Wills replied. He tipped his chin toward Kathleen. "He was just about to shoot Dr. Sainsbury here. I had no choice but to take him down."

McCreary glanced at Kathleen and then back to Wills. "Sure, of course." He nodded enthusiastically. "Good job, Agent Wills. Excellent work!" He paused a moment to catch his breath. "Where's the sample?"

Wills hesitated before responding. "I've got it."

"Good," said McCreary. "Let me have it. We need to get it to the SCIF immediately."

Wills didn't move.

"Agent Wills, did you *hear* me? Give me the sample so we can secure it properly in the SCIF. We can't risk having it out here in the open any longer."

"Actually, Bill," Wills replied in a firm voice, "I've got other plans." As he spoke, he pulled a small two-way radio from his breast pocket and spoke into it quietly. "I'm ready," he said.

McCreary was incredulous. "What do you *mean* you have other plans?"

"There's not much to say," said Wills flatly. "You and I just have different ideas about what to do with this technology."

McCreary sputtered, "Different ideas? It's not your job to—" He stopped short. "What, exactly, do you have in mind?"

"This technology's too valuable to be locked away in a SCIF, Bill. I'm going to put it in the hands of those who value it most."

"And who might that be?"

Wills shrugged. "I can't tell you yet. Right now, there's a six-way bidding war, and the Chinese are in the lead. But that could change at any moment."

Kathleen's jaw dropped and she shook her head disbelief. *Agent Wills?* She couldn't believe what she was hearing.

"Jesus Christ, are you crazy!" McCreary shouted. "Do you realize the consequences? Do you know the impact this will have on national security? On the human race?"

Wills shrugged. "Bill, those are your concerns. You dreamed all that stuff up using a bunch of fancy computer models. But this technology is inevitable. I've heard you say so yourself." He patted his coat pocket. "I've decided the time is now."

As Wills spoke, the steady thumping of an approaching helicopter arose in the distance.

Wills began backing up toward a small clearing in the cemetery.

"I can't let you do this," screamed McCreary over the noise of the approaching chopper. He tapped Goodwin on the shoulder and nodded.

Steve Goodwin—215 pounds of solid muscle—immediately charged toward Wills, hunched over like a defensive tackle, arms outstretched, legs pumping up and down.

"Back off!" Wills yelled at Goodwin, who was barreling down on him like a freight train. Wills raised his SIG and barked one last warning, "Freeze!"

Goodwin didn't stop.

Wills pulled the trigger, and a deafening report resulted. He watched in anguish as Goodwin crumpled to the ground, just inches from his feet. Then he trained his gun on McCreary. "God damn it, Bill!" he screamed over the rotor wash of the approaching helicopter. "Why'd you make me do that?"

McCreary's response could not be heard over the sound of rotors and the swirling windstorm caused by the descending helicopter.

Kathleen watched in astonishment as a blue-and-white Bell 407 touched down in the grassy clearing. Wills ran toward the chopper, bent over and hugging his overcoat to his body. The side door of the helicopter opened, and Wills climbed in.

Just before the helicopter door closed, Wills turned and gave McCreary one last look. There was nothing triumphant or gleeful in his expression. Rather, Kathleen thought, Wills looked resigned, as if he were merely carrying out the inevitable. Seconds later, the chopper lifted off with a deafening *thump-thump-thump* of the rotors, and disappeared into the night sky.

As soon as the rotor wash subsided, Kathleen and McCreary rushed to Steve Goodwin, who was writhing in pain on the ground, clutching his shattered left knee.

McCreary looked up at the blinking taillight of the helicopter as it disappeared into the sky and shook his head glumly. "God help us, the world is about to change."

"Maybe not," Kathleen whispered to herself.

CHAPTER SIXTY-ONE

BRYCE Whittaker had just drifted into to a blissful slumber, bringing to a satisfying close the best day of his career so far. He'd finally achieved his dream of breaking into television. And, according to the producer of *Randi Rice Tonight*, he'd done extremely well. "A natural" were the producer's exact words. Just as Whittaker had always known.

Whittaker's boss at the *Post* was overjoyed by the excitement and controversy caused by the QLS article. He called right after the TV segment aired to congratulate Whittaker and offer him a position at the national desk. With Whittaker's rising star power, the *Post* clearly did not want to lose him to a rival newspaper or, worse, to a television network.

It had been quite a day for Bryce Whittaker. So when the phone rang just after midnight, he naturally assumed it would be more good news. "Hello?" he answered groggily.

"Screw you, Bryce!"

Whittaker paused momentarily, confused. "Kathleen? My God, where are you?"

"Drop it, Bryce. You *betrayed* me! How could you?"

"Kathleen, I . . . I . . . had no choice."

"The hell you didn't! Do you realize what I've been through today because of your damned story?"

"I'm really sorry. I . . . I didn't know it would be such a big deal. Honestly!"

"Apology not accepted," Kathleen said evenly. "You nearly got me killed. Carlos is in the hospital. You can't apologize your way out of this one, Bryce."

Whittaker sighed. "What do you want?"

For the next five minutes, Kathleen explained in exact detail the article she wanted Whittaker to write.

"Are you kidding?" Whittaker said when she'd finished. He was fully awake now. "You're talking career suicide, you know."

Kathleen didn't hesitate. "Listen, Bryce, either *you* write it, or I'll call the *Washington Times*. Your choice."

Whittaker rubbed his temples, weighing the prospect of the rival *Washington Times* breaking the story. "All right," he said finally, exhaling loudly. "When can we meet?"

"We just did. And I want that story in the paper tomorrow morning. Front page."

"Jesus, Kathleen. Are you sure you want to do this?"

"Absolutely."

CHAPTER SIXTY-TWO

Andros Island, Bahamas.

THE Atlántic Ocean lapped rhythmically against the sugar white sand of Los Brazos beach with a soft, lulling rumble. Palm trees swayed in the warm, tropical breeze as the sun rose above the red-tiled roof of Casa de Las Rocas, a twenty-two-room mansion overlooking the spectacular private beach on the island's south end.

Guests had been arriving all night long. Several had landed in private jets on the estate's air-strip, two miles away. Others had flown in from the United States by helicopter, landing on the estate's helipad near the beach. One had arrived on *Isadora*, a 180-foot yacht, which was now moored just offshore.

At 8:00 A.M., six of the distinguished guests were assembled in the mansion's oval dining room, whose curved wall of plate-glass windows framed a view of the sparkling turquoise sea below. They sat in high-back chairs surrounding an ornate, eighteenth-century mahogany table from the British colonial period, a time of sugar plantations, rum wars, and pirates.

Outside, the twin limestone formations for which the house was named stretched out into the sea for several hundred yards, hooking toward each other at the end to form a tiny, secluded harbor where pirates once moored their sailing ships and buried their loot onshore. They called these black rocks *Los Brazos del Diablo*— "the Devil's Arms"—mainly as a ploy to keep others away.

"Gentlemen," said a tall, elegant, white-haired man who had just entered the room. "Welcome to Casa de Las Rocas." He was Guillermo de Juan Ignacio Gomez, a Mexican billionaire, and one of the richest men in the world. His snowy hair contrasted strikingly with his smooth, bronzed skin. He wore a beautifully embroidered white silk shirt, white pants, and handmade Italian sandals.

Gomez had amassed his original fortune in the early 1970s, when he'd built one of the most sophisticated drug-smuggling operations in the western hemisphere, trafficking marijuana and cocaine from Mexico into the United States. For the past five years, however, Gomez had been strictly legit, investing his sizable fortune in a string of successful resort properties on both coasts of Mexico, off Florida, in the Caribbean, and more recently in Central America. He was now a well-respected real-estate tycoon.

"Señor Wu," Gomez said warmly to the man seated nearest to him. He shook the Chinese man's hand and patted his shoulder familiarly. "I am honored by your presence."

Jin Shan Wu bowed his head slightly without smiling. He was a shipping magnate from Shanghai—one of China's new billionaires and, like Gomez, one of the richest men in the world.

Gomez worked his way around the table in similar fashion, greeting each guest warmly and with the utmost respect.

"Señor Haryadi," he said to Eswara Haryadi, owner of the largest steel company in India and also one of the richest men in the world. "Welcome, my friend." Haryadi nodded and smiled.

"Señor Nazarov," he said to Aleksei Nazarov, an oil baron from Russia, "I hope your long flight was not too uncomfortable."

Nazarov shook Gomez's hand enthusiastically and smiled. "It was very comfortable, thank you."

"Señor Glick," Gomez said, putting his arm around the shoulders of Roger Glick, CEO of WestPharma Corporation, "a pleasure to meet you." Glick nodded and flashed a courteous business smile. Glick was the only person at the table who was not a billionaire, although his personal fortune did measure in the neighborhood of 150 million dollars, depending on the daily price of WestPharma's stock. The buying power of his company, however, a 50-billion-dollar publicly traded concern, put him on par with the likes of Wu, Haryadi, and Nazarov.

Gomez continued around the table. "Señor Diakos," he said warmly to Leonidas Diakos, an old-world billionaire from Cyprus. "Your yacht is beautiful, señor. I would very much like a tour of it if that could be arranged." Diakos smiled and nodded that yes, that could be arranged. Diakos was a thin, frail man in his late seventies. His skin was tan and leathery, his thinning hair bright silver. The Diakos family had been wealthy for so many generations that no one in Greece could really recall where all that money had come from originally. Today, the Diakos family had its fingers in dozens of concerns, including banking, shipping, beverage distribution, and real estate. Leonidas Diakos, as head of the family, controlled billions of dollars in assets.

Gomez shook hands with the last man at the table, Wilhelm Van der Giesen of Capetown, South Africa. "Señor Van der Giesen," he said warmly, "welcome, my friend." Van der Giesen nodded without smiling. At age forty-nine, he was the youngest man at the table by at least fifteen years. But he, too, was a billionaire, his wealth having been acquired by his father a generation ago, largely on the backs of impoverished and abused diamond miners in Tanzania and Zaire.

Gomez positioned himself at the head of the table and remained standing. "Gentlemen, I am honored to have all of you here as my special guests. If you need anything at all during your stay, please let one of my staff know. Now, I'll turn things over to the man who called this meeting, Señor Rubin."

Elias Rubin had been waiting in the doorway just outside the dining room, and he entered the room when Gomez called his name. "Welcome, everyone," he said with a showman's flair. "And thank you for making this trip on such short notice. I believe you will find it was well worth it." He paused and nodded to each guest individually. "When I started the Olam Foundation five years ago, *this* was the day I dreamed of. The day our aspirations would finally become reality. The day that fiction would become fact. Gentlemen, it gives me great pleasure to introduce to you Mr. Anthony Wills."

Exactly on cue, Wills walked into the dining room, dressed in a light tan cotton suit and crisp white button-down shirt, open at the neck. Behind him, two hulking men in camouflage pants and tight black T-shirts also entered the room, each with a holstered sidearm strapped to his hip. They were members of Gomez's private security team, the same men who'd picked up Wills in the St. Anne's Cemetery the night before and flew him directly to Andros Island.

"Good morning," said Wills, a bit nervously. He nodded to the six seated men and to Rubin, who remained standing. "And thank you, Mr. Gomez." He gave Gomez an especially appreciative nod.

"Now," said Rubin, seating himself at the head of the table, "let's get down to business. As you know, Mr. Wills has brought with him an intact DNA sample that contains the INDY gene. That is why we're all here, of course. But, before we begin, I would like to remind all of you of the terms of our agreement, just to make sure there is no confusion or misunderstanding.

"First," Rubin said, "all transactions must be

wired directly to the Cayman Island account of the Olam Foundation. One hundred million dollars in cash goes to Mr. Wills as a finder's fee." Rubin nodded appreciatively at Wills. "The rest of the payment will be distributed equally to the members of the Foundation.

"Second, no matter who purchases the INDY gene, all of us at this table—" Rubin made a sweeping gesture with his arm around the table, ending dramatically with himself. "All of us will be granted personal access to the gene therapy at no cost. Agreed?"

Everyone at the table nodded.

"Very well then. It is now time for the first round of sealed bids—"

"Wait," said Van der Giesen, holding up his hand in protest. "We haven't even seen this DNA sample. How can we bid on something we haven't seen?"

"Of course," Rubin replied calmly. "I have a biologist here with all the necessary test equipment to confirm the presence of the INDY gene in the sample. The final bid will, of course, be contingent upon a successful test."

"Still," said Roger Glick, "shouldn't we at least see this sample before we bid?"

"Fair enough," said Rubin with a slight nod of his head. He signaled to one of the armed security guards, who exited the room and returned a minute later with a young, bespectacled man in a white lab coat. "This is Dr. Jinjung Xing, from the University of Beijing. I have retained him to help us with our transaction today."

Dr. Xing approached and spread out a light-blue surgical mat, about two feet square, in the center of the table.

"Mr. Wills," said Rubin dramatically, "the sample please."

Wills pulled the neoprene sample container from his breast pocket and handed it to Rubin, who placed it with great showmanship on the mat. The seated guests watched with acute interest.

"Open it, please, Dr. Xing," said Rubin.

As the guests watched with great anticipation, Dr. Xing snapped on a pair of latex gloves and carefully cut the Teflon seal around the lid of the container with a small scalpel. Then, he carefully unscrewed the cap, turning it slowly counterclockwise, one revolution at a time.

Everyone at the table—including Gomez and Wills—leaned in with rising anticipation. The room fell silent. After three complete turns, the lid was loose, and Dr. Xing lifted it off slowly . . . carefully . . .

"What the hell!" screamed Roger Glick—the first to react—as he fanned away the swarm of fruit flies that had just emerged from the sample container. The tiny black flies shot out like a puff of smoke and quickly dispersed all around the room.

"What's the meaning of this?" Wu demanded angrily, fanning away the flies.

"You brought us all the way here to see . . . *insects*?" said Eswara Haryadi indignantly.

"This is bullshit!" shouted Van der Giesen.

The six guests were already standing up, shaking their heads and conversing with each other in angry tones. Some were already on their cell phones, summoning their jets and helicopters to be powered up.

Gomez turned to Wills, his eyes burning with rage. "Explain this!" he demanded.

Wills shook head back and forth, mouth wide open, utterly dumbfounded.

"Get him out of here!" Gomez said angrily to the security guards.

CHAPTER SIXTY-THREE

PETER Stonewell leaned forward on his elbows and studied the front page of the *Washington Post* with great interest. In the lower right-hand corner below the fold was a single-column article, which read as follows:

LIFE-EXTENSION GENE A HOAX, COMPANY ADMITS

By Bryce Whittaker
Washington Post Staff Writer

ROCKVILLE, Md.—After a bizarre day that included an explosion at its headquarters in Rockville, Quantum Life Sciences, Inc. admitted late last night that the discovery of a human life-extension gene was a hoax, orchestrated by its president and CEO, Dr. Kathleen Sainsbury.

Carlos Guiterez, a spokesman for QLS, acknowledged that the hoax was carried out by Dr. Sainsbury in an apparent attempt to appease increasingly skeptical investors, some of whom had recently begun to question the validity of the flagging company. "There's no truth to the story about mummified remains containing a human life-extending gene," Guiterez said. "There never were any such remains, and QLS has not isolated the INDY gene in humans," he said. The "INDY" gene is a gene that has been identified in fruit flies that appears to affect their life expectancy. Guiterez added that, for the foreseeable future, QLS's research will remain focused solely on fruit-fly genetics, not human DNA.

In the days prior to Dr. Sainsbury's apparent hoax, QLS had received cash calls—votes of no confidence—from two of its largest investors, Aurora Capital and Cresent Venture Capital, both of New York City. Aurora Capital could not be reached for comment. In a statement released late last night, however, Crescent Capital said it was "deeply disappointed by QLS's apparent attempt to defraud its investors" and that it would investigate these reports promptly and "initiate appropriate civil action and possibly criminal proceedings."

In an exclusive interview with the *Washington Post* late last night, Dr. Sainsbury acknowledged carrying out the hoax but said she never intended to defraud investors. "It just started out as a joke," she said, "something I created in my own mind as an interesting theory. It just got out of hand. I never intended for it to go this far, and I deeply regret my actions."

Dr. Sainsbury resigned as president and CEO of QLS last night and said that she stands ready to take full, personal responsibility for the hoax.

"This was my doing entirely," she said. "Nobody at QLS had any knowledge of what I was doing and should not be held accountable for my actions."

Editor's Note. The *Washington Post* reported a story on the so-called "longevity gene" yesterday, having been duped by this apparent hoax. The story is hereby retracted in its entirety. The staff of the *Washington Post* wishes to apologize to its readers for any confusion the erroneous story may have caused.

Stonewell finished reading the article and leaned back with a satisfied smile. He picked up the phone and dialed Bill McCreary's number at DARPA.

"Hello," answered McCreary.

"Have you read it?"

"Yes, sir."

"I don't know how you did it, Bill, and frankly I don't care. All I can say is . . . good work."

"Thank you, sir," said McCreary blandly.

"Just out of curiosity, though, how much did this cost us?"

There was a brief pause before McCreary answered, his tone reflecting his own lingering disbelief. "One sailboat."

CHAPTER SIXTY-FOUR

One Year Later. Puerto Banús, Spain.

THE forty-five-foot sloop *Encantado* sliced smoothly through the azure Mediterranean Sea, its beautiful white mainsail neatly trimmed, its jib bowed gracefully against the stiff breeze blowing over the port bow. The sleek, fiberglass hull of the boat was heeled over about ten degrees, with just a bit of whitewater splashing over its starboard gunwale. Directly off the starboard beam of the *Encantado*, two miles north, lay the picturesque hillside village of Puerto Banús, a popular sailing destination on Spain's Costa del Sol.

Kathleen Sainsbury tweaked *Encantado*'s helm a few degrees leeward, easing the sleek craft back into its close-haul groove. The boat responded by heeling over another degree, its starboard jib sheet creaking under the additional strain of the wind.

Kathleen loved early mornings on the open water—the sun climbing above the horizon, the smell of fresh salt air, and the unique feeling of accomplishment of having safely navigated a tiny speck of sailboat through the vast darkness of the nighttime sea. It had always been her dream to make this run from Palma Majorca to Puerto Banús. Now she was living it. She breathed deeply and relished the unique sounds and cadence of open-ocean sailing: the rush of water beneath the hull; the rhythmic sound of waves crashing against the bow; the soft snapping of the jib's leech in the wind.

It had rained most of the night. As the sun rose, Kathleen observed the remnants of the night's storm clouds still hovering low above the water, tall and puffy with ominous splotches of dark gray.

She heard someone coming up from the cabin below.

"Good morning," said Carlos Guiterez as he poked his head out of the cabin hatchway and climbed clumsily into the boat's cockpit. He was yawning and rubbing his eyes.

"How'd you sleep?" Kathleen asked.

"Are you kidding? It's like a sawmill down there."

Kathleen laughed knowingly. Indeed, loud snoring could still be heard periodically, wafting up from the cabin below. "Well, you can catch some sleep up here if you want. I'm good on the helm for at least another couple hours."

"Nah, I'm okay." Carlos pointed off the starboard side toward Puerto Banúz. "Almost there, huh? I can't wait to see Ana and the girls. They got in yesterday afternoon."

"Actually, we've been tacking back and forth since about four o'clock this morning. I was just waiting for everyone to wake up before we pulled in."

"In that case, I'll go put on a pot of coffee. That should wake 'em up." Carlos disappeared below and reemerged several minutes later with two mugs of fresh coffee.

They sat in silence for a while, each sipping their coffee and enjoying the stunning view of Puerto Banúz. Whitewashed houses clung impossibly to steep hillsides that seemed to rise out of the sea. Narrow hillside streets were just visible from their vantage point, two miles away.

Before long, another head popped out of the hatchway from below.

"Oh, man, what *time* is it?" asked Jeremy Fisher, squinting at the brightening sky. He looked like a train wreck, his long hair tangled and matted, three days' worth of black stubble on his pale face.

"Just after six," said Kathleen. "We're getting ready to pull in to Puerto Banúz. See it over there?"

"Whoa, awesome!" Jeremy exclaimed, gazing starboard at the seaside village. "Here, hold this." He handed his coffee mug to Carlos and climbed painstakingly up the teakwood ladder into the cockpit, wincing with discomfort.

"How's your back feeling?" asked Kathleen.

"Stiff as hell," said Jeremy with a grunt. "But nothing a few *mojitos* won't cure." He nodded in the direction of Puerto Banúz.

Kathleen watched as Jeremy settled into the cockpit with obvious pain. She was glad he'd been able to make this trip. Seven weeks in the hospital and six months of physical therapy had taken a toll on him. At least he was walking again, which was more than the doctors had predicted just a few months ago. And to see him smiling! It made Kathleen smile, too.

"Well," said Jeremy, nodding toward shore, "what're we waiting for? Let's pull in."

"We're waiting for Paul Bunyon to wake up," said Carlos, pointing down into the cabin.

The three of them sat in silence for a few minutes as *Encantado* swooshed gracefully west along the Costa del Sol.

Finally, Jeremy spoke. "Hey, I've got a question for you, Dr. S."

"Shoot."

"I've heard bits and pieces of what happened, but I never actually heard the whole story about the DNA sample that you and Julie recovered from the thermocycler. What exactly happened to it?"

"I told you, it burned to a crisp in the fire, along with everything else."

"But, then . . . how'd you recreate the INDY sequence?"

Kathleen nodded and smiled at Carlos. "Well, that was all thanks to Carlos, here."

"How so?" Jeremy asked.

"Before the explosion, Carlos drafted a patent application. And he had the foresight to download the entire sequence—all eighty thousand base pairs—into the patent application. So, even after the fire, we had the entire sequence right there on a thumb drive."

"Ah," said Jeremy. "So there was no need for the actual sample."

"Nope. All we needed was the gene sequence. And Carlos saved it!"

Carlos shrugged bashfully. "I thought I'd saved the sample, too. Turns out, though, I grabbed the wrong container from the fridge."

"Yeah," said Kathleen with a smirk. "He grabbed a container full of fruit fly embryos. I realized it when I noticed the label started with an E instead of a J. E for embryos."

"Hey, they all looked the same to me!" Carlos protested.

"No worries," said Kathleen. "It all turned out in the end. Hey, look who it is!" Kathleen pointed at the hatchway, where another head was just emerging from below. "Good morning, Grandpa!"

"Good morning!" said John Sainsbury cheerfully. He ascended the cabin ladder steadily, coffee mug in hand, and maneuvered deftly into the cockpit. "Whew! How'd everybody sleep?"

At that, Kathleen, Carlos, and Jeremy erupted with laughter as John Sainsbury looked around, confused. "What?"

"You were snoring like a bear down there, Grandpa!" said Kathleen, still laughing heartily.

"I was? Oh, sorry."

"Don't worry, Mr. Sainsbury," said Carlos with a wink. "It wasn't really that bad."

When the laughter died down, Kathleen asked

her grandfather, "So, how's our number-one patient doing?"

"Great!" exclaimed John Sainsbury, toasting the air with his coffee mug. "In fact, I feel even better today than I did yesterday. Nothing aches; I've got a good appetite. And, most important, I'm remembering everything." He thrust a finger at Carlos's chest. "Carlos Filipe Guiterez, born April 14, 1968, in San Antonio, Texas. Graduated from St. Anthony's Catholic High School in 1986. U.S. Marine Corps, 1986 to 2001. Your wife's name is Ana, and you have two daughters, Isabel and, uh . . ." He snapped his fingers several times until it came to him. *"Maria!"*

Everyone on the boat clapped loudly and cheered.

Kathleen beamed with pride. "Wow, you're getting better every day."

"Kathleen, I feel *great* . . . like I'm thirty years old again! I don't know what's in those injections you've been giving me, but I tell you what—it's working like a charm."

"I told you, Grandpa. It's called a gene-replacement vector. It goes into your bloodstream and seeks out a specific chunk of your DNA on chromosome fourteen. When it finds it, it gloms on and expresses certain proteins. We call that chunk of DNA the 'INDY' gene, and the injections basically turn that gene on. Like a light switch."

"Well, whatever you call it, I can't thank you enough for giving it to me. Kathleen, I mean it when I say this, you saved me from a living hell."

Kathleen frowned. "Was it really like that? A living hell?"

The elder Sainsbury nodded and cast his eyes down. "It was like living in a constant nightmare. I knew something was terribly wrong, but I just couldn't wake up from it. That's the only way I can describe it."

There was a prolonged silence. Then, suddenly, Jeremy exclaimed, "Hey! Check that out!"

Everyone turned to look at the sky off to the starboard side, where Jeremy was pointing. Above Puerto Banúz, the clouds had temporarily parted, allowing a bright shaft of light to illuminate the gleaming whitewashed houses of the idyllic hillside village. High above the town, a colorful rainbow arched across the sky from east to west, ending somewhere behind the hills of Puerto Banúz.

"It's beautiful!" Kathleen whispered.

"God's bow in the cloud," said Carlos quietly.

Then, as quickly as the splendid sight had appeared, a dark, gray cloud drifted in front of the sun, casting a dark shadow over the village once again. The colorful rainbow vanished instantly.

"We'd better pull in now," said John Sainsbury. "We don't want to be out here when it starts to rain."

ACKNOWLEDGMENTS

I HOPE you enjoyed *The Genesis Key*.

Many people helped make this book possible. Thanks especially to: my lovely wife, Kelley, for her patience and support for the past nineteen years; my friend and colleague, Dr. M. Andrew Holtman, for his encouragement and advice on all things biological; Clifford S. Barney for his early comments and support; Jonathan and Colleen Barney for their kind words of encouragement; my parents, Cliff and Edna Barney, for everything; my terrific agent, Mickey Choate, for taking a chance on me; and, last but not least, Jennifer Brehl and the superb team at Harper-Collins for doing everything necessary to make this book a success.

And, of course, to those who purchased and read this book: Thank you.

TO KELLEY
with love

"My God," Sargon whispered, *utterly astonished.*

The chamber was astonishingly large, its floor measuring at least thirty by forty feet, with a high, arched ceiling. The brickwork was tight and superbly arranged in six adjacent archways, each measuring approximately twelve by twelve feet. Such technology was not known to exist in Mesopotamia for another three thousand years after Tell-Fara was built. Yet, here it was, holding up the roof of a *five-thousand-year-old* temple.

He approached the nearest niche and shone his flashlight into it. His heart leapt as he found himself gazing upon the stone likeness of a bearded man, approximately life-sized, with translucent opals embedded in his eyes. The alabaster face stared back at him intensely, as stern and commanding a presence today as it had been five thousand years ago.

He now knew that he was standing inside a *tomb,* not a ziggurat at all. Tell-Fara was a massive tomb—a concept absolutely unique in Mesopotamia in the third millennium BC.

But whose tomb?

THE GENESIS KEY

JAMES BARNEY

THE
GENESIS KEY

HARPER

An Imprint of HarperCollins*Publishers*

This book is a work of fiction. References to real people, events, establishments, organizations, or locales are intended only to provide a sense of authenticity, and are used fictitiously. All other characters, and all incidents and dialogue, are drawn from the author's imagination and are not to be construed as real.

HARPER

An Imprint of HarperCollins*Publishers*
10 East 53rd Street
New York, New York 10022–5299

Copyright © 2011 by James Barney
ISBN 978-0-06-202138-0

First Harper premium printing: July 2011

Printed in the United States of America

Visit Harper paperbacks on the World Wide Web
at www.harpercollins.com

10 9 8 7 6 5 4 3 2 1